THE GIRL *WITH NO* SOUL

MORGAN OWEN

SCHOLASTIC

Morgan Owen has always been a writer. One of her earliest memories is of sitting at her grandmother's dining table, folding pieces of paper to create makeshift books. Inside were illustrated stories of formless spirits and Sylvanian Families, which they read aloud together. A former bookseller and PR executive, Owen enjoys travelling, stargazing, eating other people's cooking, playing Animal Crossing and buying knick-knacks to put in her curiosity cabinet. She has two black cats named Salem and Binx. *The Girl With No Soul* is her debut novel. She is represented by Hannah Sheppard at D H H Literary Agency.

To anyone who has ever felt totally lost.

Published in the UK by Scholastic, 2022
Euston House, 24 Eversholt Street, London, NW1 1DB
Scholastic Ireland, 89E Lagan Road, Dublin Industrial Estate,
Glasnevin, Dublin, D11 HP5F

Text © Morgan Owen, 2022
Cover illustration by Jamie Gregory © Scholastic, 2022

ISBN 978 0702 31463 6

A CIP catalogue record for this book is available from the British Library.

Printed by CPI Group (UK) Ltd, Croydon, CR0 4YY
Paper made from wood grown in sustainable forests
and other controlled sources.

1 3 5 7 9 10 8 6 4 2

This is a work of fiction. Names, characters, places, incidents and dialogues
are products of the author's imagination or are used fictitiously.
Any resemblance to actual people, living or dead,
events or locales is entirely coincidental.

www.scholastic.co.uk

PART
O·NE
THE SPARK

1.

THE FIVE SIGNS OF SOULLESSNESS

There are many different ways in which a soul can be flawed, according to the Order.

The Spark can be too bright or the Shadow too dark; the Spirit weak, the Song discordant or the Heart bitter.

The streets of Providence were plastered with shining billboards that told us how the soul ought to look, warning of spots and scars, of cracks and fractures. But I'd never given much thought to my own soul's appearance. There wasn't much point in worrying about that. Not for me.

One damp autumn Sunday at sunset, I went to the Grand Bazaar to steal a trinket for the Countess. Thieving was how I made my living, if you could call it that. The market was full of pretty things just waiting to be nicked by a girl who kept her eyes wide open and her wits about her. Its patrons were so focused on what they wanted to buy next, they paid little attention to what they already owned. It was the perfect place to pick pockets.

The Countess had told me what to look for, and I knew I'd find it.

I always did.

Hood up, head down, I moved through the buoyant crowd, weaving between dripping umbrellas, fat drops of rain splattering me each time I stepped out from beneath the shelter of the soaking awnings.

Colourful banners hung from the towering buildings that lined the pentagon-shaped courtyard, representing the standards of the five noble Houses and marking the boundaries of the five boroughs.

The Eye of Obscura on black for the House of Shadow.

The Flower of Memoria on white for the House of Spirit.

The Harp of Harmonia on silver for the House of Song.

The Apple of Cordata on gold for the House of Heart.

The Torch of Renato on red for the House of Spark.

These were the five elements of the soul's anatomy, each with its own court of nobles to represent it. Together, the five Houses made up the Order of Providence, the foundation of our society, going back hundreds of years. Occasionally there was a revolt by discontented agitators – criminals whose souls were flawed, no doubt – but the Order could not be shaken.

Beneath the flags was a vast patchwork of clashing canopies, some several storeys high and connected by a web of rope bridges, where merchants from far across the five seas peddled the remains of the day, their sales calls reverberating in a riotous, rhythmic round.

"Torch songs! Romantic records! Half-price sale, today only!"

2

"Thinking caps, three for a crown."

"Heart food, come get your heart food! We've got sweetcakes, we've got sour breads, we've got everything!"

Here in the Grand Bazaar, you could buy not just sugar and coffee and eggs and fish, but mirrors that flattered the reflection and aroma sticks that improved the memory, sweets that made you cheerful and shoes that made you a better dancer. It was packed with shoppers, all bustling and chattering, pushing and shoving, creating a rough, undulating mass which ebbed and flowed, carrying me along with it.

A distant glimmer caught my eye, twinkling in the distance. My fingertips vibrated, tickling. *This could be it.* Cutting through a hall of hanging curtains, past a porcelain dog show and a mannequin beauty pageant, I made a beeline for the strange sparkle.

I searched keenly for the source of the gleam, eyeing each person as they passed by. A group of soldiers admired a selection of shiny weapons for sale. A couple clinked frothing glasses before a smoky stall, gazing at each other adoringly. A group of children in uniform watched a time capsule that projected triumphant scenes from the Order's history.

I spied rubies and medallions, diamonds and pearls, but these weren't the kind of treasures I was interested in. I stole that which glittered not with gold, but with feeling. The Countess paid me to steal sentimental treasures: things that meant something to someone, or had done once, long ago. Lockets and favours, souvenirs and love letters. People called them *remnants*, leftovers of the past. Each one gave me a tingle or a twitch, a pang or an itch.

On this occasion, my Lady had sent me on a mission to acquire one item in particular, but sometimes I took the initiative to go looking for myself. I enjoyed the challenge of hunting these remnants, picking through piles and rifling through purses until I found one that felt just right. The Countess paid best for remnants with dark energies, objects imbued with unpleasant memories. Murder. Jealousy. Betrayal. Death. That sort of thing.

There it was again: the glimmer that drew me in, catching on the corner of my eye. Just a faint flash in the distance. I struggled towards it, fighting against the pull of the crowd. There were too many people in the way, their heads bobbing, hands flapping, as if they had all the time in the world to waste. Finding myself trapped behind two slow walkers, I pushed boldly through the small space between them, jostling their elbows. They called after me in annoyance.

I was getting close.

The glimmer was now a shimmering aura, a floating spectral halo like a sundog, a hazy mock sun. You could tell it was other-worldly, supernatural. The magic of the soul.

"Extra, extra, read all about it," cried a paper boy on a bike, blocking my line of sight. "Chancellor Obscura promises new measures to crack down on corruption!" One of the papers fell from his bulging sack as he passed. I craned my neck, standing on tiptoes as I searched for the strange spark but I couldn't see it any more. I'd lost it again.

"Numbskull," I called after the boy, but he didn't hear me.

Sighing, I picked up the dropped newspaper, a copy of the *Daily Insight*. There was a grim-faced, goatee-bearded man on the cover, wearing dark robes with a high collar and small black goggles that shaded his eyes.

Chancellor Obscura. Our supreme leader. He had discovered the means to turn mind to matter, fuelling our fires and making the city his. Before him, the five Houses had ruled in turn, but not even the gifted luminaries of the aristocracy could challenge his rule now. The only people who dared try to usurp him were the desperate rebels with nothing to live for.

As of today, Inspectors will be granted new powers, allowing them to stop and search anyone breaking curfew without a permit. "Providence is the standard by which the entire world should be judged," said Chancellor Obscura, speaking at the Observatory last night before a crowd of employees, donors and press. "It is a city in which only the pure of soul may reside. Law-abiding citizens have nothing to fear, but those who have allowed their souls to be corrupted, be warned: we will find you."

This was followed by a series of fawning quotes from Ministers applauding the Chancellor's infinite brilliance.

Disinterested, I turned the page, skimming the house sales and obituaries, advertisements and classifieds. The society pages reported on various births and engagements among the nobles of Providence. There was a feature on the

Chancellor's spoiled son, currently on a grand tour of the continent; an engagement between two attractive nobles from House Cordata; and pictures of the latest masked ball at the Basilica, its glamorous attendees all dressed in Renato red, standing before a topiary phoenix.

I looked up from the paper as the gleam caught my eye again, peeping out from behind a stall like the sun rising on the horizon. Dropping the paper in a puddle, I scoured the crowd of bargain seekers and found the sparkle, emanating from a small woman in an ostentatious hat. She hummed to herself, rifling through trays of silverware. I pulled a picture from my pocket, a blurry sepia portrait. She looked younger and lither in the photo, but here she was.

My mark.

The hat had an ornate pin stuck in the back. It was made of brass, with a bevelled, eye-shaped bauble on the top. *She must be a Shadow soul, a servant of House Obscura.* People in Providence were defined by their soul's dominant aspect, employed by the corresponding House. They fashioned their identities around their aspects, wearing house colours and symbols, but I had no such alignment to speak of. I wore a large black Obscura coat. A ragged red Renato dress. A laddered pair of white Memoria tights. A gold Cordata undershirt. A silver Harmonia slip. All stolen.

Though unnoticed by the preoccupied masses of the market, the eye pin's mere presence made me itch and shiver. I could tell that it was rich with psyche. It was a remnant, and a powerful one at that, more precious than any gold or gemstone.

I stuck to the woman like a shadow, stalking her along the aisle. I made sure not to catch her eye but she wouldn't have noticed me in any event. Being forgettable was my gift.

The hatpin glittered incandescently. I could feel its pulsating energy from yards away. I closed in, drawn to the hatpin like a moth to a flame. The rest of the world washed away, blurring as the object sharpened in contrast...

My mark suddenly turned, and bumped right into me. For the first time, she noticed my presence, standing too close for comfort. Her face curled into a sneer. My tunnel vision receded.

"Uh, did you drop this?" I said, quickly pulling a handkerchief from my pocket, smiling innocently. But it was a flat, painted-on smile and she saw right through it, looking down her pert, piggish nose at me.

"Nice try, girlie," she said. "I know your kind, with your raggedy clothes and baggy eyes, creeping up on folks like a ghost. You were trying to steal my grandmother's ring, weren't you, soulless wretch?"

She held up her hand accusingly, showing off the golden band on her middle finger, with a single small stone of jet.

"That old thing?" I said, wrinkling my nose. "It looks like a toy from a cracker. Even a thief has better taste."

The ring was dull and flat. Whatever memories it held, they weren't very strong or interesting ... unlike the hatpin, which had a gleam so bright I'd been able to track it through the market.

"I should summon the Inspectors," she said. "See how you like that. They're clearing the streets of riff-raff like you."

Day and night, Inspectors of the Order combed the Bazaar on horseback, in their distinctive tall black hats and cloaks. If they caught me with a hoard of stolen treasures, they'd ship me straight away to the Reformatory to be purified, but I wasn't afraid. I knew her threat was empty.

"Are you sure you want to do that?" I said, leaning in closer. "They might just take a good look at you too while they're at it. Your soul better be cleaner than a washerwoman's hands."

She gritted her teeth as if holding back an avalanche of curse words. "Get out of here," she said, swatting me away like a pesky fly. "Get out of my sight, street rat."

"With pleasure," I said.

As she turned back to the stall, bending over slightly to admire a gaudy gravy boat, I swept past her like a gentle breeze, removing the eye-shaped pin from her hat as smoothly as a stage magician. She didn't feel my touch, oblivious as I melted into the crowd again. I'd be halfway across the city before she even realized it was missing. If she tried to file a report, she'd find that she could no longer recall my face and that her memory of the event was rapidly fading. There weren't many upsides to being me, but getting away with things was one of them. I had certain … talents,

8

which meant stealing and cheating came naturally to me. Like breathing.

I continued on along the road, exiting the market and heading towards the First Borough with its shiny black buildings and watchtowers. Once the flea market was out of sight, I ran my thumb over the hatpin's spike. Its energy made me shudder, caused my skin to goose-pimple. A brief prickle of something other-worldly passed through me, using my body as a conduit.

I can smell dust and dried ink. I can hear the creak of old floorboards. I can taste blood on my lips…

No wonder the Countess was so interested in it.

Was the remnant full of hatred or desire? Either way, I didn't much care. It was just another second-hand emotion I had no need for. The only time I felt anything was when I held a remnant in my hand and, even then, it was usually too faint for me to make out what emotion it was precisely.

Stuffing the pin into my pocket, I pushed on, past a butcher's and a chemist, its green glass windows full of dried herbs and apothecary bottles. Nearby, a haberdashery store had set up tables outside, all covered in boxes of bobbins and needles. I idly grazed my hand over the dusty tops of the little wooden crates until my fingertips tingled tellingly. The hairs on the back of my neck prickled: a sure sign that I'd found a remnant.

Stopping, I peered into the suspect box, where a single button shone brighter than the others. I pressed my finger into its recess, where two little holes waited to catch a thread, and it buzzed as if acknowledging me. "Hello," I whispered back. The button emanated a warmth that rippled through me in a wave: a warm, floaty feeling that made me feel safe and in my right place. It lasted only a second before dissipating.

A simple button wasn't the sort of thing the Countess would be interested in, but I was drawn to it nonetheless. The shop's owner was visible through the open door, bustling back and forth with rolls of fabric. I waited until he turned his back before slipping the button between my fingers, allowing a quivering thrill to course through my body, making all my nerve endings tingle. There was nothing more exhilarating than stealing something from someone right under their nose. In a single, imperceptible motion, I dropped the button in the pocket of my oversized coat and kept walking.

Providence was a graveyard of empires, a collection of buildings from different eras in history, all huddled together in an anachronistic muddle. The eldest and greatest of them were titanic in size, crumbling mausoleums in contrast to the shiny glass atriums being constructed with cranes. The wealthy Houses lived in its upper reaches, in columned villas high above the metropolis, while the poor lived in the grim, shadowy streets beneath, where the factory fog was so thick you could hardly peer through it.

As the sky darkened and twilight settled in, a musical tone sang out across the city, heard in every nook and cranny, every backstreet and alley. "The time is now six o'clock," came a silky female voice, ringing far and wide. "There is a curfew in place between 6 p.m. and 6 a.m. All citizens must return to their homes immediately. Anyone caught on the streets after curfew will be subject to assessment by the Inspectors, by order of the Chancellor. If you have a permit, please be ready to present your identity card."

A group of people walked past in the opposite direction, anxiously pulling out their little leather card-holders as they tried to flag down a cab. Inside was a copy of their psychograph: a picture of their soul. Such cards were crucial when navigating the city. They were mandatory for all manner of purposes, from seeing a doctor to renting a house. The only way to get an identity card was to submit to psychometric examination at one of the Order's centres, and I knew better than to hand myself over to them so easily. For someone like me, it was better to have no name, no identity.

"Your safety is our priority," continued the voice. "The Order thanks you for your cooperation."

All around me, a visceral thrum of panic gripped the city, so palpable that I could feel its collective energy. Doors slammed shut. Curtains were drawn. Folks disappeared into alleyways or climbed into carriages, directing their drivers to step on it.

Nearby, a street light came on, shining faint as a firefly through the thick, pea soup smog. Another sparked to light, then another and another, until the city centre was lit up with constellations of bright lanterns, each one shaped like the Eye of the Order. Avoiding their intrusive gaze, I turned off the main avenues and stuck to the dim, less-trodden streets walked by those who wished not to be witnessed. There were no lanterns here, only shadows. Only darkness.

Groping along the narrow alley, I waited for my vision to adjust. Most folks were afraid of the dark, frightened of what sort of people might walk the streets after curfew, but the night was my home, and the shadows my friends. Nor could I be haunted by the past, as other people were; I didn't have a past. I was comfortable in the silence of my mind.

I started whistling to keep my lips from freezing, just half a bar of a song I could no longer recall.

The sound of footsteps rumbled faintly. Ducking into a doorway, I watched as three small figures ran past. A few seconds later, bright searchlights cut through the gloom like knives. A black wagon rolled by, emblazoned with the sign of an eye inside a circle. It pulled up abruptly, brakes squealing, before a gaggle of Inspectors piled out.

"Stop right there!" came a voice.

"In the name of the Order!"

They stormed past, closing in on a trio of ragged-looking kids trying to flee the scene.

"Line up, backs against the wall. That's it."

I peered out, trying to get a better look.

"Who've we got here, then? Out after curfew?" said one of the men. He had bushy eyebrows and a bristling moustache. He was smiling but his eyes were sharp and cold as a hawk's in the bright searchlight of the wagon, circling the three youths like prey.

"Show us your identity cards."

"Lost it," said the boy, who wore an eyepatch like a pirate, while a girl with bird's nest hair said, "Left it at home." The smallest child, the one with missing teeth and bare feet, said nothing at all.

"You know what that means?" The head Inspector stared at them expectantly. "We're going to have to take a closer look. See, it's our job to keep these streets safe and clean from dirty-souled vermin like you."

Around his neck hung the pendant engraved with the Eye of the Order, marking him as a member of House Obscura, like the woman I'd stolen the hatpin from. That was the Chancellor's own house, the House of Shadows, which guarded the city from the darkness of the subconscious.

"Come on, then. If you've nothing to hide, you've nothing to fear. You don't have anything to hide, do you?"

"No," said the girl, hesitantly.

The Inspector's two subordinates flanked the kids, penning them in. I couldn't see how a couple of puny street rats could pose any threat to the all-mighty, all-seeing Order, but these Inspectors seemed to relish terrorizing them all the same.

"All you have to do is tell the truth. If you lie to us, we shall know, so you may as well tell the truth, the whole truth and nothing but."

The little boy with the eyepatch was reddening and

rumbling, on the verge of exploding like a volcano.

"Why don't you take a look at your own souls first?" he spat. "Oh wait, I know ... because you don't have none."

The girl gasped knowing – as I did – what would come next. The little boy began to cry.

"Suit yourselves," said Moustache, cheek twitching. "If you're not going to cooperate, I guess we'll just have to do this the hard way."

On his command, the Inspectors raised their shiny black bullseye lamps: magic lanterns, each one serving as an Eye of the Order. Like the eye-shaped street lights, they didn't just illuminate the city but the souls of the people who inhabited it.

The Eye network was the pride of Providence. It was what made our city the safest in the world. There was no crime here, or so the Order said, because the Eye saw everything; not just what people said and did, but also what they thought and felt and dreamt of in their beds.

The Eyes watched from every corner and courtyard, every lamp post and signpost. It wasn't just one eye or three or even a hundred eyes, but hundreds of thousands of eyes, an entire city of eyes: each with an Observer sitting behind it in a booth at the Observatory, for ever watching, always judging, tracking every soul in sight. They made sure no one disturbed the peace of Providence, or at least the illusion of it.

Now, the lanterns burst into light, triggering a magnesium flare like a photographer's flash, so bright it forced me to shield my eyes with one hand. Squinting through the brilliant glare, I saw the children frozen on the spot, like a row of marble statues at a museum. Eyepatch's lips were curled in a last-minute insult, while a tear had frozen halfway down Shoeless's face. They didn't blink or even seem to breathe, staring ahead, harshly irradiated by the glowing lanterns. And in the centre of their chests glowed a colourful orb of light.

One of the Inspectors produced a tablet, upon which the perfect soul was projected for comparison. Its five parts were evenly measured, dividing the soul into neat sections. Rumour said that it was the Chancellor's own soul.

The Shadow was perfectly symmetrical. The Spirit emitted a faint, pleasant perfume. The Song was harmonious. The Heart was sweet as sugar, its taste lingering on the lips. The Spark burned bright and steady like a candle. This was the standard by which all souls were judged.

"Look at this idiot," said Moustache, pointing at Eyepatch. "Boy's got a real temper on him. He's practically burning up inside."

His subordinate chuckled.

Along with the Inspector, I examined the boy's soul. It looked like a bird with wings of fire, caged by his ribs, casting bright sparks that spun into the darkness. A fire soul, a Spark. Its energy was so warm I could feel it from the cold of the shadows, like a hug or a warm jumper, neither of which I'd ever known, and yet, for a moment, I could imagine them vividly as if I had.

"And her? A sad little orphan, stuck in the past. Haunted by the ghosts of her lost childhood."

The girl was a Spirit soul. Her psyche was pale and misty, a cloud-shrouded moon that smelled like a musty old tomb and seemed to emanate wispy spirits, momentary sketches of memories drawn in tendrils of smoke.

The youngest boy's Heart soul glowed so gold and bright it looked as if the sun was rising inside him, illuminating every inch of the dingy alleyway. It made me feel hollow and haunted, unworthy to behold it, like looking at an angel in a stained-glass window.

The Inspectors didn't have anything bad to say about him.

The lanterns rapidly dimmed, freeing the three children from their strange, suspended state.

"You're all being arrested for the crime of latent deviancy," said Moustache. "Anything you say may be used against you in a court of law."

They were cuffed, the littlest child's cries echoing through the night.

They didn't deserve this, but there was no arguing with Inspectors. Their word was law. As they dragged the three kids towards the black wagon, they walked past me, lurking suspiciously in the darkness. I shuffled backwards instinctively, stepping on a loose tile.

One of the black coats stopped and hung back, swivelling his head in my direction, sharp as a cat that had spied a mouse.

"Who's there?" he said.

Light flooded the alley, catching upon the tip of my boot as I inched backwards, pressing up against a wall. Though obscured by shadows, I knew the Eye could see everything.

I held my breath, frozen like those children as he shone his lantern into the crack, his brow furrowed as he peered into the darkness.

The eye in the magic lantern blinked lazily, its gaze slightly off-set, as if staring straight through me.

"What's the hold-up?" came a voice.

"Nothing," said the Inspector. "Just a rat, I reckon."

"Then get a move on, boy. We don't have all night."

I watched as he retreated into the fog before I fled in the opposite direction. Half a mile on, I stopped to catch my breath in an alley plastered with posters for playhouses and phantasmagoria shows, beauty tonics and love potions, all ragged and dog-eared, rain-stained and sun-faded. They were vastly outshone by the Order's spectaculars: large, attention-grabbing billboards that hovered spectrally, playing the same scenes over and over.

A string of words popped up on screen: *prudence, patience, temperance, chastity, diligence, obedience, humility, charity.* These were the values of the Order: all our guiding principles.

I looked over at a group of vagrants huddled under a bridge. Despite these values, the Order didn't have much sympathy for those that didn't fit their flawless image. It wouldn't be long before the same Inspectors I'd just escaped from carted them off to the Reformatory so their souls could be scoured.

Another billboard showed a crowd of silhouettes waiting for a train. They had burning fireballs in their chests, symbolizing their bright, glowing souls ... all but one, who had a gaping hole instead.

On the outside, Hollows look just like everybody else, the caption warned, darkly. *But on the inside, they're soulless monsters. If you suspect that someone you know may be a Hollow, please report them to the authorities.*

The Five Signs of Soullessness flashed up in sequence.

Poor memory.

No personality.

Fearless.

Dreamless.

Unfeeling.

As I gazed at it, I couldn't help but smirk. I didn't need the Order to tell me what made a person soulless.

I knew that all too well.

I closed my eyes, listening for the sound of a fire inside. But nothing flickered, nothing burned.

That was why the Order's lanterns couldn't see me.

I had only a hole, where there ought to have been a soul.

A hollow.

2.

THE NIGHT THAT NEVER WAS

If you listened to the Order, being soulless was the worst thing a person could be, but honestly it hardly bothered me at all.

True, I had no memory beyond a year ago. I had no sense of my identity, no friends or family. I didn't fear, I didn't dream, I felt nothing but the discarded emotions captured in remnants.

But being a Hollow made me invisible, not literally but as good as. I had no presence, no trace, no energy that attracted people as others did. I was forgettable. For ever in the background. I'd go weeks without being fully seen by anyone but the Countess.

This I used to my great advantage.

Whether Countess Cavendish was truly a member of one of the Houses was unknown, though I'd heard many tall tales. Some said she had been stripped of her noble title as penance for a terrible crime. Others said she was the world's greatest con artist, and no man alive knew her true name.

I'd fallen in with her just under a year ago. I'd been

living on the streets of Providence, surviving on leftovers and bin scraps, with no memory of who I was or where I'd come from, when I heard rumours that a fancy old woman who lived in the First Borough would pay good money for stolen curios and knick-knacks. I took a trip to the Bazaar and filled my pockets with objects I thought were interesting. Little did I know I'd brought her a handful of remnants, drawn by that tell-tale glimmer.

When the Countess realized I had the sense for psyche, she paid me to fetch things. When she realized the Eyes couldn't see me, I became her favourite pet. With practice, I got better at hunting out exactly what the Countess truly desired: remnants that harboured sinister secrets.

The Countess lived in the same borough as the Chancellor himself, the upmarket First Borough, famed for its colossal sculptures. It was accessible by a set of stone staircases that always left me breathless. Her house was several storeys lower than the high-walled sky garden villa owned by Chancellor Obscura and his family, but still a good distance from the ground level where thieves like me scratched out a living.

At the wrought-iron gates, I banged the heavy brass knocker until a pair of watery eyes appeared in the sliding hatch. Her butler let me in, bowing his head and standing to one side.

"Miss Iris," he said.

"Graves," I said, nodding.

I ascended to the first floor, past antique maps, brass

busts and giant globes with the names of countries written in Latin. The panelled walls were lined with portraits of sunken-eyed, dour-mouthed nobles in ermine-lined cloaks, posing with leopards, sceptres and swords. At the end of the long corridor was a red door with a heart-shaped knob. I knocked thrice, waiting for the usual airy call of, "Come in!"

When it came, I stepped inside the familiar room. The darkened, heavily-draped parlour on the other side was an Aladdin's cave of wonderments. The side tables were cluttered with rich people's baubles, like crystal geodes and Nautilus shells, while muscular marble gods stood guard in the corners.

The Countess was a collector of priceless antiquities. Her home was decorated with invaluable heirlooms. But her most prized possession was what she called her Cabinet of Curiosities: a glass-fronted ornamental display case with many small compartments.

The items within were of little worth at first glance.

A small telescope. A rusty harmonica. A perfume bottle with a tasselled atomizer. A pair of worn velvet gloves. A chipped porcelain tea cup...

To the layperson's eye they were just meaningless trinkets, but I knew better: each was a memento of a particular event. The Countess collected them, blackmailing their owners for money or favours.

She played their memories for me sometimes when she was in a jovial mood, like a film night at the picture house, while we ate chocolate and gossiped about the Order's misdeeds. The telescope contained the memory of a military massacre. The harmonica held the memory of an innocent man sentenced to the gallows. The gloves told the story of a forbidden love affair, while the chipped tea cup had witnessed a grisly poisoning.

A slight, elderly woman with piercing blue eyes, her hair covered by a veil, the Countess sat before the roaring fireplace, dressed all in black – as if she was on her way to a funeral or a wake. I'd asked her once if she was mourning someone or something. "My youth," she'd responded, dryly.

I leant against the door, closing it. The scene I'd witnessed with the street children was still fresh in my mind.

"You'll never guess what—" I began.

"Hush," she said, as I entered.

I sat down beside her on the chaise longue, crossing my ankles and hugging a silk cushion. "What are we watching?" I whispered.

"The memories of a snow globe," she said.

Propped on the lace-dressed table beside her was a magic lantern, the metal, bullseye kind carried by the Inspectors. Under its jewelled light, psyche could be revealed, projecting the memory of the person who owned the object, putting on a show for us voyeurs. I didn't know where she'd got it, and I didn't care to ask. It made a low, juddering noise.

In the dusty beam of the lantern's bulb was indeed a snow globe, with miniature carved figures skating on a lake.

The flickering spotlight projected moving shadows on the wall. They acted out dioramic scenes as if imbued with a mind of their own, forming vignettes and silhouettes, like the puppets of a shadowbox show. Two young lovers danced in a bandstand pavilion, surrounded by the vignette of a rose garden. They whirled and twirled as he dipped her slowly at the waist. Laughing without sound, they stood upright again, leaning in for a slow kiss as fireworks formed roses in the sky above.

"Doesn't seem like your sort of thing," I said.

"Wait for it," she said.

The lovers broke apart, beginning to argue. The boy stormed off in a rage, as the girl ran after him in tears.

I shivered, involuntarily.

I knew nothing of love other than what I'd learned from remnants, and what I did know was dreadful. Such bitter pain and broken longing, making me sickened and dizzy. Love was a madness, a catastrophe.

The lantern stuttered and dimmed as the remnant reached the end of its imprinted memories.

"Well, don't keep me in suspense," she trilled primly.

Digging eagerly into my pocket, I pulled out the hatpin.

"Very good," she purred. She turned it over in her lace-gloved hands, using a jeweller's loupe to examine it. "You've developed quite the eye for this, haven't you, dear?"

"I should hope so," I said, folding my arms proudly. "I've nicked enough of them for you now."

"Do the honours, won't you?" she said.

I removed the snow globe from the little tray in front of the lantern's beam, replacing it with the hatpin. Its shadow fell upon the wall in front of us as we sat in anticipation, like spectators at a theatre. The Countess peered through her opera glasses.

At once, the darkness came alive.

The slender shadow of a petite, well-dressed woman skulked in an open doorway, spying on a bearded man sitting at a desk. She removed the pin from her hat before creeping up on him, plunging the pin into the side of his neck. Black shadow blood gushed from the wound of the faceless victim. He turned to his killer, whispering something unheard before slumping to the ground. The silhouetted murderess watched him coolly a moment. Then she wiped the pin clean on the man's shirt, stuck it back in her hat and departed the scene. The shadows dissipated as the spotlight faded.

"How delightfully morbid," said the Countess. "I'm sure dear Lady Cleary will be willing to pay a handsome sum to get it back. She wouldn't want this to fall into the wrong hands, would she now?"

She fished around in her purse, a beaded, tasselled thing she kept beside her on the chaise longue, pulling out a handful of coins.

"I'll give you half a crown for it," she said.

"Is that all?" I said, my face spoiling.

"What did you expect, dear?"

She pressed the coin into my palm and gestured at the

hatpin. "Put it away for me, won't you?" she said. "The snow globe too."

"What am I, your servant?"

The Countess gave a musical chuckle.

I approached the Cabinet of Curiosities, pulling open its glinting glass doors and moved the assorted curios around to make room for the pin. When I turned back to face her, the Countess looked me up and down, tilting her head from side to side.

"You know, if you're looking for a proper windfall, I have just the job in mind," she said.

"I'm listening," I said, after a beat.

"I need you to procure something very special for me," she said.

She pottered around busily, rooting through the drawers in her writing desk. Triumphantly, she pulled out a silver fork.

"A fork?" I scoffed. "Are you looking for the knife to match?"

"No, dear. Do not be fooled by its humble appearance," she said, "for it contains the memory of a most mysterious event."

"Go on," I said.

She propped the fork up in front of the lantern, where it projected the vignette of a lavishly decorated room with vine-wrapped pillars. I felt a flicker of interest, despite myself.

"A winter ball at the Basilica of All Souls, held on

December 24th last year," she said. "That night, something happened. Some say there was a battle. Sirens rang for hours. The streets were cordoned off by Inspectors, as attested to by many witnesses, but the following day everything was exactly as it ought to be – or so it appeared."

"What does *that* mean?" I said.

"There were rumours. Some of the guests were left with strange feelings they couldn't explain. Things they had seen, which were now forgotten, as if they never happened at all. They could not properly recall the evening. And stranger still were the things left behind that could not be explained. A broken window. A lost shoe. A trail of blood… A single fork, found in a flower bed."

On the wall, a group of elegant, stuffy-looking silhouettes took up their cutlery, delicately dissecting miniscule desserts as servants whisked away empty plates. There was no sound but I could see a commotion unfurling in the background. People turned their heads and stood up, flocking to the front of the ballroom. I couldn't see what they were looking at, nor the expressions on their faces, but the memory's maker hastily backed out of the room, almost as if they had been expecting trouble.

The vision faded out.

"This, as far as I know, is the only remnant that exists from the ball on the night of December 24th. The Night That Never Was. I have yet to identify the person who created it."

"Not very illuminating," I said.

"Doesn't that seem strange to you? A room full of wealthy, highly important people and pretty, expensive trinkets and only a single fork can be found to testify that it ever happened at all? Probably overlooked due to its apparent unimportance. I've acquired several artefacts from that night and all of them are curiously blank, wiped of psyche. All but the fork."

"What do you think happened that night?" I asked.

"Something the Order wants covered up if they removed all traces of it. Naturally, I want to know what they're so keen to hide."

"So what is it you want me to steal, exactly?" I said.

The memory played again. This time, the Countess pointed to the silhouette of an older woman in a dress with many ruffles, sitting in a wheelchair, her hair piled up on top of her head in a beehive fashion.

"That's Lady Rubella Renato," she said. "Her son Ruben is the Chancellor's right-hand man."

"I know who he is. I read the papers. What about her?" I said.

"Ever since that night, Rubella has worn a particular ring. Venetian gold, set with stones of amberic and ruby. Amberic is known for its psychometric properties, of course, being an ideal material to hold a memory. I am certain it's a remnant, and a powerful one at that."

The Countess turned to me, her pale eyes boring into mine.

"I believe it may conceal the truth about the Night That

Never Was. I believe it may be hiding a terrible secret. According to my spies, that secret involves nothing less than the destruction of a human soul."

"The Order can do that?" I said, breath catching in my throat.

"They can do anything," she said.

"I thought they were purifying souls," I said. "Why would they destroy a soul when they could save it instead?"

"Perhaps you don't know the Order as well as you think," she said.

The weighty statement hung in the silence between us.

"I'm willing to pay five crowns for the ring," she said, coaxingly. She pulled a small velvet money bag from her purse and tossed it quickly in my direction, so I had to fumble to catch it. I eagerly loosened its neck, gazing down at the shiny gold coins inside.

That same old thrill coursed through me, spiking my adrenaline.

"Lady Renato wears the ring everywhere she goes. She'll be at the Golden Gavel tomorrow night, in the Fifth Borough, near the harbour."

"If the Inspectors catch me skulking around after curfew they'll make sure I end the night in the back of a wagon," I said.

"The Inspectors won't be stopping anyone near the Golden Gavel. It's an auction house. A respectable establishment. You won't have any trouble so long as you're rubbing shoulders with the right people. Collecting remnants is the latest fashion among the nobles of Providence, including the wealthy donors who keep the Order's caviar flowing. They'll bid extraordinary amounts to possess an object that keeps the memory of a military battle or a royal wedding, just so they might show it off on their mantelpiece."

I slowly shook my head. "So, let me get this straight," I said. "You want me to steal a priceless ring off the finger of a member of the illuminated nobility in the middle of a crowded room full of loyalists? All because it *might* contain the memory of a night no one remembers in the first place?"

She gave a barking laugh, in amusement or disdain, I wasn't sure.

"That's right," she said.

I licked my lips, considering her proposition. Five crowns was a lot, but was it worth the risk of getting caught, however small?

"Think of it this way," she said, circling me. "Lady Renato is older than half the antiquities in Providence. She could pass over at any moment and who knows what would happen to the ring then? It would be a tragedy for such a treasure to be buried six feet under. Then we'd never know the truth about the Order's misdeeds. How could you live with yourself?"

"It's not my conscience that's troubling me," I said. "It's my common sense. I'm quite fond of my freedom, you know, and this sounds likely to get me robbed of it."

The Countess clucked her tongue, batting her hand.

"You needn't worry. You're hardly even a person, Iris. Not even the ghosts will know you were there. You're the only person in this city that the Eyes can't see. Besides, it would please me. You want to please me, don't you?"

The Countess knew my secret. She'd guessed I was Hollow when I'd arrived at her doorstep with no name, no memory and a handful of trinkets. She'd named me Iris because of the odd keyhole shape in one of my eyes. She kept me close, knowing I'd be useful. Besides that, she was my only source of income. If I didn't do what she wanted, she might turn sour on me.

"You know, I'm not sure five crowns will cut it after all," I said. "This sounds more like a ten-crown job."

"Six crowns," she bartered.

"Nine," I said.

"Seven crowns and fifty cents. That's my final offer. Do we have a deal?" The Countess removed one lace glove. "Any agreement needs a proper handshake to seal it."

Reluctantly, I put my hand in hers.

In the space of a heartbeat, she'd snatched the money bag back, prying it out of my hand with ease.

"Hey!" I said, reaching out to grab thin air.

"You'll get paid when you deliver what has been promised."

"That's not fair."

"That's how business arrangements work, dear. But first, we must do something about your unsightly appearance."

I gazed down upon myself, taking in the muddy boots I'd stolen from a sleeping tramp under a bridge. I didn't put much thought into my appearance. What was the point when no one paid me any notice?

"We can't have you turning up like that," the Countess said. "They'll think you've come selling matchsticks or begging for scraps. No, you can borrow some of my old clothes. Come."

She gestured for me to follow.

Upstairs, the air was stale and every surface was thick with dust. In the Countess's dressing room, a beam of dusty light bounced off the cloudy vanity mirror on the dressing table. From the branches of a jet and ivory tree hung many earrings and bracelets and necklaces.

I reached out curiously but she quickly slapped my hand away. "Did I say you could touch anything?" she said.

She disappeared into her closet, rifling through dusty garments and sending out moths. "Ah! Here it is." She shoved a garment bag into my chest.

At her insistence, I retreated upstairs to the box room she let me stay in on occasion. It would have been foolish to call it "my room". I knew well that it didn't belong to me. Its walls were empty. Its drawers were empty. But I knew its lumpy mattress. I knew its creaks and draughts. It was as close to a home as I could remember.

"What's taking so long?" called the Countess.

I put on the black velvet mourning gown, grumbling all the while. It had a black velvet bonnet to match, which I tucked my tangled red curls into, tying its ribbon beneath my chin.

When I looked in the mirror I saw ... the Countess. Rich. Elegant. Morbid. Empty.

Would I end up like her one day, hoarding remnants in cabinets and paying street kids to steal for me? I could think of worse things, I supposed.

I opened the door to reveal myself.

"Well?" I said.

"Hmm. You'll do. But your posture is all wrong, dear. Straighten your back. Hold your chin up." She demonstrated the correct stance, seeming suddenly younger than she ever had before. "You're not a street rat now, you're a woman of society."

"No one will notice me anyway," I said, dismissively.

"Let's hope not. If our plan is to work, you must remain unseen and unheard. You should do nothing to draw attention to yourself. There will be a soul lantern on the door but it shouldn't pick you up, Hollow as you are. Beyond that, trust no one. Do you understand?"

"Is it really worth it?" I said. "All for a ring? Why do you care so much what happened that night?"

The Countess hesitated a moment before answering. "If a secret is worth obliterating the memory of everyone in the vicinity, it's priceless to those who wish to keep it hidden. Nothing is more precious than the truth in a world of lies. Think of the power I could attain with that knowledge at my fingertips."

It always came back to blackmail, in the end.

To power, to knowledge.

Later that night, once the Countess had retired to bed, I snuck downstairs again and slipped into her parlour, pulling out the button I'd stolen earlier. It was nothing special, just a simple brown tortoiseshell type.

Running it between my fingers like a coin, I tried to draw out the warm, safe feeling I'd experienced, but it wasn't as strong as before. A remnant was never as good as the first time you touched it.

I turned on the lantern, placing the button in its tray. Its shade took form, branching into swirling patterns that reassembled themselves into two new silhouettes. This time, a mother and child. The mother bent down to fix the collar of her daughter's cape. She repeated the action again and again as the nights and days passed in cycles behind her. Then the seasons, as the birds and blossoms of spring and summer made way for the falling leaves of autumn and snowflakes of winter.

The two grew old before my eyes, for even when the girl became a woman her mother still fixed her collar, replacing a new button with the old one she'd worn all her life, until the elder woman grew hunched, her hands withered, until she sank into a chair and never got up again.

The shadows flaked to dust, dispersing into nothing,

until only the silhouette of the button remained.

I retrieved it, cradling it in my palm. I closed my eyes, imagining what it must be like to be that girl, whose mother cherished her so much she buttoned her collar every day.

What it must be like to be loved.

To be treasured.

The snow globe glittered nearby. Swapping it for the button, I watched the shadows dance again. Holding up my arms to mimic their pose, I waltzed with an invisible partner, fantasizing about what it might feel like to be in love. Maybe it didn't matter that it ended in tragedy. Maybe it was worth experiencing anyway. I watched the couple kiss and quarrel over and over again, but my heart was still dry and empty, cold as stone, matching my Hollow soul.

Back in the spare room, I placed the button in the old shoebox under the bed, where I stored all the things I'd stolen that the Countess had no interest in. They were the happy memories she thought boring. The plain, uneventful days of ordinary people. Joy. Sorrow. Nostalgia. Contentment... These common, everyday feelings were just as alien to me as the jealousy and vengeance that drove people to murder their husbands with hatpins.

I often tried to imagine myself in those serene, domestic scenarios. Sitting down for dinner. Flying kites in the park. Sweeping ashes from the fire. Yet each time, it was a disaster. The dinner became a food fight. The kite got stuck in a tree. The fire burned down the house.

The harsh truth was that I didn't belong in the happy, shiny, normal world. I belonged here in the shadows, where all the thieves and rebels and broken, corrupted souls lived in secrecy and anonymity. I'd been lost and alone in the darkness for so long that I'd become a part of it now.

I was Hollow.

Empty from the inside out.

I was soulless and I was glad of it, for it protected me from the worst that the world had to offer.

3.

THE MEMORY THIEF

Graves drove me to the scene of the crime-to-be, travelling through the First Borough, past the Observatory where the Order's servants watched through the Eyes, and on to the Fifth Borough, home to the Reformatory, where souls were cleansed.

Passing over a latticed iron bridge lined with torch fires, we joined the queue of carriages that crawled along the high road, looking down above the harbour where cargo ships ferried luxury goods out to the colonies and factory chimneys belched thick black shadow smoke.

The Order ruled half the world, from Providence in the East to Constitution in the West. Back in the Middle Ages, five scholars from Providence had performed an alchemic experiment that illuminated the dark matter of consciousness – psyche – allowing them to harness its power. They were the founders of the Order and the five Houses, promising to shine a light on the secrets within the hearts of men and use their knowledge and power for good. From their discovery came the Enlightenment where the tenets of the Order were forged – that only the pure of soul were worthy of a place in society. The same belief that guided the Order today.

An imposing-looking building with marble columns, decorated with gold filigree, the Golden Gavel was busy with bidders: oily, moustachioed men in top hats and pinstripes; extravagantly-fashioned women in diamonds and furs; foreign dignitaries in ceremonial robes and aristocrats in avant-garde accessories.

I peered through the carriage window, steamy with condensation. As the Countess had said, there was a glass lantern above the entrance, reflecting the Eyes of the Observers who watched from the First Borough. The lantern illuminated the soul of each person as they entered, displaying their psychograph in its panels. Fire soul. Shadow soul. Song soul. Each one was approved and certified to be within the desired limits of balance, the lantern glowing green.

A group of Inspectors talked among themselves nearby, ready to cart off anyone who got rejected, but again the Countess was correct – they didn't seem to be expecting any trouble here tonight.

Graves pulled up, jumping out to open the door.

"I'll be waiting here when you return," he said.

I gave him a stiff nod before climbing out awkwardly, laced into the dress so tightly I couldn't breathe. Looking back over my shoulder, I watched as the carriage disappeared down the road, leaving me alone.

You're invisible, I told myself, as I waited in line.

Forgettable.

A ghost of a girl.

Stepping beneath the lantern, I lifted my chin, not pausing to watch if its light turned red before boldly striding forth as if I belonged there. Only when no one stopped me did I realize I'd been successful.

The lantern glowed neither red nor green but remained dark, as if failing to register my presence at all. It was exactly as the Countess had said: the Eyes didn't seem to see me.

Exhaling, I pushed on. Inside, the auction was already in full swing. The room was thick with wealthy patrons, all seated in rows and holding numbered paddles. I joined the loose group of spectators standing at the back of the room: important enough to be there but not important enough to get a chair. None of them paid any mind to me, too busy leafing through their pamphlets, boasting about how much they wanted to spend.

On a raised stage at the front of the room, a dandelion-haired gentleman in a silver suit stood at a small podium, gesticulating wildly with a golden gavel.

"Our next item, number 83, is this charming statuette depicting a young bride and groom," he said. A soft chorus of oohs filled the room as a smiling, white-gloved assistant placed it on the auction box. She slowly turned the rotating cabinet, showing off every angle.

"Eighteenth century, fine porcelain, hand-painted. Recovered from a house sale. As per the catalogue, it contains a nine-minute memory of the ill-fated wedding between Charles Vandergriff the Third and Veronica Sophia Beaumont, which can be revealed with a magic lantern or psychoscope."

A scandalized murmur rippled through the crowd.

"As you may recall, the ceremony was interrupted by a male servant claiming to be the groom's lover, leading to a brawl in the aisle. The Vandergriff and Beaumont families were subsequently expelled from the Order. The memory is clear, high quality, with only minor corruptions due to improper storage. Starting at ninety crowns. Do I have any takers?"

"Ninety crowns," I whispered bitterly beneath my breath. I could rent a room at an inn for a year if I had ninety crowns in my pocket, but these people were willing to spend it on a gossip-filled trinket.

The Countess paid me in pretty words and wind. I had to find a better job, a more rewarding profession.

The auctioneer's sparkling eyes swept the room. "Yes, I see ninety," he said, nodding at the man in the top hat who raised his paddle aloft.

I stuck close to the wall, squeezing through the crowd, murmuring polite apologies to the people I pushed past.

"Do I hear one hundred? Yes, thank you, madam."

Three bidders continued to battle, as the heads of the audience swung back and forth. Scanning the crowd, I spied Lady Renato, recognizable by her silhouette, sitting in a gold wheelchair with a red blanket on her lap. She was being chaperoned by a grim-faced nurse.

"One hundred and fifty over here, thank you sir."

I spied the ring sitting pretty on the Lady's thin, wrinkly finger, loose enough that it hung crookedly. It was even more impressive in person, its flame-shaped jewel catching the light of the chandeliers as if it were burning. As I looked at it, I felt myself sucked in as the room faded out and I was rocked by a surge of feeling – a prickly, tingly, skin-crawling sensation.

There were dozens of remnants on display, all of which twinkled deliciously under the light of the chandeliers, but none gave me such strong feelings as the ring. My spine rippled, as if an invisible musician was playing a symphony on my vertebrae. My heart sped, racing so fast I thought it might crash and burn. *Ba-dum, ba-dum, ba-dum.*

The closer I got to Lady Renato the stronger the ring's energy became. It was a turbulent, tumbling, manic and maddening sensation, a terrible restlessness that made me want to tear off my skin. I longed for it, hungered for it, though I couldn't say why.

Lady Renato was starting to nod off. Her head bobbed, her hands crossed over the paddle in her lap.

"Are you in, madam?" called the auctioneer. "Are you certain? What about you? It could be your lucky evening, sir. What about two hundred and ninety? Do I hear two hundred and ninety? Anyone? No? Then we're going, going, gone!"

Another sort of thief might have constructed an elaborate

plan, mapping out all of the possibilities and anticipating them simultaneously, but I had no talent for imagining outcomes or inventing master strokes. I would make it up as I went along, just as I always did.

The auctioneer banged his gavel on the desk and the statue was whisked away. The white-gloved assistant brought out the next item: a fancy blue and white plate. Sidling up to the Lady's nurse, I tugged urgently on her coat-sleeve and put on my best, most upper-class voice.

"Excuse me, ma'am. You're a nurse, aren't you?"

"What of it?" she snapped.

"So sorry to bother you," I said, "but I'm here with my sister. She's pregnant. She went out for some air and fainted. I sent for a doctor but he'll be some time. Please, could you help?"

"I wish I could, I do," she said, pulling an exaggeratedly sympathetic face, "but I'm not trained as a midwife."

"Please, I'm worried it might be an emergency," I tried. "She's far along. The baby might be coming…"

The nurse gestured at her now sleeping charge. "Even if I wanted to, I'm on duty," she said.

"Sold for seventy crowns, to the man with the purple cravat!"

"I can watch her," I said. "It's no problem. No trouble. I look after my grandmother all the time."

The nurse snorted. "That's Lady Renato, honey, the matriarch of one of the five great and noble Houses. Not your old nan. I'll be swimming in seven shades of hell if anything happens to her."

41

"But what if there's something wrong with the baby! You don't want a stain like that on your soul, do you?"

Her face wrinkled, as if she'd sucked on a lemon. I could tell she was weighing up how this might play out, and what sort of punishment she'd face if ever the Order caught wind of it. People had to act as if the authority was always watching. Probably because they were.

She looked me up and down, taking note of my fine clothes.

"All right, all right," she relented, grabbing her coat. "Where is she?"

"We walked a little way around the corner."

"Stay here and keep an eye on her," she instructed, gesturing at Lady Renato. "If she wakes up, tell her I won't be long. That I'm going on a worthy errand. I'll bring your sister back here if I can rouse her."

"Of course. Thank you, ma'am."

As soon as she disappeared through the doors, the phony smile slid off my face like butter on a hot plate. I picked up a printed catalogue someone had dropped, outlining the particulars of the items for sale. Kneeling down next to Lady Renato, I dropped the pamphlet into her lap, hiding her hands.

"I agree, ma'am, that *would* look lovely on the mantelpiece," I said.

As my fingertips grazed the gold band, a static shock pinged sharply against my skin.

"Ouch," I hissed.

I tried again, and this time a wave of vibrating energy passed through the empty shell of my body. I gasped as fragmented visions flashed in my mind, like reflections in the broken shards of a mirror.

White marble, red velvet, gold, fire...

A masked figure in a black hood...

Panic closed my throat. A sharp pain tore through my chest. Gritting my teeth, I managed to wriggle the ring down her finger.

Lady Renato snorted awake, startling me.

"Wha'sgo'n?" she muttered, clutching my sleeve. I froze, the ring in my hand. She blinked at me as I attempted to gather myself. I straightened up, hiding my hand behind my back.

"You're not Doris," she said.

I surreptitiously slid the ring into my pocket.

"Where's Doris?" she demanded.

"Doris had to step out. Someone took sick in the street. She asked me to keep an eye on you."

Her brow furrowed.

"Don't I know you from somewhere, girl?"

Taking one step backwards, I shook my head.

"I doubt that, ma'am," I said. "I'm no one. No one at all."

The old lady's wrinkles deepened as she peered at me suspiciously, then down at her hands in her lap.

"I have to go," I said. "Nice meeting you."

I backed away hastily, squeezing through the gaps between chairs.

"My ring!" she shouted. "Where's my ring?"

Pushing through the dense crowd of bargain-hunters, I threw open the doors. The cold air stung my cheeks like a slap. To my horror, the lantern overhead glowed red, making a dull, droning noise. The Inspectors looked over.

No. No. That couldn't be right...

I was supposed to be a ghost.

The ring was glowing red as a fire iron, too. It was warm to the touch, burning through my coat pocket like a hot coal. I hurtled down the street, frantically looking for my Lady's carriage, but it wasn't there.

"Oi! You!"

I looked behind me and saw the auctioneer and two of his white-gloved assistants running down the street in my direction. Lady Renato wheeled herself out after them.

"That's her!" she called, as Doris reappeared, looking furious. "That's the little rat who stole from me!"

I put my head down and ran for my life, speeding up until the streets became a blur. A group of Inspectors poured out of the station on the corner, pounding down the road towards me, some on foot, some on horseback. Rubberneckers flooded the pavement, pointing as the Inspectors pursued me, splitting into factions so they could surround me from all sides.

So much for not attracting too much attention.

I bolted, headed towards the Lower Lanes of the Fifth Borough, causing bystanders to scatter like bowling pins.

"Don't let her get away!"

"Someone stop her!"

Escape route blocked, I headed towards the bridge, where trams and omnibuses roared past at high speed. Horse-carriages rode in-between them, ringing bells and cracking whips.

Two Inspectors burst through the crowd behind me. Stumbling, I ran straight into the road, narrowly avoiding being mown down by a bus, darting through the speeding traffic. The Inspectors hesitated behind me. A carriage missed me by an inch, honking violently.

"Watch where you're going, numbskull!" called its driver.

Diving on to the pavement on the other side, I scrambled to my feet and staggered down the endless stone steps into an alleyway, winding through an obstacle course of descending streets lined with slop bins and puke barrels, mangy cat gangs and overflowing drains.

I found a good hiding-spot beneath the bridge, where I could climb up into the rafters with the birds. The black coats charged underneath, their beams scouring the ground, not noticing my legs dangling overhead. I waited until they were out of sight before letting out the breath I was holding in. Climbing down, I fished out the ring.

"Bloody thing," I muttered. "You almost got me killed." It was still warm, though its heat faded in my palm. "What's so special about you? What are you hiding?" Curious, I slipped it on, finding that it snugly fit the middle digit of my left hand, like Cinderella's slipper.

All at once, the world bled away.

I was tumbling, falling, somersaulting backwards inside myself, plummeting into that deep, dark place where people lose themselves. I was floating in the middle of an abyss. There was no land, air or sea, only a dense, dark mist through which I could neither walk nor swim.

A speck of light emerged from the murky depths, like a single burning ember in a pile of spent ashes. It called to me and I struggled towards it, watching as the tiny spark grew stronger and brighter.

As I drew closer, the ember burst into a pulsating ball of flame that crackled and flickered, illuminating the darkness around me and revealing swirling bioluminescent patterns. Strange tremors passed through all the pores and ridges in my skin, every part of me fizzing and tingling, every cell singing, from the follicles on my scalp to the tips of my toenails.

In the fire, a picture developed like a photograph from a negative. My own face stared back at me, a mirror's image.

A river of pictures flooded through the empty pit of my head, winding and snaking, its current too quick to keep up with.

Green fields. Clean sheets. Falling rain. Dark birds.

A freckled woman with tears in her eyes, mouthing a silent warning.

Burning embers, a painted phoenix…

Blood drops on snow…

A masked figure, raising their arm as if to strike.

I felt myself drawn back to reality, yanked backwards as if by a leash. Forced back into the vessel of my body. Into a new reality.

I was alive.

I existed, and it was very strange.

4.

BORN AGAIN

The sudden sound of an approaching wagon startled me. Panicked, I fled my hiding spot, trying to lose myself in the shadows of the deserted streets. The ring on my finger seemed to throb along with my heartbeat.

"What just happened?" I whispered.

Adrenaline surged through my blood, catching like fire.

I felt like a wick that had just been lit.

As I ran, I became acutely aware of the pattern of my breathing and the steady rhythm of my own heart beating.

The bitter wind howled wolfishly, tossing up dead leaves. A barking dog jangled my nerves. A singing child sent a chill through me.

I had the feeling I was being watched.

Panting, I slowed to a fast walk. The streets were almost empty this late after curfew, but there were still a few grimy ne'er-do-wells hanging about, smoking pipes in alleyways and talking in hushed, furtive voices. They looked at me hard as I hurtled past.

I told myself it was the outfit. In the Countess's funereal

dress, I must have looked conspicuous lurking around in the Lower Lanes. Or maybe it was the ring that people were sensing. I took it off and stashed it away, deep in my pocket, but it didn't seem to change anything. People stared just the same.

Looking up, I spied an eye-shaped glass lantern, tracking the souls on the street. As I passed, it whirred to life, a beam of light sweeping towards me. I flung myself behind a pile of stinking rubbish to avoid its sight.

That was new.

The lanterns had never tracked *me* before.

Shivering, I moved on. Everywhere I turned, there was another eye to spy on me. There were eyes moulded on to lamp posts and painted on to walls, eyes embroidered on to flags or sculpted in relief. They were etched in brass and landscaped in grass, carved in wood and laid in mosaic.

Each one seemed to fix on me as I walked by.

Unless it wasn't the dress or the ring. Unless it was me. Deep within me, something had sparked into existence. I was used to being invisible, a spectre of flesh and bone, but ever since I'd stolen that ring, I'd felt … seen.

Now here was the proof: the lanterns could see me too.

I didn't like it one bit.

I made my way back to the home of the Countess, all the while looking over my shoulder to make sure I wasn't being followed. When Graves opened the door, his face rumpled with relief.

"Miss Iris! I'm so relieved you're all right."

I glared at him. "What happened to you?"

"I apologize. The harbour was crawling with Inspectors."

"The Countess is lucky I made it out alive with the prize," I said, shaking off the rain. I took one last look at the street before stepping inside, but I didn't see any Inspectors lingering.

As usual, I'd got away with it somehow.

Upstairs in the parlour, my Lady was waiting for me, surrounded by a dozen empty chocolate boxes. She blamed her sweet tooth on being a Heart soul, a weak excuse I'd always thought.

"*There* you are!" she said eagerly, standing up. "It's about time! What took you so long?"

I closed the door, listening to the whispers of the remnants in her cabinets. Their energies felt stronger than usual tonight.

I paused, deliberating over how much to tell her.

"I might've got here sooner if my ride hadn't bailed on me," was all I admitted.

"Tell me you have it," she demanded.

"Of course I have it," I said, holding the ring out for her to see.

She snatched it from my hands, inspecting it intimately.

I watched on, feeling oddly jealous. I wanted it back, like a woman letting a stranger hold her newborn baby.

"You weren't seen, of course?" she said, still peering at the ring.

I knew I ought to warn her just in case they tracked me

back here, but I was afraid she wouldn't pay me if I did.

"Oh, I don't think anyone noticed," I lied.

The Countess placed the ring in the tray in front of the lantern. "And now, for the moment of truth," she said.

In silence, we waited patiently for the shadow show to begin, but nothing developed. Grunting, she gave the lantern an energetic thump. "Come on. Stupid contraption," she chided. It rattled and juddered, spewing sparks. The seconds stretched out, long and taut. The machine whined unnaturally, before clapping out with a puff of acrid-smelling smoke.

Tutting, the Countess swapped the ring for the fork, still propped up nearby. Its psychic shadows came to life as normal, re-enacting the same scene at the ball as before. She returned the ring to the tray once more, yet still it failed to produce any imagery.

"I don't understand. Why isn't it working?" I said.

The Countess turned to face me, hands on hips.

"Perhaps you can tell me, Iris?" she said, sharply.

"Wait. You think this is *my* fault?"

She retrieved the ring from the lantern's tray.

"Who else?" she said, examining it again. "Are you trying to hoodwink me, girl? You think you can trick me with some counterfeit so you can sell it to one of your friends on the black market? I may be old but my mind is still sharp as that hatpin. Never trust the soulless, that's what people say."

My cheeks grew warm. "You trusted me to steal your

precious treasure, didn't you?" I said. "When have I ever failed you before? That's the real deal right there. Straight from the hand of Lady Renato herself. You'll be reading all about it in the papers tomorrow, trust me."

"I thought you said you weren't seen," said the Countess, her eyes narrowing suspiciously.

"They'll know it's been stolen by now," I said. "They'll be probing the memories of everyone in attendance."

"They'll be looking for a girl with no face. A girl with no name. If they remember you at all, if they even saw you in the first place."

"If they catch me, they'll come for you," I said. "They'll know you had me fetch it as soon as they start groping around inside my head."

The Countess chuckled airily.

"Hollows can't be probed," she said. "Nor can their image be captured permanently in memory. As far as they'll know, we've never met. That's why the soulless make such good confidantes, and rather useful accomplices."

I'd always known she was using me, but now it bothered me. She'd sent me into hell to fetch her a trinket and now she was complaining about it. Fire rising inside, I couldn't prevent the truth from blurting out.

"I'm not Hollow any more," I said. "The Eye can see me now."

"You're lying," she said, after a pause.

"It's true. The lantern picked me up on the way out. They might be able to access my memories too."

She watched me intently for a moment, before raising the loupe to her eye with a shaking hand. Whatever she saw, it made her jolt reflexively.

"Foolish girl," she hissed, pushing the ring back into my hands. "And you led them right back here? You must go. Right now."

"What about the Night That Never Was? What about—"

"It doesn't matter now. You'd do well to be rid of the thing, before it lands us all in the Reformatory."

"Get rid of it?" I said. "You promised me seven crowns and fifty cents for it! You should at least pay half."

"Didn't you hear what I said? No pawnshop in ten miles will touch it once the Order reports it stolen. They'll put a trace on it soon enough. Perhaps they already have. Throw it in the river for all the good it'll do us now. Gather your things and don't come back. Now, I must send one of my servants out to see whether the Order are on your tail yet. I want you gone by the time I return."

She hurtled down the stairs, calling for Graves. I stared resentfully at her back before sighing and jamming the ring back on my finger.

In the Cabinet of Curiosities, I spied the hatpin, which seemed to glitter at me mischievously. Maybe I could pawn that instead. It would serve her right for going back on our agreement.

"Finders keepers," I whispered.

I reached out for the pin. As soon as my fingers touched it, I plunged inside myself again – just like I had when

53

I had first put the ring on my finger, careening through the darkness. Suddenly, without explanation, I found myself standing in the dioramic scene of the hatpin's murderous memory.

It wasn't just a feeling or a vision. I was right there, transported to an entirely different place and time.

I am standing in the doorway of a house I've never been to, some years in the past, watching a bearded man I've never met scribbling at his desk.

Gazing through a stranger's eyes like windows, I watch my victim sign his signature. Unspeakable hatred floods through me.

I am the murderess.

Her thoughts echoed in my ears, as if they were my own.

That dirty, rotten cheater. I've given him the best years of my life, I've carried two of his sons into this world, and this is how he repays me? Writing love letters to another woman? I'll kill him. I'll kill him.

I prize the pin from my hat and step forward. He turns to greet me and I bring the weapon down without hesitation, into the soft flesh of his neck. The sound and feel of it is sickening but much worse is the blood, dripping down my hands as I pull it out again.

"No!"

His face wrinkles in disbelief and something else … remorse, or regret.

"Why, my darling," he croaks, lying even now. "Why?"

"You know why," I hiss.

With a gasp, I pulled away from the scene, scrambling

back into the Countess's parlour and slamming my back against a table.

The cabinet rocked from the sudden motion.

The snow globe toppled out, crashing into the corner with a rumble. Its glass sphere cracked, starting to leak. I dived to save it, gingerly picking it up, but it was too late. Tiny trees and fawns and skaters all came pouring out of the star-shaped hole I'd made.

Against my will, I was again sucked into a panorama of a borrowed past, taking the creator's place in their own memory.

I am in a bandstand under a canopy of roses. Beyond, a ring of snow-capped trees surrounds a frozen lake beneath a star-crossed sky. The scene is vivid, teasing my senses. I can smell a pig roast and taste mead, fresh on my lips. I can hear a string quartet playing a soft, heartsick symphony. I can see every icicle, every petal, every stitch on my ostentatious white gown, which floats around me like a cloud.

My thoughts are fast, loud, strong, desperate. Excitement, dread, fear, desire, all war chaotically within me.

I have to tell him.

Lost in a crowd of waltzing dancers, I duck under flying elbows and dodge twirling skirts, searching the crowd for the one I want. The one I need.

"There you are," comes a soft voice.

A strange boy's arms wrap around me in a dance, encircling me tightly from behind.

In this brief moment, I am home.

I am whole.

I am … in love.

The weight of it presses down on my chest, a burden so great it takes my breath away, making me light-headed. I feel so small and so huge at once, so empty and so full. As if I might burst.

He takes my hands and spins me out, then back towards him. I have no worries, no cares, all of my urgency dispersing as he dips me, just like the shadows on the wall.

I look up at him, but his face is blurred. The music is contorted, echoing oddly as if we are dancing on the bed of the ocean floor.

The memory was disintegrating as the snow globe's water leaked out. Its vessel had been broken, its psyche escaping.

"No, wait…"

I didn't want to let go, but I had no choice. Blinking rapidly, I landed back in the parlour, once again empty and numb.

It wasn't the ring sending me back to the past.

It was me.

I'd changed.

I turned to face the chaise longue, where the Countess had left her purse. Tipping it out, I retrieved the velvet bag with five crowns in it as well as a pair of gloves, which I pulled on before grabbing the hatpin. The gloves seemed to offer some small degree of protection from the onslaught of memories. Now, when I touched it I sensed only the outline of its psyche, the faintest tug towards it, instead of being completely consumed by it.

Lingering at the doorway, a tickle at the back of my neck

alerted me to my box of trinkets under the bed upstairs. I could feel it calling to me, even from a distance. I couldn't leave them behind.

Creeping up into my room, I tipped the box's contents into the stolen purse as sirens wailed like out-of-tune violins.

I moved to the window in time to see five shiny black wagons pull up on the road in front of Cavendish House. A battalion of Inspectors poured out. One of them marched up and hammered on the door.

Heart seizing, I backed away, my mouth dry, chest heaving. I didn't want to think about what they would do if they caught me.

I could hear the Countess shrieking downstairs as the Inspectors pushed their way into the hall.

Inching forwards along the landing, I peered over the banister into the foyer below, flattening my body against the wall.

"What did you do with the ring?" barked one Inspector.

"What ring?" cried the Countess.

"Lady Renato's ring," he said. "Don't play dumb with me, you old battle-axe. Where's the girl?"

He turned on his lantern, casting a holographic scene upon the wall. It was the memory of Lady Renato at the Golden Gavel, seconds after I'd snatched the ring. The image closed in on my face and froze in place.

A cold draught passed through me.

"I've never seen her before in my life," said the Countess.

She was protecting me. Even after everything. I was gripped by some untraceable emotion: gratitude, perhaps.

"She's lying," he said. "Bring her in."

"This is all a terrible misunderstanding," shrilled the Countess, as Inspectors cuffed her. "A case of mistaken identity."

"Sure. Haven't heard that one before."

Graves was escorted outside too, manacled and mute as more Inspectors poured inside.

"Search the house. Detain the rest of her staff."

I didn't wait to hear any more. I ran back into the room, grabbing the purse and pushing a chair against the door. My hands were clammy. My legs were soft and slippery like noodles.

Someone rattled the door handle.

"Open up, by decree of the Order!"

Darting over to the window, I climbed out on to the roof. Birds scattered as the wind whipped my skirts. I stood at the edge, looking out over a sea of slate tiles and brick chimneys, turrets and vents, terraces and terrariums, some with washing lines or wooden walkways between.

The roof opposite was only about six feet away. As the Inspectors broke through the door, splintering wood, I took a running jump, launching myself over the edge. I easily cleared the pitch of the roof opposite, sliding down the slate awning on the other side and catching on the leaf-filled gutter. The Countess's purse slipped off my shoulder but I caught it at the last second.

Scrambling up, I walked along the rooftops, inching along sills and down fire escapes until I reached the bottom and fled, disappearing into the deepening dark.

I ran until I no longer heard sirens.

5.

CURIOUS AND STRANGE

I believed that the Eyes would have a harder time keeping track of me if I kept moving, so I didn't stop, travelling through the Second Borough, rich with the perfume of flowers, into the Third Borough, where the National Anthem rang out from speaker towers. I pulled up behind a music hall to catch my breath, panting and shuddering as I tried to think what to do next. My eyes caught on a loose drain cover, and the answer jumped out at me, loud and clear.

The Countess had mentioned the black market. I had no plans to sell the ring, at least not until I'd unlocked its sinister secrets – but she had given me an idea. The black market was the sort of place where people knew things. Things the Order would never share. And if I wanted to find the black market, I'd have to descend to the World's End, a labyrinth of tunnels where all of the sins of the city converged in one place, located in the underworld slums beneath the five boroughs.

Looking left and right to make sure I wasn't being

watched, I heaved the drain cover aside, staring into the dark hole. If anyone could help me understand what was happening to me, they would surely be found here, in this murky and forgotten place. However, it wasn't a very inviting entrance. Taking a deep breath, I climbed down the rickety ladder that clung to the shaft wall, disappearing into the darkness beneath the ground, taking it step by step, rung by rung, until my feet found the bottom. The strong scent of sewage and sulphur assaulted me as I staggered through the pitch black. Here, the smog was so dark and dense people said that not even the Observers could peer within.

No wonder the Order never sent Inspectors down here.

At first, the tunnels appeared abandoned, but I knew they were not. The World's End was home to all the people the Order had left to rot. The people who couldn't get jobs because their souls were too flawed. The people who couldn't rent houses. The people who didn't have identity cards. It was a lawless den of thieves, where no one cared what happened to you. The Order used it as an example: look at what could happen if we were not in power. This was life without surveillance. This was society without the science of the soul.

I'd never had reason to visit before, not when I was running errands for the Countess in the First Borough, but I had nowhere else to go now. I staggered forwards, coughing, trying to find my way through the gloom as the passages opened into wider roads, with decrepit buildings and shopfronts beginning to emerge from the darkness.

Shielded from any natural light, the World's End was illuminated by a series of flickering antiquated lanterns. Endless tenements further cast the roads in shadow, carved into the walls of the tunnels like caves. The narrow, puddle-strewn under-streets were clouded with a putrid, chemical-smelling fog, and sparsely scattered with people.

I struggled past a group of grimy fellows who glared at me from beneath the peaks of their flat caps, past a building with broken windows from which dirty-faced urchins stared out. Scantily clad women loitered in doorways, while the tunnels between neighbourhoods were full of rough sleepers, dozing and dazed.

Further on, tiny houses lined the makeshift pavement like crooked teeth. Some were sinking into pits, their timbers sticking up like skeletal ribcages, while mountains of ashes and refuse were heaped high on every corner. Winding deeper into the slums, the tunnels grew dark and cold as midwinter. The walls were plastered with missing person posters, crudely drawn from memory.

I kept my head down and kept walking. One passage opened out on to a pentagon-shaped courtyard, an underworld version of the Grand Bazaar, lined with shady-looking establishments, alehouses and pawn shops, bustling with shabby vagabonds. Peddlers traded in stolen remnants and dark, disturbing items for which they most certainly didn't have a permit. Something told me not to trust them, so I continued on.

Now that I was no longer running for my life, I found

myself flooded with strange sensations. Feelings I wasn't used to fluttered inside me. A spike of anger. A sob of grief. A tickle of delirious humour. A dull longing lingered like the remains of a stomach ache; the stolen memory of being in love, maybe. It was terrible, but it was wonderful too. Hadn't I hungered to feel something, even bad things?

All of this strange and unexplained psychometry seemed to be connected to the ring. There was something wrong with it, and yet it had chosen me as its conduit, flooding me with memories and feelings. Was that because I was broken and corrupted too? Or was it just because I was the only person stupid enough to steal it?

Every street down here seemed to resemble twelve others. In every possible direction, another thin, unnumbered tunnel awaited me, growing ever more deserted as I strayed from the centre. I could hear only my own scattered footsteps, echoing through the subterranean sprawl. My breathing quickened. Blood rushed in my ears. I was being watched again, I was sure of it. I spun around and spied a figure, a silhouette loitering a few yards back, cast by the light of a broken lantern. I clutched my stolen bag tighter.

"Hello?" I called.

No one responded. The shadow remained still.

"Who's there?" I called again.

Silence.

Heart pounding, I turned and walked faster, zig-zagging through the tunnels. Still, the shadow trailed me. I broke into a run, peeling down a squalid lane lined with shuttered shops and salons. When I next risked a glance over my shoulder, the shadow seemed to have vanished.

I waited for my pulse to slow, still alert to every chitter and rustle, every spider and every moth, but gradually my breathing evened out.

I found myself standing in front of a shop with a starry blue awning. A painted banner above the doorway read "*The Emporium of the Curious and Strange*", in a curly gothic font. In the window, framed by black curtains, was another, smaller sign printed in neat calligraphic letters, which read:

We deal in lost memories, broken hearts, bad dreams, haunted houses, cursed objects, spooks, spectres & more. Scholar of psychometry in residence. Rates negotiable. Enquire within.

It sounded like exactly the sort of place a girl might bring a stolen ring with a violent memory trapped inside it.

I caught my reflection in the glass — red-headed and wide-eyed with a constellation of freckles scattered across my cheeks. Fixing my hair, I took a deep breath and pushed open the door, causing a small bell to ring out. The shop had a musty, fusty, slightly flowery aroma. Inside, time-yellowed junk was stacked to the ceiling in precarious piles. Wooden cabinets created a maze of aisles, some so narrow they could only be navigated sideways, like a crab. Every single shelf was crammed with unnerving oddities. Masks, fossils, statues, grisly-looking specimens in formaldehyde...

I wove past bookcases and dressers, trying not to knock things off shelves as I squeezed past. At the back of the shop was a counter, scattered with books and papers, but there was no shopkeeper in sight.

"Hello?" I called.

When no answer came, I jammed my hand on the bell with a label that read, "Ring for service", holding it down.

From the darkness in the corner, a person emerged. I was expecting a wizened man with a plaited beard or an elderly woman wearing too many necklaces. Instead, I saw a boy, not much older than me, although I didn't know how old I was exactly. Having no memories didn't make it easy to remember birthdays. I guessed I was sixteen or seventeen, perhaps.

The boy was lanky and bespectacled. He had olive skin and a large, dignified nose. His thick, dark, overgrown hair had a streak of white in it, as if induced by fright, and it was tousled as though he'd only just got out of bed.

"How did you get in?" he asked, narrowing his eyes.

"Through the door?" I said, confused.

I got the distinct impression that they didn't get many customers at The Emporium of the Curious and Strange.

"What do you want?"

"I need to speak to your scholar of psychometry," I said.

"That … that would be me," he replied, clearing his throat.

"Are you sure? You look a bit…"

"A bit what?" he said, quirking one dark brow.

"A bit … young."

"Do you want my help or not?"

"Yes," I mumbled, grudgingly.

"Let's start over. I'm Evander Mountebank, and you are?"

"Iris. Iris … Cavendish."

The Countess's surname was the first that came to mind, along with the name she'd given me. I had no idea what my real name was. For the first time, this felt odd. Unnatural. What sort of person didn't know their own name?

"So, what is it you need assistance with, Miss Cavendish?" the boy asked.

Tentatively, I pulled off my glove and removed the ring. "This."

I watched him carefully. His expression seemed to flicker as if intrigued, but he didn't gape in shock or horror. He didn't seem to recognize the ring as stolen. I guessed the news of the robbery hadn't filtered down to the slums of the World's End yet.

"It's a remnant," I said. "There's a memory inside it. It's trapped or damaged, I'm not sure, but I have to find out what it is."

"Where did you get it?" he asked.

"Family heirloom," I said.

"I see," he said, warily. I wasn't sure whether he believed me or not. "Let me take a look."

He pulled out a loupe with a dark glass lens, much like the one the Countess used, inspecting the ring through its eye. His stiff, guarded posture seemed to relax slightly.

"Fascinating," he murmured.

"What can you see?" I said.

"Nothing… That's what's so fascinating."

"Come again?"

He tilted the ring gently back and forth. "Wherever the soul goes, it leaves a trace. Through the eye of a shadow glass, almost everything you can see is covered in soul dust. Yet this ring has been wiped clean. It has no trace at all, not even from your touch."

Just like the remnants the Countess had collected from the Night That Never Was – all except that single fork.

"Here." He passed the loupe to me. "See for yourself."

I raised it hesitantly to my right eye, like a monocle. Through its dark lens, the ring was pure black, while the rest of the room glittered with white, dusty spirit matter.

"I believe your ring has some kind of concealment on it, to keep it from prying eyes," he said. "Someone wanted to ensure that, whatever memory this remnant contains, it remains a secret."

I recalled how the Countess had inspected me with her own shadow glass after I'd told her that I was no longer Hollow, and how she'd recoiled. I wondered what she'd seen. Impulsively, I turned the lens on the boy, but he reached out a hand to stop me.

"What are you doing?" he said, covering the lens.

"Nothing." I flushed.

He looked displeased. "You know, it's not polite to spy on someone's soul."

I'd given myself away. A person with a soul wouldn't have done such a thing. I had to be more careful.

He placed the ring in my gloved left palm. "Sorry Miss Cavendish, but I can't help you."

"Why not?" I said, staring down at it.

"I really can't risk getting mixed up in, well, whatever this is." He gestured vaguely at me. "I think we both know that's not a family heirloom. Not belonging to your family, anyway."

Panic spiked, making me sweat. Panic was another new sensation the ring had sparked in me, and one I wasn't at ease with.

"What? Why do you think that?" I said, forcing a laugh.

"It has the Renato House seal on it, for one thing, and you don't look like a Renato to me," he said.

"That's rude of you to presume," I said.

"Well, we don't get many nobles down here. I prefer to stay out of sight of the Eye, you see, and this seems like exactly the thing to draw attention. You'll just have to find someone else to dig out whatever dark memory your stolen ring contains, I'm afraid."

That was inconvenient. Evander Mountebank had seen through my ruse, which made him a threat. He might report me to the Inspectors, even anonymously. Now I had to find a way to cajole him into helping me, through bribery or blackmail. Whatever it took.

"Why are you so keen to stay hidden?" I said. "Are you hiding out from the Order? You must be, if you're working down here."

I watched his Adam's apple bounce up and down.

"That's really none of your business," he said.

"To get a job up there, you need to provide a psychograph. I bet you don't want to show your identity card, do you? If you even have one."

He opened his mouth and closed it again.

"I'm right, aren't I?" I pushed, feeling a sudden sense of kinship with him. "What did you do? Burglary? Assault? Impersonating an officer of the law? I'm not judging, I'm just curious, that's all. You don't look the type for it."

"I didn't say I did anything," said Evander cagily, his cheeks slightly flushed. "You're making assumptions."

"Oh, you did *something*," I affirmed.

It was just a question of working out what it was.

That was when I saw his Shadow behind him, stretched thin upon the wall. As he stood there, outwardly calm and still, his Shadow gesticulated wildly, its lips parting and closing as if engaged in an argument. It didn't mirror him as shadows were meant to. It moved all by itself.

It didn't occur to me to run away. I wasn't afraid so much as captivated. I'd never seen such a thing, only the shadows of memories cast by the Countess's magic lantern. But I knew it wasn't right... Wasn't ... *normal*.

His silhouette saw me looking and brought a finger to its lips, as if signalling a secret between us.

"*Ohhh*, I see," I said.

Evander followed my line of sight to the wall, where his

Shadow quickly slipped back into place.

"What?" he said.

"It's your Shadow. It's acting with a mind of its own. I saw it, just now. That's why you're living down here with the rats."

His expression hardened, brows sloping.

"You must be mistaken," he said, firmly.

"I know what I saw. Your soul must be out of balance."

By the look on his face, I was right.

"The Order would want to reform you, if they caught you. They might even lock you up for good," I said. "Lucky for you, all I care about is that memory. If you help me out, I have no reason to think about you ever again. I'll be on my way and forget you in a heartbeat, but if you don't, I'll make sure to remember everything. In photographic detail."

I fixed him with a stony, threatening glare.

His eyes darted back and forth, as if debating with himself, before he sighed resentfully.

"You have five minutes," he said. "That's all."

He opened a door, ushering me into the cobwebbed back room. It was filled to the rafters with even more weird garbage than in the main shop, including a painting of a sad clown and a doll with no eyes.

"You've sure got a lot of junk, haven't you?" I said, taking it all in. Creeping across one wall was a collage. I could see blueprints of buildings, maps, pages torn out of books, diagrams and press clippings, all pinned to corkboards. I pulled up in front of it, eyes roving. "What's this?"

He quickly pulled a string, and a roll-down map blocked my view of his wall of conspiracies.

"Nothing you need to be concerned with," he said.

Curiouser and curiouser.

In the opposite corner of the room was a bulky object, covered over with a faded floral throw. He pulled the sheet off, revealing a strange machine that resembled a slide projector, sitting on a trolley. It was a lantern, although not like any I had seen before. It was ancient and rusted, made of brass with three telescopic lenses.

"It's a psychoscope," said Evander, though I hadn't asked. "Five times more powerful than a magic lantern. They're used by the Memorialists, to access deeply repressed memories. If the ring has any kind of concealment on it, this ought to break through it."

"Where did you get such a thing?" I said.

"A junkyard," he said, in an unconvincing tone.

Behind him, his Shadow mimed sealing its lips again.

Evander rolled the trolley into the centre of the room, then placed the ring into the tray before its middle lens, fiddling with knobs and levers. The rusted old machine began to whirr.

I heard the ticking of clockwork and the flicker of gas, the squeak of brass and the whistle of steam. Yet within seconds, the machine powered down again, reclining into a sedentary hum.

"Nothing," said Evander. Just like the Countess's lantern, the psychoscope couldn't reveal the ring's memory.

He tried the machine again, to no avail.

"Looks like you're out of luck," he said. "If a psychoscope can't reveal the memory, nothing can."

I felt my chest getting tight and heavy. A dreary, shivering sort of cloud descended over me. I was ... disappointed. That was the word for it, this feeling breaking through my emptiness.

"Guess I'll never know the truth now," I said, morosely, trying out this brand new emotion. "Maybe I'm not meant to."

I stepped forward, crossing into the line of the psychoscope's bulb to retrieve the ring, sliding it back on my finger.

As I did, a beam of light flickered from the lantern, hitting the wall opposite. An eye-shaped peephole appeared there as images began to bloom.

"Don't move!" said Evander, holding up one hand.

Turning my eyes to the wall without stirring a muscle, I saw the light shining through me.

At first, the patterns were just nonsensical shapes metamorphosing and deconstructing, but soon they took on clarity, like scenes from a moving picture, projected as if from a soul's eye view.

The person whose memory I was watching stood before a roaring hearth in a room with red velvet curtains, burning a letter on the fire. I caught a glimpse of the date before flames ate the paper.

December 24th.

The Night That Never Was.

A sinister figure emerged in the doorway, wearing long black robes with a hood and a featureless white mask, its face eerily smooth and still.

I'd seen that figure before.

I'd glimpsed them when I first touched the ring.

They looked like an Observer, one of the watchers who monitored the visions of the Eyes.

As the robed intruder inched closer, the other retreated, glimpsing her own horrified reflection in the ornate, black-framed mirror on the wall. My breath caught noisily. My own face stared back at me.

It was ... me.

I was watching my *own* memory.

The realization burned right through me. The memory was crystal sharp and clear now, shining through the fog of forgetfulness.

It clicked into place in my mind, as if it belonged there.

I was close to the age I was now, but cleaner and better-groomed, in a red embroidered dress with a neat, braided hairstyle.

Evander looked back and forth between me and the girl on the screen, blinking rapidly.

"Isn't that...?"

Before he could finish this sentence, the masked intruder lifted a strange weapon. A black, twisted staff with a bevelled stone of jet on top, shaped like an eye, like the hatpin.

Something invisible shot out from its dark jewel, pulsing

through the air with a glimmer and striking past-me right in the heart.

"Oh!" I cried out.

Even in the present, I felt the suppressed memory of its pain, raising my hands to the offending spot.

"Miss Cavendish, are you all right?" said Evander.

I barely heard him, transfixed by the image. In the memory, the mirror cracked in its frame, breaking into five pieces. Past-me slumped to the white marble floor, twitching, her hand stretched out before her.

The Renato ring was on my finger. The same ring I'd stolen. The same ring I wore now.

I'd worn it before. No wonder it had called to me.

The peephole rapidly closed. The psychoscope smoked, shuddering violently before clapping out. For a long moment, neither of us spoke.

"Did you see?" I said, hoarsely.

"I saw," said Evander, darkly.

"That was *my* memory." I gasped for air, but air wouldn't come. "I can't … I can't breathe."

I clutched at my throat as I dropped to my knees, wheezing and rasping for a long moment before I saw Evander kneeling beside me.

"Tell me five things you can see," he said.

"What?" I choked. "How will that—"

"It's an exercise, to re-orientate yourself in reality. Just try it."

I gazed around, trying to isolate individual objects as the world spun and slipped, like bare feet on a wet floor. "I see, uh, I see a sad clown, a doll with no eyes, a taxidermy crow, and what looks like, is that … a skull?" Evander turned to see what I was looking at.

"Yes. Yes, it is. In retrospect, perhaps we shouldn't have done this in here," he said, mildly.

"I see … you," I said, turning to face him. The newly-familiar planes of his face were like an anchor, keeping me centred in a tilted world.

"Now tell me four things you can hear," he said.

"A clock ticking. A train rumbling overhead. Music, in the distance. My own heart beating. It's fast."

"Now three things you can touch," he said.

"Myself," I said, patting myself down.

"What else?"

"The floor…" I planted my palm on the wooden floor, reassuringly cool and solid. I groped around for another object to touch. "And this…" My fingers touched a dirty wet rag.

"Ew," I said, dropping it instantly.

"Now two things you can smell," he said.

"I smell … rising damp, and cologne. Mmm." I closed my eyes briefly, breathing it in. "It smells nice, kind of musky and spicy."

Beneath Evander's collar, his neck turned pink.

The room slowly returned to normal as my lungs opened up, allowing air to rush in. My heartbeat slowed, quietened.

"The last one is something you can taste," he said.

"I taste … rusty pennies. I think I bit my tongue."

The silence between us expanded, inflating like a balloon.

Evander stood. I wobbled to my feet, swaying slightly.

"This ring, where did it really come from?" he said, holding my gaze so tightly I felt claustrophobic.

"I stole it," I confessed. "From Lady Renato, at the Golden Gavel."

"Lady Renato, of the Order?"

"That's right."

"You stole this … from Lady Renato?"

"That's what I said, isn't it?"

"But why?"

"Someone hired me. I have a talent for stealing remnants. That's what I do. I can sense them." His brow puckered with curiosity but he didn't say anything. "I didn't know it was mine," I continued. "I didn't know it belonged to me. I don't remember being attacked. I don't know what happened to me."

A sharp, hot thought struck me like lightning.

"Maybe this is why," I whispered.

"Why what?" he said.

The truth poured out of me like an unstoppable landslide, raw, ugly and uncensored.

"I can't cry. I can't laugh. I can't dream. I have no feelings … or at least, I didn't. I have no memory of my life beyond a year ago."

Evander said nothing, his face infuriatingly blank. I couldn't guess what he was thinking, but I doubted it was good. When he failed to respond, I filled the silence myself.

"Before today, I was invisible, asleep, but as soon as I touched the ring, a spark was lit inside me, making me feel things, making me sense things. Now the Eyes can see me. Now I'm … awake."

I stared at him.

"Aren't you going to say anything?"

"Give me a moment," he said. "I'm trying to take it all in."

I paced back and forth, unwilling to wait for him to catch up.

"What if that person, whoever they are, the one in the memory, the one in the mask – the Observer – what if they did this to me? What if they took my soul, and destroyed it somehow?"

"You're not soulless," he said, gently.

"You don't know that."

"If you were soulless, you would feel nothing."

"There's no need to rub it in," I said.

He shook his head. "If your soul had been destroyed, you wouldn't be able to sense the psyche in remnants, like you said. You wouldn't be able to sense anything."

I pulled up, ceasing my wild striding.

"Then what happened to me?" I said.

Everything was unfolding too fast and too loud and in too many directions. I was starting to feel woozy again. Walking over to the grimy window, I combed my empty head for a memory, but every time I grabbed at some faint and fleeting recollection it drifted away from me again, vanishing back into the void. It was like I was stuck in a dream. The harder I tried to clear my head, the cloudier it became.

"Maybe your soul wasn't destroyed," said Evander, quietly. "Maybe it was just broken."

I turned to face him again. "Broken?" I echoed. I pictured the cracked mirror I'd seen in my memory. "A soul can break?"

"Souls can be chipped, cracked, split, fractured. It's uncommon for a soul to break entirely into pieces, but then nothing about this is ordinary."

He rooted around in a cupboard and pulled out a book, which he handed to me.

"*The Anatomy of the Soul*," I read aloud.

Its cover showed an object shaped like the anatomical heart organ, divided into five sections, like butcher's cuts.

"You know the basics, I'm sure," said Evander, adjusting his glasses. "The Shadow is the subconscious. The Song is the personality. The Spirit is the memory. The Heart symbolizes raw emotions and the Spark is the vital fire of life that connects all living beings. It's more complicated than that, of course. Each part is intertwined. One cannot exist without the other. But for the purpose of classifying souls, the Order devised this simple system when they first came to power. It's still in use today, centuries later."

"What's your point?" I said.

"This is just a theory, but perhaps that weapon caused your soul to shatter, breaking into its five anatomical parts."

I wrapped my arms around myself. I felt fragile, just then. It would be so easy to break me all over again.

"Why would someone do that to me?" I said.

"I don't know," he said. "But when you were attacked, you were wearing that ring. When you put the ring on again, maybe the part of your soul it was protecting was returned to you. The Spark, I assume, given that the Spark is associated with the sense of touch and the ring is worn on the hand."

I twisted it around my finger.

"If that's true, the other four parts of your soul might be contained within treasured objects that were nearby when you were shattered, much as remnants are created through proximity." He hesitated, catching on a thought. "Although technically, they'd be reliquaries. A remnant contains only a memory. A reliquary contains part of a person."

"There's a word for that?" I said.

"One not used in modern parlance, but yes. I've read about such things in old texts, folktales, and so on. That's probably why the lantern had so much trouble revealing it," said Evander.

I paced back and forth again as my mind whirred into action like a machine. My thoughts were coming in quick and thick, filling my head with questions. I tried to sort through them, seeking the most urgent.

"If the ring contained my Spark and the Heart is the seat of emotion, then why am I ... feeling things now?" I said.

"The Spark is connected to the Heart. The Spark is

connected to everything," he said.

"Five pieces of the soul," I said, nodding slowly. "Five reliquaries. My Shadow, my Spirit, my Song, my Heart."

If Evander was right, the pieces of me were out there somewhere, just waiting for me to find them, like lost children. Where were they? Who had them? Were they safe? How would I find them again?

"I can't even remember *myself*," I said, thinking aloud. "How am I to remember my belongings?"

"Think of it like a treasure hunt," said Evander.

"If it were a treasure hunt, I'd have a map marked X," I said.

"True, but you do have one clue."

He nodded at the ring. I removed it again, examining its ruby jewel and the Renato seal. I hadn't noticed the seal before, but now it stood out starkly. Had such a precious thing truly belonged to me?

Evander stared at me intently, as if considering the same.

"You must've been a member of Renato House," he said.

"A servant, you mean?"

"You were wearing their ring, and that was a fine room you were shattered in. You must've been someone important." He frowned. "Though if so, I have no knowledge of you. I don't recognize you."

"Why would you?" I said. "Go to many society balls, do you?"

"No," he said, defensively, "but I read the papers. There are no Renatos of your age. The youngest is Lord Ruben and he's in his forties. Plus, the Renatos are rather notorious, with their propensity for torturing folks and all. You know what the Renato Method is, don't you?"

I stared down at my hands.

"Yes," I said, recalling what the Countess had told me.

"They can kill with a graze of their fingertips, or cause so much pain they'd make a person *wish* they were dead," he said. "They could make you feel like you were drowning or burning or bleeding from a thousand cuts. A family like that has plenty of enemies. Almost as many as the Obscuras, since they're the ones in charge."

Lady Renato's face popped suddenly into my mind, wrinkling as she scrutinized my face in the overheated auction room.

Don't I know you from somewhere, girl?

"You know, I think Lady Renato recognized me," I said, excitedly. "She said as much."

"She did?" he said.

"I have to go find her and talk to her, figure out what she knows."

I pulled on my right glove, but Evander laid a hand on my arm.

"Is that wise?" he said.

"She's my only clue."

"You just stole from her. Besides, it's nearly midnight. I doubt she's taking visitors at this hour."

"I don't need an invitation," I said. "I'll wake her up if I have to. She'll be at Renato House, in the Fifth Borough.

I've walked past it before."

"You're going to break into Renato House?" said Evander.

"It won't be the first time I've burgled a noble's house to rummage around their drawers, and probably won't be the last."

He held my gaze for a moment, before reaching into his pocket.

"Here." He pressed something small and dark into my hand.

The shadow glass.

"Don't you need it?" I said.

"I have a spare," he said. "It might come in useful."

"Thanks," I said. "And ... sorry." I had never said that before and meant it. It felt wrong on my lips. "I wouldn't really have told the Order about you. I just needed you to think I would, so you'd help me. I'll be sure to forget about you, should the Inspectors catch up with me."

He didn't respond to my apology.

"You should be careful," he said instead. "You're playing with fire, digging into the Renato family's secrets."

"I'm not scared of a little fire," I said.

I followed him back through the shop to the entrance, watching his Shadow on the wall.

It was the same mysterious shadow that had chased me before. I recognized it now. It was tall and lean. It moved like him. But why had his Shadow followed me? Was it trying to keep me away, or lure me in?

With one last inscrutable look, Evander closed the door between us. I watched him disappear into the dark. Turning around, I looked out on the endless, unknowable gloom of the World's End, wondering how I was going to find my way out again. For some reason, I thought about the Countess. Was it just a coincidence that she had bid me steal back the very vessel that contained my own lost memory?

Her words echoed in my ears.

According to my little spies, it involves the destruction of a human soul.

The destruction of a human soul.

I just hadn't expected it to be my own.

PART
TWO⊙
THE SHADOW

6.

HEART OF DARKNESS

Through the eye of the shadow glass, the city was illuminated by soul dust. Sparkling trails and silvery threads lit up the night, from the person-shaped splatters in the darkest alleys to the sylph-like spectres who re-enacted their last moments, over and over, all unseen to the naked eye.

The human soul left its traces everywhere, but there was only one soul I was interested in. My own soul still existed, though broken in pieces and scattered. I could almost feel the edges of those fragments, distant but resonant. The idea of them kept me company as I climbed up to the streets and crept through the shadows towards Renato House, past the Golden Gavel, now roped off by Inspectors, and the Reformatory, where the flawed were brought in black wagons to be purified.

What must it feel like to have a whole soul? I was getting a tantalizing taste of it now. Words gathered inside me, waiting to pour out. Impulses swept over me. When an empty, aching feeling gripped me, I recognized it as loneliness. When my skin prickled and made me tremble,

I identified fear. Now, when I heard the Order's sirens, it was as if a switch had been flicked, telling me to run. Now, if the Inspectors came too close, my body responded, heart flapping its wings like a bird trapped in a cage.

Around the corner, I came face to face with myself. This time, my mugshot was broadcast on a spectacular, my gigantic face staring down from the wall. It was the exact same memory projected by the Inspectors who'd raided Cavendish House.

"Have you seen this girl?" announced a velvety, disembodied voice as I approached. "Described as small and slight with red hair, she is wanted for the theft of a precious ring belonging to Renato House."

A picture of it popped up.

"Last seen in the Fifth Borough. Categorized as extremely dangerous. Do not approach if seen."

My blood ran cold, veins full of ice. Fear, again.

A trio of Inspectors approached and I skittered away, hiding behind a pillar. My heart pounded painfully, so loud I feared they'd hear it. Every second I spent on the streets, I was closer to being captured. A smart person would go bunker down in some hidey-hole until the heat was off, but I couldn't wait. I couldn't let fear stop me. I wanted answers.

Renato House sat on top of the hill overlooking the Reformatory, its hanging baskets blooming with pink bougainvillea. Its campanile contained not a bell, but an eternal flame that shone through the night, signifying both the fire of the Spark, and the strength of the Order.

I stood at the foot of the cliff, looking up at it through the smog, trying to scour my hazy memory for knowledge of the Renatos. I knew that the head of the house was called Ruben Renato, the Chancellor's right-hand man. The head of the military. One of his ancestors had discovered the famous Renato Method, a system of psychometric pressure points that could be used for hurting or healing. No longer did soldiers use swords to cut flesh but batons forged by the fire souls of Renato House, batons that burned into the psyche. Once, the Renatos had been the most powerful House, until the Chancellor came along and turned mind to matter.

According to the papers, Ruben was away visiting the colonies. That meant his House wouldn't be as closely guarded.

I followed the winding road that led upwards, keeping my head down until I was standing right outside the hedge wall that surrounded the house. I circled the perimeter, searching for a way in. Up front was a guard hut with a sleeping man in a red tunic inside. The gates were locked, too high to scale.

Around the rear of the property, however, part of the hedgerow was withered, turning brown and leaving a weak spot. I pushed through, getting my hair tangled in its branches. On the other side, immaculately manicured lawns were patrolled by peacocks, their tail feathers glinting under the moon. They stood still, watching me as I crept towards the house. I tried the glass patio door and, to my surprise, it was open. Clearly the formidable Renatos had no need to lock their doors. I boldly slipped inside, letting the intoxicating kick of entering a place I absolutely shouldn't run through me, making me giddy.

I found myself in a finely-appointed, high-ceilinged drawing room. This single room was bigger than an entire hovel in the World's End. On the walls hung landscapes in oil. Leaning in, I spied the scrawled signature on the nearest painting, which depicted an apocalyptic-looking sunset: *R. Renato.*

That could've been the Lady, or even Ruben himself.

A platter of fruit and cheese had been laid out on the table for some time, attracting flies. For several minutes, I didn't move a muscle, listening for the sounds of occupation, but nothing came.

I drifted along the hall like a phantom, gently pushing open any doors left ajar.

The villa was quiet, *too* quiet. Wasn't this the stately home of a great and powerful dynasty? Where was the hustle and bustle of servants turning down beds? Even if Ruben was away, he must've had assistants, underlings, people paid to run his business while he was gone.

Halfway down the corridor, I pulled up, spinning slowly on my heels to face a dark doorway. The room within looked horribly familiar.

Swallowing several times in succession, I entered.

The room had a white marble floor and a balconette with pillars that overlooked the gardens outside. With growing dread, I walked towards the hearth. The image of a letter being thrown in came to me.

I'd seen it in the ring's memory.

A sharp pain surged through me and sweat slicked my skin. This was it. The room where I was shattered.

My room.

I forced myself to draw a ragged breath, to calm myself, to look around for clues. It was definitely the same room, but it didn't look like it had that night. Everything was new, unused. There had been a phoenix on the wall in the memory, and now it had been painted over. There was no cracked mirror on the wall either. The furnishings were different, too. There were no clothes in the dresser, which had the strong scent of fresh varnish. The desk was empty, with no stains or scratches on it.

Fishing out the shadow glass and holding it up to my eye, I examined the room, watching for the glitter of psyche. But there was only a single, faint glimmer. The room had been wiped clean of psyche, just like the ring, all but for one single, forgotten object.

On hands and knees, I peered under the bed, stretching out my arm until my fingers closed around something. A small bronze bobby pin, wedged between two floorboards. Flashing back to the ring's memory, I recalled the elaborate plaited up-do I'd sported that night. I rolled the pin between my fingers, but despite the soul dust, the accessory didn't give me any feelings in particular. I had owned it. I had worn it. That was enough to make it shine. But I hadn't treasured it. I hadn't forged a strong emotional connection to it. It wasn't a remnant. There were no memories imprinted on it.

Standing up, I dropped the bobby pin into my purse. I backed away from the room, continuing along the hall. My skin was burning. My heart was hammering. I'd never felt closer to the truth, and yet it remained obscured.

Passing by another open door, I pulled up abruptly. Lady Renato sat facing the wall with her back turned to me, dabbing drearily at a crude oil portrait, less like the masterpieces on the wall in the drawing room, more like the finger-painting of a toddler. I knew I should run right there and then but I didn't. Curiosity pulled me in, like a fish on the hook. Step by step, I neared, until I stood alongside her.

Her head turned slowly towards me.

I expected her to scream or at least gape in shock at this criminal in her boudoir, but she merely stared at me placidly.

"Do you remember me?" I said.

"It's nearly time for dinner," she said, dreamily, though it was long past the hour.

"What?"

"I think I should like a leg of lamb tonight, Margery."

"I'm not Margery."

"Thank you, dear."

"Can you even hear me?" I tried.

"It's nearly time for dinner," she repeated.

"You said you recognized me," I tried, desperately. "Lady Renato?"

I gently shook her shoulder, and her head wobbled like a jack-in-the-box toy. I saw a shimmer in her eyes, making her pupils and irises misty. Whatever spirit lived within her, it wasn't home right now.

"You," came a shocked voice.

A stocky, apple-cheeked woman in a maid's uniform stood in the doorway with towels piled in her arms. Margery, perhaps.

"It's you." She gasped. "I saw you on the spectaculars. You're the girl who stole the ring!"

She backed away, no doubt ready to summon the Inspectors. In a moment of blind panic, I grabbed the poker from the fire, its tip burning red hot, and held it out at her like a sword.

"I just want you to answer some questions," I said. "Tell me what I want to know and no one gets hurt. I'm a Hollow, in case you didn't hear, so I won't think twice about killing you ... or her."

I didn't mean it, of course, but by the look on the maid's face, she was sure I did.

"What do you want to know?" she said, in a tremulous voice.

"What happened to her?" I said, nodding at Lady Renato. "She wasn't like this before."

"I don't know! Inspectors came earlier, to take her statement about the theft. They took her off to the Reformatory and she came back like this."

Lady Renato hummed to herself, blithely. She was in

some sort of state of oblivion. Clearly someone was trying to make her forget something.

Forget … me?

"What about her nurse?" I said. "Doris, her name was."

"I haven't seen her since. Think she got fired."

"And where's Lord Renato?" I asked.

"No idea. I've never met the man. I haven't seen him the whole time I've worked here. One night they got rid of the entire staff and brought us in new. I don't know anything else."

I swallowed. "One night? When was this?"

"Last year. December 25th."

The day after the Night That Never Was.

"And you haven't seen Lord Ruben in all that time?" I said.

"No. I know how it sounds, but I swear it's true."

The curfew announcement resumed its half-hourly chime, like church bells or prayer calls. A moment's hesitation on my part was all it took for her to flee down the hall, calling out for help. It would be enough to wake that guard I'd seen out front. I retreated in the opposite direction, running along the corridor and dropping the poker with a clatter by the door. In moments, I was down the lawns and out through the hole in the hedge, pounding pavements as I followed the road down, spiralling into the smoky streets below.

Rounding the corner, an Inspector loomed in front of me.

"I've got her!" he hollered, reaching out to grab me.

I backtracked, dodging his grasping mitts, but two others appeared from the opposite direction, cornering me.

"We found her, Sarge!"

The moustachioed Inspector I'd seen before emerged from the dark.

"Well, well, what have we got here?" he leered. "We've been looking all over for you, little lady. Been thieving again, have you?"

"I haven't done anything," I said, reflexively.

Hands moved over my skin, unpermitted. They tore the purse from my shoulder and rifled through it. I watched as my treasures were tossed into the back of a van. The Inspector held up a lantern, showing me the holographic scene of myself running off with the Renato ring.

"Look familiar?" he said.

"That ... that's not me," I said, in a higher pitch than usual.

Grunting, he grabbed my wrist with one hand and pulled off my gloves with the other.

"Then why is the ring on your finger?" he said.

Moustache nodded at his subordinates, clutching their soul-baring lanterns. The eyes of their lamps flicked open in sync, emitting four beams of light that imprisoned me like bars of fire. The Eye of the Order looked right at me this time, emitting a blinding beam. Its light was so powerful it lifted me off the ground, just like those street kids I'd seen. I'd never been the one in the sight of the Eyes before. It terrified me.

I was trapped in a paralysing bubble that slowed and muffled everything around me, like an insect immortalized in amber. I saw the Inspectors huddled together, whispering as they inspected my soul's anatomy. I felt naked and small. No rosy ball glowed in my breast. No jewelled reflections told the story of my life. There was nothing but a tiny Spark, with a dark, whirling abyss around it, like a crater on an alien planet.

"I've never seen such depravity," breathed Moustache.

They could see all my secrets, all my lies, all the darkness in my scant excuse for a soul. They were going to take me to the Reformatory and wipe my mind clean as a kitchen counter, just like they'd done to Lady Renato. I could do nothing to stop them as these strangers gawped over the eyesore of my psyche.

"Doctor Stanford is going to want to see this one for himself," said the Inspector. "Take her to the Reformatory."

As they lowered their lanterns, releasing me from their hold, the temperature in the alley suddenly plummeted. A strange, prickly silence followed. Moustache flung out one arm, shining his lantern into a dark corner.

"What's that?" he said.

"What, boss? I can't see nothing," said another man.

"Don't move!" barked Moustache, waving his nightstick. "Hands where we can see them." The darkness shifted once more. "I said, '*don't move*'!"

One of the men swung his lantern just in time to see something emerging from the gloom. The shadow of a horrific, nightmarish, hell-born creature appeared on the wall, creeping slowly towards us. It had the curled horns of a ram, leathery bat-like wings and knife-sharp fangs, dripping with blood and bared in a gruesome howl. At first, it was just a flat, black silhouette, like the dancing shadows on the wall in the Countess's parlour, but as it moved closer it seemed to fill out, becoming a body of swirling ribbons of black smoke. It became material, became real, from mind to matter, as shadow turned to smoke and smoke to flesh.

The monster rounded on the Inspectors, driving them towards the dead-end. One of them dropped his lantern, causing its glass panels to shatter. I tried to make a break for it while they were distracted but Moustache was still fixed on me. Turning back on myself, I crawled on hands and knees over to the abandoned lantern, clasping it in my hands. As he lunged for me, I raised it up, catching him squarely on the temple.

Before the Eye faded out, I caught a flash of his gnarly-looking soul in his chest, covered in ugly bumps and bloodied bruises. He toppled to the ground like lumber, passing out at my feet.

The monster of smoke and shadow charged at the rest of the Inspectors, hurtling towards us at lightning speed. Caught between a beast and a wanted criminal wielding a blunt object, the rest of the black coats bolted, running until their cries faded out. Left alone, the shadow monster turned to me. Damp with sweat, knees shaking, I stumbled backwards.

"Nice … monster," I said, gingerly holding out one hand. But the creature fell still and slack, like a puppet with no master, its flesh rotting and flaking away, until it was just a flat black shadow again.

A corporeal figure rounded the corner. "Evander?" I said, in disbelief. "Evander Mountebank?"

His eyes were wholly black, with no whites at all… And his Shadow was the monster.

7.

OBLIVION

As his Shadow metamorphosed, reforming to take his regular human shape, Evander blinked back at me, his eyes returning to their normal brown. He looked at me in surprise.

"Iris Cavendish?" he said. "What are you doing here?"

He gazed around in confusion.

"What am *I* doing here, for that matter?"

I examined his face for signs of humour.

"You're joking, aren't you?" I said. I wasn't very good at working out what people did and didn't find funny but his expression was blank, free of malice. "You just..." I spluttered, trying to summon the words to describe what had just happened. "You cast a monster with your Shadow!" I waved my hands wildly. "You just scared off the Inspectors!"

A look of utmost despair crossed his face. "Oh no. Not again," he said, shaking his head.

"*Not again*?! What does that mean, *not again*?"

I could hear distant shouts and oncoming sirens. I grabbed my gloves and purse from the back of the van, left abandoned with its doors still open. The ring was gone, taken by one of the men who had fled.

I pulled us down the alley and through the streets, away from the sirens. I missed the ring already, feeling its absence growing inside me like a void. When I judged that we were far enough away, I ducked into a shadowy alcove. Crammed together in our hiding spot, so close that we were almost touching, I stared at him expectantly.

"Well? Explain yourself," I said.

"I'm not sure that I can," he said.

"What are you, or rather, what is *your Shadow* doing here in the nick of time to save me from a one-way trip to the Reformatory?" I said. "Not that I'm not grateful, obviously, but it is a bit creepy, you have to admit."

"I can assure you, it wasn't intentional," Evander said, holding up his hands. "I don't know what happened. The last thing I recall was drifting off by the fire in the shop, and now I'm here."

He went to adjust his glasses, except he wasn't wearing them. He seemed to see fine, I thought.

"What did you mean, 'not again'?" I pressed.

"We shouldn't talk out in the open," he said, gesturing at a stone eye on the corner of a nearby building.

"I don't have anywhere else to go," I said.

He looked at me and tilted his head. "Come on," he said, at last.

"Where?"

"Back to the shop. It's safe there."

"Safe how?"

He began to walk on again, not answering my question. I walked after him but he stared ahead, as if deep in thought.

"You're helping me again?" I said.

"It looks like it, doesn't it?"

"But I thought you didn't want to get mixed up in whatever this is. That's what you said."

"That was before my Shadow sought you out in the middle of the night. I must be out here for a reason, even if I don't know what it is yet."

I walked faster to keep up with him, my little legs working twice as hard as his long ones.

"When I first met you, I had this strange feeling that I was supposed to help you," said Evander. "That was why I gave you the shadow glass. But, apparently, that was not enough to satiate my subconscious."

Once more, my mind filled with questions, like a swarm of bees, buzzing between my ears.

"So you followed me?" I said.

"My Shadow must've trailed you, after you left the shop," he said. "It must've known that you'd get into trouble."

"Guess it's my lucky day," I said.

He led us on to a drain cover, heaving it aside and gesturing for me to climb down. I descended and he followed, directing us through the warren of grimy sewage tunnels that sprawled beneath the streets. He held one finger in front of his lips as a group of ragged people passed by. Curfew didn't exist down here in the World's End, apparently.

"I found the room I was attacked in," I whispered, after they'd passed, unable to hold it in any longer. "It had been redecorated, everything new, as if someone was covering something up. I saw Lady Renato too but she wasn't herself any more. She hardly seemed to know she was alive. The Order must have got to her already."

"You *must* have been a Renato," said Evander. "Perhaps the ring was a family heirloom after all."

"Maybe I stole it," I said. "Maybe that's why I was shattered."

"The Order does a lot of things but they don't go around smashing thieves to smithereens," he said. "They'd have you arrested and put to trial if that were the case, to make an example of you. The Order is a lawless beast, but they at least like to keep up appearances."

He led us back to the dingy square I'd visited before but now, instead of the Emporium, I found a used bookstore.

"Wait, where's the shop?" I said. "It was right here before."

"Keep looking," he said, with a hint of pride.

As Evander drew closer, the shopfront rippled, shimmering like a mirage. Gradually, the Emporium shone through.

"Wow," I breathed.

"An illusion," he said. "To keep the Inspectors at bay, just in case they track us down here. It's never happened yet, but there's always a first time."

"It's so realistic," I said, as we passed through the filmy, sparkling veil. "How did you do it?"

"It's just a trick of the eye. Psychological deception. When you look at an object, light reflected from it enters the eye through the cornea, the window of the eye, if you will. The cornea bends the light rays in such a way that they pass freely through the pupil…"

I could feel myself glazing over.

"The iris works like a shutter in a camera," he went on, evidently enraptured by the subject. "It has the ability to enlarge and shrink. Psychometry allows us to control that process to create false images, which trick the brain into accepting it as real…"

He had fully lost me.

I followed him into the shop as he talked about truth and illusion, refraction and reflection. I couldn't stop thinking about what the maid at Renato House had said: *One night they got rid of the entire staff and brought us in new.*

They'd been fired after the Night That Never Was, right after I was shattered in Renato House. Why hadn't Ruben been home since? It was all highly suspicious, but I couldn't make sense of it yet.

"Do you drink tea?" asked Evander, as we climbed the stairs.

"Not really," I said, mildly irritated. Things were too serious for tea.

"Everything is better with a cup of tea," he said. "Three to four sugars is best, I find."

"That sounds like a lot."

"Moderation is for the weak," he said.

I raised one eyebrow at him.

Evander led us up into a large living room, which was faded and chintzy with net curtains and a mish-mash of furniture in clashing colours and styles. There were porcelain ducks flying on the walls and ceramic plates on the fireplace, with a cuckoo clock hanging above it, framed by flowery lampshades with frills and bobbles.

"Is this your house?" I said, picking up a kitschy statue of a milkmaid and pulling a face.

"It belongs to the store's proprietor, Arjun Sharma." He gestured at the framed portrait on a side table, showing a man in a jewelled turban posing in front of the pyramids. "He's the owner of the Emporium, and something of a father figure to those of us who are wanted by the Order."

"So you *are* a fugitive," I said. "I knew it."

"Everyone here is," he said, casually. "Especially Mr Sharma. Unfortunately, he's away right now. A shame, because he knows far more than me about this sort of thing."

"What will he think of me stopping over uninvited?" I said.

"He won't mind. He likes to help all the waifs and strays. Why do you think I'm here? There are four of us living here, hiding out from the Eyes. Five if you're going to be staying."

As he talked, Evander filled the kettle and put it on the hob. He did so clumsily and I noticed that he spent some time hunting for sugar. Clearly he was not usually the one in the household who made the tea.

"If you're here, it's because you're meant to be here," he continued. "It's been said that those who have need of the Emporium will find it, one way or another. You're not the first person to turn up unannounced."

As the kettle whistled its jarring melody, I watched him out of the corner of my eye. He seemed nervous, tugging at his sleeve and looking to the door as if he half-expected the Chancellor's vanguard to pour in at any moment.

We sat down in threadbare armchairs, sipping tea from cups with price labels still tied to their handles.

"Go on, then," I urged. "Start talking."

He nodded, grudgingly.

He remained silent though, staring into the darkness of the corner, tongue-tied. I waited and waited for him to speak, but he didn't.

"What's wrong with you?" I said bluntly, increasingly impatient. "How is it that your Shadow can wander independently from your body?"

"Remember I told you before about the five parts of the soul?" he said. "Spark, Heart, Shadow, Spirit and Song. All souls are dominant in one part or the other. Well, I'm a Shadow soul. The Shadow is the subconscious, the dark double that accompanies us through life, embodying all that lies hidden beneath the surface. My mastery of my soul's dominant Shadow allows me to create mirages. To disguise objects, places, even people."

He held out his hand, and the air in front of us began to warp and shimmer, taking the form of a single red rose.

As he pressed it gently into my hand, one of its thorns pricked my thumb. A bead of blood swelled in the spot.

"Ouch," I said, as pain spiked enticingly.

The rose blackened and decayed to dust, leaving my skin unmarked. I stared into the darkness of his pupils, seeing myself reflected in them. As far as I knew, there were only two kinds of people who possessed such powerful gifts: members of the illuminated nobility, belonging to the five Houses, or those who worked for them. But most of the Order's servants used devices like lanterns to tap into the network of psyche; they were not naturally gifted, as Evander was.

No wonder he was a fugitive.

"And it's not just illusions," he said. "I was always able to send out my Shadow to spy on people, to gain useful information. But lately it has started going on its own sojourns, wandering free of me. Sometimes, such as tonight, it even, well, takes over my body. I wake up in strange places with no memory of where I've been. I can't control it."

"Is that why you're wanted by the Order?"

Evander laughed bitterly, shaking his head.

"Not quite. I worked for them, once." He didn't elaborate, and his expression told me not to ask. "My point is, people like us threaten their rule. Not just because we defy them, but because we have the gifts to do something about it. We have a power to match their own."

I frowned at him, not understanding.

"People like us?" I said.

He looked pointedly at my hands crossed in my lap.

"You can sense remnants by touch, Iris. You can channel the psyche in objects. Your soul may be incomplete but you're powerful, and here you are on the wrong side of the Order."

Once he'd said it, it seemed perfectly obvious. Hadn't I been able to sense remnants this whole time? Even before I'd recovered the ring? Other people used loupes and lanterns to reveal them but I'd never needed such accessories. I'd always known, in some small part of my mind, that I was different somehow, and here was the proof. The idea of being gifted, special, filled me with pride and excitement.

"I think that's why the Order is hunting you down," he said. "Not because you stole a ring, but because of what you can do."

Or because of what I had done, as a member of Renato House.

My excitement dissipated. Perhaps I was even more dangerous than I thought, more dangerous than I felt.

"It's not a coincidence that you're here, or that we met. That must be why my Shadow came after you, to protect you," Evander said. "Because you're one of us. You know, we have more in common than you think. You can't remember yourself, and I'm forgetting things too."

"You are? Like what?" I asked.

He leaned forwards, putting his head in his hands, but his Shadow missed a beat, failing to mimic his actions for just a split-second. It was spying on us again, listening in. Evander noticed me staring at the wall.

"My soul is damaged. Out of balance. The Shadow is expanding, bleeding into my memory, my personality, my feelings. Where once there were bright scenes full of detail, there's now only darkness. I can remember the bare bones of my life, but I can't really see it any more. I can't feel it. What people said, what we laughed about, what it was like to be alive in that moment… It's all numbed, faded. And I don't believe that's a coincidence either. I think it was done to me deliberately."

A deep, dark wave of foreboding washed over me.

"It's not just us," I said. "There's a whole night in history the Order is trying to erase. December 24th. The night I was shattered."

"The Night That Never Was," he said.

We stared at each other, wide-eyed and open-mouthed.

"What do you know about it?" he said.

"That's why I stole the ring in the first place. The Countess I worked for was looking for traces of a mysterious event, to blackmail the Order with. The ring and a fork were the only clues she could find – everything else to do with that night has been obliterated."

"A fork?" he said.

"It showed some kind of commotion at a fancy ball."

"That's right. There was a party that night, at the Basilica."

"Countess Cavendish thought the ring might contain the truth about the destruction of a human soul, and it did. It was *my* soul she was talking about, but I don't know how she knew. And I can't ask her about it now. The Order took her." I tipped my head at him. "What about you?"

"That's the night my memory loss began," he said. "Everything before that and after that is affected too, as if the damage is spreading, taking all other associated memories with it. I can't remember the Night That Never Was either, but I know something bad happened. I can feel it."

The cuckoo clock hooted, its clockwork bird popping in and out. We watched as two tiny figures appeared from two doors, running along a track until they met in the middle to shake hands.

"Whatever happened the night you were shattered, it was removed from my memory," he said. "Your mystery and mine, I'm sure they're connected. I know they are. I don't know how yet, but I'd like to find out. Wouldn't you?"

His eyes were so dark I couldn't tell the pupil from the iris.

"I'm proposing that we make a pact," he said.

"What sort of pact?" I said.

"We should work together to find out what happened. Help me piece together what happened on the Night That Never Was, and I'll help you find the rest of your soul's lost treasures. Maybe then we'll both remember exactly what it is that we've forgotten."

He held out his hand for me to shake.

"What do you say, Iris?"

I'd wanted a friend, and here he was. He might be able to help me, if I let him. Though he was a stranger, I trusted him more than anyone else I could remember, which wasn't saying much.

Without thinking it through, I pulled off my right glove, clasping my hand in his, skin against skin. Emotions rushed through me, as though I'd touched a remnant.

A painful wave of longing and regret washed over me. I felt Evander's loneliness, cold in my bones, and all the hard, rough edges of the walls he'd built to keep people out. I felt the pain he nursed for his mother's loss, picking at it nightly like an open wound. I felt his tightly-held pride, clashing with his youthful awkwardness, his yearning for freedom and desire for acceptance. I felt his self-loathing and his melancholy, growing deeper by the year, consuming him entirely. I felt his desire for a person unknown. I felt all the terrible complexity in his heart, and all the fears that ate away at him.

As he loosened his hold, the sensation faded. It clearly wasn't just objects I could sense but people too. I hadn't touched anyone with my bare hands since I'd put on the ring. He was the first.

Apparently oblivious, Evander stood up.

"Let me show you upstairs," he said. "You can stay here for now and work in the shop to earn your keep, like the rest of us."

Still reeling, I shadowed him up another staircase and then a third, final set of rickety, pull-down steps.

Glittering dust motes filled the air. Evander found a match and a gas lamp, igniting the wick. A tiny spark bloomed, filling the bulbous glass lantern with light, tainted sepia by the oily smears on the glass. It illuminated the contents of the shabby attic. A low, rusty bed. A dresser with a mottled mirror. Moth-eaten drapes. An ugly painting of a horse.

We stood close together in the confined space, him bending slightly to avoid hitting his head on the low-hanging beams. In this low, scattered light, his warm brown eyes looked to have flecks of amberic in them.

"Well, goodnight," he said. "Sweet dreams, as they say."

"I don't dream," I said.

"Sweet oblivion, then," he said.

"Sweet oblivion," I said.

Evander descended, closing the attic trapdoor behind him.

I watched him disappear into the dark, bleeding into the night until it was as if he had never existed at all.

8.

THE IRREGULARS

When I next awoke, it was ten past ten according to the old alarm clock on the dresser, yet the room was still dark. It took me a minute to remember where I was. Underground it never really got properly light, but the World's End outside was already long awake. Trains and trams rumbled on the streets overhead and the shouts of wandering peddlers echoed from the tunnel below.

Hugging my knees and gazing around, I took in the attic, focusing on the ugly horse painting. It felt as if aeons had passed since yesterday, as if the world had been turned upside-down and me inside-out. I had learnt so much. Evander was forgetting things too; he was damaged, like me. Something had happened to us on the Night That Never Was. Ruben Renato had disappeared. And I … I might be a member of the nobility.

I tried to make sense of the mess of my hair before barrelling down the attic stairs. The sweet sound of someone singing caught my ear, drawing me in; a girl's voice, high and clear.

Your soul's Song is in harmony,
A sweet orchestral symphony,
Every note and line is in tune and in time,
It sounds like you're in love with me.

Following the noise to an open door, I spied a girl my age with a cloud of black hair, sitting in the window sill with a wistful expression on her pretty face. She didn't notice me at first, launching into the second verse before she turned her head, trailing off. Her last note hung in the air between us.

"Oh, hello Iris," she said, standing up to greet me. "I'm Octavia. Octavia Belle."

She must've been one of the others Evander mentioned: the gifted waifs and strays who worked at the Emporium.

"How did you know my name?" I said.

"I heard it in Evander's thoughts. I'm a Listener, or I used to be."

I tried to empty my head, afraid she could hear me.

"The Song of my soul is too loud, so they say. But I can tune into any stream of consciousness for ten miles around. It's amazing what a girl can learn when she pays attention." She tapped her right ear, which had a silver ring in it. "Except for you. Your mind is as silent as the grave, Iris."

"You can't hear anything in me?"

"Not a whisper. It's highly unusual." She flashed a dimpled grin.

I was oddly relieved.

"But don't worry. All of us here are unusual. Irregular,

113

some might say." Octavia talked fast and made herself familiar, hooking my arm as if we were old-time friends as she led us downstairs. "We're all wanted by the Order, too. We'll look after you, c'mon."

She wore a necklace with a birdcage pendant on it. The cage was empty, with no bird inside. The birds were printed on her yellow tea dress instead, flying free, their wings spread wide.

In the kitchen, a boy in a white chef's apron was cooking eggs and bacon on the stove. He smiled at me lazily as I entered.

"Iris Cavendish, meet Gus Han," said Octavia. "His soul's Heart is too strong. The Order said he possessed dangerous amounts of enthusiasm."

"Nice to meet ya, Iris," he said.

Gus was a broad, muscular youth with symbols illustrated on his biceps, including a heart with an arrow through it.

"Gus has the best gift of all," said Octavia. "He's what we call a gourmand. He has the gustatory gift. He can cook food that makes you laugh, or brew beer that makes you cry."

I blinked at them, overwhelmed. It was like being invited to the reunion of a family I didn't know I had.

"You hungry?" said Gus, nodding at me.

My stomach grumbled on cue.

"Starving, actually," I said.

"Good. Comin' right up, red."

I pulled out a chair, sinking into it while looking

around. Like every room in the Emporium, it was a mess of mismatched goods and furniture. The walls were splattered with mysterious stains, the crooked shelves stacked with herbs and spices. Potted plants lurched askew on every surface, their leafy green entrails dangling everywhere. It wasn't like any place I'd ever been before. Stranger still, they all seemed calm, casually making breakfast even as the Order hunted for them. It felt safe here, and yet I struggled to relax.

Sitting opposite me was a pale young woman in a voluminous fur coat, like the skin of a bear. Her eyes were made-up with kohl and mascara and she wore a headband with a white flower on it.

She stared at me coldly.

"So this is new girl," she said, drumming her long, white-painted fingernails on the table. "She's much littler than I was picturing."

She had a strong eastern accent I couldn't quite identify, her speech fluid yet slightly broken.

"Iris, this is Perpetua Blavatsky. She's a Spirit soul," said Octavia.

Perpetua flared her nostrils at me in greeting.

"Top notes of blood and petrichor," she said. "Heart notes of sugar and incense. Base notes of grass and milk. You know what this tells me?"

"Not … really?" I said.

"Violent act happen to you. Your childhood stolen from you. You were betrayed by person you love."

"You can tell all that from a smell?" I gaped, breathing into my cupped palm self-consciously. I'd only just woken up and already someone had tried to read my mind, smell my soul and fill my heart.

"Every soul like a perfume. It can tell you past, present, even future. Some very faint. Some pungent, like rotting corpse. Your soul's scent practically non-existent, but I can make out just a whiff."

"Way to make our guest feel comfortable, Perpetua," said Octavia, widening her eyes at her accusingly before turning to me. "Don't mind her, Iris. She simply can't help herself."

Gus placed a plate down in front of me. Two eggs and a strip of bacon formed a smiley face.

"Bon appétit," he said.

"Thanks."

I heaped food on to my fork, shoving it eagerly in my mouth. It was hot and tasty, filling my belly. Gus watched me eat, hovering expectantly like a child awaiting praise. He'd only just met me, and yet he craved my approval. I gave him a thumbs-up. Smiling, he turned back to the stove.

"Come on, then," said Octavia, mouth full. "Tell Iris your stories – she already knows mine."

I didn't. Not exactly. Though I went along with it for now.

"My Papa was Order soldier," said Perpetua. "I was born on base in Moscovium until Papa was stationed here, to protect Chancellor Obscura. But Papa joined side with

116

rebels. He plot against Order, tried to kill his bodyguard. Chancellor stamp out all embers of revolution swiftly. He killed them right in front of me. Now I wait every day for revenge."

She grabbed the butter knife, stabbing it violently into the wooden slats of the table. No one commented, though our plates trembled.

"I used to work as a kitchen boy at the Basilica of All Souls," said Gus, "cooking up fancy canapés for the Order's soirées. Until they put me in the Reformatory and tried to purify me. Guess it didn't stick."

"How did you get out?" I asked.

"They gave me a job in the prison kitchen, didn't they? That was their first mistake. I met the cook, an old friend of Mr Sharma's. He sent a wagon disguised as a delivery truck to break us out."

Mr Sharma sounded like quite the character.

Gus looked past me and I turned, curious. Evander loomed in the doorway. He looked like some frightful vampire, dark circles under his eyes, hair everywhere, as if he'd been out all night gallivanting.

"Morning, sunshine," said Octavia.

"Ugh," he said, by way of greeting.

"I'll make you some tea," said Gus, patting him on the back.

Evander sat down, completely ignoring me. The kitchen was quiet but for the boiling kettle.

"Yes, he *is* always like this in the morning," said Octavia.

"I thought you said you couldn't read my mind," I said.

"No, but I can read your face. Don't worry. Evander's always a total gargoyle before noon."

"I can still hear you, you know," he said, frowning.

"Not me, I'm an early bird," she said. "Nothing better than getting up early enough to watch the sunrise."

"Where did you go last night, anyway?" asked Gus, of Evander. "I went to the bathroom and saw your Shadow slip outside gone three o'clock."

"I went to the Observatory to see what they know about Iris," he said, "but I didn't learn anything useful."

Finally, he looked me in the eye.

"You broke into the Observatory?" I said, impressed.

"Not in person. Just my Shadow. It's a lot easier when you can walk through walls."

Octavia gave him a disapproving look.

"It's still risky," she said. "They could use one of their lanterns to sense you. Or the Chancellor himself could spy you!"

They fell silent, exchanging a cryptic look. Whatever she heard in his mind, she didn't share it with the rest of us.

"Are they looking for me?" I asked.

"Yes, but they're only trying to catch a thief," he said. "Now they have the ring back, they've scaled back the search, it seems."

I exhaled in relief, enthusiastically clearing my plate.

When breakfast was finished, Octavia lingered.

"I don't mean to be rude," she said, quietly, "but you

smell like a dead rat in a bin fire, Iris. You really ought to run yourself a bath."

I sniffed one armpit, recoiling. I couldn't recall the last time I'd washed myself properly. No wonder Perpetua could smell my soul, if it smelled anything like my body.

"And what's with the black clothes?" Octavia said. "Did you bury someone recently? I think you need a fresh dress. Fresh dress for a fresh start."

She ushered me into a white-tiled bathroom with exposed pipes and a damp-stained ceiling. She pushed a bundle of towels and toiletries into my arms and departed. "I'll be waiting when you're done," she called through the wall.

Turning back to the tub, I ran the taps. After brushing my teeth at the basin, I tore off the black gown, removed my gloves and climbed in. I sat motionless, shaking though the water was warm. I stared up at the ceiling, eyes following the trails of mould that sprawled out like the tributaries of a river.

Untangling myself like a knot, I retreated to a horizontal position, sliding lower and lower, until my chin dipped under the surface. Here, it didn't seem to matter who I was, or wasn't.

Was this what a home felt like?

I scrubbed myself thoroughly, from my scalp to my toes. After drying myself off, I wrapped a towel around my body like a toga. When I opened the bathroom door, Octavia was standing there, hands on hips.

"Doesn't that feel better already?" she said, assessing

me with a keen eye. She grabbed my hand, pulling me into her room.

Her feelings flooded through me in a wave, just as Evander's had done before. She was lonely, but there was a hopefulness beneath it that shone through. She was happy to have a new friend, excited to have someone to talk to, afraid that I wouldn't like her. I could sense something darker too, something more discordant and bitter, swimming just beneath the surface, at odds with her sunny disposition, but she dropped my hand before I could feel any more.

The mildewed walls of Octavia's room were plastered with pictures of pin-up girls: performers in variety shows. Several posters depicted a woman with an hourglass figure and dangling silver earrings, pictured singing onstage to an audience of luminaries. There was a mannequin in one corner and a standing mirror in the other. She disappeared into her closet, throwing out an assortment of garish garments for me to try on: dresses with ruffles and beads and billowing sleeves. I vetoed them all.

"What about this one?" she said.

This dress was purple with a lacy blouse and frilled skirts. "It's not very me," I said.

"Me is who you make it. Just try it on."

I changed behind a screen, which doubled as a clothes horse, piled with unfolded garments. Admiring myself in the mirror, I saw a stranger. It was a nice enough dress, but miles away from what I would have chosen. Then again, Octavia was right. I didn't know who *I* was to begin with.

Maybe I could be someone different now, someone better...

Cupping my hands to my chest, I was comforted by the flickering feeling within, the Spark of my soul burning. This one small piece had changed everything. Who knew what I'd be capable of being with a whole soul again?

"You should get rid of those old gloves, too," came Octavia's voice. "You look like you got lost on your way to the debutante ball." I opened and closed my hands before pulling them back on.

"The gloves stay on," I said, firmly. I didn't want to get sucked into someone's psyche again.

"Fair enough," she said, amiably. "Let's see you then."

I stepped out, feeling clumsy and gauche. I was unsure how to stand or hold myself, so I copied the pose of one of the girls on the wall.

"Perfect," she said, clasping her hands together. "You just need to fix your hair now. Come on, sit."

She pushed me down into a chair, grabbing a brush from the dresser and dragging it through my scarlet curls, untangling the knots as she chattered about everything and nothing. I watched myself in the mirror, trying to memorize my own face, wondering who it belonged to. Maybe I'd find a clue in my key-hole shaped iris, or by joining the dots of my freckles. Maybe I'd hear a rumour hidden beneath my tongue, or unlock a memory caught in my hair like a leaf.

I saw myself again in the ring's memory, in the mirror that had shattered like my soul. My hair had been fashioned in a high society style that night. Had I done it myself? Did I have servants who'd dressed me, or a friend or sister like Octavia to care for me? Under her quick hands, the tangles were soon a shiny auburn waterfall.

"There. I think you're ready to find your soul now," said Octavia. "You can't have a clean start while you're still caked in the dirt of the past."

"How do you know what I'm looking for?" I said.

"I heard it in Evander's thoughts," she said, chewing her bottom lip. "Again. Sorry, I didn't mean to pry. Well, I did, but I feel bad about it now. An old habit. Back when I worked for the Order, it was second nature, tuning into the stream. I find it difficult to stop myself."

We stared at our reflections in the mirror, me in purple and her with the birds on her dress.

"We should go open up the shop now," she said.

I followed her downstairs.

"What is this place, really?" I asked, picking up an ugly stuffed fox. "It's not just any old curiosity shop, is it?"

"We sell things and buy things, but really it's just a cover. Ever since the Order came to power, there has been an Emporium, to shelter those they hunt. Its location may change, even its name, but it's existed for centuries. It has outlived many Chancellors, and will probably outlast many more to come, unless we have anything to do with it, of course."

She turned the sign on the door from CLOSED to OPEN, looking out at the empty street.

"We?" I said.

"The resistance," she said. "Welcome. You're part of it now."

I hadn't agreed to any such thing but I liked the idea of it, being a rebel on the run from the law.

"Is this it?" I said. "Or are there more of us?"

"More than you could ever imagine," she said. "Plenty have been captured. Plenty have died. But there are plenty more still living, still fighting, all hiding out across the country, waiting for the right moment to strike."

Her words roused me, making me want to fight too.

"What was it like, working for the Order?" I asked.

Octavia's posture stiffened, defensively.

"It was fine, at first. I lived in a fine place, wore fine clothes, and went to lots of fabulous parties." She smiled, eyes glittering as she remembered, before a serious expression clouded her face. "I worked at one of their Listening Posts, using amplifiers to hone in on thought patterns. But when they discovered that I could hear the stream without the need for their equipment, they made me one of the Chancellor's personal Listeners."

I tried to imagine her standing at the Chancellor's side, listening out for signs of insurrection. She was only a little older than me, still barely out of her teens. And yet the all-mighty Chancellor had needed her for his ears.

"So why did you run?" I asked.

"I may have heard a few things I shouldn't have, working for the Chancellor. I might know a few secrets the Order would rather keep hidden, the kind of secrets people kill to keep quiet, if you know what I mean."

"Secrets? About the Night That Never Was?"

She slowly shook her head.

"I remember that there was a ball that night, and that I accompanied the Chancellor to the Basilica of All Souls, but that's all I know. Evander has already probed me about it a dozen times."

I felt my face fall. Octavia seemed to notice, fixing on a more hopeful expression. "But with so many people missing their memories, it's plain to see that the Order is hiding something," she said. "It wouldn't be the first time. They have a habit of burying their secrets so no one can spill them. There are things I don't dare talk about, even now."

I wanted to know about the dangerous secrets she knew, but she didn't volunteer them, even though she talked so freely about everything else. I decided to wait. I would ask her again when she trusted me.

"How did you end up here?" I said, instead.

She didn't answer for a while, twisting a lock of curly hair around her finger. "Evander, he ... worked for the Order too. We knew each other from the courts. We decided to run away together."

I found myself flushing, surprised. "Are you and he...?"

She read the end of my sentence in my expression.

"Oh no, honey. He's not exactly my type, if you know what I mean," she said, winking at me. "I just became a friend to him, in the months before we left, and he to me.

We decided we wanted out. Evander's Shadow made contact with Mr Sharma, a former servant of House Obscura. He'd fled the Order himself over a decade earlier. Now he runs an underground network, using his abilities to keep an eye on people in danger. He brought us here where we'd be safe. But it was all in vain because the Order put a tag on me."

"A tag?"

"It's like having my own personal fire alarm. The Order can't hear me down here, it's out of their range, but the second I reach the surface, they can hear my soul coming a mile off. That's how they track down fugitives. I have to stay here underground, day in and day out, until the end of time."

She sighed, propping her chin in one hand. Her eyes drifted to me, her brow furrowed. I got the feeling that Octavia was used to being able to read people's minds, that she used this as a way to navigate conversations. Without it, she seemed unsure of herself.

"Anyway, that's enough about me," she said. "Let's talk about you and the search for your soul. It's all so exciting, in a terrible sort of way."

I told her everything that had happened, filling in the gaps of the things she hadn't already eavesdropped. She responded dramatically to each revelation, gasping or clutching her chest.

"If the other parts of my soul are hidden in objects that were present when I was shattered, I need to work out what they are," I finished. "But I can't remember the memory too well. It's already fading in my mind."

"Then perhaps you need to refresh it," she said.

Of course. The psychoscope, that large, clearly-stolen lantern that had revealed my soul for the first time. Maybe if I stood in front of it again, I could see the recollection more clearly. I might notice something different this time.

"I'll be right back," I said, hurrying off.

In the back room, I found Evander, standing in front of his wall of papers and frowning deeply. He was transformed from earlier, his dark hair slicked back, his clothes pressed and clean. He looked … nice. It was hard to believe he'd cast such a horrifying monster with his Shadow. When he heard me approach, he looked up and caught me watching him, pausing a moment to register my altered appearance, before turning back to his thoughts, in apparent disinterest.

He'd seemed a lot friendlier yesterday. It was almost as if something else was now occupying his mind.

"I want to see the memory again, through the psychoscope," I said, without preamble. "There might be more to be gleaned from it."

"Go ahead," he said, casually.

He removed an object from the tray and switched the lantern on again, allowing me to step in front of it. I waited for a picture to develop. At first, it showed only my small, rosy Spark, a distant glimmer with a burning centre. I felt suddenly embarrassed, that he could see how puny and incomplete it was.

Nothing happened.

"Think about the memory you saw in the ring," said Evander.

I tried to recall it as vividly as I could. Gradually, the room I'd been in yesterday at Renato House appeared, only in its pre-renovated state.

I watched myself.

There I was, hurriedly burning a letter on the fire. My hands were shaking. I moved back and forth erratically. An empty suitcase on the bed. Open drawers. I appeared to be packing, in the middle of fleeing. That's when I spied the intruder at the door. In the mirror, I saw my eyes widen. The painted phoenix loomed on the wall behind me.

"Well, that's definitely Renato House," I said, watching myself be shattered again. "And I'm certain that the room was mine. I think I remember painting that phoenix. I used to enjoy painting. Lady Renato taught me…"

This trickle of dormant recollections poured out of me without much coaxing, and then stopped, dying out like embers in the dark of my mind.

I played the scene again. And again. Rather than focusing on the action, I searched the background for objects that might be remnants but the image was fuzzy and askew, blurred in places, blackened in others. The memory was becoming less distinct with each viewing.

"It's no use," I said, growing frustrated. "This isn't telling me anything I didn't already know."

"Try examining the suspect instead," said Evander. He

was busying himself, writing something in a book, but he kept looking over.

"Well, it looks like a man to me," I said, "though it's hard to tell with those shapeless robes. Their hair is covered by the hood. They're wearing the same mask the Observers use. And look, the eye atop the staff. Isn't that the symbol of House Obscura?"

"I've seen weapons like that before," he said. "Only the most senior Observers carry them."

I realized that, as a Shadow soul who previously worked for the Order, Evander had likely served House Obscura, the Chancellor's own House. But he said nothing of it, offering up no personal connection.

The memory restarted once more.

"Wait! Go back," he said.

"What do you mean, 'go back'?"

"Think about the fire again."

The image on the wall flitted back and forth, jumping around before settling on the hearth. "There," said Evander. "Stop."

I had no idea how to operate my own mind like a projector but for some reason it worked, perhaps because I *wanted* it to work. The image froze, fixed on my hand clutching a piece of paper, moments from tossing it into the flames. It was covered in frantic, barely legible writing.

"Forgive me," said Evander.

"Forgive you for what?" I said.

"That's what it says," he said, squinting to make out

the faint, scrawled sentence just-visible. "'Forgive me.'"

I stood closer, tilting my head back and forth. He was right.

"But did I write it, or did someone write it to me?" I said.

"Either way, it's suspicious."

"I must have had something to hide, something I didn't want people to find," I said. "I was packing. I think I knew they were coming for me. I knew my life was in danger, even before they showed up."

The memory resumed, playing out to its bitter end again. The image focused in on the Renato ring before fading out.

"Everything keeps coming back to the Renatos," I said.

I didn't feel refined or important. I didn't speak like the highly educated luminaries who made up the five Houses. I didn't know anything about psychometry, or art, or even the history of the world.

"Why isn't anyone looking for me?" I said. "If I were a Renato, it would be all over the news. A missing debutante."

"Maybe the Renato family is covering up your disappearance. Maybe you did something that threatened their position in society."

"Maybe." I chewed my lip, thinking of that strange, silent house. "Or maybe something else is going on. Ruben hasn't been seen since the Night That Never Was, according to that servant."

"Yet according to the papers, he's away touring the colonies," said Evander, passing me this morning's copy of the *Daily Insight*.

"'Ruben Renato gives rousing speech at military ceremony,'" I read from the front page. "Then why hasn't he been home in a year?"

"The Order has its ways and means of making people be seen where they're not. The Chancellor knows how to project such illusions and control them. He is a Shadow soul himself, after all."

"You mean, Ruben might never have been at that ceremony, or in the colonies at all? He could be dead, or imprisoned?"

"It's entirely possible."

I flicked through the paper, hunting for further clues. Evander inched closer to read over my shoulder, but nothing jumped out at me.

"Maybe he fled that night," I mused, putting it down and turning to face him. "Something clearly happened at Renato House. We might all have been running for our lives."

"By all accounts, Ruben is deeply devoted to the Order," said Evander. "I can't imagine him doing anything to upset the Chancellor. He could just as likely be the one responsible."

"Either way, I need to find him," I said. "He's my only lead."

"Let's watch it again," said Evander.

This time, I slowed the memory down to a crawl, grinding my teeth with the strain of concentrating. On the wall, I saw my own face captured in the mirror's reflection. I watched it crack the moment the weapon's surge struck me, fracturing into five equal–ish pieces of glass.

"The mirror," I said. "Why didn't I think of it before?"

"You think it's a reliquary?" he said.

"How many times would I have stood in that room, gazing into it?" I said. "Thinking, feeling, remembering. Happy, sad, angry. I would've had a strong connection to it, don't you think?"

Evander was quiet, seemingly lost in thought again.

"But the room has been renovated since," I continued. "The mirror was broken. They got rid of everything. If a reliquary is destroyed, what happens to the soul piece inside?"

"It would die," said Evander, holding my gaze, "and your body would follow. Since you're still alive, I think we can assume it still exists. It could've been fixed, I suppose, or maybe someone rescued it."

"Who would save a broken mirror?"

"I don't know. Someone who knew you and loved you, perhaps. If your gut is telling you to look closer at the mirror, I say we listen to it."

My gut? Was that what it was, that impulse, that instinct, that feeling I couldn't prove to anyone, including myself?

"How?' I asked.

"We can try and track it, by diving deep into your own psyche. We'll start tomorrow."

"Why not now?" I said, impatient to begin.

"The Shadow can be ... volatile. It will take a lot out of you. It's best that you're well rested."

His expression was drawn, his eyes dancing back and

forth as if recalling something he didn't share. Once again, I found myself wondering what he'd done for the Order, and what they had done to him.

I moved to stand beside him, looking over the papers he had pinned to the wall. A floorplan of the Observatory. Pictures of the villas of the five Houses. A map of Providence. A family tree.

And a boy in hiding.

"You want to bring down the Order, don't you?" I said, gazing at him admiringly.

He clenched his jaw.

"Don't you?" he said.

For the first time, I considered it seriously. What would the world be like, without the Order to spy on us? I couldn't even imagine it.

"My memories were taken from me. I want them back," he said, in a carefully-controlled voice, not meeting my eye. "The Order did something to me and I want to make sure everyone knows about it. If I can prove it, perhaps I can show the world that the Chancellor isn't fit to rule." Finally, he glanced at me. "You could help."

"I want my memories back too," I said, "but I remember even less than you do. I don't see how I can help anyone, least of all myself."

"That's why we need to focus on finding you that next reliquary. You're the key to this, Iris. I'm sure of it."

His attention was fully fixed on me now, his dark eyes glistening, but still I didn't know what he was running from.

That night, I fell asleep with the button in my hand and woke up hours later, tangled in the sheets with a painfully full bladder. I rolled over, trying to convince myself that I didn't need to go, but the harder I tried to ignore it, the more it bothered me. It was the call of nature. I knew I'd never be able to go back to sleep unless I answered it.

Grabbing the gas lamp, I tiptoed out into the corridor, trying not to tread on the creaky boards. The wind was howling outside, causing the branches of the trees to tap and scratch the glass. The lamp created a floating sepia vignette around me, illuminating the brown, patterned walls, their paper peeling.

I felt my heart quickening.

"No!" came a cry, echoing through the quiet.

Breath catching in my throat, I moved along the hallway, raising the lamp, ready to use it as a weapon if I had to.

The door to Evander's room was ajar. I tiptoed towards it.

"No, no…"

I peeped in, the light of the lamp spilling on to his bed. Evander wore a thin white nightshirt, his chest partially bare, his dark hair comically mussed, even messier than usual. As he stirred, his silhouette acted out his nightmares on the wall. The monster he'd cast before loomed over him, its wings outstretched as it opened its fang-filled mouth.

"Oi!" I hissed, as if scaring off a scavenging dog.

Startled, the Shadow turned its dark head to me,

metamorphosing back into its normal silhouette.

"Evander?" I said, but the Shadow shook its head. Evander was asleep, yet his Shadow was awake, roaming free.

The realization dawned on me, strong and clear and shining bright, illuminating everything.

His Shadow had led me to the Emporium.

His Shadow had saved me from the Inspectors.

His Shadow *knew* me.

"You remember me, don't you?" I whispered.

Unable or unwilling to answer, the Shadow broke apart into a hundred shadow birds that flocked across the walls. I ran to the window, watching them scatter across the city.

In seconds, they were gone.

9.

THE SHADOW REALM

I couldn't get back to sleep, my head too full and noisy. How did his Shadow know me? Perhaps it wasn't so surprising. If I had been a Renato, and Evander had worked for the Order, some trace of me might remain in his subconscious, even if his waking mind didn't remember me at all.

The next day, I followed him into a warm, wood-panelled study, ready to deep dive into my psyche. Its walls were hung with pinned, framed butterflies. I hadn't told him what I'd witnessed in his room. It was a secret between me and his Shadow.

Evander produced a golden metronome, setting it down on the table beside him. It began to tick steadily.

"What's that for?" I said.

"To trigger a sleep state," he said. "Today, we're going to try and make a connection with your subconscious by entering the Shadow realm, the ethereal plane made of dreams and nightmares, fears and fantasies…"

I looked at him blankly.

"But I don't even have the Shadow part of my soul, just my Spark."

"The Spark is the fire, the powerhouse of the soul. Every part is connected, so everything is within reach. The Spark is connected to the Shadow. Maybe your Spark will lead us to it. That's the idea, anyway. We're in unchartered territory here, as far as soul searching goes."

"So what you're saying is, you don't know what you're doing or whether it will work?" I said.

The corner of his lips tugged into a smile. A fluttering feeling filled my chest, tickling me on the inside.

"I have years of experience traversing the Shadow realm and I still don't understand how it operates. But we've exhausted the memory in the ring for clues, so now we must go hunting in even murkier aspects of the mind. You must battle your own subconscious to remember what it's suppressing. Only you can win the war within yourself."

"I didn't realize I was at war," I said.

"But you are."

"Then I'll need to know how to fight, won't I?"

"Right. First, you have to learn to 'fall into yourself' at will. To look inward. There's no way of knowing what you might find in your subconscious once you go looking. I'll be here to wake you up if your soul wanders too far from home – but you must go alone."

I took a deep breath, setting my shoulders.

"I'm going to try and induce you into controlled sleep, allowing you to journey in a lucid state. When you get there, you'll want to think about the mirror and see where your mind leads you. I have no idea where your psyche will take you from there, but it might trigger something. Are you ready?"

He took my gloved hands. I could feel the warmth of his skin even through the thick material.

"I ... I think so," I said, flushing nervously.

"Look into my eyes, Iris. Keep looking into my eyes."

I resisted, feeling myself falling into him instead. His psyche was strong, like a hurricane dragging me into it. I pushed against it.

"Don't look away. Keep your eyes focused on mine. Now, take a deep breath. Fill your lungs."

I could see myself reflected in his pupils again.

"Now, exhale. Take a second, deeper breath. Inhale ... and exhale. In and out. You'll begin to notice your eyelids becoming heavy."

Tick, tick, tick.

My eyelashes were frantically fluttering, the sound of the metronome becoming a lullaby.

"Soon, they'll become so heavy that you can barely keep them open. You can feel the muscles around the eyes getting weak. Your eyes are getting heavier ... it's getting harder to resist. This is the place where the Shadow can spirit you away, when you're open and vulnerable to its influence."

Tick, tick, tick.

The shadows of my body bled into the shadows of the world.

I felt myself losing form, becoming nothing at all.

"I'm going to count down from five. By the time I reach the count of one, you will enter a subconscious state."

I fell backwards then, letting myself cartwheel through the darkness, unbound by gravity.

"Five, four, three, two, one…"

All light and sound extinguished like a snuffed wick.

When I opened my eyes again, I was standing alone in the dark place.

The void of my soul.

I walked back and forth, trying to find the edges of the darkness. I searched for a window or a door but there was nothing but empty space.

Walking turned to running. Frustration turned to panic. No light. No sound. No way in or out. I was trapped deep inside myself. I stopped and tried to calm myself. I was here for a reason.

"The mirror," I recalled.

Focusing on my recollection of the object, I spied a glint. A distant shimmer, like a remnant on the horizon, calling to me. As I floated closer, I saw that it was the mirror from the wall of my room at Renato House – but a giant version, as big as a door. I stood in front of it, watching as it cracked slowly, the splintering sound echoing. Its five parts fell away, disintegrating to dust and revealing the black abyss beyond.

I gazed into the gloom. Swirling mists formed a wooded clearing where a bonfire waited, its flames illuminating the darkness all around me. A shadowy figure stood on the other side, obscured by fire.

I saw that it was a girl. Not just any girl. Myself. It was creepy, seeing myself in the flesh – not as I appeared in a mirror or glass, but through the eyes of another person. The Other Me was dressed in the Countess's black gown. Her hair was black too. She was made-up like a body at a funeral parlour, with thick rouge and lipstick, her face powdered, like the hatpin's murderess.

When I raised my arm to wave at her, she copied. When I took a step backwards, she did too. With every move, she mirrored me perfectly, imitating me as I advanced towards her.

"Who are you?" I said.

I am you, she replied, her voice a low rumble in my head. *I am the darkest part of you.*

She entranced and repelled me. I wanted to befriend her, but I was frightened of her, too. I held out my hand for her to take but she merely stared at it, her face a mask of antipathy. Her skin hardened, forming the smooth white mask worn by the person who'd shattered me. She raised her arm to strike…

The blow took me off-guard, causing me to stagger to one side.

Before I could recover, she launched herself at me, knocking me over and rolling on top of me.

"Stop! What are you doing?"

We tumbled around on the ground. She was frighteningly strong. Her hands clasped around my neck, squeezing until I gasped raggedly for breath.

"Why are you fighting me?" I rasped.

Her eyes turned black, like Evander's when he cast the monster. Looming over me, she began to cry mockingly. Black tears splattered down into my face as she laughed, blocking out the light—

Shouting out loud, I jolted upright.

I was back in the butterfly room with Evander.

"You're OK, Iris," he said, holding up his hands as one might try to contain a frightened animal. "You're safe."

I stood up and spun around, convinced this was still a fantasy and that my Shadow self would spring out at any moment to attack me again. My breathing slowed as the clammy sweat on my neck dried.

"What did you see?" he said.

I licked my dry lips.

"I saw the mirror. I saw it shatter, and I walked through it."

"Then what?"

"I saw ... myself."

"Your Shadow?"

"She attacked me. She wanted to fight. She was trying to kill me."

"I thought this might happen," he said.

"A little warning would have been nice," I said, sharply.

"I wasn't sure what would happen," he said. "We're in the realm of experimental psychometry now, like I said."

I sank into the armchair, cradling my head in my hands.

"Why does my subconscious hate me?" I said.

"She is the manifestation of your forgotten self, and she alone holds the secret of the mirror's location," he said.

"Can't she just tell me? Why do we have to fight?"

"For all of us, the battle against our darker sides is a lifelong struggle. We must constantly reaffirm our superiority by taking control of ourselves, over and over. You must exert your authority, show her the power of your Spark."

"How am I meant to do that?" I snapped.

"I don't have any easy answers for you."

"I thought you were an expert, a scholar of psychometry."

"The battle is won differently depending on the person. The key to defeating her is within you somewhere. The only solution is to persevere until you identify that weakness, that flaw you can exploit."

"I have to fight her again?"

He nodded.

"You must keep fighting her until you win, no matter how long it takes," he said. "You must keep searching for yourself, Iris, or who knows what else you might lose."

I caught a flicker of regret in his expression, a sadness in his eyes.

Had he lost something? Some*one*?

"I don't have much to lose," I said.

"You'd be surprised," he said. "Sometimes you don't even know what you have until it's taken from you."

Resigned, I returned again and again to my subconscious, battling my Shadow. Each time was the same: I met my dark double before the fire and fought off her assault. She kicked and bit, she slapped and spat. She pulled my hair and scratched my skin, and always with the same dead-eyed glare.

"What is your problem?" I shouted.

She threw me head first into the fire.

I woke myself up violently again, crying out as I shook in the chair. Evander appeared out of nowhere, handing me a cloth to mop my brow and a glass of water to quench my thirst. I glugged at it, parched, as he held my gaze.

"You OK?" he said, his eyes soft, his brow wrinkled.

"Physically, yes," I said, inspecting myself.

Though I had no scratches or bruises, though our fights made no physical mark, I could still feel the sting and the ache they left behind.

"Mentally, no," I added.

The fear lingered, hauntingly. Part of me felt like curling up into a ball and hiding away for the rest of the day. If I'd known how to cry I would have done it, I was so exhausted.

"You're getting closer, I'm sure," he said. "You have to keep going. You have to break through."

"Is it worth it?" I said, my voice croaky. "I think I preferred being Hollow to this."

"You really want to go back to feeling nothing? Knowing nothing?"

"How many times am I going to let her grind me into the dirt?"

"That's up to you. Remember, it's *you* you're fighting with. You have the power to end it."

"Then why do I keep losing?" I said.

"Don't you want to find yourself?" he said.

"You know I do."

"Then fight. Trust me, this is a battle you have to win."

His words irked me. It was easy for him to say, just sitting there.

"You're one to talk. You can hardly control your own Shadow," I said in a flash of temper.

Evander gave a short, dry, bitter laugh, shaking his head.

"Sorry," I said, regretting it instantly. "I didn't—"

"It's fine. It's true enough."

He pinched the bridge of his nose, as if he had a headache.

"If I can't set a good example, then consider me a terrible warning. Do as I say, not as I do."

"So I can beat my Shadow, but you can't beat yours?"

He didn't answer.

"I'll wait here and keep watch," he said, instead.

I set my jaw, shaking off the sense of hopelessness that had set in. I wanted to know myself more than anything. I couldn't quit at the first hurdle. I had to be tougher, stronger, smarter than I'd ever been. I went into the dark place, not once or twice but so many times I lost count, but every time I thought I was winning the war, she tripped me up or tricked me.

I forced myself back again.

This time her eyes were wide, appealing.

We don't need to fight, she said.

"I'm not falling for that."

We can both exist.

"No, we can't."

With an animalistic cry, I launched myself at her, pummelling her with my fists in all the places I knew from experience hurt most. As before, she quickly regained control, knocking me to the ground and standing over me to gloat. She was arrogant, too confident that she would defeat me. I writhed beneath her, letting her think she'd won.

You'll never be whole, she said. *You'll never be loved. You're worthless. Hardly even a person.*

Now was my moment. I jammed my foot into her shin, causing her to fold at the middle, then kicked the other shin, driving her to her knees. I threw myself at her like a missile, pushing her face into the dirt as I raged.

"You're ... not ... me!" I said.

I felt the edges blurring between her and I, as pure,

white-hot fury coursed through my veins.

"Help me," I demanded, shaking her. "Help me find my Shadow."

My newborn soul was a fire raging out of control. Soon, there would be nothing left of me but ashes.

She began disintegrating into nothing, flaking into a cloud of dust as her dark energy flowed through me. A stream of fast, jumbled pictures rushed through my head. Here was the masked figure who'd shattered me. Here was the staff, raised to strike. The cracked mirror un-broke itself.

The memory jumped, skipped, replaced by the dark exterior of a government building. I recognized it as the Observatory. Inside, black coats sat around glass orbs, watching the projections of the city's Eyes. They wore blank-faced white masks. Each one was the spitting image of my soul's killer.

I floated away down the corridors as if I already knew the way, passing through a dusty library, past a dark door. On the other side was a jumble of items with cobwebs between them, but all were blurred except for one.

I focused in on it.

A cracked oval mirror with an ornate black wrought-iron frame, obscured by glittering dust. The masked figure flashed through my mind, causing me to jolt. Suddenly I was toppling backwards, plummeting through the dark place as I clawed at thin air.

My Shadow was imprisoned in the Observatory.

I stood up with a gasp, waiting for the dizziness to reside as the butterfly room flew into view.

I was alone.

Knees shaking, weak from hunger, I searched the Emporium for Evander, finding only Gus drinking solo and Perpetua whispering to plants, growing increasingly agitated when I couldn't find him. His bedroom door was open but he wasn't in his room. He wasn't in the kitchen, or the living room, or down in the shop.

I found him in the back room, where he was sitting on the floor in front of the psychoscope. It was projecting memories – his memories – through his body on to the wall, as it had mine before. I caught a glimpse of a girl in a white dress. The memory was garbled, corrupted, skipping every few seconds, but I could just about discern her through the haze, laughing without sound. She had pale blue eyes. Long blonde hair. A wide, pearly smile. Silver bangles on her wrist. She looked like the kind of girl who might appear on a billboard, a model of perfection. She reached out for his hand, enticing him to join her.

I didn't know this girl, had never met this girl, but I disliked her instantly. She was the opposite of me in every way.

I watched Evander's face, cycling through a series of different emotions, from joy to sorrow to fury then back to his usual stoic hopelessness. Sensing my presence, he looked up, causing the image of the girl to fade.

I swallowed, gripped by an unpleasant sensation I couldn't name.

"You're awake," he said.

"I thought you were supposed to be standing by, in case I got lost in my own mind," I said.

"Sorry, I ... I thought you'd be out for a while."

His dark eyes drew me in again. I looked away, forcibly.

"Well, I did it," I said. "I beat my Shadow. She showed me where the mirror is. You were right ... you really *are* a scholar of psychometry."

He looked surprised.

"Well, look at that," he said. "Where is it?"

"In the Observatory."

Neither of us spoke for what felt like a century.

"You want us to break in there, don't you?" he said in a dull voice.

"I don't *want* to. I have to."

He shook his head vehemently.

"That's a bad idea," he said. "A very bad idea. The Observatory is closely guarded, and it's full of spies."

"My Shadow is in there," I said. "I have to get it back."

"You can't just walk right on in."

I thought of the papers on his wall, the blueprints. He had all sorts of plans but no action by the looks of it.

"You went there the other night, didn't you?" I said.

"As a Shadow," he said. "It's different. It won't help us here. I can't bring anything back with me."

I found myself getting annoyed by him, unreasonably so, maybe. It bothered me that he had a secret life that I knew nothing about, working for the Order and dancing with blonde girls.

"Then I guess I'll have to go fetch it myself," I said. "I need to know what happened to me. I need to be whole again, more than anything."

"I want that too Iris, but you don't know what you'd be up against. The Order can haunt your dreams, or hypnotize you into believing a falsehood. They can tamper with your memory, or make you forget yourself. They can torture you with your own emotions, forcing you to relive your most painful moments, over and over again."

I got the sense he was speaking from experience here.

"We're both wanted," he said. "If we go to the Observatory, we could get caught. We could expose everyone else."

I nodded as if I was listening, but it didn't make any difference. For me, there was no question. It wasn't whether I would break in or not, but when and how and whether I'd be doing it alone.

"Please, Evander. You said you wanted to help me, and I can't do it without you," I said. "You've been there as a Shadow. You know the layout."

"I'm the absolute last person who ought to be creeping into the Observatory in person," he said. "Trust me."

"Why?" I said. "I know there's something you're not telling me."

He didn't answer for a long time, staring into thin air with a pained look on his face.

"I worked for House Obscura, using my gift for illusion," he said at last, between gritted teeth.

"I figured as much," I said. "So what?"

"The Order taught me everything I know. They were … like a family. But then they took someone from me."

I opened my mouth to ask more but he cut me off:

"*Don't* ask me to talk about it," he said, holding up one hand. "I just want you to know how high the stakes are. I defied the Chancellor's orders. He'll remember me. If I set foot in the Observatory, they'll recognize me."

"You don't have to show your face."

"They have my psychograph on record. It's … distinctive. I'm sorry Iris, but I can't. I just can't. And you shouldn't either."

At my sides, my hands clenched into fists.

"Then what else am I do?" I said. "Maybe once I would've been happy to spend my entire life not knowing who I am, but not now. Not any more. They have my soul, Evander. They have a piece of me locked away like a prisoner. How can I live without it? There's no other way to get myself back. No other way to save myself. Don't you see?"

I closed my eyes, listening to the roar of the Spark inside. I was flawed and incomplete, I was shattered and scattered, but I could still fight for my life. For my soul.

"You told me to battle my Shadow and I did. You told

me it would show me where the mirror is, and it did."

"I know, but—"

"We had an agreement, didn't we? A pact. You can't back out now just because it's getting complicated. But if you really won't help me, I'll go alone. I'm breaking into the Observatory tonight, with or without your help."

Evander ran one hand through the white streak in his hair, shaking his head softly as if he didn't want to hear it.

"I can't change your mind, can I?" he said.

"Not even a little bit," I said.

I held his gaze mercilessly. I watched his shoulders slump, his arms unfold, his face soften. He shook his head in resignation.

"Fine," he said.

"You're in?" I said.

"I'm in." He sighed.

I'd won, but it didn't feel like a victory.

What was he hiding from me?

Who was she?

10.

WHAT THE EYE SEES

Beneath a full moon, we stood before the Observatory, where all of the city's psychographs were filed for reference. Pictures of the souls of citizens were archived here on glass slides, ready to be dissected in dark rooms. They were printed on papers to be carried by law, presented to doctors and judges and landlords and moneylenders. This was where the Chancellor's Observers monitored the visions of the Eye, flagging up anything that pointed to deviancy or insurgence, and we were about to burgle it.

"I can't believe you talked me into this," said Evander. "We'll never get away with it."

I gazed up at the perpendicular Gothic façade of the building, made of sandy limestone with two square towers and a spire.

"Thanks for the show of confidence," I said, dryly. "That's just the pep talk I needed before breaking into a government building."

"I said I'd help. I didn't say I'd be happy about it."

"We'll be in and out in a blink," I said, trying to convince myself. "Even faster since you know the way. They won't be expecting a thief to break in and steal a mirror, will they?"

"I suppose not," he said, grudgingly.

Privately, though, I was already beginning to have second thoughts. The pull of my Shadow was even stronger now. I was definitely in the right place, but what if it cost me everything? What good would a subconscious do me if I was sitting in a cell, or worse, six feet under?

Either way, it was too late to turn back now.

Slowly, we moved towards the side of the building, avoiding the main entrance. Evander had used his skill with the Shadow to disguise us, him as an Inspector whose notebook I'd pocketed on the way, allowing Evander to cast the spectral impression of his face, and me as an Observer, my features hidden behind the mirage of a mask, the same blank-faced mask as my shatterer. But we could not obscure our souls, he reminded me.

"Does the Eye really see everything?" I said, staring up at the network of lanterns that guarded the front door. We were out of their line of sight, but who knew how many more there would be to spy on us inside. It was like creeping into the lair of a hundred-eyed monster.

"The network has many blind spots," said Evander. "The idea of total omniscience is just something the Order uses to discourage insurrection. There are more Eyes than they have people to operate them."

He knows so much about the Order, I thought.

"Won't we be seen sneaking around inside?" I asked.

"The Eyes are looking outwards, not inwards. They're paying much greater attention to what's happening out here than what's happening within. Once we're inside, we stand half a chance of getting away with this."

"What are you saying?" I said. "People out here are terrified to so much as think the wrong thing for fear of Inspectors locking them up, but the Order barely spare a glance at their own?"

"Basically. That's power for you."

I made a disgusted noise.

Evander manifested a shadow sketch of the building's blueprints, roving one finger over its spectral plans.

"Here's the library you saw, at the end. We need to try and avoid the two main chambers inside. There are Inspectors with lanterns on all three doors. Here, here and here, look. They search everyone who passes through these points. Our disguises should be enough to buy our way in but if they decide to take a closer look, we're in trouble."

Evander held out one black-gloved hand.

"What're you doing?" I said, staring at it in confusion.

"Just take it, and hold on."

I let his fingers curl around mine, my stomach tipping in response. He fixed me with a cold, expressionless gaze before turning back to the corner, raising his other hand. The whites of his eyes turned black, as if the inkpots of his pupils had burst and spilled over. The shadows began to bleed out, forming thin filmy ribbons, like spools of black silk. They shot out like grasping arms and wrapped around us, pulling us into the yawning mouth of the darkness. I was in that same dense black abyss I associated with the dark place inside myself, except this time Evander was right beside me.

I couldn't breathe. I couldn't talk. I could barely place one foot in front of the other. I could feel myself stumbling, falling, losing my centre of gravity, but Evander had my hand, holding on tight. The darkness appeared to yawn, forming an arch we could walk through. As we emerged into a cool, stony hall, the shadow portal closed in, leaving us alone and in silence.

Evander remained still, tendrils of shadow still weaving around his body like curls of smoke. I watched as the light returned to his eyes.

"Act natural," he said.

I didn't know what natural looked like, so I opted for my usual self.

"How did you do that?" I hissed, still reeling from the mind-bending sensation of travelling through a solid wall.

"We don't have time for a physics lesson," he said, curtly.

He was avoiding the question. There was no way he was just a lowly underling in his former life. He was someone of consequence. The Chancellor's personal Observer, maybe.

We crept past the spiralling cast-iron staircase, sneaking past rooms full of historical archives, divided into wings dedicated to the five Houses. Their ancient scrolls rolled up like carpets in cabinets. Entering a luxurious black and gold foyer, we ducked behind a pillar as a group of Observers bustled by in the distance, headed towards the gallery.

We waited until they were out of sight before moving on, drifting into a gilded room, its walls lined with Renaissance friezes: chiaroscuro scenes symbolizing the five aspects of the soul. A beautiful woman gazed into a mirror, in which she saw her own fantasies and fears. The Shadow. A group of scholars listened to the song of a harpist. The Song. Noble folk sitting at a long table ate an extravagant feast as painted courtesans flocked around them with baskets of fruits. The Heart. Two children collected flowers in a meadow, watched over by the cloudy memories of their ancestors. The Spirit. A young couple lay on a chaise longue before a fire as a storm raged outside. They were partially nude, electricity sparking between their fingers and lips … The Spark.

For a moment, I saw my own face in place of the painted young woman, and Evander in the place of the half-naked man.

I flushed hot behind my mask, trying to shake the image out of my mind. *It must be my Shadow playing tricks on me*, I thought.

"Come on," said Evander.

In one of the dimly-lit side rooms, a group of Observers watched the projections of dreamers, far away in their beds. The masked employees were manipulating the sleeping people, closing their eyes as they touched glowing orbs with both hands, orchestrating what happened in people's minds like directors in a theatre play. They were torturing them with endless nightmares. I stared at these poor souls open-mouthed before Evander pulled me on again.

Through another doorway, I gazed upon a dark chamber lined with upholstered black benches, on which sat a dozen scattered Observers, reading and conversing and making notes. In the centre of the room was a gigantic floating orb. Images floated across the surface of the bubble like open windows, showing scenes from across the city.

A huddle of guards in red armour. A glamorous-looking woman surrounded by reporters. A group of homeless people under a bridge. A sewer grate that led to the World's End…

We passed through another door into a narrow corridor. On either side, there were many red velvet compartments in which Observers watched the reflections of glass globes. They sat talking, dozing, doing the crossword in the newspaper, some hardly paying attention to the visions at all.

At the end of the hall was a grand, oversized oil painting of the Chancellor, looking down his nose at us. A tall, thin man with shaded goggles and many rings on his fingers. There was something hard about him, something sharp and twisted. I shivered, face curdling, as a feeling of foreboding puckered my skin. He must've been capable of anything, if he could turn mind to matter. How could any rebellion ever compete?

Evander moved on quickly, past a smoking room thick with fumes, into a series of chambers, windowless and heavily-curtained, where Inspectors were filing psychographs, drinking coffee and monitoring the orbs. There were wanted posters on the wall, including one of me.

My hands grew clammy inside my gloves, but no one recognized me beneath the mask. Some of the Inspectors even nodded at us as we passed, including a grey-haired cleaning woman.

"Long night, huh?" she said.

"Aren't they always?" I said.

Around the corner, a group of Inspectors stood gossiping around a water fountain, talking in hushed voices.

"Did you hear?" said one to another. "The Chancellor is sending a thousand soldiers to all five boroughs."

"What for?"

"I don't know, do I? They won't share it with us dogsbodies."

"He must be planning something."

I exchanged a dark look with Evander before we continued along the hall, trying to look as if we belonged there.

The walls beyond were lined with racks of alphabetized glass slides, with magic lanterns set up at desks between them. In one, I saw a psychograph imprinted on the small see-through square, like a pressed flower. It cast the image of an unknown soul on the wall, a person whose Shadow was so powerful it leaked out in curling streaks, while darkness bled through its branching veins.

We hurried through the second door on the right. On the other side was an enormous wood-panelled room, a grand library with a mezzanine level, rolling ladders and gold spiral staircases. A single Observer sat at a table in the corner, surrounded by piles of fusty tomes and water-damaged manuscripts.

My memory tugged, twigged, dragging me back to the vision I'd seen after battling my Shadow.

"This is it. This is the place I saw the mirror," I whispered. "The Shadow of my soul is here somewhere. I can feel it."

My vision tunnelled. My ears began to ring. I drifted forwards, following the invisible pull as Evander trailed after me.

The library was full of peculiar compendiums and encyclopaedias, with names like *A Beginner's Guide to Dream Walking and Soul Sailing*, *The Scent of War*, *The Gastronomic Guide to Fine Dining* and *The Symphony of the Soul: A History*.

A red book caught my attention: *The Renato Method*.

Unable to resist, I stopped and picked it up, trying to look like I was browsing as a librarian passed by with a trolley. Evander pretended to be looking for a manuscript from a box of scrolls.

I opened the red book, leafing through it. It contained instructions with illustrated diagrams on channelling lifelines, using the hands to activate different pressure points on the body and stimulating the nerve endings to mimic different physical sensations.

Turning a page, text jumped out at me:

By pinching a particular spot on the neck (see diagram) a user of the Renato Method can make their subject feel as if they're being suffocated. By placing the palm on the chest with fingers splayed, the user can cause the subject to lose consciousness.

I shuddered, skipping ahead.

But the Renato Method is not just a means for torture. Its usefulness transcends discipline and interrogation. There are parts of the body a user can touch that will make the subject laugh, cry, or confess to their deepest secrets. It can also be used to heal injuries, or even revive a patient's heartbeat. The advanced branch of the Renato Method is explored in the next section. For experienced users only.

I turned the page, examining a diagram that depicted all the lifelines in the human body.

Evander nudged me, urging us on.

Replacing the book on the shelf, I advanced to the rear door.

Looking back over my shoulder, I tried the handle. It was locked, but I'd had the foresight to bring two bobby pins to pick it: the one recovered from Renato House, the other borrowed from Octavia. The Countess had trained me in how to access remnants that were locked away safe and sound.

The door was stiff, making a loud noise as it sprang open. I slipped inside and Evander closed it behind him, submerging us in the pitch darkness beyond. Stumbling around, I found a glass lamp, turning it on. My eyes gradually adjusted, revealing a gigantic version of the Countess's Cabinet of Curiosities, each item carefully labelled and dated, like exhibits at a museum.

From the ceiling, a large sign hung, reading **LOST AND FOUND**.

Somehow, I was both.

I felt at home here amongst the forgotten detritus of the past, moving along the aisles and reading some of the labels.

Murder on the Orient Express, read a faded green leather suitcase.

Jilted at the aisle, on that of a bride and groom cake topper.

Grief, said a small knitted pair of mittens.

Here were the remnants with no owners, memories whose makers could not be identified.

"Iris, over here," came Evander's voice.

I followed it to a cabinet of dusty curiosities that were unlabelled, an unsorted pile of miscellanies. Here, in the middle, was the mirror.

Suddenly afraid to face whatever it had to teach me, I hesitated. Evander looked frightened too, though of what I didn't know. Maybe being back here in this place he'd run from.

As I neared the mirror, heart throbbing, the Shadow trapped inside it began to leak out through the crack, forming a streaky fog. Its tendrils wrapped around my arms and legs, pulling me towards it.

As soon as I saw my frightened face reflected in the shattered glass, with Evander standing behind me, I plummeted deep inside myself, hurtling through the chaos of time and space until I crashed down into the dark place.

I gazed upon the bonfire again, realizing only now that it was the Spark of my soul, its flames changing colours. This time, my Shadow stretched out beside me. Where I ended, she began.

When she held out her hand, I took it.

My head filled with a glittering, swirly darkness that took shape and form of its own volition.

It was my imagination. My subconscious.

The Shadow of my soul.

Together, we sought the memories I needed.

A mirror on the wall, its glass not yet cracked. My past self is standing in it, well-dressed and groomed again, staring fixedly into my own face as if in search of answers. A man comes to stand behind me. It's Ruben Renato, dressed in embroidered red robes with flame patterns on the sleeves. He grips my shoulders, turning me to face him.

"If you want to set the world on fire, all you need is a tiny spark. One spark is all it takes. A single ember can reduce an entire city to cinders, turning even the greatest of empires into tinder." He's smiling, but his eyes are burning. "The world is all yours, my Ruby. All you have to do is reach out and take it."

Ruby?

He reaches into his pocket, pulling out a small red box and handing it to me. I open it shakily, revealing the Renato ring.

"What's this?" I say, looking up at him.

"It belonged to your grandmother. Now she wants you to have it. You are the crown jewel of our House now."

Ruby Renato. I was Ruby Renato.

I see myself reflected manifold in its facets.

Tentatively, I pull the ring out of its box, tilting it between my thumb and forefinger. It's a bit gaudy, but its amberic glitters mystically under the light of the chandelier.

"First, I will need to train you," he says. "That means you will live here with me, in Renato House. Your mother raised you well but there are things only I can teach you, tools you will need if we are to avenge her."

Ruben holds up his palms, allowing little fires to dance over his skin.

"Trust in me, and you will know all the secrets of the soul. Trust in me, and your life shall be your own."

I stare into the mirror again, face skipping between joy and pain.

"There is no one else I would trust with such an important mission but my own flesh and blood. My daughter. Will you help me?"

I set my face with a steely expression, lifting my chin.

"I'll do it," I say, turning to face him again with a nod. "I'll help you bring down the Chancellor."

"That's my girl," he says, proudly. "My jewel. My Ruby."

I slide the ring on to my finger.

All the world begins to tremble.

A dozen different reflections appear in the same mirror, one after another. I see myself reading the red book I leafed through in the library. I see myself sitting with Lady Renato as she reads my palm, teaching me the lifelines through which the Spark is conducted. I see myself fighting a boy in a red tunic, my hands strapped. I see myself laughing and dancing and painting a phoenix on the wall. I see myself crying and lonely and screaming into a pillow on the red canopy bed. I see myself winding the key to a music box, watching the dancing figures spinning as a haunting melody plays…

A music box…

The final reflection shows me sprawled on the floor as the hooded attacker looms over me. In the mirror, I watch the darkness spill from my right pupil, creating the distinctive keyhole shape that earned me the name Iris.

My memory hurtled ahead, dragging me like wild horses back to the present of the Observatory.

I blinked, and I was back in the library, sprawled on the floor as Evander bent over me, speaking without sound, his face creased with concern.

Regaining my vision, I saw my dark double projected against the wall, cast by the lantern's light, moving with me in synchronicity. I'd always had a Shadow, but I'd never paid it much attention before. It had never felt like a part of me. Now I knew better.

Still dozy, I moved my hand back and forth, making shapes with my fingers as she matched me perfectly. We were one. United, in harmony, Shadow and Spark. If before, my body had been little more than an empty shell with a Spark in it, now it was filling with the richness of Shadow.

The electrifying realization washed over me again. Ruben Renato, the Chancellor's right-hand man, had groomed me to fight. I was a rebel born and bred. My mission?

To destroy Chancellor Obscura.

PART
THREE
THE SONG

11.

SOUL GAZING

"Iris. Iris. Iris."

Evander's voice broke through the fuzzy memory fog that made my head heavy, my wrong name echoing.

"Iris, get up. We have to go."

The sweet, alluring voice that announced the nightly curfew rang loudly through the Observatory, sobering me up instantly.

"This is a security announcement. The Observatory has been compromised. Please make your way to the nearest evacuation point."

A grinding, bone-shaking alarm sounded as Evander and I stared at each other in horror.

The mirror was too big and heavy to take with me, but my Shadow was safe within me now. I followed Evander out of the room and back into the library, now swarming with black-coated guards.

"Any ideas?' he said.

"Just … act natural," I said.

We mingled amongst them, joining the exodus flooding

down the nearest staircase.

"Please be on the lookout for an intruder," continued the voice, with eerie cheerfulness. "The suspect is approximately five feet two inches tall and dressed as an Observer. Be vigilant."

I felt as if I were shrinking, as several pairs of eyes landed on me. Beside me, Evander appeared to be flagging, stumbling slightly.

"Are you OK?" I said.

I watched as his spectral disguise began to fade, allowing his real face to shine briefly through the false one. Turning to the nearest window, I saw my own Observer's mask bleaching away to nothing.

The illusion he'd cast was failing.

One of the Inspectors pointed at me, his hand shaking.

"It's her!" he hollered. "The girl with no soul!"

As he broke through the crowd, trying to grab me to make an arrest, I pushed him in the chest, trying to force him away. Without thinking, I made a palm shape, fingers splayed, copying the diagram I'd seen in that book, the movement coming to my fingers unbidden. One touch from me and his eyes rolled back in his head. He toppled backwards over the railings.

I peered over, watching as he hit the floor with a thud. No sound or movement followed.

The gathered crowd paused in shock. In that suspended moment, another Inspector grabbed hold of me. I threw up my fists, ready to fight him before I recognized the stranger's face, stopping myself just in time.

Evander raised his voice, sounding every inch the Inspector he looked. "Stand back, everyone. The fugitive is coming with me."

He pulled us through a fire door and down a flight of steps before pausing, reaching forwards to touch my face softly.

"What are you doing?" I said, flinching as the cold skin of his hand rested on my hot cheek.

"Creating a makeshift disguise."

Turning to spy my reflection in a nearby panel of glass, I saw an entirely different face looking back at me: a mousy woman with a pinched mouth and sunken eyes. He tossed aside the security badge he'd used to draw her picture in his mind, and we stumbled down another staircase.

A small group of Inspectors followed in quick pursuit.

We burst through the nearest door, flying into another identical-looking corridor full of black busts on pedestals, flattening ourselves against a painting just in time to miss another group of patrolling Inspectors. We emerged into the lobby with its black-tiled floor, where people crowded beneath the hanging lanterns. Footsteps thundered in the distance.

"Well, that's that," said Evander. "We're doomed."

"No. We're not giving up that easily," I said.

He looked pale. His nose was bleeding, causing the illusion that disguised his face to falter again. We didn't have long.

"Stop! Stay where you are!" came a shout. "We have a warrant to search everyone in the room."

Inspectors threaded through the crowd, looking through binoculars and swinging their lanterns. Listeners accompanied them, holding up their silver ear trumpets. It was only a matter of time before they spied us. I dragged Evander on towards the double doors but another troop of Inspectors charged down the staircase. They locked their arms together to create a chain of bodies, blocking off our escape route. Flashes of light lit up the hall as lanterns scoured souls.

Someone was shrieking.

"Hold still, ma'am."

"Just do as you're told, sir."

Turning back on myself, I spied the dark entrance at the top of the stairwell at the other end of the room, currently unguarded. I jerked my head towards it and Evander nodded. Creeping along the perimeter of the room, trying not to bump into anyone, I led us towards it. We stumbled up and into the dark empty room on the other side. It was some sort of gallery, its walls lined with paintings of members of the five Houses. Breathless, I pulled us on, or tried to, but Evander stood stubbornly in the middle of the walkway.

"We have to go," I said, tugging his sleeve.

He didn't seem to hear me. He was staring at a portrait of the Chancellor – a different painting this time, depicting the woman I assumed to be the Chancellor's late wife and their son as a baby, swaddled in a black blanket. Darkness crept into Evander's eyes, blackening out the whites.

"Evander?" I said, voice tremoring.

The shadows around us began amassing, becoming material. They circled him like greedy birds. Dark smoky tendrils broke free, wrapping around him. He was immobilized, trussed up in a suffocating web of darkness, like a spider's prey.

Shouting his name, I pulled and tugged with all my might to free him from the mass of swarming shadows. He did nothing to stop it. He was in some kind of trance, just letting the darkness take him.

"Evander, wake up!" I cried. "Please wake up. Snap out of it!"

I tried to tear the shadows away, ripping them up like spools of fabric, but they grew thicker and tougher, like tree branches. As I grappled with them, my hands touched his skin, pulling me into him again. Fragmented visions washed over me, tarnished with a blackness that obscured everything, spreading like rot or mould.

I am small, sitting alone in a dark room full of toys. I cry and cry but no one comes to check on me. Locked away for days on end, with only my own Shadow to talk to. Over time, it comes alive, waving to me. My Shadow, my only friend.

The images broke apart, moved faster, mixed together, creating a chaotic mosaic of moments.

I punch a hole in the wall. I smash a window. Balls. Feasts. Dances. Rooms full of people in glittering gowns, their faces painted like masks.

There she is again. The pretty girl with blonde hair, this time standing on the opposite side of a ballroom. The crowd parts to reveal her. It's like nobody else exists.

"I'm Lily," she whispers in my ear. "Don't tell anyone."

Now we're dancing outside in the snow, beneath a bandstand covered in roses, dipping and whirling, swaying and spinning as lovelorn music plays.

The Night That Never Was.

I'm kissing her, and she's kissing me. Our bodies are intertwined. We become a part of each other.

Like spilled ink, spreading darkness blotted out the memories.

I'm screaming, banging on a black door…

I'm running through the woods at night…

Blood drops on snow.

Something yanked me away from Evander, back to the present. He stood apart from me, glassy-eyed and bleeding, swathed in shadow. Out of nowhere, a crackly image of the Chancellor's face flickered on to the wall in front of me, cast by a lantern in an alcove.

"Hello, Ruby," he said, his shaded stare boring into me as my throat closed up. "So we meet again."

I backed away from the distorted, flickering image.

"And Oliver. How nice. It's been far too long."

Oliver? I turned to Evander just as the shadows retreated, his eyes returning to normal, revealing his horrified expression.

"We're going to have ourselves a little reunion," the Chancellor said. "You, me, and my son."

His … son?

No, no, no…

"I suggest you both come quietly, or this won't end well for either of you. Stay where you are. My Inspectors are on their way."

The picture fizzled out, leaving Evander and I alone again.

"It's not what you think," he said, before I could speak, but I didn't know what I thought yet.

My eyes stung bitterly, blurring my vision.

I tried to speak but nothing came out.

A black hole opened up before us, sucking all the shadows into it before a single figure stepped out on to the balcony overhead. Entering the room just as Evander had entered the building, the Chancellor appeared in person as Inspectors loomed in every doorway, blocking us in.

"Guards! Seize them," he said.

Evander's face bore a terror like I'd never seen before.

"Now, Evander! Through the shadow," I said.

He froze up, as Inspectors pounded towards us.

"You can do it," I said firmly, unsure whether or not it was true.

Holding my gaze, he hesitated for only half a second before complying, grabbing my hand as we tumbled head first into darkness.

The void expelled us into a street outside. I landed face down in a puddle, spluttering. Catching my reflection in the settling water, I saw that the illusion Evander had cast had vanished. I was myself again.

I hauled myself upright, finding Evander slumped over nearby and helping him to his feet.

"You OK?" I said.

"I think so."

Five brilliantly-bright beams of light shot up into the sky, roving around as they probed the night skies on all sides of the Observatory, in every angle and direction.

"Uh oh," I said.

Every single Eye lamp in the city began rotating too, searching the empty streets after curfew. Every spectacular illuminated with a deep surging sound. A thousand pictures of my face popped up, captured in the split-second when my disguise faltered. Simultaneously, every listening station in a five-mile radius began playing the same, automated message, its cacophony deafening.

"Please be on the lookout this evening for the Order's Number One Fugitive," came the usual voice. "Going by the names Ruby or Iris, this soulless Hollow is guilty of capital crimes and considered extremely dangerous. Do not approach if seen. Please report to Inspectors immediately. Thank you for your cooperation. Have a pleasant evening."

I cursed.

"This way," said Evander. Or ... Oliver?

He didn't speak again and neither did I, running wordlessly through the warren of pitch black streets as we tried to avoid the light. He seemed a little unsteady on his feet. A small trail of blood ran from his nose to his mouth.

I had so many questions, all running around and

screaming inside my head, but none of them made their way to my lips, getting stuck in my throat, making it hard to breathe.

"You … you're…"

"Not now," he said.

The Chancellor's son. How had I not seen? How had I not realized? Wasn't he supposed to be on a grand tour of the continent?

Evander slowed a bit, clutching his side as if he had a stitch. I limped behind him, trying to catch my breath.

"I told you … we shouldn't have gone," he panted.

"I had no choice! What else was I supposed to do?" I said. "Write the Order a nice letter, asking politely for my soul back?"

"It's still a capital crime."

"No. What *they're* doing, that's a crime," I said. The Spark inside me bloomed to a flame. "Torturing people, wiping their memories, shattering souls, making us live in fear. They're not purifying souls … they're pure evil. They were hunting me before and they're hunting me still. So what? Let them come at me and show their faces. I want to look directly at the ones who shattered me and show them they didn't break me."

Evander didn't reply. He didn't look as if he had the energy to.

Down the road, he began to sway, turning grey before collapsing on to a bench.

"I just need a minute," he said.

"We don't have a minute," I said, hearing the rumbling of oncoming wagons, all ringing their bells.

"You should go... Go on without me."

"I can't do that."

Despite everything, I needed him. I still wanted him around.

I tried to pull him up and on to his feet, but he was heavy as lead, dragging me down with him.

"Evander, Oliver ... please! Get it together!"

His eyes were pure black again, as if the Shadow was trying to commandeer him. He slipped into unconsciousness. Blood trickled from his nose, dripping over his lips and splattering down his shirt.

"Oh god," I said.

Scarlet drops speckled the ground, reminding me of the image I'd seen in his memories. *Blood drops on snow.*

I was a wanted fugitive and I was stranded, responsible for the life of a boy I wasn't strong enough to carry. Not just any boy, but the Chancellor's son. What was I supposed to do now?

Help, I thought, as loudly as I could. *Help!*

A dark carriage approached at speed, horn sounding, swerving around a bicycle to pull up beside us. I froze, thinking it was all over, but then Perpetua's head popped out of the driver's window.

"Get in, idiots," she said.

I couldn't have been happier to see her pale, stony face.

With a sudden spurt of strength, I heaved Evander inside,

slamming the door behind us. The wagon sped off again with squealing wheels, just as the other carriages caught up. Perpetua rang the bells and operated the searchlight, pretending to scour the streets for us like all the other black wagons.

Evander collapsed into his seat as we sped around a tight corner.

"There's something wrong with him!" I yelled over the roar of the road. "I don't know what to do!"

"Here," said Gus, in the passenger seat, leaning back to hand me a glass bottle. "This will help."

"What is it?" I said.

"Medicine. It's safe. I made it myself."

I pulled out the cork, holding the little bottle up to Evander's lips and dribbling it into his mouth. It had the strong smell of ether or some other spirit, mixed with a sharp, aniseed scent. Evander's eyes emerged as the darkness dissipated, locking on to mine.

Slowly, he slumped forwards with his head wedged between his knees, moaning softly. Instinctively, I patted his back to comfort him. His clothes were soaked through with cold sweat. My heart tugged with sympathy, but I shook it off. No, I was supposed to be angry with him. He had lied to me, and not in a small way. He had lied about something gargantuan.

I pulled back my hand.

"He'll be all right in a little while," said Gus.

"How did you know we'd be here?" I asked. "You

couldn't have arrived at a more perfect moment."

"Octavia," said Perpetua.

"She read Evander's mind?"

"No, she heard you whispering in corridor on your way out to break into government building, so we stole Inspectors' wagon to come rescue you." She scoffed. "I know you only have part of soul, but you have whole brain. No excuse for such stupidity."

"I didn't mean to cause so much trouble," I said, as we zipped past another parade of wagons heading in the opposite direction.

"Really? What did you think would happen, new girl?" she said.

"Not this, obviously," I said.

"Did you get what you were looking for, at least?" asked Gus.

I told him about finding the mirror with my Shadow in it, and how Ruben had called me his daughter. I hoped to impress upon them the urgency of my act, but this only deepened Perpetua's scowl. I didn't tell them about my vow to destroy the Chancellor, nor the part about Evander's identity. I didn't know what they knew, and I needed to talk to him alone first.

"I knew you were trouble," said Perpetua, with a sniff. "But I didn't know you'd be *this* much trouble."

"I guess we should start calling you Ruby now, huh?" said Gus, amiably. "Or is it Lady Renato?" He performed a comical bow.

I thought about it, saying the name over and over in my head. "I don't know about that," I replied. "I feel more at home with Iris, even if that isn't my real name. Maybe I should just pick a new one and start over."

I watched Evander under cover of my eyelashes as the colour slowly returned to his cheeks. He sat up and blinked, his eyes meeting mine.

"I'm sorry," he mouthed.

Frowning, I looked away.

We'd pulled it off somehow, at least in the sense that we were still alive, and yet I could not feel triumph. We were just starting out on a long walk through the dark, without a coat or a map. The Chancellor had come within six feet of us. We had certainly caught the Order's notice now. And Evander wasn't the person I thought he was.

Perpetua abandoned the wagon in an underpass and we climbed out. Down a narrow, shadowy lane, we approached a drain cover.

"Give me a hand," directed Perpetua, as Gus propped Evander up.

I helped her heave it off, revealing a deep shaft. She nodded for me to go first. Stepping carefully on to the creaky ladder, I took it backwards, step by step until I reached the cool, cavernous hollow at the bottom. Perpetua followed, then Gus helped Evander down, replacing the heavy cover. Perpetua picked up a lamp and held it out before us, illuminating a tunnel that seemed to stretch infinitely beneath the city.

We made our way through the World's End, past ragged stalls and grimy alehouses, past a dozen tunnels filled with dozy, grubby people trying to scratch out a living selling stolen goods.

Back at the Emporium, Octavia was waiting in the sitting room upstairs, knitting furiously, but her anger seemed to melt away when she saw us, dropping her half-a-scarf. She hugged me first, my arms pinned to my sides in surprise. After a moment, I hugged her back, relaxing into the embrace, careful not to touch her bare skin. I couldn't bear to fall into someone else tonight.

"Did you find it?" she said, pulling back to hold me at arm's length. "Your Shadow?"

When I nodded, she squealed in excitement. She began talking a mile a minute, praising my bravery on one hand and admonishing my foolishness on the other, but I couldn't concentrate, getting lost in my own thoughts again. Ruben's words echoed in my mind.

The world is all yours, my Ruby. All you have to do is reach out and take it.

He had been training me – his own daughter – to bring down the Chancellor. I stared at my hands, thinking about the guard I'd knocked over the balcony. What else was I capable of? What terrible things had I done?

Octavia pulled Evander in next for a hug but her joy lasted only a moment before turning to anger.

"Look at you!" she said. "Didn't we talk about this? You're putting too much of a strain on yourself."

"I'm fine," he said. "It's nothing. Just a little blood, that's all."

"You have to take better care of yourself, Evander. Please. If not for yourself, do it for me. For us."

Brushing her off, he retreated upstairs with one last glance at me. Octavia looked after him, biting her lip. I wondered if she knew. Hadn't she said they'd fled together? That they knew each other from the courts?

When she turned back to me, I gave her a purposeful look.

"What?" she said.

"I know," I said. "About Evander."

"Oh," she said, collapsing into her chair again. "Well, that's a relief. It was a struggle to keep it in for so long."

"You met me yesterday."

"Exactly. This is the longest I've ever kept a secret to myself."

"What's wrong with him?" I said. "Why is he bleeding like that?"

Blood drops on snow.

"It's complicated," she said, evasively.

"Tell me," I said. "Please. I need to know."

Octavia checked the hall outside was empty before the dam broke. "I don't know what he's already told you… But something happened to him, something that damaged his soul."

"Lily, you mean?"

She looked surprised that I knew the name, though she shook her head. "No, much earlier than that. It's not my story to tell, but it caused a crack. Everything that came later only caused that crack to grow, letting the darkness in more and more. The Shadow of his soul is so powerful, but that power can easily overwhelm a person."

I pictured myself battling my dark double, and how Evander had told me it was a fight I had to win.

"On top of all that, turning mind to matter is as great a strain on the soul as you can imagine," she said. "Even for him to send out his Shadow, it takes its toll. But to create tears in the fabric of reality by turning darkness to black holes? If he carries on like that, he'll kill himself one day."

Guilt and regret churned within. I'd begged him to use his power to get us in and out tonight. What kind of damage had it done?

"I've tried to help him," she said, "but I can't get through."

Octavia's eyes filled. The emotions inside her were so close to the surface they were at constant risk of spilling out, whereas mine were buried deep, so deep I could hardly access them. I almost envied her.

"What can we do?" I said, feeling helpless.

"Only Evander can save himself from that darkness inside, but he doesn't want to," she said.

Maybe now I knew why.

Octavia drifted off to bed, leaving me alone. I sat in silence for a while, trying to work out how I felt, but I couldn't untangle one emotion from the other, all of them distant, removed, not quite a part of me but close enough to ache. Leaping to my feet, taking the stairs two at a time,

I hammered on Evander's door. He opened it and saw me, greeting me with a self-pitying sigh.

"We'll talk tomorrow," he said.

He tried to shut the door again but I stuck my foot in the gap.

"You said later. This is later."

Pushing past him, I looked around at his room. I'd only been in here once before and it had been dark. I took stock of the desk covered in angry scribblings and screwed-up balls of paper, the pile of dirty clothes on the floor, the empty bottles in the waste bin, and the bloodied rags in a bucket.

What a mess.

His glasses were on the bedside table. I picked them up, looking through the thin lenses. Just another part of his disguise.

I whirled around to face him.

"Why didn't tell me you were the *Chancellor's son?*" I hissed.

He looked away again, shaking his head as if still trying to deny it.

"Answer me, Oliver," I said.

"Don't call me that," he said.

The silence was suffocating.

"I just want the truth," I said.

"Look, I know you're upset with me right now," he began.

"I'm not *upset*. I don't get upset," I said.

"Are you sure?" he said. "Because you look upset."

I bristled, folding my arms.

"Why didn't you tell me?" I said. "Answer me."

"I should've told you," he said. "I *wanted* to tell you. I thought about telling you quite a lot."

"Then why didn't you?"

"I don't know. I don't know!" His voice cracked. He threw up his hands in frustration.

Behind him, his Shadow reclined lazily against the wall, seemingly at peace when he was not. It had wanted me to know all along.

"At first, I wasn't sure I could trust you," said Evander. "You did try to blackmail me, to be fair. Then I wanted to protect you. It was safer, for you to know nothing. But then, well, I ran out of excuses after that. I didn't tell you because … I don't *want* to be him. I don't want to admit it, not even to myself. I didn't want you to see me that way."

"Why do you care what I think?" I said.

"I don't know … I want you to like me, I guess."

Despite my anger, I felt the urge to be closer to him, to comfort him or even hug him, like Octavia had done. I resisted it, sitting down on my hands on his bed. I wanted to tell him that I *did* like him, that I didn't like many things in this world but he was one of them. But the words didn't come.

"I wouldn't want to be the Chancellor's son either," was all I managed, in the end.

Evander stood stiffly at the window, looking out into the moonless night of the underworld.

"Were you lying about your memory being damaged too?" I said.

He turned around quickly. "No! No, that was all true. I really can't remember the Night That Never Was, or the time around it. Everything I told you was true, I just didn't disclose this one particular part."

"It's a pretty big part!" I said.

"I'm sorry," he said, quietly. "I'm sorry, Iris."

I believed him. I'd seen his corrupted memories. And I hadn't told *him* certain things, after all, like the fact that I had fallen into his mind. That I'd looked through his eyes and felt his feelings. That I knew about *her...* Trusting was tough, especially in our position.

"I want to know you," I said. "The real you."

"No, you don't. You really don't. Trust me."

"Isn't that for me to decide?"

"There are things I've done, in my past ... if you knew them, you'd think of me differently," he said. "I was a different person then, but still I have to live with what the old me did."

I thought of all the things I'd stolen and all the lies I'd told.

"I'm not exactly a paragon of virtue, am I?" I said. "I've done things I'm not proud of too. And that's just what I can remember."

"It's not the same," he said. "I'm a bad person, Iris. You have no idea what I'm capable of."

"Then tell me," I said.

After a moment, he sat down beside me, wringing his hands. Silence settled between us again, like falling snow.

At last, he spoke.

"My father taught me the world was full of things to be afraid of, and that only the Order could save us from them," he said. "He never seemed to like me much, and yet he controlled every aspect of my existence. He tried to make me exactly like him. He taught me how to cast my Shadow, how to use darkness to create illusions and manipulate the subconscious of his enemies. But he said I had to learn to control my gift. He said the gift of the Shadow had driven my mother mad and it would do the same to me if I let it. People say she killed herself, but I don't know any more. One day she was there, and the next she wasn't. My father forbade me mention her name. After she died, I was just ... so lost. The Shadow grew too strong within me, just like he said it would."

This must be it, the old wound Octavia talked about, that opened up the crack that let the darkness in.

"He came to fear whatever he saw in me, afraid that I might hurt him, or worse, embarrass him." He laughed, bitterly. "As the Shadow grew stronger, I started rebelling against him. I did things, things that made people think I was unstable. Unbalanced. He didn't like that. Finally, I did something so terrible he had no choice but to lock me away while he projected a simulacrum of me enjoying myself at every social event in Europa. As far as everyone else is concerned I'm still there, having the time of my life."

The quiet enveloped us, swallowing us whole. I thought about what I'd seen in his memory, the smashed windows and stolen bottles. Was that what he meant by *something so terrible*, or was there something else?

Something worse?

"He conspired to cover up any evidence of my shortcomings," he said. "The Order is supposed to be pure, immune to the sickness of society. Especially the Obscuras."

I felt so far away from the rest of the world.

"How did you escape?" I asked.

"My father ordered his personal Listener – Octavia – to keep an ear on my thoughts and report back to him, but we became friends instead. She heard the doubt in my mind and she wanted out too. So I tunnelled through the Shadow, just like we did when we entered the Observatory. My father didn't know I could do it. It was the one thing he'd never taught me. I was drawn here, to join Mr Sharma, once I'd made my escape. He'd been watching out for me for years, ever since he left my father's employ. He always knew I wouldn't follow in the Chancellor's footsteps. I didn't plan to hide away for ever but once I started living as someone else, I found that I liked it. I liked being Evander Mountebank. He was better than Oliver Obscura ever was. I thought I could really become him, and forget the old me entirely. Like I never existed."

"Why aren't they looking for you?" I said. "There should be soldiers searching every house."

"My father doesn't want to admit I fled. How would that

look? A Chancellor who can't control his own son? That's why he uses the simulacrum. He can puppet it perfectly. I think part of him hoped the real me had gone for good. No more scandals." He paused, shook his head. "But tonight I risked his whole house of cards falling down, showing up at the Observatory like that."

We stared at each other wordlessly for a while. Finally, I dared to ask the question I had been wondering about most of all.

"Evander, who's Lily?"

His face paled, his eyes widening.

"How did you…"

"I saw her in your mind when I was trying to fight those shadows. I can do that now apparently, channel psyche by touch … even with people."

"What else did you see?" he said.

"Not much. That's why I'm asking. Tell me," I pressed.

"Lily," he said. "Of House Memoria. We were at the Academy together, the Order's prestigious school of psychometry."

Lily.

I saw her spinning and smiling again. Blonde hair. Pink lips. White dress. She was tall and sinewy, graceful, learned, elegant. Everything that I was not. Everything I'd never be.

And yet … she was nowhere to be seen.

"What happened to her?" I asked, afraid of the answer.

"She died," he said.

I watched the hurt break on his face, a wave of pain. His eyes seemed to fill, shining in the light, but he didn't shed a tear.

I didn't know what to say so I reached out to him with my bare hand, letting his grief run through me instead. At once, I could feel it: that terribly strong, terribly painful, terribly permanent love. His sorrow was a heavy black wave, dragging me under.

I'd thought perhaps I could share his pain somehow, so he didn't have to endure it alone, but it was too much for me to bear. I could withstand only a few seconds of it before breaking away.

"You ... loved her," I said.

The words felt strange and out of place in my mouth, causing me to cringe internally, as if I were talking about fairies or unicorns or any other such made-up, nonsense thing.

"I love her still," he said.

We didn't speak for a tortuously long time, as I battled with the increasing confusion I felt inside.

"How did she die?" I asked.

"I killed her," he said.

I don't know what I'd been expecting him to say, but not that.

He spoke quietly, as though he had been over this many times in his mind. "It was the Night That Never Was and we were at the Basilica of All Souls. There was a ball, as you know, the annual winter ball. Lily and I were outside, dancing in the garden. The last thing I recall was us arguing."

Something caught in my memory, snagging, spooling. But I couldn't untangle it just yet.

"It was snowing... I blacked out... I don't remember anything after that. I have this vision of seeing her lying on the ground, but that's all. All of my memories from that night are fragmented."

Evander wrung his hands anxiously.

"I remember my father telling me it was my fault, that my Shadow took over me. He said I lost control of myself. He had her buried and mourned in haste, then no one ever talked of her again, just like with my mother."

"But – but you didn't kill her, right?" The longer I waited for him to answer, the more excruciating the wait became.

"I can't see any other explanation for it," he said, eventually. "Why would my father lie about something so damaging?"

I spluttered. "Because ... because he's a liar! He's the liar of all liars! How can you believe anything the Order says?"

His memories of that night replayed in my mind:

Screaming, banging on a black door...

Running through the woods at night...

Blood drops on snow.

My eyes rested on the bloodied rags. No, no it couldn't be. I refused to believe it.

"I don't think you did it," I said.

"Well, I can't prove otherwise."

"You can't accept what you don't remember. And that night, of all nights? It's all too much of a coincidence. Lily died at the Basilica and I was shattered at Renato House, both on that same evening? The same night you started to lose your memory? It sounds like a conspiracy to me. All of our stories are connected. We just have to work out how."

Evander's grim expression brightened slightly.

"I really want you to be right," he said.

"Of course I'm right. Don't you remember what you told me before?" I said, nudging his shoulder slightly to show I was not afraid of him. "The Order can haunt your dreams, or hypnotize you into believing a falsehood. What if everything we think we remember is a lie?"

He fidgeted beside me, his brow furrowed.

"I thought you wanted to remember what happened?" I said. "How can you, if you're pretending to be someone else? You're the *Chancellor's son*. If you wanted the truth, you could walk right into House Obscura and get it."

"No," he said, forcibly. "I already tried. That's why I fled. The longer I stayed, the more confused I became. I wanted to know the truth, and I knew I'd never get it from my father. I want to know exactly what happened, no matter what. But if I go back, he'll take control of me again, he'll take away the only memories of Lily I have left. I can't go back, but I can't pretend any more either. I thought I could bury the person I used to be, but I think it's just killing me slowly. Does that make sense?"

It did. He wasn't the only one running from the past.

"There's something I need to tell you," I said. "When I looked into the mirror, I regained some more memories. One of them showed me talking to Ruben. He was training me for something. A mission."

"What sort of mission?"

"Let's just say, I think I know why the Order shattered me."

He held my gaze, and I knew he could see the truth in it.

Octavia appeared at the door, breathing hard. "They're raiding the World's End," she said.

A gust of wind blew the fire inside me out.

12.

SANCTUARY

Evander and I moved to the window, watching clouds of smoke blooming in the far distance.

At once, we ran into the living room, where Gus and Perpetua were waiting, dressed in their bed clothes. Every few seconds, bangs ricocheted through the rickety building.

"The Order never raided World's End before," said Perpetua. "All these years, and now this?"

"Do you think they're here for me?" I said.

"Or me?" said Evander.

"Does it matter now?" said Octavia. "What are we going to do?"

"Get the hell out of here, obviously," said Perpetua.

"We should go to the Sanctuary, to Mr Sharma and the other rebels," said Evander. "We're in over our heads."

Finally, I'd get to meet their mysterious mentor, though it wasn't under the best of circumstances.

"I can get us out," said Evander. "Maybe. I've never transported more than two people before, but it should be possible, theoretically."

Perpetua didn't look convinced. Nor was I. If just travelling with me caused him to bleed, what would happen if he transported five people?

"No," I said, firmly. "We'll find another way out."

"What about me?" said Octavia. "Won't it activate the Listeners' tag as soon as I leave the World's End?"

"We'll just have to take our chances," said Evander. "We don't have much choice."

Octavia swallowed nervously, staring at her feet.

"I don't want to put you all in danger," she said.

Though I knew leaving the World's End was her dearest desire, now the moment had arrived, she seemed afraid.

"When we get to the Sanctuary, we'll be well-protected," said Evander, squeezing her shoulder. "We'll be safer than we are here. And you'll be with Rani there. Don't you want to see her again?"

I didn't know who Rani was but Octavia gave a small smile.

"OK," she said, decisively.

Evander handed us each a suitcase from the back room and told us to fill it, quick. We dispersed at speed to our rooms.

I pushed aside the gnawing, guilty feeling in my gut, that this was all my fault, pressing it down, down, down. I didn't have time for that now. I had to pack. I had only a couple of outfits and the Countess's purse full of remnants to fill my case.

The memory the ring had returned to me flashed through my mind. I'd been packing on the Night That

Never Was. I must've planned to run away. While Oliver danced with Lily, I was fleeing the city.

I dug the broken snow globe from the purse, still leaking water into the embroidered silk lining.

Blood drops on snow.

Snow.

My brain was trying to tell me something, trying to join the dots.

Evander had said that it was snowing on the Night That Never Was.

An image tumbled through the darkness of my mind, like a trapeze artist at the circus. A girl and a boy dancing outside in the snow, beneath a bandstand covered in roses, swaying and spinning beneath a star-crossed sky.

The boy in the snow globe was Oliver Obscura…

The girl *had* to be Lily.

When I touched it, I felt nothing but cold steel and sharp glass, even with my bare hand. Maybe it was already too late, but I had to try. Running back downstairs, I held it out to Evander.

"Do you recognize this?" I said.

Its globe was partially smashed, its figures broken and drowned in what remained of its melted snow.

"The Basilica was decorated with snow globes that night," he said, taking one step backwards, as if afraid of it.

"There was a memory in it. It's damaged but I think it might be Lily's. We have to access it now, before it's too late."

Another distant explosion ricocheted.

"Now? Really?" he said.

"Yes, now. We might not get another chance. It's not as if we can take the psychoscope with us, it's too big, and the snow globe is already broken. The memory is fading."

Evander exhaled, nodding. "Do it. Quick."

I placed the globe in the tray, reflecting its remains upon the wall. When I wound up the lantern, reigniting its spark, the snow globe's shadow broke apart, casting images on the wall. They were clouded with a sepia tone, just enough to discern certain blurry, twisted, desaturated forms.

At first, the memory was even more degraded than before, missing parts and pieces, like an upright jigsaw puzzle that was gradually collapsing, but slowly the picture cleared, sharpened, settled, taking the form of a ball. People were dancing on the polished floor of the Basilica as a band played a silent song onstage. A grand clock overhead read 9.37 p.m., DECEMBER 24TH.

I hadn't noticed that before.

The memory's viewpoint moved through the room and out into the gardens, where two young lovers danced in a bandstand.

We watched them not from their own eyes but from the outside, as if the memory didn't really belong to either of them.

Here was the faceless boy I now knew was Oliver Obscura. His real identity shone through the haze, the picture filling in.

And here was Lily. She was ethereal, every part of her

sparkling, shining, alive. She smiled widely, her eyes slightly narrowed with desire.

"Lily," Evander whispered, beside me.

She fluttered her thick dark eyelashes, her plump lips glistening. It was clear to see the hold she had over him, that quiet, secret power that made him look at her as if he were her servant, not the Chancellor's son and heir to all the world. Like he would've given up everything for her...

I hated her.

Here was the kiss, the fireworks...

I turned to watch Evander's reaction, illuminated by the lantern, swallowing down the bile that rose in my throat.

"You were in love with her," I said, gesturing at the wall. "It's plain to see. Why would you have killed her?"

The memory skipped forwards, showing the couple breaking apart. Lily's eyes were wet, appealing, her palms raised. Evander's face curdled with hurt and fury. He threw up his arms before stalking away.

The memory ended abruptly.

"I was angry with her," said Evander. "Maybe I *did* do it. Maybe my Shadow took over me, acting on some subconscious impulse—"

"Your Shadow took over you before, but you didn't hurt *me*. In fact, your Shadow came to protect me."

"But my father—"

"Evander, your father is lying."

When he met my eye, I felt myself falling into him again, pulling back to spare myself.

"She loved you too, you know," I said.

"How do you know?" he said.

"When I first touched the snow globe, I felt her feelings."

"Tell me," he said, eagerly.

I hated the idea of telling him such private things. Of being the messenger between him and a dead girl. But I knew he needed to hear it. I closed my eyes and dipped once more back into the memory.

I have to tell him.

"There you are," comes a soft voice.

A strange boy's arms wrap around me in a dance, encircling me tightly from behind.

In this brief moment, I am home.

"She wanted to tell you something that night," I said. "She was looking for you. But when she found you, she forgot whatever it was she wanted to say. She was just happy to be with you, in your arms. It felt like…"

My mouth dried up.

"It felt like coming home," I said.

I could feel it, that love, like electricity flowing through a conduit. I didn't know a lot of things but I knew theirs wasn't the sort of love that got spent up overnight. It was the sort of love that burned for ever.

"Thank you," Evander said.

"I didn't do anything," I said, in a small voice.

"You've done more for me than you'll ever know."

He held my gaze but I looked away, my stomach churning. I had never felt worse in all my memory, and it was only partly because of the growing ruckus outside. Sirens in the streets, sirens in my head.

"Come on," he said. "We need to get moving – if we're going to get out alive and find our answers."

"Right," I said, remembering our dire predicament. I watched as he resumed packing. I was still stuck in the moment, unable to move. "I meant to tell you… When I looked into the mirror, I saw a music box."

"A music box?" he echoed.

I nodded. "The Spark is the sense of touch so I put the ring on my hand. The Shadow is associated with the sense of sight, so I looked into the mirror. If the Song represents the sense of sound, I'd have to listen to it, so a music box would be the ideal vessel, right?"

"Time to go!" shouted Gus.

I grabbed my suitcase. Evander put the ruin of the snow globe into his, his expression troubled yet dreamy.

We assembled in the hall. It wasn't easy convincing Octavia to leave; she'd talked herself into a paranoid frenzy by then.

"We're all going to get arrested because of me," she said, clinging to the doorframe like a cat being forced into a bath. "They're going to surround us as soon as we leave the World's End and take us all to the Reformatory. You should go without me. Save yourselves."

"Don't be so dramatic," drawled Perpetua. "You think a little thing like a tag can stop us?"

"You're in just as much danger here, if not more," said Gus.

"I've got a bad feeling, Evander," said Octavia.

"Change is frightening, I know," Evander said gently, "but you're just going to have to be brave. You've done it before. You can do it again."

She hesitated, then took his hand, smiling gratefully.

"OK. I trust you," she said.

A shuddering boom threw us off our feet.

The smoke outside grew thicker. The fires drew closer. The tunnels outside were thick with crying, screaming people.

I could hear shattering glass and tumbling brick.

One by one, the gas lights that kept the World's End illuminated were extinguished, plunging us into pitch blackness. The screaming reached a fevered pitch, bringing me out in goosebumps.

I grabbed a lantern from the stoop, turning its knob. A single, flickering flame lit our way as we escaped.

As the tunnels around us gradually filled with smoke, we fled, taking one last look at the Emporium. Slipping out through a sewage pipe, we joined the queue of people fleeing the underground but every street exit was barricaded by Inspectors, swinging their lanterns and driving folks to the ground, arresting all those who tried to escape.

"This way," said Perpetua.

We hurried on through a complex warren of stony catacombs with wooden beams, as the darkness grew heavier and the air thick with dust and a strong, sulphurous smell.

One by one we climbed up, popping out from a grate

near the Auditorium, from which the sounds of the national anthem played. There were soldiers on the steps, armed with batons, which they swung at the angry masses who'd managed to escape the World's End.

Nearby, an Order wagon had been abandoned, presumably by the Inspectors currently battling with a growing mob.

"Why'd you attack the World's End?" one woman shouted. "There are kids living down there, you bastards!"

"All this because some girl stole a ring?" ranted a man.

Perpetua broke into the carriage with the crowbar she fished from her purse, taking charge of the steering wheel. Gus sat up front and the rest of us squeezed in the back. It was cramped and stuffy. We drove along a long, bumpy road that rolled my stomach.

No one spoke. None of us knew what to say. Each time an Order wagon rolled past, we all held our breath, hearts pounding in synchronicity.

But none of them stopped.

We passed by a series of sky-grazing towers with circular silver dishes fixed to their outsides. Octavia gasped and practically climbed over me to look out of the window.

"That's the station where I used to work," she said, "before the Chancellor made me spy for him alone."

"What was it like?" I asked, staring out at the iron towers and shiny silver parabolas.

"Imagine vast banks of people holding ear trumpets, sitting in front of radios tuned to different brainwaves," she said. "If they listen in on something interesting, they start recording. You'd never know until you got hauled to court on a warrant and they played it back to you."

"How do we know they're not listening right now?" I said.

"We don't," she said, looking pointedly at Evander.

I shivered, shrinking back into myself. How long before they caught up with us again? We couldn't run for ever.

"What's the plan, anyway?" I said. "Say we make it to this Sanctuary, what then?"

"Mr Sharma will know what to do," said Evander. "He was once the Chancellor's own personal Observer, a member of his private staff, like Octavia was. Now he leads the rebels. He has long plotted to remove the Chancellor from power, amassing an army from all the lost and broken souls the Order cast aside. But all previous attempts at overthrowing the Order have failed. He says he's been searching for years for proof that will reveal the Chancellor's true nature to the world – a particular memory Mr Sharma was party to in his previous life as a servant of House Obscura. But so far, he has been unable to locate it. The Chancellor is careful to remove all incriminating evidence of his misdeeds, directly from people's heads if need be."

"Then what?" I said. "We can't just hide away."

"Some would say it's only a matter of time. The Order is escalating. Regular, law-abiding citizens are being hauled off for trials, Inspectors sent into schools, carting people's children off to the Reformatory if their souls aren't in balance. Soon enough, we won't be able to stop them from storming the streets. Maybe then, it will finally be time to act. Until then, we should focus on staying alive. We're no help to the resistance if we're all in the ground."

Half an hour down the road, Evander sat upright with a start.

"I think we're being followed," he announced. In the rear mirror, a discreet black carriage trailed us at a distance.

Octavia concentrated, closing her eyes and putting her hands over her ears, tuning into the stream of consciousness.

"They know who we are," she said.

"Everyone hold on," said Perpetua.

The vehicle veered dramatically as we left the road. A sharp right turn threw me to the floor. I got tangled up with Octavia, her arm thwacking against my face as I kneed her in the side.

"We still have company," said Perpetua. "Hold tight."

Crawling back to the window, fingers clutching the sill, I peered out to see three carriages following where before there was just one. We careened down a bank and splashed through a shallow river before rising on the other side, but they doggedly followed.

"We're going to need a bigger distraction," said Evander.

I watched as his eyes grew dark, his Shadow stretching out before breaking apart into birds. Carried by the wind, they plastered the windows of the carriages behind us.

Blinded, one vehicle bumped into another, tipping it on its side and forcing it to skid in a ditch.

The remaining two carriages continued pursuit.

Evander's Shadow grew enormous, a cloud of ephemeral matter that reassembled behind us, creating the mirage of a closed-off road with a barricade. One of the black carriages pulled up, tyres screeching, but the other barrelled straight through the illusion, ignoring the make-believe warning sign.

"They're closing in!" bellowed Gus.

Evander redirected the cloud of dark matter. It transformed into a deep crack, which grew larger as the ground behind us caved away, creating a bottomless pit. But the last wagon drove right into it, appearing to float mid-air as it continued along the road.

"It's not working," said Evander, looking increasingly frantic.

"What should we do?" I shouted.

"Let's all try. Psyche is stronger when combined."

"The Shadow is my weakest aspect," said Gus.

"It's worth a shot. Everyone, picture a fire: flames curling around the trees, burning hot and bright, destroying everything in their wake…"

I gave him a doubtful look and he added:

"You're a Renato, remember. Fire is your element."

I recalled what Ruben had told me in my memory, about the gift of the Spark being in my blood. I imagined balls of flame in my hands. I imagined myself throwing them into the path of the Order wagon, setting the ground alight. When I opened my eyes again, we were speeding through a forest on fire, as a thick cloud of black smoke suffocated everything in sight.

"It's actually working!" Perpetua said. "I can't believe it."

Gus and Octavia cheered, slapping hands.

But the last wagon was undeterred, appearing through the dense dark fog and trailing us relentlessly.

"These fellas just won't quit," said Gus.

The smell of the illusionary fire was so strong, it was making me cough and splutter, its perfume clinging to my hair.

A deafening crack signalled a toppling tree. We just made it past, but then it crashed down behind us with a ferocious, sparking thud, creating a burning blockade the last Order carriage couldn't pass.

"It's a real fire!" I yelled, over the roar of flames.

"Did we do that?" asked Gus.

"I guess it worked a little too well," said Evander.

We had collectively turned mind to matter.

Gus opened the window, reaching out his hand before drawing it back with a sharp hiss, cradling his hand against his chest.

"It's real all right."

The inferno we'd created now threatened to consume us, its smoke filling our field of vision. The carriage ignited, its wooden walls catching alight.

"Everyone, out!" yelled Evander.

"My dresses!" cried Octavia, watching her bag turn to ashes.

"No time for that!"

I lurched out, coughing. The thick smoke blinded me and I stumbled. Evander grabbed me around the waist. "I've got you," he said. He dragged Octavia behind me as Perpetua pried Gus from the wreckage.

In seconds, our carriage was a skeleton of iron. We began to run, the white of the sky breaking through the smoke, creating a tunnel.

"Everyone OK?" asked Octavia, as we ran.

"Just a little singed," said Gus.

We kept running until the burning wood was far behind us, slowing as we traversed down a series of country lanes. Everyone was dusted with ash and soot, giving us a shabby, dishevelled look. Evander wiped clean his glasses. Gus dusted off his spiky hair. Perpetua stood calmly, unbothered by the dirt.

At last, we reached a village, which appeared to be abandoned.

"Where is everyone?" I said, shivering.

"Villages like this were practically abandoned when the mines closed down," said Evander. "The Order doesn't need them when it has the Obscura method to turn mind to matter, does it? They can turn any old rock to coal or gold from the comfort of their mansions."

"How does it work, anyway?" I asked. "Turning thoughts into ... things? I hardly understand it."

"It can happen if there's enough psychic energy, but it's forbidden," said Gus. "Or something like that. We learned the theory behind it at school, but I wasn't really paying much attention."

Evander rubbed his forehead. "It's simple, really. All matter is made up of atoms. They form everything you can see and everything you can't. Advanced psychometry allows us to assemble those atoms into the desired form simply by imagining them, be that a diamond or a weapon so fearsome it will destroy any enemy – or a forest fire. Very few people can do it alone, which is why the Order has entire factories dedicated to the task."

"*You* can do it alone," I said.

"I can, but it's generally not advised."

I pictured him bleeding and falling, and me helpless to stop it. I shivered again, unsure whether it was due to cold or fear, or both. A moment later, I felt something gently draped over my shoulders.

"Here," said Evander, "take my coat."

"Won't you be cold?" I said, holding it at the neck like a cloak. "I'm a fire soul. I probably run hotter than you."

"Just take the coat, OK?" he said, smiling.

"Thanks," I said, growing warm.

For a moment, I was happy, returning his smile as a giddy feeling bubbled through me, but then I thought about Lily.

What if she was still alive? What if he found her again, hidden away by the Order? They'd be together and I … I would be alone again.

One by one, the bubbles burst.

"Don't worry," he said, misinterpreting the look on my face. "We're almost at the Sanctuary, according to Perpetua."

"You haven't been there before?"

"No. Most of the people there don't know who I really am, and I doubt they'd like it much if they did."

On a hill in the distance was a mound, with five trees atop it. At the foot of the incline was a small village of thatched houses, with a brick well and a cobbled courtyard at the heart of it. We climbed past fields of sheep and ponds with ducks, past an aviary and a bell tower, until we reached a stately house. It looked abandoned, run down.

But when Perpetua stepped up to the doors, the illusion faded, revealing the hidden grandeur behind it.

"What's the magic word?" came an amplified voice.

It was silky, familiar.

"Encore," said Octavia, listening in to the stream.

The grinding sound of a lock followed.

"Welcome to the Sanctuary," came the voice.

13.

IN OUR DREAMS

The door slowly opened out into the foyer. It had ceiling-high stained-glass windows depicting triumphal scenes from the Order's history, with silver marble floors and glittering chandeliers. A grand piano stood quietly in one corner.

"This is your rebel base?" I said, raising one brow.

"Appearances can be deceiving," said Evander. "You ought to know that by now."

A small group of people awaited us, including the man in the turban I'd seen in the photo at the Emporium, posing in front of the pyramids.

"We've been expecting you," he said.

"Mr Sharma!"

Octavia ran to him, wrapping her arms around his belly.

"Hello, Via," he said, patting the top of her head.

He had a waxed moustache and beard, styled into curly tips. He wore a smart linen suit with a handkerchief in the pocket and a matching turban, teamed with a monocle with a black glass lens.

"I'd say I've missed you but I've been keeping an eye

on everything from afar. It helps when you can split your psyche in order to be in several places at once, of course."

He greeted each person in turn, bumping fists with Gus and bowing to Perpetua, before patting Evander's shoulder with a fatherly affection.

"I'm relieved to find you well. When I learned that the Order was on its way to raid the World's End, I tried to make contact but I was unable to reach you," he said. "Now I learn that you were not asleep in bed as I expected, but busy breaking into the Observatory."

"About that," said Evander.

"No matter. We'll discuss it later," said Mr Sharma, lightly.

Finally, he set his kindly eyes on me.

"Iris," he said. "Dear Iris. I've been hearing so much about you. What a pleasure it is to make your acquaintance."

"You only just met me," I said, disarmed.

"Since when has that stopped anyone becoming friends?" he said, smiling at me.

A young woman with long black braids burst through the group, flying at Octavia and wrapping her arms around her.

"Rani!" said Octavia, her face bursting into a brilliant smile.

They looked at each other like Evander looked at Lily.

"This is Mr Sharma's niece Rani," Octavia explained, grinning. "She visits the shop sometimes. She has the gift of the Shadow, like Evander and Mr Sharma. She can part her mind from her body. Rani, this is Iris."

"Oh, I know who you are," said Rani, shaking my hand vigorously like a businessman making a good deal. "You're already legendary."

"Where's Birdie?" asked Evander.

"You know our Songbird," said Mr Sharma. "She always likes to make an entrance."

As if on cue, a high-pitched whistle drew our attention. Beneath an imposing archway, another corridor stretched out, with many rooms branching off. An hourglass silhouette waited at the end of it, arms spread wide as she stepped into a spotlight. She had long brown hair piled up in a bun on her head, and she was wearing a dazzling pair of earrings.

It was the woman I'd seen on Octavia's wall.

"Hello, my darlings," Birdie said, nodding at Perpetua and Gus. "It's so good to see you again. I must admit, I was somewhat delighted when I heard word from one of my little feathered friends that you needed help."

She held out her arm, whistling.

A pretty songbird came to perch on it. She sang to it in a wordless language, and it chirruped back.

I stared at her. "It's not just humans who have souls, though of course, ours are among the most complex," said Birdie, answering my unspoken question. "A person with a gift of the Song can communicate with other animals whose psyche is musically attuned. Birds are highly skilful spies, and their range is larger than even the Listeners."

The bird's wings fluttered as it nuzzled her fingers with its beak before flitting off out the window.

When Birdie clapped eyes on Evander, she looked suddenly tearful, drawing a ragged breath.

"Hello, Oliver." She glanced briefly at me. "Oliver's mother Nadia was one of my dearest friends, long ago. Such a beautiful soul. You look more like her every time I see you." She touched Evander's cheek fondly.

His expression grew drawn as he looked down at his feet. The room seemed to grow colder.

"I'm sorry. I didn't mean to make you sad," she said.

He nodded graciously. "It's fine. It's nice to hear people talk about her, actually."

"Birdie, you remember Octavia Belle," said Mr Sharma, changing the subject. "And this is Iris."

Her gaze drifted to me curiously, just like her avian friend.

"You must be the Renato girl."

"You remember me?" I said, eagerly.

"Unfortunately not, but there are rumours. Plenty of them. I tend to hear things, in my line of work."

"*You're* the voice," I said, putting the pieces together – that smooth, lilting voice that had so often punctuated my day. "You're the voice of the curfew announcement, the voice of the Order."

"I'm afraid so, darling."

"But how?"

"I was hired for my dulcet tones, but being able to hide one's thoughts from the Order has its advantages," she said. "By running in the elite inner circle of Providence, I can use my power to harbour unfortunate souls such as yourself, opening up my house to offer them shelter. Come, meet the others. Everyone is quite excited to meet our mysterious midnight guests."

The room began to fill with people, a colourful cast of folks who seemed somehow at odds with the glamorous setting of a mansion. Mr Sharma introduced some of them.

"This is Ash," he said, of a tall, slender person whose head was shaved but for a strip in the middle, their hands covered like mine. "A runaway Firestarter." Mr Sharma gestured next to the long-haired fellow in a flowery shirt. "Vincent, a perfumer. He can extract and modify memories ... And this is Cook, our resident chef and smuggler."

A small, portly woman with missing teeth and one diamond earring greeted Gus warmly, slapping his back. She was the prison chef with whom he'd escaped the Reformatory, I realized.

"I can't believe they raided the World's End," said Ash.

"Long story, but we might've broken into the Observatory and stolen a reliquary," I said.

"Wait. Is that Oliver Obscura?" said Vincent, spying him standing sheepishly at the back of the crowd. "Well I never."

The bustle of the crowd died down as everyone turned to him.

"I thought you were on the continent?" asked someone else.

"I saw you swanning around Roma in the papers!"

One woman drew a weapon, holding it protectively at her side.

"All a lie, I'm afraid," said Evander, nervously rubbing the back of his neck. "An illusion. I fled nine months ago."

"You kept this from us, Arjun?" said Cook. "I thought we had no secrets between us?"

"I did it only for his own protection," said Mr Sharma. "There are many who would plot to harm him, even within our own circles."

Disapproving voices rose in volume.

"How do we know we can trust you?"

"Yeah, you could be here snooping on us for him!"

I reached out and squeezed Evander's arm gently, as I'd seen him do to reassure Octavia before. He gave me a thankful look.

"Look, I know there's nothing I can say to make you believe me right away," said Evander, raising his voice, "but I hope to earn your trust in time. The Chancellor ruined my life just like he's ruined yours."

"He is here to help, to use whatever knowledge and abilities he has to aid the resistance, just as he has been doing for the past nine months," said Mr Sharma. "I know that many among us have grudges to bear, but this young man is not the Order. He is not his father. He is one of us, and I expect you to treat him with the respect you'd give any other lost soul who found their way to our Sanctuary in need of help. If any of you take issue with that, please kindly direct your complaints at me, and not him."

Some of the runaways glanced uncertainly at each other but no one openly protested. The woman who'd drawn her weapon put it away.

"Well, I say welcome to the club, kid," said Cook.

"I never expected the Chancellor's own son to stand against him," said Ash. "The tides really must be turning."

"We're not done yet," said Evander. "This is Iris. Otherwise known as Ruby Renato, daughter of Ruben Renato."

This didn't cause as much of a stir — merely a confused murmur.

"I didn't think Ruben had a daughter," someone said.

"If he does, I don't remember her," said someone else.

"The Order has tried to make us forget her," said Evander. "But on the Night That Never Was, her soul was shattered by a person dressed as an Observer at Renato House."

"Shattered?" someone echoed.

"We have proof of it in the memory she retrieved from a ring. The Renato ring."

"We're still trying to track down the missing pieces of my soul, trying to piece together what happened," I said, "but I can tell you that Ruben Renato was plotting against the Order."

Silence fell.

"He trained me for something. I just can't remember what it was. But I swore I'd help bring down the Chancellor."

Now the crowd seemed curious.

"I thought Ruben was loyal as a dog."

"It *was* a bit strange, him suddenly being sent to the colonies."

"Ruben isn't all he seems, I can vouch for that," said Birdie. "He and I have had previous ... interactions. But he hasn't been seen often in public of late, and when he has, he seems preoccupied. His thoughts cannot be overheard. Word comes from overseas that he's a shadow of his former self."

"Well, if the Chancellor created a simulacrum for me, there's no reason why he couldn't have done the same with Ruben," said Evander.

"Look at us. It's no mistake we're all standing here today," said Cook, "and with the Chancellor's boy and this Renato girl? Maybe it's a sign."

"A sign of what?" I said.

"A sign that it's time to seize the moment," she said, raising a fist. "There are people who've been waiting for this all their lives."

"Hear, hear!"

"With the World's End gone, there will be plenty of survivors with nowhere to go but the streets," said Ash.

"I'll make contact with the other bases," said Birdie. "Rally the troops. Make sure they're ready to move if we do."

"They're ready," said Cook. "We're ready. How long have we waited? If not now, when?"

But Mr Sharma continued to look thoughtful. He held out his arm for me to take. "Walk with me, Iris," he said. "There is much to discuss."

He led us away from the others, all talking over each other, and out into the gardens, where automated instruments played by themselves and musical fountains sprouted water in great arcs.

Mr Sharma began to speak. "One of my gifts is that I can see a person's subconscious. In the darkness of the pupils is a stage, and upon that stage, all of their fears and fantasies play out."

I felt exposed and looked away.

"It is a gift I once put to work on behalf of Chancellor Obscura. For many years, I was his servant, his second pair of eyes, which is why I know all too well the darkness in his own soul."

"Is that how you know Evander and Octavia?"

"I didn't meet Octavia until after she defected. Evander was just a child when I fled the Order, but I kept an eye on him from afar all these years, as his late mother asked me to. When I learned that he too had made his escape, I made contact with him through the Shadow. I took him in, and Octavia too. I gave them a place to live and work."

"Why did you leave the Order?" I asked.

"As the Chancellor's own Observer, I saw many things that shook me to my core. They haunt me still, at night, as the past tends to, but one in particular is key to the Order's undoing."

Was this the proof Evander mentioned? The thing he'd been looking for all this time? I waited for him to elaborate.

"When Oliver was five years old, his mother died."

My throat ached, the resonant reverberation of having lived his pain, mixed with the mystery of my own lost mother.

"The official story is that she fell. A tragic accident. But rumours circulated that she jumped from the balcony by reason of insanity. That day, I was called away to spy on one of the Chancellor's many enemies. When I left, she was alive and well. When I returned, she was dead."

A picture bloomed briefly in my mind. An elegant woman wearing a headscarf, posing for a portrait. I must've glimpsed her in Evander's memory.

"Naturally, I suspected that something was amiss. Oliver seemed disturbed, but I couldn't get anything out of him. The Chancellor asked me to interrogate his staff. I knew that eventually he would probe me too, and if he did, he'd see that Nadia had confided in me at times about her contempt for him. It had become too dangerous to stay, so I risked everything to escape. If the Chancellor had been a cold, controlling man before, he grew even more monstrous after his wife's death. It has been my deepest regret that I didn't take Oliver with me that day."

He fell quiet, ruminating on his own weighty words.

"I am convinced that Oliver witnessed his mother's death, but the Chancellor had it removed from his mind. Perhaps we shall never know what happened to Nadia Obscura."

He gazed at me calmly.

"Perhaps *you* are the key to the Order's downfall instead."

"You think so?" I said, frightened and flattered in equal measure.

"If the Chancellor had you shattered, you must've been dangerous to him. Unfortunately, I can offer no more information as to what happened on the Night That Never Was, nor to your identity. I remember no child at Renato House. It was known that Ruben and Lady Renato had no children, that they were, in fact, incapable."

I thought for a moment. "So Lady Renato is not my mother?"

"Ah, well." Mr Sharma looked somewhat flustered. "Your father was … how can I put this? A great appreciator of the female form. I think we can assume that you were born outside the marriage – and you could have been born to any number of women from all walks of life, such was Ruben's talent. As one with the tactile gift, he was very popular, shall we say?"

"I see," I said, feeling small. No one in all of Providence seemed to recall my existence; I had no place in the Renato family. It was hard to believe I was ever there at all – but for the memory of me lying shattered on the floor of Renato House, and Ruben calling me his daughter.

His words floated back to me.

"Your mother raised you well but there are things only I can teach you, tools you will need if we are to avenge her."

If I was to avenge her, my mother must already be dead. I thought of the button, and how I'd never experience that love for myself. But the pain was distant, numbed. I couldn't remember what I'd lost.

"I have spent over a decade assembling knowledge of the

Order and recruiting those who would work against it both inside and outside of its walls. And yet I had no inkling that Ruben Renato – the Chancellor's most trusted advisor and friend – was plotting against him. I am most intrigued to find out more – and why he was so sure you were the one to act."

"Maybe it has something to do with the Renato Method," I said. "I knocked a man unconscious with just a touch of my hand."

He frowned. "Though the Renato Method is indeed a powerful skill, it can be emulated by a simple baton these days. The Order is constantly finding new ways to amplify psyche through technologies. No, I think you were destroyed for another reason."

"What?" I said eagerly.

"Knowledge," he said. "Knowledge can be the deadliest weapon. I think you knew something about the Chancellor, and he sought to destroy you for that knowledge. We must remember what it is. That's why it's imperative that you seek the shattered pieces of yourself. There are many people you can help, Iris, if only you can remember yourself."

I nodded. "I want to help. Whatever you need me to do, I'll do it."

"And we will be glad of it. In the meantime, I shall do my best to locate your father. If your memory is accurate, he could be of great help to us."

That was something. Maybe I'd get the chance to quiz him myself one day. We joined the others, back in the main lobby.

"You must be exhausted," said Birdie. "You should retire to bed and get some sleep. We can regroup tomorrow."

I trailed Octavia and Rani, heads close together, busy chattering, as we set off towards our guest rooms, trailing along an endless series of corridors. The Sanctuary was ten times the size of Cavendish House and three times more grand, and yet there were signs of rebellion everywhere. A protest slogan sprayed on to one wall. A room full of gunpowder barrels. Boxes full of pamphlets. A closet with Inspector uniforms hanging in it.

We walked past a marble statue of an Order soldier and a painting of the five founders. The Songbird had a penchant for pictures of herself, posing in dramatic scenes with creatures of all kinds. Birds were everywhere, loose from their cages, sitting atop wardrobes and chandeliers, gathering in stairwells and congregating in cupboards.

Different music played in every room. In the kitchen, it was a brisk, lively song that sounded like springtime. In the ballroom, a grand, operatic symphony. In the drawing room, a sombre piano melody.

There were almost as many people living here as birds, setting up camp in antiquated rooms with poster beds. There were people playing games, smoking hookah pipes, talking in different languages, play fighting, rolling dice. All of them were runaways, fugitives, like us.

Passing by a closed door, I heard muted voices within. Evander, and Mr Sharma. Slowing, I let the others walk on, leaving me alone in the hallway.

"You needn't worry so much," said Evander.

"It sounds like he was able to take control of you through your Shadow at the Observatory," said Mr Sharma. "Of course I'm concerned."

"We were in close proximity. He can't reach me ordinarily."

I lurked outside, knowing I should feel guilty for eavesdropping but doing it anyway.

"Are you sure about that?" said Mr Sharma. "For safety's sake, I want you to be extra vigilant in the coming days. There's no telling what kind of traces they might have on your psyche now. If you feel yourself sliding into that dark place again, I want you to reach out. Don't keep it all inside."

"I understand."

"I'll leave you to rest."

I bolted, continuing on until I found an empty suite. It was richly decorated and adorned with pictures of Birdie, performing for the Chancellor, or singing before crowds of soldiers. Pulling the old button out of my pocket, I held it tightly in my hand, grateful it hadn't burned with the rest of my meagre belongings in the carriage fire. I threw myself down on the squeaky bed and stared at the ceiling, turning the button over and over in my hand.

My mother was dead and I couldn't mourn her. I didn't remember her well enough to miss her.

I lay there for hours, not-thinking. Every time a thought popped up, I pushed it away again. For a moment, I missed the days when I thought nothing, felt nothing, feared nothing, the days when I was all alone and didn't care to be known. Now my thoughts and feelings seemed to overwhelm me. But as painful as it was, deep down I was glad. Relieved that I could feel anything at all.

My own misery was intoxicating, and I indulged it, letting myself sink deeper and deeper into myself.

My father had groomed me to kill the Chancellor and my mother was a nameless ghost. A stranger. And yet I longed for her. I wanted a mother to hold me, to tell me everything was going to be all right, to button my coat and keep me warm from the cold.

At some point, sleep took me.

That night, I dreamt for the first time in memory.

In the dream, I woke up in a small, dilapidated house, its windows clouded and cobwebbed, decorated with a few sparse furnishings. I didn't know it was a dream at first, confused as to where I was and how I got there. The cracked mirror hung on the wall … and I was wearing the ring.

I attempted to get my bearings, but when I opened the door, there was no street, no world, no nothing. Only a void. Only now did I realize that I was in the dark place – the Shadow realm. The subconscious realm of dreamers. As I gazed into the gloom, a narrow, heavily forested lane appeared, as if I'd imagined it. I followed the winding path to an unknown destination, past the burning bonfire of my Spark, where I'd battled my Shadow before. Eventually, I reached a barrier; a thin, shadowy curtain, ragged and tattered. Passing through it, I found myself in a different place entirely.

It was a warm summer's day and the air smelled like honeysuckle and jasmine. I was in a pretty green park I didn't quite recognize, with fountains and statues, and a lake with white swans. There was a carnival in the background, its revolving wheel visible over the tops of the trees, fairground music echoing, fairy lights twinkling alluringly.

Evander was sitting under a tree nearby, his eyes closed. He looked uncharacteristically peaceful. I was dreaming about him, without even meaning to. He heard me approach as my shadow cast over him.

"Of course you're here too," he said, with a dry laugh.

"Huh?"

"Didn't you get your fill when you gazed into my soul?"

"What are you talking about?" I said. "This is my dream."

"No, it's mine," he insisted.

I looked around, suddenly unsure.

"Then what am I doing here?"

"I don't know. Are you the real Iris?" he said. "Or just a figment of my imagination?"

"How can I *prove* that I'm real?" I said, in frustration.

"That is the ultimate question," he said.

"What if I told you something you didn't know?" I said.

"How would I know what you say is true?"

"You can check with me, when you wake up."

"All right, go on."

I screwed up my face, trying to think.

"I stole a button," I said, "the day before we met."

His lips quirked with humour, along with his brow.

"A button?"

"It contains the memory of someone's mother buttoning their coat. I kept it because when I hold it in my hand, I can feel safe and warm and loved for a minute, even if that love was really meant for someone else."

His expression softened. He ran one hand through his unruly hair.

"Maybe when we … when you accessed my subconscious before … maybe it created a channel between your mind and mine," he said, awkwardly. "I suppose that means you have a key into my head now … and vice versa."

"In that case, you should definitely give me a tour," I said. "Show me the sights. I don't recognize this place, so it must be your mind we're in."

He smiled slightly, looking behind me as if picturing something.

"I came to this park with Lily once, on a date," he said.

I bristled at the mention of her name.

"I've never been on a date," I said, airily. "Not that I can remember. What do people actually *do* on dates?"

"That depends on the date. But at the carnival, people talk, play games, eat, buy each other gifts … kiss."

"Sounds nice," I said, turning my face so he wouldn't

225

see me blush. "The Countess always said love was a waste of time, that it sucked your Heart out of your soul and left you empty."

"She's not wrong."

"I think I'd like to experience it anyway."

We ambled around the fairground, checking out the ring toss and the coconut shy, the milk bottle stand and the carousel, past a kissing booth and a stall selling fancy candies and chocolates.

"I come here a lot," he said. "It's a comfort to me. This was one of the only times in my life I ever felt truly happy and at peace."

"Can you control it?" I asked. "Can you direct your mind to create a different place?"

"Sure. Where would you like to be?" he said.

"Paint me a picture, of the sort of place you wish you were in right now."

I wanted to forget about Lily.

I wanted it just to be us.

Evander closed his eyes and the carnival music stopped abruptly. A moment earlier, the fairground had been full of dream-people, all screaming and laughing and holding balloons but now it was abandoned, its rides empty, their carriages rocking in the growing breeze. They faded away, into nothing, until we were standing in the infinite darkness.

"Hmm, let's see. We're somewhere warm. On a hill overlooking a vast cloud forest, with trees as far as the eye can see."

As he described it, the scene around us transformed, taking on the appearance of his words.

"The air smells like vanilla, like coconuts, like the ocean."

I watched reality colouring, filling in, like a watercolour painting.

"You're looking out over a beautiful waterfall. The sun has just set. The sky is so clear you can see every star that ever existed. You can hear birds singing and the sound of running water."

And there it was, as if for real. I could see every droplet of water, every feather, every leaf.

"In the distance, a single guitar is playing a beautiful song. It sweeps and soars, filling your soul with its sound. It makes you feel alive. It makes your heart ache, but in a good way. Everything is perfect. Everything is in its right place. No one or nothing can harm you. There's nothing you'd change. You have everything you need here. Everything you desire."

The hairs on the back of my neck stood on end, in a manner that was both disturbing and delightful. For a fleeting moment, I felt something suspended between us like a string, as fragile as spider silk. I was drawn towards him, as if he were magnetized, my body leaning in all by itself. The world slowed to a halt, as time itself seemed to stop.

But then Evander frowned, his expression clouded.

The beautiful vision he'd created wasted away to nothing again as another scene took its place. The ground froze over beneath our feet. Snow began to fall in flurries. Now we were standing in front of the Basilica of All Souls on the eve of December 24th.

"Why did you bring us here?" I said, shaken.

"I didn't mean to," he said.

"This is the snow globe's memory. This is the Night That Never Was. Your subconscious must still be stuck on it."

"I've never seen it this clearly before," he said.

The Basilica looked like a giant wedding cake, dressed in a thick, glittering blanket of snow that blunted its features like marzipan. Palatial ice formed spires and curlicues, like sugar spun decorations. Every curve and cornice had a frosty whip on top, like cream on cocoa, and every surface was dusted with powder, like a baker's table. The moon was reflected on the surface of the lake, a luminous orb through which people skated in figure-of-eights.

In here, the memory wasn't corrupted. It was as pristine as the fresh white snow. The echoes of a haunting tune reached my ears. A string quartet launched into a familiar swooning tune. It was muffled and muted, slightly distorted, as if played beneath a bell jar on the bottom of the ocean.

Beyond, I saw the rosy bandstand rimmed with icicles, its interior decorated with snow globes and illuminated by candles.

Here, Oliver danced with Lily, re-enacting the scene as fireworks lit up the sky…

"Lily," whispered Evander.

Her white dress ballooned around her as she spun under

his arm, laughing like a bell. I could see his face now, and hers, both of them enraptured by the other, their eyes locked in an intense, heated gaze. As if enchanted, Evander glided towards them. He circled the dancing couple, memorizing every move, every look, every moment.

For what felt like an eternity, I watched him watch them dance, before tearing myself away from the scene. This was their moment, their memory, and I didn't belong in it. My gaze drifted to the deep and growing patch of darkness on the horizon, slowly sucking everything into it.

A black hole.

It inched closer and closer, making a ripping, crackling sound as it consumed everything in sight. When I looked back to the Basilica, the snow was melting, washing away the memory. The sky grew dark, as clouds blocked out the moon. The bandstand crumbled away to dust as Evander backed away, leaving us standing in the darkness of the Shadow realm.

"What's happening?" I said.

Three blank-masked figures appeared from the black hole, gliding slowly towards us, moving unnaturally.

"Observers," said Evander, grabbing my arm.

We started to run.

"Are they real?" I said.

"As real as we are. The Chancellor must've sent them."

The Order had found us, even in our dreams.

The ground vibrated. A low, moaning groan shuddered the earth.

"We have to wake up," he said.

I pinched myself, but nothing happened.

"How?" I said.

A giant crack appeared, branching out quickly, growing wider and wider, opening up a yawning crevice that split us apart. Dark waters flooded out, sweeping us off our feet and carrying us away with it. Evander reached out for me, his fingers grazing mine, but it was too late…

He was gone.

I watched him disappear beneath the surface before my head was pulled under. I took my last breath.

I sat bolt upright, shouting. I was back in the room at the Sanctuary. Music played softly somewhere deep within the building, barely audible. Pulling the covers up to my chin and hugging my knees, I gazed around the dark, empty bedroom, listening as the frantic pattering of my heart gradually subsided.

"It was just a dream," I told myself. "It was just a dream."

My heart was beginning to return to its regular sedentary tempo when a soft knock sounded on the door. I crawled out of bed to open it, revealing Evander. When he looked at me, it was as if he forgot what he came to say.

"Did we just…" he started.

"You remember it too," I said.

I could tell by the rapt look on his face.

"Vividly," he said. "I just wanted to check that you were still here."

"I'm here. You're here... We're here. Wait, I can prove it."

I patted myself down, looking for something, before I pulled out the button, grinning. When he saw it, he smiled wider than I'd ever seen before.

For a moment, I forgot about Lily.

14.

THE VOICE

Mr Sharma was keen to help me locate the next part of my soul, and he had at his disposal various means to attempt this. He delved personally into my psyche while Vincent burned smelling salts intended to trigger my memory, but we uncovered nothing new. I had no meaningful recollection of the music box, and I had no proof that it was the reliquary I was looking for in any case, only the gut feeling Evander told me to listen to.

Meanwhile, the Sanctuary buzzed with talk of an uprising. The plan had snowballed overnight. Now people talked of ransacking the city, of imprisoning the Chancellor, of burning down the Reformatory. I learned that the Sanctuary was in contact with other rebel hideaways, some far away in the north, or in the small islands to the west. They too had been galvanized by news of the Chancellor's son and a Renato heir joining the cause.

"My plan has always been to seize control of the Eye network," said Mr Sharma, "broadcasting the truth about the Order to the people of Providence. But the Chancellor is skilled in smoke and mirrors. Whatever we cast must be undeniable, shocking enough that it will draw the people to the streets. If Providence were to fall, news would spread to the colonies. The kings the Order bribes into serving them might consider reclaiming their lands. But the Chancellor has many powerful tools at his disposal. And that's before we address the small issue of accessing the Eye network. It's nestled deep within the Basilica, its operations so secretive only a small number of people know what goes on within. But we may be forced to act before we're ready. The Order already raided the World's End. There's no telling what they might do next."

The following evening, Birdie insisted that we dress up for dinner.

"This might be our last chance," she said. "Our last dance. You never know what tomorrow might bring."

Some of the rebels weren't used to parties, like Gus and Perpetua. They hovered uncertainly, not sure what would be involved. For others, like Octavia and Evander, this was second nature, a throwback to their former lives.

I found myself somewhere in between.

Birdie invited us into her room to try on outfits. She had quite the selection from her days of throwing elaborate society events, including a range of Bard play costumes. I picked a red one, a floaty, fairy-like gown. Birdie gave me a pair of sandals to go with it but they were too small, cutting into my feet. I fished a pair of old work boots out of a cupboard.

"I'll just put these on instead," I said.

Birdie raised one eyebrow, suggesting she had serious reservations about my fashion choices, but she didn't say anything.

I primped myself in the mirror, pulling faces. I wanted to have a dazzling smile that left an impression, to be the kind of girl a boy might fall in love with, even if I couldn't love him back. That bubbling feeling returned, making me light on my feet.

Octavia went for a silver dress, with so many ruffles she looked like a metal rose unfurling.

"This is so much fun," she said. "I can't believe I'm out of the house, meeting new people, going to parties, seeing Rani again…"

She spun around, twirling her skirts.

"I was frightened at first but now I just feel energized, like I'm ready to live on the edge and let down my hair, you know?"

"Then let's make it a night to remember," said Birdie.

Octavia painted my face. We styled our hair in the mirror together like sisters. My head throbbed from all of the bobby pins she'd stuck in it, but she ensured me the effect was worth the discomfort.

All of this felt horribly familiar. Perhaps Ruby Renato had indeed attended many parties – and perhaps she hadn't liked them much.

Birdie cheered my spirits, telling secrets she knew about Order soldiers and ministers to entertain us. "You should've been at the party they threw for the bicentennial. They brought in a horse. It took a ginormous dump on the marble floor. Oh, the Chancellor's face!"

Downstairs, an orchestra of automated instruments played a lively tune, animated by psyche. Everyone was sitting around a long table in the dining room. They were all dolled up, Birdie most of all, in a feathered dress that made her look like a peacock. But there was a nervous energy present, an unspoken fear. We should not be celebrating. People had died. People were missing. The Order might catch up with us at any moment. But for now, for tonight, we were all still alive and we were going to have a party.

I took a seat next to Octavia, opposite Evander, though I didn't dare to look at him directly, spying out of the corner of my eye only.

"Wow, you look amazing!" said Rani, a little too loudly.

"So do you," said Octavia, admiring Rani's tux. "Black is definitely your colour, girl."

Perpetua was still wearing her bearskin coat but she'd teamed it with a sparkly headband and a white slip. Mr Sharma was wearing a black top hat with the price tag still on it, Gus wore a gold waistcoat, and, when I finally risked looking at him, Evander was wearing a black tuxedo with tails.

My heart pounded, drowning out the sound of my own mind.

He looked just like he had in the snow globe. It wasn't

difficult to imagine him being a member of the nobility, dressed like that.

"You look nice," he said, almost as if he were surprised.

"You too," I said.

My words came out shaky.

"I like the boots," he said.

I could feel myself getting warm.

"They're … not mine," I said, awkwardly.

The silence stretched out, practically to breaking point.

Cook brought out a platter of delectable entrées: cured meats and rare fruit, fresh bread and fancy sweets. We attacked it like a pack of lions, tearing at bread and cutting up meat. Despite our grim situation, everyone was laughing and bonding, connected together, but I felt even emptier than I usually did. The Heart food they were serving didn't seem to work on me.

I watched Evander from across the table. He looked more relaxed now, exchanging jokes with Ash. Octavia was talking excitedly to Rani, her hands flying. Gus was giggling with Cook. Perpetua was talking to the woman who'd drawn her knife. I felt on the outside of things, like I was gazing through the window into a room where I wasn't invited. The absence of my soul's Heart ached more noticeably than usual.

Soon, the adults in the room were enjoying many beverages, filling their glasses with wine as soon as they emptied, while the younger members of the group seemed to prefer the fruit punch served in a bowl with lemon slices.

It made them giddy and shiny-eyed, but it did nothing for me. I found one of the wine chalices left unattended and downed it, but it tasted like bitter vinegar.

"Enjoy yourselves now, kids," said Cook, raising a glass. "The life of a rebel is short and violent, a bit like me. If you're in this, you've gotta be all in, or you won't last half a second out there."

"Out there?" I said.

"On the battlefield. One day you'll come face to face with the Order again. That's why you've got to believe in what you're fighting for, so when the time comes, you'll fight with all you've got.

"Live fast, fight hard and leave behind a funny epitaph, that's my motto," said Ash.

"That's enough," said Birdie, clapping her hands. "If you're quite finished traumatizing our new friends, I suggest we dance away our troubles."

She stood up, shooing us out of our seats.

"Come on, people. I need energy. I need atmosphere. We shall dance the traditional House dances. No excuses! If you don't know the steps, I will teach you."

Birdie shepherded us to the dance floor, like we were her flock.

"First, the House of Song," she said.

Looking around the ballroom, she strode over to Octavia, gently taking her hand and leading her into the middle of the floor.

Octavia looked equally thrilled and terrified.

"I've never danced it before," she said. "I was only there to snoop, never to dance."

"No matter. I will lead," said Birdie, shaping her partner into the right stance. "The echo dance involves performing the same routine flawlessly. The lead dancer is the voice, and their partner is the echo. The voice goes first, while the echo follows after a count of ten."

Mr Sharma put a record on the gramophone, a silver tube taken from a cabinet full of cylinders in paper sleeves. As its sweeping melody rang out, Birdie launched into an elaborate sequence of twists and turns, near impossible for Octavia to memorize on the spot but she gave it her best shot, moving smoothly in time with the music.

"Marvellous. Magical," said Birdie, applauding. "The rhythm in your soul is impeccable." Octavia swaggered away, grinning widely.

"Do the mirror dance next," hooted Mr Sharma, waving his glass.

"Ah, yes. The House of Shadows is known for its mirror dance," said Birdie, grabbing Evander and pairing him with Rani. "Face to face, your partner must mimic your movements perfectly in turn, as if you are a reflection of one another. Here, let me put the right tune on."

Evander clearly knew the dance, reluctantly taking the lead, but Rani did not. According to Octavia, Rani had grown up away from the Order, protected by her uncle. She picked the moves up quickly with Evander's gentle encouragement though, blooming into herself until she smiled confidently.

"Go, Rani!" said Octavia, whooping and clapping.

Birdie continued with the bouquet dance, partnering Perpetua with Vincent in his flowery shirt for a ghostly waltz, then what she called the dessert dance, partnering Gus with Cook for a buoyant boogie.

"Finally, we have the burning dance," she said, grabbing me and yanking me and Ash into the middle of the dance floor. Birdie signalled for us to join hands, which Ash did, though they looked somewhat horrified.

"The burning dance is about heat, about passion. It is about the urges we feel that we cannot fully understand. Iris, you are the moth and Ash, you are the firelight."

I wasn't sure how to dance like a moth, but Birdie made it look more beautiful than I could have imagined. As she instructed us, keeping the time by clapping, I found that I knew the steps, guessing several moves ahead. As if the song was written on my body.

"Iris! You're a natural at this," she said.

Ash, being rather gangly and ungraceful, was not.

"Sorry," they said. "Sorry."

After they tripped over my feet for the third time in a row, Birdie threw up her hands.

"No, that won't do! The two of you have no chemistry." She gazed around the room flirtatiously, batting her long eyelashes. "Evander!" she said, pointing at him. "You must know this one."

"Me?" he said, as if there were another.

Birdie beckoned him. After looking left and right in search of escape, he sighed and joined me on the dance floor. I prickled in annoyance. Was I really such a terrible partner?

Birdie pressed us tightly together. Our hands entwined, creating a spark that pinged my skin like a static shock, even through the gloves. My head barely reached his shoulder.

I felt strange, awkward. I couldn't explain it. I wanted to run away, but also … not.

"And again! One, two, three four…"

Evander took the lead, gliding us into the first move, faltering slightly as if out of practice. He held my eye, dipping me at the waist. He steadily regained his nerve, spinning me under his arm and back again, as I tried to imagine myself the most beautiful moth that ever lived.

"You *are* good at this," he said in a low voice.

"I know, right?" I said, surprised.

"You must've danced the burning dance before at Renato balls."

His hand seemed to fit perfectly at my waist.

"It's as if my body remembers what my mind can't," I said.

I was in my element, letting the fire of my soul move through me. I soon forgot that everything else existed, dancing through the void of the dark place, with only the light of our souls to guide us.

Mine was small and fiery, with a rosy, flickering hue. His was larger, shrouded in shadows, but glowing through like the spotlight of a distant moon.

A beautiful scene formed around us like a watercolour painting, with suggestive streaks of blue and impressionist dots of green, applied in washes and layers until they formed vivid imagery, more like a canvas by the old Masters.

Now we were dancing beneath the open skies at night, in a field full of pale, delicate flowers.

"Are you doing that?" I said.

"I just thought you might appreciate some scenery," he said.

As we danced, fireflies formed constellations, while a shower of comets lit up the night. I wanted to fall into him again, to swim through his memories and feelings.

Distracted, I missed a step and stumbled into him. The bare skin of my neck met his.

Lily's face shone through, blinding me.

He was dancing with me, but he was thinking of her.

I looked at him, and he looked at me, and I knew at once that he knew what I'd seen.

The song seemed to end abruptly, transplanting me back in the ballroom as the dream scene faded out. I grew painfully aware of the rest of the party again, looking up to see everyone watching us with wide, questioning eyes. Rani whistled, her eyebrows lifting.

Before I could speak, Evander quickly turned and peeled out of the room, grabbing a bottle of wine and disappearing into the gardens. After a long moment, I followed, picking my way through an elaborate hedge maze, getting completely lost as I tried to find my way to him. Eventually I located him sitting in front of a fountain with frolicking cherubs, his dress shirt untucked, drinking straight from the bottle.

"Why did you run off like that?' I said.

"I'm not really in the mood for conversation," he said. His voice was slurred, the words indistinct.

The fire inside me roared, its flames rising up and burning my face. I had never felt so stupid.

"Oh, really?" I said, wanting to say something but not knowing what to say. "Well, excuse me for existing!"

I clenched my fists, struggling to hold back the scream that arose. Face twisting, I turned and walked briskly back towards the house.

"Wait!" he called after me, standing up. "I'm sorry! I didn't mean it like that. Lily, stop."

I pulled up, spinning around on my heels to confront him.

"*Lily*? Did you just call me Lily?"

Evander looked mortified.

"That's not my name," I said.

"Sorry, that was … that was my mistake."

"I'm not her," I said.

"I know…"

I turned around and ran on, not giving him the chance to make a fool of me again.

"Iris!"

I didn't even know why I was so upset, only that I was. Maybe I was angry at myself, for daring to think he could ever care for me like he cared for her. Or maybe I was angry at him for letting me think it.

Stupid, so stupid.

I couldn't compete with Lily. Dead, perfect Lily. She'd always live in his heart, in his head, no matter what I did.

I stormed into the foyer, unsure what to do with myself, when Birdie approached me from the stairs with an eager expression.

"Can I talk to you?" she said. "Now, while no one is here."

Mr Sharma lingered behind her, his face conflicted.

I forced myself to look calm. "What is it?" I said.

She signalled for me to follow.

"I have been in two minds as to whether to share this with you," said Mr Sharma. "Part of me fears it may be a trap, a red herring perhaps. But Birdie is quite insistent that she knows better than me on this occasion."

He smiled at her fondly, and she returned it.

"Go on," I urged.

"A couple of days after the Night That Never Was, I received a mysterious parcel from a Renato messenger," said Birdie. "She risked her life to get it to me, and all she said was, 'keep it safe'. After that, she disappeared."

"What does that have to do with me?" I said.

"Well, I recognized Ruben Renato's handwriting on the envelope."

I frowned. "You recognized his handwriting?"

Birdie gave a faint shrug. "Ruben and I used to be close, once upon a time. He had a habit of sending rather risqué letters with instructions to burn them afterwards."

Burning letters. Was that a habit he'd passed on to me?

"He confided in me. He knew I kept friends in low places. Ruben had little sympathy for the rebels the Chancellor had him torture and kill. He thought them foolish. But he feared his House was losing all control, that the Order was now a one-man operation. I was surprised to hear from him after so many years, but more surprising was the fact that, when I tried to open the package, I could not. Ruben Renato had sent me a parcel I couldn't open. It was a mystery to me — until now. I think you might be the true recipient."

"Oh," I said, my bad mood forgotten as curiosity took over. "Well, let's take a look then."

Birdie led us to a door with a glittering star on it, like a dressing room at a theatre. She flicked on a light and her private parlour came into view, decorated with yet more artistic interpretations of herself.

In one corner of the room was a cabinet full of remnants, much like the one owned by the Countess, a selection of treasures that I assumed contained the memories of Birdie's life in and outside of the Order.

"I have my doubts as to Ruben's true allegiance," said Mr Sharma. "I often warned Birdie against trusting him completely. But rebellions make for strange bedfellows. I trust in you, Iris. If you say he was plotting against the Chancellor, then perhaps we find ourselves fighting on the same side after all."

Birdie disappeared into her closet, throwing out a series of hats, scarves and handbags, before emerging with a small square package wrapped in brown paper and string, attached to a letter.

"Here it is," she said.

I hesitated, afraid that I might be wrong, that my memory might not be true, that nothing I knew was real. And yet … I felt it.

A small sound caught my ear. Its melody stirred my heartstrings, connecting me to something I didn't yet possess.

I opened the letter first, easily breaking its wax torch seal and pulling out the folded sheet of paper inside. It was an unsigned note that read: *If you've got this far, you're closer to the truth than you think.*

Excited, I unwrapped the parcel with shaking fingers, letting its paper fall away like a shed snakeskin.

Inside was the music box I'd glimpsed briefly in my memory, with pearly panels and filigree, decorated with dancers in formal dress. I reached out with exploratory fingertips. I could sense its hidden, inner vibrations. I turned the wind-up key and the box sprang open with a clatter, revealing two miniature figures, dancing together in a rosy bandstand.

A dark-haired boy in tails.

A red-haired girl in a scarlet dress.

I could see its cylinders turning and its hammers banging, striking off the grooved notes in sequence. With a crackle, a song rang out:

"Let the night take me,
Your spectre is taunting me,
Darling, the shadows
I live with are haunting me."

"I know this song," I said. I began to sing along, my voice croaky and out of practice.

"Sweetheart, don't cry for me,
Don't tell me it's time to go,
I live in the past where I know
You still love me so."

I found that I recalled the words perfectly.

"For as long as I live, in my dreams, I'll be kissing you.
With the last spark of my soul, I'll be missing you."

The lullaby sound became a full orchestra.

It was the Song.

My Song.

Each instrument was a part of my personality. The drum was my determination. The horn was the convictions of my beliefs. The piano was my sense of humour and the violin my passions. My quirks were the flute and the cello my insecurities.

I felt myself filling in, colouring, becoming three-dimensional.

As the music climaxed, my soul's Song emitted a deep, harmonic hum, a vibrating wave of energy that used my bones like a xylophone. The earth trembled. A flood of recollections coursed through me, swallowing me up and spitting me out in a different place and time.

Lost deep inside myself, I stand in front of an old, cupola-topped building, its windows softly illuminated. The Basilica of All Souls.

It isn't the Night That Never Was for there's no snow on the ground but the Basilica has a similar buzz about it, full of people coming to and fro. A painted banner decorated with a phoenix reads "Burning Eve".

It's the Renato House holiday.

Inside, dancers in bright, outlandish costumes twirl like spinning tops as servers carry silver platters and cut-glass decanters. Moving through the crowd, I find myself standing in front of Oliver Obscura. Chalice in hand, he appears to be looking for someone when his dark eyes catch on me.

Evander's former self wears tailored, night-black robes to match his raven hair, missing its familiar streak of white. An eye-shaped pendant hangs on a chain around his neck. He looks like an entirely different person, from his posture to the pinched, haughty expression on his face.

"My father sent me to speak with you," I say.

"If he wants to dance, he really ought to come over and ask me himself," he quips, smiling at his own joke.

"Just humour me, please. He's trying to find me a husband, I think. He wants me to be seen as desirable to all the other young bachelors in court. If you smile and act polite, we can both move on and enjoy our evening."

"I doubt that," he says.

"Why? I thought you liked parties?"

"Who told you that?"

"Ruben said you had a taste for vice."

"Well, he would know," he says, swigging from his glass. "The man is a master in all seven sins."

I look around for a source of small talk, watching people dancing to the melodious refrain of the orchestra.

"Maybe you just need to get into the spirit of things," I say. "From the look on your face, you may as well be at a funeral."

"A funeral I would prefer."

"Everyone else seems to be having a good time."

"That's because they have the collective intellect of a bowl of grapes," he says, in a drawling voice. "It doesn't take much to placate them, especially if the drinks are flowing."

I splutter, choking on laughter.

"You can't say that."

"Why not? I can say what I like. You think they're going to punish the future Chancellor for gossiping? There's a ball here every day, and if not a ball then a banquet. The novelty soon wears off. Once you've been to enough of them, there's very little enjoyment to be derived from it."

He points across the crowd, at a dancing couple in gold.

"Lord and Lady Cordata, blind drunk and draped over each other like barnacles," he said. "Later, they'll be at each other's throats, no doubt. Last I heard, the Lord was having seven separate affairs."

"Seven? Really?" I say lightly. "Where does he find the time?"

Placing one hand on my shoulder, he turns me slightly to face a man and woman in white. "Lord and Lady Memoria, two of the dullest people ever to walk the earth," he says. "All they ever talk about is how much better things were in the good old days."

He points at the couple in silver.

"Lord and Lady Harmonia. Never a kind word to say about anyone. Their only joy in life is gossiping."

"Isn't that what we're doing?"

"Touché," he says.

He moves us through the crowd, across the dance floor.

"You know Lord and Lady Renato of course. The worst of the five Houses, by most accounts."

"You dare to say such a thing to my face?"

"You're not really a Renato. No one even knew you existed until a month ago."

"Ruben is my father, and he's been nothing but kind to me."

Oliver looks pointedly at the ring.

"You're illegitimate. A love child, born to a servant

woman. He's only interested in you because you're gifted. If you weren't, he'd have you sent to the Reformatory."

I burn shamefully, my brow wrinkling.

"You were lucky to be born out of wedlock," he says, "to grow up as a commoner away from all of us."

"A commoner?" I say. "Is that how you think of me?"

His cheeks tinge pink as he realizes he's said the wrong thing.

"No. You know what I mean," he says, defensively.

We watch Ruben's wife Valeria throw a drink in a waiter's face, remonstrating him for getting her order wrong.

I need to take charge of the situation.

"Let's get out of here," I say.

"And go where?" he says.

"Who cares? Anywhere is better than staying here. If I have to listen to these people a minute longer, I might just start screaming obscenities."

I look at him, and he looks at me, the tension stretching between us deliciously.

"Or are you worried you'll upset your little girlfriend?" I tease. "Doesn't seem like she's too interested in you, though."

I look across the dance floor, nodding at a blonde-haired girl in white with her back to us, dancing with another boy.

Lily.

Oliver follows my line of sight, a miserable look clouding his features for a moment.

"Let's go," he says.

With a theatrical flourish, he grabs a cut glass decanter full of ambrosia and hustles us outside into the landscaped gardens of the Basilica with its many sculpted topiaries.

Everyone we pass gawks at us unabashedly.

"Every ball, a different girl on his arm," someone whispers.

There are rumours about Oliver Obscura, and I listen to all of them. That he's a playboy love rat who tells girls what they want to hear. That he's a drunkard, a wild child. That he's deranged, dangerous even. There are signs for everyone to see. I pay attention, but I ignore all the warnings.

We sit on the steps of the rose-covered bandstand. Oliver swigs straight from the neck of the decanter then passes it to me. I copy him, glugging it hungrily before slamming it back down on the wooden steps.

"Don't look so surprised," I chide. "I'm from the north. We drink fancy boys like you under the table."

He gives a throaty chuckle. "Is that so?"

His eyes bore into mine, like a key in a lock.

"So, what else do you do with your time?" I say, inching my fingers closer to his. "When you're not being forced to attend terrible balls, I mean?"

"I like to do as little as I can get away with," he says.

"Will you really be Chancellor some day? I can't imagine it."

"I don't really have much choice in it."

"I'm not sure you're cut out for it, the way you talk."

"No one is," he says. "Least of all my father."

"What about what *you* want?"

He shrugs.

"There must be something you want," I press. "Everyone wants something, don't they?"

Something flickers briefly in his eyes, something that makes him look vulnerable and bereft, a boyish yearning. It quickly fades and he laughs. "I just want to be left alone."

"Oh, is that right?" I say, pretending to get up. "Because I can go."

"Not you," he says, quickly. "You can stay. You're the most interesting person I've talked to in a while, and I only met you a few days ago."

The sound of the burning dance floats over from the Basilica.

"Shall we?" he says, standing up to match me.

It's a good thing Lady Rubella taught me the steps before sending me out into society.

Tentatively, he clasps my right hand with his left one. I place my left hand on his shoulder. He gently clasps my waist, a delicious thrill coursing down my spine. When he steps forwards, I step back.

He's taller than me, making our movements stilted and sloppy but both of us are laughing, oblivious to the narrowed eyes and wrinkled lips, clucking tongues and furtive whispers. People talk. They always talk. The song ends all too soon and another begins, this time an old torch song: one of those yearning melodies about heartbreak and unrequited love.

"Let the night take me,
Your spectre is taunting me,
Darling, the shadows
I live with are haunting me."

Oliver twirls me under his arm before pulling me close again, until we're only an inch apart.

I'm not supposed to like him.

I'm not supposed to be having fun.

The song continued to play as the scene faded away, leaving me standing alone in darkness until another vignette gradually built up around me, constructing itself piece by piece.

Now I'm unwrapping the music box, this time in the room I was shattered in. I turn its silver key, listening as the jingle-jangle of "The Haunted Heart" plays. The miniature figures dance on loop.

I know Oliver made it for me himself, from mind to matter, but whether his heart is really in it remains to be seen.

In the mirror on the wall, I spy Ruben at the door, catching the look on my face before I conceal it.

"Getting gifts already?" he says, crossing the room towards me. "You're even better at this than I imagined."

I stare hard into my reflection.

"About that... I was thinking—"

"We have no more time to waste. We're going to have

to up our game. Strike while the iron is hot, so to speak."

In my reflection I see doubt.

"But how am I supposed to hide the truth from him?" I ask. "Rumour is he sees everything."

"Deception is an art," says Ruben, "and you are a painter. Do what I told you to do, and he'll soon forget his own name."

"It still feels wrong," I say.

"This is our chance to undermine the Chancellor. Sometimes fighting for the right thing involves making difficult decisions."

I open the card, seeing the name written inside it.

Oliver.

"The boy is incapable of ruling House Obscura," says Ruben. "His mother's death ruined him. He is unstable, delusional, prone to psychosis. He cannot be trusted to lead us. That is why you must help us destroy him."

He raises my chin with one red-gloved finger.

"He's dangerous, Ruby."

"So am I."

"You're the only one who can do what needs to be done when the time comes. Don't forget what the Chancellor did to your mother."

I clutch at the necklace I wear, hidden beneath my blouse.

"What better way to honour her than to destroy the man who took her from you?" he says. "And Oliver is key to the Chancellor's downfall."

Sighing, I nod, throwing the card on the fire.

"I'm listening," I say.

"Find out what he remembers of the night his mother died. If we can prove what the Chancellor did, we can take down House Obscura. His reputation will be irrevocably damaged. He will be subject to an investigation. Renato House will be poised to seize control. For the good of the nation, we must remove the Chancellor from power, whatever the cost."

Ruben departs, leaving me alone with the music box.

I turn its key, listening to "The Haunted Heart" again.

The picture was filling in, the jigsaw puzzle assembling.

The terrible thing Ruben said only I could do...

It was to betray Evander.

The sound of Mr Sharma's voice drew me back, dragging me into the real world as the aftershocks of this revelation continued to quake me.

"Iris? Talk to me."

I was sprawled on the floor and Birdie was leaning over me.

"Are you OK, my love?" she said. "You had a funny turn, and you're white as a sheet."

I held out the music box.

"My Song," I said, trembling. "My Song was in it."

"Oh my," said Mr Sharma.

Birdie helped me to my feet, checking me over.

"I can't believe it was here all along," said Birdie. "No wonder you felt so familiar to me when we first met."

Before I could process this, the sound of banging interrupted us from deep within the house, like a heartbeat buried under the floorboards.

Mr Sharma's eyes turned black, as he looked within.

"They're here," he said. "The Order are here."

15.

THE SOUND OF THE SOUL

Abandoning our conversation and the music box, I joined the group of panicked people gathered in the upstairs foyer.

"How did they find us?" asked Birdie, in fury.

"They already knew our location. We must've been compromised," said Mr Sharma.

A fearful hush descended as everyone looked around at each other.

"So there's a spy in our midst," said Cook.

"Don't look at me," said Evander.

"I'll be exposed," said Birdie. "We'll lose our contacts, our cover, everything. What should we do, Arjun?"

Mr Sharma closed his eyes, looking deep within.

"There are seventy-five of them, and only thirty of us."

"The Chancellor is here too," said Octavia.

All of the Spark seemed to drain out of Evander's body, leaving him empty as a glove.

As we advanced towards the kitchen, we saw black wagons surrounding the house on every side.

"There's no way out," said Rani.

"What about travelling through shadows?" said Evander.

"You can't possibly transport everyone," said Mr Sharma. "It would kill you. I won't allow it."

They exchanged a long, inscrutable look.

"Then we have no choice but to fight," said Perpetua.

Mixed terror and thrill spiked in my veins.

"We won't win," said Evander. "This is it. The end of the road."

"Don't say that," I said.

"He's here for me. I'll go to him, give myself up. Maybe then he'll spare the rest of you."

"What if he's really looking for me?" I said. "He wants to make sure I don't remember myself completely. I should be the one to hand myself over."

"Neither of you are going anywhere!" snapped Octavia.

"Didn't you escape the Order before?" said Mr Sharma, gripping Evander's shoulders firmly. "Didn't you break into the Observatory? We can't become disheartened before we've even begun, can we?"

Another wave of banging erupted.

"We always knew this was a possibility. An eventuality, some might say. And we are not entirely unprepared."

Birdie led us to a study. She stalked over to a bookcase lined with leather-bound tomes, running her hands over their spines. Resting her fingers on a single book, she pulled it out. It acted as a lever, causing a series of clunking clogs to grind as the heavy bookcase swung open like a door. It revealed a cavernous room in which many strange weapons were displayed in cases.

"Everyone, grab something to fight with!" said Mr Sharma. "We don't know if they'll battle us with minds or bodies. Probably both."

"What are they?" I said, inspecting the array of strange weapons.

"Experimental technology," he said. "Made by the Order."

"I've sung many sweet songs to many powerful men, and some of them gave me gifts," said Birdie. "Others I stole and squirrelled away whenever I had the chance. Each one is designed to amplify the psyche of a particular user."

She gestured at a red baton with a strap.

"That right there is the same baton used by the Order's soldiers. You should take it. As a fire soul, you should find it easy to use as a conductor for channelling life force."

I removed the baton from its hook, weighing it in my hand. It was cool and smooth, engraved with the fire sign.

It sparked involuntarily, showering embers.

"Sorry!" I said.

Ash took the other fire weapon: a bow with arrows that could be ignited telepathically. Birdie gave Octavia a bell that could discipline soldiers like dogs, while retrieving for herself a bullhorn type device that she said could break the sound barrier. Mr Sharma instructed Rani on using orbs like those we'd seen in the Observatory, which could be used to enter a person's Shadow. Perpetua inspected a smoking lantern with incense that haunted all those who smelled it with their own memories. Cook and Gus stuffed their pockets with potions and poisons, to be used as projectiles.

"Up to the roof," called Birdie. "They're almost through the door."

Looking over the balcony in the hall, I saw a horde of Inspectors overflowing into the house.

Mr Sharma hung back, creating a fiery blockade with my help. Bounding up the stony spiral staircase, we climbed the highest tower of the house as footsteps thundered below, bursting out on to the roof.

"This way!"

Edging along a narrow precipice, past statues of black, bug-eyed gargoyles, we headed for the most protected area of the rooftop, surrounded by turrets and spires, startling as a volley of shouts ricocheted below.

Down on the ground, Inspectors piled out of wagons, black boots crunching on gravel as they marched in lines towards the entrance. Standing in formation, they worked together to turn mind to matter, producing an enormous crane that lifted them up to the roof.

"Do whatever you have to do to defend yourself and others," said Mr Sharma, puffing up his chest.

He turned to Birdie, taking her face in her hands and kissing her lips with great tenderness.

"Arjun," she said, fondly.

Watching on, Octavia turned to Rani and followed suit. Rani looked surprised for just a second or two before kissing her back.

Evander and I merely looked at each other, the unspoken rippling.

I wondered what his lips felt like. Had I kissed him before?

"We'll be OK," he said, though his face didn't look as if he believed it. "I'll do whatever it takes to keep you safe."

"I can protect myself," I said. "It's you I'm worried about."

I felt that invisible thread stretched between us again.

"Don't die, OK?" I said, feeling the irony in my words after the dreadful realization my Song memories had stirred.

"I'll do my best," he said. "Don't do anything stupid."

"I can't promise that," I said.

The thread promptly snapped as the Inspectors flooded the roof, roaring towards us. I watched as Evander's pupils expanded, drowning out the whites. His Shadow grew enormous, wrapping around the intruders like a ragged black cloak. Scrambling, stumbling, the blinded guards crashed into each other, yelling out in confusion. One plummeted over the side of the building. At the same time, Birdie projected waves of sound, an eardrum-splitting wail I could only hear faintly. The Inspectors clutched at their ears, screaming in pain.

The Chancellor emerged through dark clouds, flanked by a woman in a white doctor's coat and a man in a silver tunic wearing an earpiece. The woman went after Evander. The man went after Octavia. The Chancellor headed straight for me. His presence made me feel cold, sickened, naked, a thousand eyes on my skin, their shadowy tendrils bleeding into the cracks of my soul. In his hand, a familiar dark staff glinted, the same staff that had shattered me.

Swinging it, he manifested serpentine monsters that attacked me in a swarm. They tore at my hair and clothes, blinding me with their dark, streaky tails. He was channelling the Shadow, weaponizing it.

Mr Sharma charged forward to meet him, blocking the Chancellor's path to me, but a red-coated army cadet loomed out of nowhere.

He was holding a baton identical to mine. Its golden light spread into branches, forming a sprawling, web-like pattern that stretched through the air. Soul fire. It was the same energy that ran through me, the same energy I'd channelled to create the carriage fire.

The crackling lightning snaked forth, striking me in the chest.

"Argh!"

It coursed through my veins like fire in my blood. Bright stars scorched the surface of my retinas. My ears rang at high pitch. I could smell something burning and taste the rusty penny kiss of fresh blood on my lips.

Setting my jaw, I allowed my Spark's energy to flow through my own baton, creating a web of energy that matched his. Crying out, I imagined a fire that would burn his skin, causing him to scream in pain. But somehow he directed the energy back on me, forcing me to my knees.

The cadet dragged me up off the ground, reeling me towards him as if caught on a fishing line. I managed to wriggle away from his invisible pull, bolting on to the narrow walkway that surrounded the roof. Thick black smoke obscured my vision, but I could make out a glimpse of the Chancellor, using his staff to direct the smoke like a hurricane.

"You know, everyone is getting real tired of chasing you around," said the cadet, following me.

"Then why don't you stop and save yourself the trouble?"

Part of the narrow ledge crumbled. I took one hesitant step to the left and the walkway dropped out from beneath my feet. As I struggled to catch on to something solid, the baton plummeted to the ground below, shattering.

When the cadet threw out his weapon, I ducked and rammed him in the stomach with my head, slamming into him with as much force as I could gather from my own soul's tinder. It poured out of me, a tsunami of soulfire, coursing into his body and knocking him out instantly. His eyes rolled back in his head as he tumbled, falling through the air until he hit the ground below with a squelchy, bone-cracking thud.

I winced, looking away. I should have been disgusted, remorseful, but I was merely relieved, relieved that I didn't have to fight him any more. Picking up his dropped baton, I crawled over to the other side of the roof, searching through the smoke for the Chancellor.

Some of the Inspectors were hallucinating, haunted by the spectres of their own memories.

"Rosie," one cried, chasing after the ghostly spirit of a

woman cast by Perpetua. "Come back to me, my love!"

"You're supposed to be dead!" screamed another, backtracking from the vision of an elderly, cackling woman.

Gus ran through the throng, throwing potions like bombs, casting bright explosions of multi-coloured smoke that sent Inspectors to sleep. Ash fired a flaming arrow in the Chancellor's direction – which grazed the padded shoulder of his jacket – before being disarmed by two soldiers in red tunics.

In a pool of shadow, I found Evander half-conscious, bloodied and murmuring to himself.

"Evander!"

I knelt down beside him, trying to rouse him. He opened his eyes, seeing me kneeling over him, and reached for my hand, his face softening.

"I wanted it to be you," he said, cryptically.

"Evander, please! We need you. I need you!"

He drifted away again.

Covering him over with a dropped coat, I moved through the fog. I saw Ash on the ground, now being pummelled by guards. Perpetua was in spectral cuffs, swearing up a storm. A smashed orb leaked more shadows into the air, while Octavia screamed for Rani, unseen.

Mr Sharma stepped into the fray, fighting serpentine shadows with spectral illusions, each permeating the veil between fantasy and reality. Cannons. Lightning. Swarms of locusts. All becoming real.

But the Chancellor barely flinched.

"I see you've gathered quite the army, Arjun," he said, his voice unnaturally loud. "So many people, and not a soul worth saving."

Silence descended on the battlefield as the smoke began to clear.

"Hand over my son and Ruby Renato, and I will only imprison you. Resist, and I will kill you and your families. You will be branded as traitors for the history books to immortalize. No one will mourn you. There will be no one left to remember you."

No one moved, although some of the runaways looked at each other, considering it.

"You've stolen too many lives already," said Mr Sharma. "I won't let you take any more."

With a sudden thrust of his arms, he cast a spectral tsunami of dark matter, which washed over the Chancellor. Yet he emerged unscathed, protected by a ring of empty space.

"You're wasting your time," said the Chancellor. "The battle is already fought, and lost. You missed your chance. You've become slow. You're too old for this, Sharma. It's time to stop dreaming."

He gestured lazily around the roof. I realized with growing horror that he was right. Cook had been hit with one of her own potions, her mouth foaming. Octavia was being tortured by her own supernatural screams. Gus and Rani had been captured, carted off into black wagons, the doors closing behind them. We were losing. We were losing badly.

"This was but one battalion of soldiers and yet it was enough to defeat you with ease. I have hundreds of thousands more troops at my disposal. Don't make this any more embarrassing than it needs to be. You are but a servant, and a poor one at that. You are no rebel, for there is no resistance."

"You think those people out there are happy under your rule?" said Mr Sharma. "You're wrong. You have no idea how wrong. There are more of them than you have loyalists. One day, if not today, they shall rise up, and burn your Order to the ground."

Snarling, the Chancellor bombarded him with shadows in the form of knives and arrows. Mr Sharma struggled to take control, rising to his feet as the muscles in his arms tensed, his fists clenched.

He released a howling, tornado of shadow matter that tore up the roof, tossing Inspectors aside and throwing the woman in the white coat back against the wall, but the effort lasted only a moment before the Chancellor held out his staff, manifesting a gigantic wrecking ball that hit Mr Sharma at full force, almost pushing him off the roof before it disintegrated into nothing.

Two Inspectors seized a bloodied Mr Sharma, pinning him in cuffs.

Evander was barely conscious.

It was all up to me.

Roaring, I charged towards the Chancellor, my hands outstretched, my mind hot and white with rage. I was ready to do whatever it took to destroy him, even if it meant sacrificing myself.

He casually threw out an arm in my direction, tensing his fingers as if gripping an object. Kicking and screaming, I was dragged towards him by shadows, my hands and feet bound together.

I felt the fire inside me draining away, leaving me weak and thick-headed, making me want to give in. Looking up, I saw those dark tendrils cast by the Chancellor trying to creep into my head, snaking into my ears.

"Get away!" I cried, shaking them off.

The Chancellor gazed at me impassively through his shaded lenses, slowly tilting his head to one side.

"There you are."

Two Inspectors materialized, stepping through shadow portals, pulling me up and holding me in place.

"Bring forward the traitor," said the Chancellor, clicking his fingers.

The man in the earpiece produced Birdie, now restrained with black shadow chains, and dropped her at his feet.

"Get off me, you ugly brutes," she said. "Where are your manners? This dress cost more than your parents paid to raise you."

"Let her go!" warned Mr Sharma.

"Of all the people who've turned against me, your betrayal is the least surprising," said the Chancellor. "I never trusted you."

"Then why did you invite me to your birthday soirée?"

Birdie pouted, dramatically. "Didn't you enjoy the private performance I gave you?"

The Chancellor's face soured, hand twitching on his weapon.

"Don't you dare hurt her," said Mr Sharma.

"Oh, don't worry. This won't take a minute. I just wanted to make sure she saw this," said the Chancellor.

In one swift, smooth movement, his staff whirled through the air.

"No!" I yelled.

The motion was horribly familiar...

Before anyone could stop it, a black beam shot out from the eye of the staff, striking Mr Sharma in the chest.

"Arjun!" yelled Evander, roused from unconsciousness.

A rosy, glowing ball of psyche shone briefly through Mr Sharma's shirt. As he looked down, his chin pressed against his chest, the light broke apart into five beams. I could see his Shadow and his Spirit, flanking him on either side. I could hear the harp in his Song and the fiery Spark that sat atop his golden Heart, shining through his shirt.

It was just like my shattering, but the staff didn't drop at the last minute, as it had in my memory. It remained in place, its beam surging, gradually gaining in power until a deep resounding boom reverberated.

Mr Sharma's eyes fixed on me. "Find ... him," he gasped.

Was he talking about Ruben? He must be.

The light inside him died out, the pieces of his soul's

anatomy flaking away to dust. His lifeless body toppled to the ground.

I stared at it numbly, in total shock.

A long moment of silence followed, before it was punctuated by Birdie's ragged, murderous screams.

"You … you *killed him!*"

The Chancellor applauded her, mockingly.

"Yes, very good. You always did have a talent for theatrics but your performance is over now. It's curtains for you."

Trembling, she struggled against the chains to get to her feet. Her pretty face twisted.

"Then surely I must be allowed one last swansong," she said.

A wailing, soul-tearing lament, the sound rang out across the roof, causing everyone to cease fighting.

"Darkness descends upon our land,
Ruled by men with bloody hands.
Their secrets control our minds,
Their lies keep us hypnotized."

Transfixed, the Inspectors lowered their lamps and dropped their weapons, standing stationary in a daze.

She was taking control of them, enchanting them with her song, like a siren from legend.

Even the Chancellor appeared immobilized by the gut-wrenching sound, struggling slowly towards her and raising his staff.

"It's time to rise up and shine a light,
We'll take our freedom back tonight..."

The Inspectors pivoted on their heels, marching towards the Chancellor as if to seize him instead, their eyes glazed.

Your evil reign is coming to an end,
The soul of the nation we will——"

Cut off prematurely, the last note rang out.

The Chancellor's arm was frozen in position, the staff still smoking.

I watched the parts of Birdie's soul divide and die. I watched her eyes cloud over, raising one hand helplessly. It was the same method used to kill Mr Sharma, the same weapon used to shatter me.

I should have been killed. I understood it now. Instead of fading out, those pieces of me had been protected, given sanctuary by my possessions somehow. If only I knew how, I could have saved them both.

They'd given everything to the Sanctuary, to protect people, to protect me, and now they were dead because of it. It wasn't fair. It wasn't right.

Birdie tumbled to the floor, lying prone next to Mr Sharma, their hands only inches from one another, twitching.

Silence.

No encore.

In the distance, a musical chittering began to grow.

With the smash of glass, one of Birdie's feathered friends soared through a broken window, mimicking her swansong.

Inspectors ducked as birds zoomed at them like fireworks. Another followed, then another, until the skies were full of music. They flew off in every direction, spreading the resistance anthem across the village and beyond, echoing Birdie's last song.

Evander struggled to his feet. His enlarged Shadow shot out, grasping his father around the throat and raising him off the floor. The Shadow streaked through his veins, creating sinister-looking tributaries beneath the skin.

The strain caused him to bleed again, this time from his eyes, spilling crimson tears that left a trail of blood across the rooftop.

Several guards stepped forwards, ready to defend their Chancellor, but he shook his head slightly, signalling for his men to stay back.

"Oliver. Son," rasped the Chancellor.

"That's not my name," said Evander. "Not any more."

His voice was different, more baritone. Deeper and rougher, as if dug up from the grave. His white dress shirt was splattered in blood now.

The Chancellor clutched at the Shadow hand now throttling him.

"Come with me," he forced out. "Come home. The darkness inside you is corrupting your soul. Your Shadow is taking over you, just like it did with your mother. You're becoming a monster."

Evander's Shadow transformed again, becoming the same demonic beast that had chased away the Inspectors, sprouting horns and wings.

"*I'll show you a monster,*" he said.

"You mean to let it kill me?" gasped the Chancellor. "Your own father? Without me, you will die. Only I can help you. Only I can hold back the darkness that consumes you. That's why I was able to enter your Shadow, how I used it to locate you, because deep down inside, you wanted to let me in."

Evander staggered slightly, the monster devolving. "No."

"Ever since we crossed paths at the Observatory, I have been watching you. You allowed me to share your memories. Your feelings. You showed me this hiding place."

"It's not true," Evander chanted, shaking his head. His eyes were brown again, his voice his own. "It's not true."

His hold on the Chancellor loosened, allowing his father's feet back on the ground to support his weight.

"Your Shadow was so weak, so susceptible to influence. It was so easy for me to commandeer it. It showed me the real desire in your heart … to come home, where you belong."

"No, no, no…"

I shook my head along with Evander. "Don't listen to him," I said firmly. "You don't belong with him. You're not him."

Evander turned to me, haunted, his expression pleading.

"She can't help you," said the Chancellor. "She betrayed you. Used you. All because her father told her to."

Evander's monstrous Shadow retreated further.

"What?"

The Chancellor removed his dark glasses.

"Here. Let me show you," he said.

Whatever Evander saw in his father's eyes, I wasn't privy to it, but his mouth hardened.

I watched him grow cold.

"How could you?" he whispered, turning back to me.

There was nothing but steely hatred in his voice. His words were a knife, plunged into my chest.

"Evander," I gasped. "I didn't..."

When he turned to me, his black gaze was a void.

"Let's go," said the Chancellor, casually stepping over Birdie's body. "Bring the girl."

"Yes, father," he said.

Evander reached out his hand as if to take mine, but darkness streaked out from it instead, overcoming me.

The light of the world went out.

PART
FOUR
THE HEART

16.

REFORMATION

For a long time, I thought I was dead.

I didn't think anything.

I didn't feel anything.

I didn't want to exist any more, so I didn't.

Gradually I became aware of a bumpy, rocking rhythm and realized I was on the move. It was so dark I couldn't see anything, but I could sense other people in close quarters, breathing, shivering, whimpering.

"Iris?" came a whisper. "Is that you?"

"Octavia?" I said, recognizing her voice.

"I can hear your thoughts now," she said.

It must have been because I'd got my Song back, though the music box was surely in the possession of the Order now.

"What happened?" I said, still groggy.

"I don't remember," said Octavia. "My head feels heavy and full of fog. I can't hear the stream outside very well."

"Where are the others?" I said.

"I'm here," sniffed Rani.

I could just about see her, on the other side of Octavia,

her face tear-stained, rocking gently back and forth.

"Rani," I said, hoarsely. "I'm sorry."

"I can't believe he's dead," she said. "Gone. Just like that."

"I know," said Octavia, rubbing her arm. "I'm so sorry, honey."

"He looked after me my whole life after my parents died," said Rani. "He taught me how to use the Shadow, how to escape reality in dreams. He was all the family I had left."

"That's not true," said Octavia. "You still have us."

"But for how long?"

"It's all my fault, isn't it?" I said.

"Of course it's not," said Octavia. "Don't be ridiculous."

"I was the one who insisted we break into the Observatory. The Chancellor wouldn't have found Evander if not for me. He wouldn't have been able to spy on us through his Shadow, and identify our location."

"No!" said Rani fiercely. "That's enough! That's what they want. To tear us apart and make us as cynical as them. We have to stick together and focus on the real enemy. The Chancellor. He was the one who killed them. That's what Uncle Arjun would've wanted. Birdie, too."

"Poor Birdie," said Octavia.

Her voice broke. Her hand found mine, taking Rani's hand with the other. I let their feelings drift through me. The aching sob of grief stuck in my throat. The freezing terror. The numbness that held me in its grip, making me feel as if none of this was real at all.

We felt it together.

I thought about the button, long gone now, and my mother along with it. I mourned the idea of her.

"Did anyone else make it?" I said.

"They captured Perpetua, Ash and Gus. Cook is dead. The others are dead," said Rani.

"Evander went with the Chancellor," I said.

Octavia's lip wobbled. She bit down on it, trying to dam the tears that threatened to spill over, making my eyes sting vicariously.

"His father still has a hold on him somehow," I said. "He's still controlling him through his Shadow."

None of us spoke for several long minutes.

"Where are they taking us?" I asked.

"The Reformatory, probably," said Octavia. "If we're lucky, they'll only try to purify us. They can retune the personality. Edit the memory. They'll make us forget ourselves."

"And if we're unlucky?" I said.

"Then ... it was a pleasure to know you, my friends," said Rani.

A lump got stuck in my throat.

"They must've kept us alive for a reason," I said, wanting to believe it. "The Chancellor could've killed us there and then."

Silence.

"I need to tell you something, before I can't remember any more," said Octavia, gravely.

"You'd best be quick," I said, as the carriage slowed.

"Remember I told you I knew a few things the Chancellor would rather I forget? One of them is about the Chancellor's wife. Evander's mother."

"Nadia," I said. "Mr Sharma told me about her."

Rani nodded.

"He always thought Evander witnessed what happened that day. But he could never recover the memory. Evander is convinced that his father removed it, but he's wrong. I know that memory still exists in Evander's mind, just deeply repressed, buried within his subconscious."

"How do you know?" I said.

"The mind doesn't always quiet when people sleep," she said. "Sometimes I can still hear their stream of consciousness as they drift into dreams. I've heard him cry out for her. I've heard him scream. One time he said, 'Papa, no! Stop! Don't hurt her!'"

I thought of the nightmare I'd seen acted out on his wall.

"What are you saying?" I said, letting the pieces fall into place. "That the Chancellor hurt Evander's mother?"

"I'm saying that Evander can prove his father killed her. That's the memory that Mr Sharma has been trying to uncover." said Octavia. "And I know, as the Chancellor's Listener, he was obsessed with finding everyone who worked for him at the time of Nadia's death, including Mr Sharma, though he could never find him. Another was a maid who quit six months later. When I started working for him, he tracked her down at long last, all these years later.

He had me eavesdrop on her thoughts. She recalled that the Chancellor and Nadia quarrelled that day. Nadia told him she was leaving, taking Oliver with her. The Chancellor refused. His eyes turned black. His Shadow manifested, becoming material. It threw her from the balcony. The maid saw it all."

"People might not care what the Chancellor does to us rebels, but to kill his own wife? It would ruin him. If we could prove it, we could broadcast the memory through the Eye network, like Mr Sharma planned. We could show everyone the truth, like Evander always wanted," I said.

"What happened to that maid?" asked Rani.

"The Chancellor killed her for what she knew, like he kills every witness to his cruelty, leaving no evidence behind. Evander is the only one left who might remember and he can't help us right now."

Ruben's voice echoed in my mind.

"Find out what he remembers of that night. If we can prove what the Chancellor did, we can take down House Obscura."

Was this why I'd been chosen to infiltrate Oliver's mind? His heart? To expose his repressed memory of his mother's murder?

And if I'd recovered it once, did that mean I could do it again?

"I should've told you before," said Octavia, reading my thoughts. "I thought we'd have longer. But every time I brought it up with him, he was insistent that he doesn't remember anything."

The other prisoners were starting to stir now. The carriage pulled up, brakes squeaking. The doors of the wagon swung wide open, allowing a lighthouse-bright spotlight to spill into the back of the cab.

I squinted, my eyes burning.

"Where are we?" asked one of the others, sleepily.

"Rise and shine," said an Inspector. "Welcome to the Reformatory, your new home sweet home."

As my vision adjusted, I made out some other faces from the battle at Birdie's house, dirtied and bloodied, groggy and disorientated.

Dragged out into the cold night, the Inspectors unclipped our ankle cuffs, leaving us bound by the wrists. They herded us into a flock, standing before the entrance.

"Stop that snivelling," said the head Inspector, giving Rani a little push. "Why, anyone would think you're off to the gallows."

"Leave her alone," said Octavia.

"Did I hear something?" said the woman, turning on her. "I didn't give you permission to speak, did I?"

"N-no," she said. "No, ma'am."

When she walked away, Octavia's eyes were as sharp as knives.

The giant doors were creaked open by winch, revealing the dirty yard on the other side. They marched us in rank and file past the Gatehouse, where a group of men in tall black hats stood still as statues of soldiers.

"Those fine fellows are the gatemen, the Keepers of the

282

Keys," said the Inspector. "They make sure no one gets in or out. No point trying to run from here on in, boys and girls. If you even think it, we'll know about it."

Built into the exterior wall were four turreted towers, looping around a paved path.

"This is the Listening Post," she said, of the tower with a mast-like spire. "You'll answer to them if they hear divergent thoughts in your stream of consciousness. No cusses. No violence. No filth."

Octavia and Rani huddled together, as if for warmth.

We watched as dark birds flocked overhead in a large noisy rabble, frantically flapping as if fleeing in haste. It made my chest ache to see them flying free, wondering if I'd ever walk out of here.

A nurse in grey glided past in the opposite direction, arm in arm with a pale-eyed patient who stared right through me, as if I were a phantom.

"This is the Infirmary, where you'll come for memory edification, so that's something to look forward to, eh?" said the Inspector of the industrial-looking keep surrounded by grimy fountains.

As I passed by a ground-floor window, I looked through to see rows of pupils chanting monotonously, all dressed in identical grey tunics.

"Prudence, patience, temperance, chastity, diligence, obedience, humility and charity," they droned.

The Inspector led us inside, into the spacious foyer, where a series of statues symbolized the five stages of the soul's Enlightenment, from the blindfolded peasant who stood cowed and naked in shadows to the golden winged goddess with a crown of stars. Around them, youths sat plucking harps and arranging flowers, fencing and painting watercolours.

"Here are some of our recently Reformed students."

A trio immediately stopped what they were doing to wave at us, flashing wide, toothy smiles.

I recognized them right away: Eyepatch, Bird's Nest and Shoeless. The three children I'd seen dragged away by Inspectors the night this all began, when the Countess first told me about the ring.

"Once, they were fantasists and deviants, liars and thieves. They were unhappy, unworthy, un-whole. Just like you."

There was something quietly sinister about their glassy gazes and the way their body language mirrored one another.

"They've been purified," whispered Rani. "Their souls cleansed of everything that made them *them*."

I tried to make eye contact with the littlest one. It was as if all the real golden light had been drained from him. I clasped my hand over my mouth, my stomach seizing as if I were about to start retching.

"Soon, they'll be valuable members of society," said the Inspector. "Maybe, one day, you will too."

She signalled for us to follow, and we walked in silence.

The Inspector brought us to a tower with shaded porthole

windows and a watch post lined with brass telescopes.

"This is the Watchtower, where we keep an eye on everything. Even when you're sleeping at night, the Observers will be watching in, so don't even dream of escaping."

She herded us into a corridor.

"The Order helps people become the best version of themselves, to elevate them above the base impulses that make humans act like animals. That's what the Reformatory is for. To *reform* people. Our mission is to help you become valuable members of society. It's for everyone's benefit. In time, you'll see that."

I wondered who she was trying to convince, us or herself. In either case, she was lying through her teeth.

"The time has come for you to get your psychograph taken," she said. "Form an orderly line."

One by one, they took us into a dark room. Every few minutes, I heard a bang as the bright flare of magnesium shone through the door cracks, filling the staircase with sulphurous smoke trails that made us all cough and splutter in sync. Each time, the noise startled me.

With every passing second, I grew more afraid, as if tied to a train track watching a locomotive hurtling towards me. Unstoppable and inescapable. There were too many soldiers and not enough exits. Even if I could manage to lay my hands on one of them, I wouldn't make it out of the corridor.

Something was crawling through my guts.

Why was I here, anyway? Why hadn't the Chancellor

just destroyed me there and then? He must be keeping me alive for something.

They announced us by surname. As a Belle, Octavia was one of the first to go in. She went through the door with one last look at me, seeming younger and smaller than she had before.

As a Renato, I was one of the last.

The fire inside me was reduced to ashy embers, making me feel weak and helpless, soft and pliable as putty in a warm hand.

A doctor beckoned me.

He was small and bald as an egg, wearing funny little glasses with adjustable lenses. The placard on his desk read DOCTOR STANFORD.

I'd heard that name before. The Inspectors had told me he'd want to see me for himself. Whatever that meant.

I gazed around at the pictures on the walls, wetting my dry lips. There were dozens of them: brilliant spectral orbs of many colours, shining and swirling like galactic nebulas. The man nodded blithely, gesturing at the spotlight. Though he smiled at me in a kindly manner, his eyes were flat and penetrating.

An assistant handed me a placard with a number on it.

RENATO, RUBY. PRISONER 509431.

Side-stepping, I stood in the glare, holding it up.

The assistant wound a wooden box with silver discs

that started spinning. I heard the ticking of clockwork, the flicker of gas and the whistle of steam as the projectionist held something aloft in his hand.

"Watch the birdie," he said.

A blindingly bright spotlight burst forth from the lantern. Its dazzling beam struck my chest above my folded arms, bouncing off to form a peephole vignette on the blank wall behind me. I heard a rattling whirr as the projectionist rotated five coloured lenses in front of the bulb in turn, like an eye doctor giving an examination.

The first lens was black, casting my Shadow. The second lens was pearly and frosted but it projected nothing but the lantern's light. My missing Spirit, I presumed. The third lens, a shiny, metallic disc, caused the music box version of "The Haunted Heart" to play as the image vibrated. The projectionist moved on to the fourth lens, a golden circle that cast shining sunlight, but the wall stayed empty. A hole where my soul's Heart should be.

The fifth lens was red as blood, turning the spotlight crimson and projecting the image of a raging inferno.

My Spark.

The doctor murmured to himself in shock, fascination perhaps. I smiled into it, warmed by its fire, empowered by its strength. The Order could try their best but I wasn't going to let them put that fire out again.

The spectral glimmers cast by my Spark metamorphosed, casting frantic disordered shapes that rapidly multiplied. Dancing flames ripped through the hazy reflections, leaving scorch marks like burning celluloid. But when I recalled the Chancellor's greedy, gleeful expression as he destroyed Mr Sharma's soul, when I remembered the hateful way Evander had looked at me, that fiery courage withered away, diminishing.

The flames retreated.

With the sound of a shutter, the booth flashed bright. The lantern fizzled out, leaving the room full of smoke.

"Next," he said.

I filed out, joining the others waiting in the yard. We moved on, to the complex in the centre.

"This is the Mess Hall. You'll come here twice a day, for breakfast and dinner," said the Inspector.

In a stone-clad room with a burning hearth spitting embers, they sat us at wooden benches with tankards of lemon water and stale sweet bread to share, with stringy mystery meat that had an acrid tang. The Inspectors didn't free us from our manacles, leaving us to struggle to pick up our knives and cups.

I gazed around at the faces of my fellow prisoners, some barely older than seven. The only sounds were of swallowing and chewing. Down the table, someone loudly yawned.

It caught on, spreading like a fire.

"They… It's…" said Octavia.

She trailed off, blinking dazedly.

"Are you feeling all right?" I whispered.

"The food," slurred Rani.

They'd laced it with something to make us docile, but

like the Heart food, it didn't seem to be working on me.

"Time's up," shouted one of the Inspectors.

They ushered us out into the yard, leading us towards a squarish building lined with guards.

"Octavia," I hissed, tugging at her sleeve. "We have to try and work out a plan. Are you listening to me?'

"Huh?" she said, dreamily.

She stared straight ahead, eyes glazed. Rani was the same way.

Two young cadets in red military tunics loomed in the doorway, wearing copper helmets and leather half-gloves.

"Have that one transferred to solitary," said the lead Inspector, nodding at me. "Chancellor's orders."

The two guards in red coats dragged me away. I struggled against them as Octavia and Rani watched emotionlessly.

"You're hurting me," I said, as one guard twisted my arm.

They brought me through another giant set of wooden doors, which were opened by many iron gears and levers.

Rows of cells were stacked up on top of each other like birdcages at a pet shop, stretching all the way up to the ceiling. They faced the watchtower in the middle, connected by a grid of scaffolding patrolled by Inspectors with bullseye lanterns. The cells had only one wall. The other three sides were barred and open to view by any of the hundreds of other cells that looked upon them.

Here, *we* were the Eyes, spying on one another.

"Privacy is a privilege to be earned, so keep your noses clean," one guard was telling a group of new initiates.

"The first night is the worst. I suggest you start by reflecting on how you got here."

"The sooner you come to terms with the corruption in your soul, the sooner you can heal from it," a chaplain told another group of recruits.

The red coats hauled me all the way to the top, along a mezzanine. We passed a series of cells, revealing the sunken-eyed living skeletons inside. Some were curled up in corners, or laid flat on the floor. Others rocked back and forth, or banged their heads against the wall.

They hauled me into an empty cell, slamming the door behind me.

I could hear crying, rattling, shouting, praying: the sonata of a thousand souls in torment.

All of the emotions I'd been holding back overwhelmed me now. With a dry sob, I threw my fist at the wall, pain surging through my bones. Then I sank to my knees, curling up on the floor, trying to drum up the will to keep fighting, keep believing. I longed to break down but I felt too numb to fall apart.

Octavia, I thought, as loud as I could. *Octavia, can you hear me?*

In my mind, I called out for her for hours, hoping to hear her voice in my head, but I didn't. Eventually, I drifted off into a fitful sleep, calling out Evander's name, like I had Octavia's.

I searched my dreams for him, following a thin, spiderweb thread into the dark. I chased him like I'd chased my own Shadow, but I could never catch up to him.

17.

REMEMBER ME

Time in the Reformatory was relative, yet regimented. There were no clocks, so I measured time by watching the shades of the sky and listening to the bells that rang upon the hour. In solitary, my only company was the howler next door. Night and day, they screamed into the void.

Sometimes I thought about joining them, but I clung to one last crumb of hope. There were too many unanswered questions. Too much unfinished business. I couldn't die without finding the rest of myself, without apologizing to Evander and identifying my mother, without finding out what happened on the Night That Never Was and finishing what my father started.

I had too much still to do.

From my cell, I saw groups of prisoners crossing the yard at regular intervals, Octavia and Rani among them, but they didn't pick up on my loud, urgent thoughts, nor did they hear me banging on the window and whistling. I saw Perpetua on occasion, Gus just once, but their eyes were clouded. Whatever powers the Reformatory was using to "purify" them, it was making them forget themselves ... and me.

I soon lost track of how long I'd been in solitary. Days? Weeks? Months? There were no markers, no signposts in the dark, just bowls of slop through the hatch in the door, over and over, until two guards came to fetch me in the middle of the night.

One walked in front of me and the other behind, both holding their batons close in case I tried to fight them again, but I was still sore from the last failed attempt. Every part of me ached. They ushered me to a tower full of white coats and padded cells and walking dead patients, with a strong antiseptic smell.

In a clinical examination room decorated with anatomical posters and exotic plants, a doctor waited for me. I recognized her from the rooftop of the Sanctuary. Her blonde hair was scraped back severely into a bun.

DOCTOR MILLEFLEUR read the badge on her coat.

"Hello, Ruby," she said. "We meet again."

As the guards strapped me into my chair, she placed an empty vial in a peculiar gold machine covered in various knobs and dials.

She stuck a small needle in my arm.

A psychoscope, operated by a silent projectionist beneath a curtain, shone upon the wall.

"Begin session," she said, and two golden discs on the wall began to rotate, crackling like gramophone records.

My fear peaked, though I tried to look calm. She sat in

the armchair opposite, delicately crossing her legs.

"I'd like to start by getting to know you," she said. "Why don't you tell me about your childhood?"

I pressed my lips together.

"I asked you a question. Now answer it."

"I don't know," I said. "I don't remember anything."

"You must remember something."

Green fields. Clean shirts. Dark birds.

Standing up, she picked up a cut glass crystal decanter, pouring a see-through liquid into a chalice.

"Spirit serum," she said. "Helps to retrieve repressed memories."

"Too bad I don't have a Spirit," I said, desperately trying to sound braver than I felt.

"Oh, don't worry, your Spirit is still out there somewhere," she said. "Even in your fragmented state, the connections between your soul's parts are palpable. My job is to make contact with it, tuning into the energies of what's left of your memories."

She poured the liquid down my throat as I spluttered, massaging my neck and forcing me to swallow. The acrid taste lingered. It tasted as if my brain was on fire, as if all my nerves were sparking like lightning bolts. Despite my resistance, a memory appeared in the peephole on the wall, clouded and partial as my soul. It had picture but no sound, like a silent movie.

Like a film played backwards, it began with me sitting in the chair and reversed down the hall with the guards, running through my Reformatory orientation and my conversation with Octavia in the wagon before re-enacting the deadly rooftop battle. My memory slowed when we reached the Observatory break-in, and the snatches of memory I'd recalled about Ruben.

Here I was, vowing to destroy the Chancellor again.

"Copy that," the Doctor instructed her assistant.

The assistant held up his clicker and took a picture before plunging deeper, reliving the Observatory break-in, which she similarly marked for copy.

But after viewing my conversation with Oliver Obscura, in which we'd mocked the leaders of the other Houses, she said, "Mark for deletion."

The assistant nodded and made a note.

She viewed the theft of the ring, going all the way back to when I first met the Countess. I was trying to fight her but I was weak and sleepy.

Out of nowhere, a small house atop a green field popped up, with washing strung out to dry and dark birds on the roof. A freckled woman appeared, her eyes shining with love. It was the woman I'd glimpsed briefly before. She looked like me, wide-eyed and round-faced. She beckoned me to come to her. My viewpoint was low, my stance wobbly, my limbs chubby and short. I jumped into her arms. She whirled me up into the air, spinning me around in circles as the sound of our laughter broke through the silence.

"Mama!" I squealed, giggling.

My mother.

My baby hands clutched at a thin glass tube on a fine-linked silver chain around her neck, decorated with ornate flowery patterns.

I could see something glimmering inside, catching the light.

The picture morphed, surging ahead through a dozen different images of the same woman, showing her aging, her happy face becoming harried and lined. The stream of memories slowed, fixing on a particular picture of my mother, standing at the window of a darkened attic. It was blurry at first, but gradually came into focus.

"Show me this day," said the doctor.

I didn't want to show her but curiosity won out. My resistance waned. I let myself be drawn in.

Downstairs, someone is trying to break in through the front door, creating a relentless *thud, thud, thud.*

A single tear rolls down my mother's cheek, which she captures in the glass vial around her neck, sealing it tight. With trembling fingers, the nails bitten down almost to the cuticle, she drapes the necklace around my shoulders, fiddling with its catch as the banging grows louder.

"A memento, to remember me by," she says. "Keep it close to your heart and I'll always be with you."

She takes the vial in hand and brings it to her lips, sealing it with a kiss before tucking it beneath my blouse.

"Look at me, baby," she says, gripping my cheeks. "Listen to me very carefully. There are things I never told you, things about your father… I wanted to keep you safe, do you understand? I managed to keep you away from him all these years. I didn't want you to be drawn into the Order's world, but there is no escaping it now. They will imprison me, and claim you as their own."

"My father?" I say, in disbelief. She never speaks of him. She gets angry with me when I ask about him.

"He's an important man, a powerful man of the Order," she says. "The ruler of Renato house. You will live well under his care, but he will try and mould you into a facsimile of him. Don't let him."

"I thought the Order was evil?"

"They are, which is why you have to take everything that matters to you, everything that you are, everything you love, and lock it away deep inside yourself. Put it in a box, in a chest, and throw away the key. Hide it away so they can't hurt you with it. Then one day, you can return to me… Promise me."

I give a terse nod, chin wobbling.

"As long as you keep hold of this tear-catcher, you can find yourself again when the time is right. Even if they take your name from you, your Spirit will lead you back to it."

I hear raised voices, chased by heavy, pounding footsteps. I throw myself at her, wrapping my arms around her like a buoy. Her tears drip on my skin, bleeding her feelings into mine.

The pain of losing a child… My tears pierce like needles.

I am mourning myself.

We sink down to the floor, holding our last embrace. We remain frozen that way, like a tragic statue in a lonely chapel, listening to splintering wood and smashing glass.

"Mama," I whisper.

The memory was already fading, bleaching into oblivion.

She told me not to forget myself, as if she knew what was to come.

She told me I could find myself again, even if all seemed lost.

Now the all-too-familiar scene of the room in which I was shattered emerged, a new memory forming.

Here are the velvet drapes, the white marble floor, the burning hearth, the balcony, my half-empty suitcase on the bed.

The mirror is already cracked, and I'm lying on the floor.

I can't move... I can't speak.

The time is 10.05 p.m., according to the clock in the courtyard.

I blink heavily, sensing myself losing consciousness before I feel myself rising, floating up like a balloon. I look down upon my own broken body on the floor, to which I am attached by a thin, silvery thread.

I watch as my right pupil bursts, spilling into the iris.

I'm still wearing the necklace my mother gave me.

A figure appears in the doorway, crying out in alarm. They run over to my body, trying to wake me.

"Ruby! Ruby!"

It's Ruben Renato, dressed in red formal attire.

And outside, it's snowing.

Removing his gloves, Ruben lays his bare hands on my upper chest near my collarbone, murmuring unintelligibly. He's using some form of the Renato Method, taking those thin, fiery threads into his hands and weaving them together, like a cat's cradle.

As he chants, reviving me, my chest begins to glow.

The five shattered pieces of my soul rise up into the air, orbs of light in five different colours: red, black, silver, white and gold.

The Spark goes first, its rosy burning fire drifting down like a single ember, settling into the ring. The silhouette of my Shadow disappears into the mirror. The haunting Song of my soul retreats into the music box. My soul's Heart shines round and full, captured by the heart-shaped box hidden beneath the bed: white with a red velvet ribbon. Finally, my Spirit turns to vapour, seeping into the tear-catcher necklace.

Ruben sweeps these objects into a sackcloth bag as the memory stutters to a close.

"Mark for copy," said Doctor Millefleur.

Heart hammering, I tried to fit these new pieces in with the old, to make a whole picture. Ruben had saved my life. It was him who'd forged my shattered soul into reliquaries. He had sent the music box to Birdie, and given the ring to his mother.

And yet. My mother had hidden me from him for years, warned me about him. She told me I'd lose my name and forget myself ... that one day I'd be hunting my true identity.

And here I was.

Every time I felt myself drawn in one direction, something came out of the blue to yank me back in the opposite.

"Summon the Chancellor," said Doctor Millefleur to her assistant.

The guards began unfastening my cuffs.

As they walked me out of the room, my gaze caught on a photo. A happy family portrait, framed on the desk.

Doctor Millefleur, her husband, a little boy – and a teenage girl.

The girl had pale, wavy hair with a pearly smile that shone brightly, demanding your attention. Graceful in her white dress, bangles on her wrist, just like in the memory I'd seen. Identical, in fact.

Lily.

"Is that your daughter?" I said.

"I don't see that it's any of your business, but yes." She gave a haughty sniff. "She's in her final year at the Academy," she added, as if she couldn't help but boast.

Before I could ask any more questions, the guards tugged me on, back to my cell.

Lily was alive. Lily Millefleur, of House Memoria, was alive.

All of my jealousy paled in comparison to the idea of being able to bring Evander some peace. I had to find him and tell him, even if that meant me losing everything. It was the least I owed him.

I tried to pry myself from their grip, twisting around to interrogate the interrogator, but one guard sparked me with a baton. Losing all the strength in my arms and legs, I lost consciousness, plummeting deep inside myself again. I sunk to the bottom of the dark sea inside me, where I slept dreamlessly.

Hours later, I awoke to the sound of keys in the lock.

Three guards appeared, all holding batons.

"Stand up," they said. "It's time for your trial."

"*Trial*?" I said, fighting against them as they dragged me to my feet and out the door. "What trial?"

They marched me still half-asleep through the endless web of cells. I didn't fight. I was wet-palmed and weak-kneed, fading to grey. There was barely anything left in me to try.

A sea of faces watched me through iron bars, blankly observing. One was familiar…

"Octavia!"

I called out her name, my voice broke.

She stared at me without expression, without attachment.

It wasn't that she didn't recognize me. She just seemed entirely indifferent to my existence.

"I just want you to know," I shouted, as they hauled me on, "you were the first and best friend I ever had."

A flicker of something unnameable passed over her face before the guards pulled me out of sight.

18.

THE TRIAL

Penned into a windowless cell, I was left in darkness for what felt like centuries. At long last, a red light on the wall was illuminated, accompanied by a grinding noise. A window of light appeared as a door slid open, revealing a large amphitheatre-like space. I'd never been here before but I knew what it was. The Auditorium, where criminal trials were held.

It looked like a giant theatre, with me centre-stage.

Every seat in the upper circle was filled. As I came into view, the murmurs of an expectant crowd grew louder.

"Step forward, prisoner 509431," came a voice.

Taking a deep breath, I slowly ascended the stairs. The symphony of whispers drowned out my heartbeat. When I reached the top step, I found myself standing at the dock in a court. The door closed behind me. A metal bar slid out, holding me in place.

Around the oval room sat the audience: members of the Order who served as the court's jurors. They held paddles engraved with the word Justice on one side and Mercy on the other. Divided into five sections, the gallery was filled with the representatives of the five Houses, with the Chancellor in the very middle, gazing at me coldly.

Bile rose in my throat as I stared at him. He had held the staff that shattered me. I couldn't prove it, but I knew it was true. I sensed it. His lips curled into a hollow smile.

But then I saw Evander by his side, and all of my anger washed away, putting out whatever fire still burned in me. He was dressed all in black, as at the Burning Eve ball, his hair slicked back. He was wearing no glasses, which gave him a sterner, more severe appearance.

He glared at me with absolute revulsion.

At once, he was a stranger again.

Five judges lined the long table at the rear of the floor, in robes of gold, red, black, white and silver, with matching white wigs. A gavel rapped impatiently as the black-robed judge pulled out a lengthy scroll.

"Prisoner 509431, you are accused by the Order of Providence of the following crimes," he said, his voice amplified by a loudspeaker.

On the wall behind him was a giant eye in a circle. Its pupil was a shiny, round, black bevel-cut circle, reflecting the courtroom.

"Treason, insurrection, illegal psychometry, attempted murder, assault, theft, grievous bodily harm, breaking into a government building, arson, blackmail, intimidation, public indecency, selling and receiving stolen property, impersonating a federal employee, sharing state secrets, resisting arrest and twelve other misdemeanours we'll summarize as 'miscellaneous'. For the record of the court, do you plead guilty or not guilty?"

People were gasping, fanning themselves as they stared at me with revulsion, like a cockroach they planned to stamp on. I was shivering, though the room wasn't cold. I looked to Evander, screaming "help me" with my eyes, but he looked away mechanically.

"Not guilty," I said, my voice echoing.

Several people in the audience shouted out in disbelief.

"Let us begin with the psychometric evaluation," said the judge in black, his voice monotonous.

The dock slid open as two ushers shepherded me down the steps, and into the centre of the court. Ears ringing, I stood in front of the giant eye. Its shiny black pupil began to buzz as it caught me in its sights. A spotlight burst forth, passing straight through me to form a peephole vignette on the curved viewing screen behind me.

Here was my incomplete soul, a glowing ball of fire and shadows.

My Shadow didn't mirror me as it was supposed to. Instead it silently raged and roared, clutching at her hair and clothes. The Song played off-key. The Spark raged like an inferno.

Horror rippled across the faces of the audience. I crossed my hands over my chest, colouring shamefully, but it did nothing to stop the projections.

The egg-headed doctor now took a seat in the witness

box, ready to testify to my great depravity.

"Doctor Stanford, can you please give your assessment of the accused's psychograph?" asked the judge.

"Of course, your honour. The unsymmetrical Shadow, as we can see, suggests that the subject will tend towards crime and vice. She is paranoid and cynical with a negative self-image, making her a potential danger to society. The subject has no Spirit, possibly as the result of a failed attempt to wipe her own memory ahead of being apprehended. Such practices are common in criminal circles."

"That's not true," I yelled.

"Do not speak unless you are spoken to," said the judge in black, banging his gavel, "or I shall add contempt of court to your charges."

"The Song is dissonant," the doctor continued, "an indicator of abnormal behaviour or an unsavoury character. She has a very obstinate personality, as you can see. This is someone who won't be bound by social norms and, as such, shows potential for depravity."

I opened my mouth but shut it again at a look from the judge.

"Of most concern is the total lack of a Heart," said the doctor. "Subject shows no emotion. She is incapable of human attachment. The subject entirely lacks temperance and poise. Such a person will struggle to curtail their anger or inhibit their compulsions, for the Spark is burning out of control."

I dug my fingernails so deep into the skin of my palms,

they left an arc of little crescent-shaped marks.

"In my opinion, the accused is incapable of reformation," said the doctor. "She poses a clear and immediate danger to our society."

As the gallery murmured, Doctor Millefleur took his place, her eyes catching on me only for a moment. I glanced at Evander to see whether he had registered her, but he stared ahead blankly, as if he wasn't really in there.

Doctor Millefleur pulled out a manila envelope, spreading several small glass slides beneath a magnifying lamp. When she wound its handle, a bulb projected the image on the viewing screen.

"Your honours, I present the following evidence."

The slide revealed a capture of my face running from the Golden Gavel. The girl in the first picture was unmistakably me, with a distinctive keyhole spill in my right eye and curly red hair.

The doctor lifted a pointer. "Let us begin with the theft of the Renato ring," she said.

I gasped along with the rest of the gallery as my former mistress was led into the courtroom in shackles.

"Countess," I breathed, palms slick with sweat.

Her gaze met mine but she didn't appear to recognize me. Her eyes were sunken, her bones protruding painfully through her translucent skin, as if she was half-starving.

"Countess Cavendish is unable to give direct testimony due to poor health, but we have retrieved the memory of the accused bringing the stolen item to Cavendish House."

It played on the wall, projected by the black shiny eye.

My own words echoed back at me:

You trusted me to steal your precious treasure, didn't you? When have I ever failed you before? That's the real deal right there. Straight from the hand of Lady Renato herself. You'll be reading all about it in the papers tomorrow, trust me.

The crowd burbled.

"I'd next like to summon Lady Rubella Renato," said the doctor.

My grandmother was wheeled into the witness box by the nurse I'd hoodwinked. Her expression was blank, just like the Countess's.

"Can you identify the person who stole the ring from you?" asked the judge in black robes. "Are they here in this courtroom?"

"Yes," she said mechanically, pointing at me.

"Lady Rubella identifies the assailant."

Listeners were recording everything, sitting at banks before small gramophones.

"Can you also identify the person who broke into Renato House on the evening of November 3rd?"

Lady Rubella pointed at me again.

"Do you have anything to add, Mrs Radley?" asked the judge of the nurse I knew as Doris.

"The accused persuaded me to leave my lady by telling me a pregnant woman was in danger," she said. "Whoever could do such a thing?"

The parade of witnesses was never-ending, from the

moustachioed Inspector I'd hit with a lantern to the Observer I'd pushed over a balcony and the cadet I'd thrown from the roof, who wore a sling and received sympathetic glances. Each one testified to my cruelty and depravity.

Doctor Millefleur played a series of selective memories showing me intruding in the Observatory, though conveniently none of them showed my accomplice, who was sitting across from me in this very room.

Instead of watching the slides, I watched Evander. No expression crossed his face. He seemed ... Hollow.

"We have proven that the accused stole the Renato ring," said Doctor Millefleur, "but the question is – why? She received no payment for the ring and stole nothing from the Observatory. So what did she have to gain?"

Her eyes glittered as she surveyed the gallery, as though on the precipice of a great and terrible revelation.

"I present to you that the accused is in fact Ruby Renato, the illegitimate daughter of Ruben Renato."

Someone in the gallery fainted.

Doctor Millefleur displayed the memories she'd made copies of. Every single sordid moment played out in the amphitheatre for all to see, including Ruben instructing me to get close to Oliver.

I tried to catch his eye but he refused to look at me.

My soul cried out for him, and it was unheard.

The courtroom erupted in cries of horror, with jurors taking to their feet and waving their fists.

"Order!" yelled the judge in silver. "We must have Order!"

"Lord Renato was also caught in possession of an incriminating remnant," said Doctor Millefleur, gesturing for an usher to step forth. He carried the heart-shaped box on a red velvet cushion. "From this evidence, we retrieved the following memory."

The eye-shaped peephole appeared again, revealing my room at Renato House, its mirror un-shattered.

The cordate box sat on my desk. When the door opened, I quickly folded away a letter, replacing the cover and stashing it beneath the bed.

Ruben Renato entered.

"Tonight is the night," he said.

"Tonight?" I said.

He was wearing the same red robes as when he'd revived me.

"You did what was needed, and so have I."

He held up a small brooch, made of shiny black jet.

The Chancellor's face was reflected in its facets.

At this point, the memory appeared to skip ahead a few seconds, cutting off whatever Ruben was about to say.

"This is all we need to take down House Obscura, to incapacitate the Chancellor in full view of the rest of the court. Everything is in place."

"What about Oliver?" I said.

"If he fights, if he tries to defend his father, you must do whatever it takes to ensure he isn't capable of taking his place."

His expression hardened.

"It is up to you how you do that."

"And what if he doesn't fight?" I said.

"He will," he said. *"His father is all he has left."*

The room erupted again. I watched Evander as he watched past-me, the pain of my betrayal barely registering on his face. The Chancellor leaned closer to him and whispered something. Evander nodded, impassively.

The judge made a winding motion with his hand, and the memory show ceased. The uproar of the gallery faded away to a worried whimper.

"We assert that Ruby Renato did, along with her father Ruben, plot to destabilize the Order and seize power through illegal means by manipulating Chancellor Obscura's son Oliver," said Doctor Millefleur. "Through this ruse, Miss Renato was able to gain access to classified information. She and Ruben intended to reveal that information to the Order's enemies, risking our national security in an act of treason. But their plan failed. We can confirm that Ruben Renato is currently incarcerated. His trial will be held in three weeks' time."

The gallery broke into pandemonium.

"Do you have anything to say for yourself, Miss Renato?" asked the black-robed judge.

I cleared my throat as the hubbub died down. It was so quiet you could hear a pin drop. I focused on Evander, as the rest of the Auditorium faded away. There were many things I wanted to tell him, like "I'm sorry" and "I cared for you, I think," but there was only one thing he needed to know.

"Don't trust the Chancellor," I said quickly. "Lily is still alive. He killed your mother. There was a memory in that brooch. *Your* memory—"

One of the guards struck me with a baton and I immediately lost my voice, clutching uselessly at my throat.

"I think that's enough, don't you?" said the judge.

"The accused and her father conspired to commit a capital crime, a fact to which we have provided ample evidence," said Doctor Millefleur. "Your honours, I rest my case."

The head judge nodded.

There was no defence.

"Let us first take a public vote," he said. "Members of the gallery, please give your verdicts."

The jurors conferred, murmuring softly. One by one, every last paddle turned to Justice as the roar of the mob rang in my ears.

"Death to the traitor!" someone yelled.

"Long live the Order!" cried someone else.

The judge and his fellows exchanged a curt nod before he banged his gavel.

"We have deliberated and, in this case, we unanimously agree with the court of public opinion. Ruby Renato, you are guilty as charged."

I wanted to protest, to scream and swear, but I was still mute. The Chancellor smiled at me as he rose to leave the Auditorium. Evander merely looked bored, as if there was somewhere else he'd rather be. Anywhere, maybe.

"Sadly, not every soul can be saved," said the judge.

Later, barely conscious in my cell, a new memory played in the dark theatre of my mind.

Fireworks explode in the sky as Oliver kisses me, making me forget what I came here to say, lighting up the banks of white snow all around us. Bright, glittering gunpowder flowers bloom and fizzle out.

It's the Night That Never Was, and we are dancing our last dance.

As music plays, we waltz slowly in the bandstand, surrounded by ornaments and candles and … snow globes.

Each one captures our last moments of happiness.

"It's our song," says Oliver softly, as the band plays the first notes of "The Haunted Heart". I don't know where I end and he begins. His feelings are my feelings. His memories are my memories.

I want this moment to last for ever, and yet…

I look up at the clock tower, watching as time runs out. 9.38 p.m.. The reveal is planned for 9.40 p.m.. In two minutes, Ruben will broadcast the memory of Nadia's murder to the court. I have to warn Oliver. I have to prepare him for what's to come.

I touch his face, no barrier between us. His soul plunges deep into mine, swimming through the seas of me. I lead him down into the lower chamber of my soul, to the locked chest I keep deep inside me, the one where I keep all of my darkest secrets, just like my mother taught me.

I know never to let anyone get so close as to open it.

I know never to give anyone the key to my Heart, but my Heart is working against me now. Willingly, I open it … and he sees everything.

The recollections of my betrayal move slowly through his psyche, showing my vow to destroy him, to use him, to manipulate him for my own intent, leaving no conversation unrecited. Oliver breaks apart from me, ending our dance. His face is taut with shock, hard for me to read.

The night grows colder, snowy flurries gusting.

"Please, let me explain," I say, reaching out for him.

His nose starts to bleed, speckling the white ground.

Blood drops on snow.

"I have to warn my father."

He tears away, down the bandstand steps, and I follow.

"Oliver, wait!" I call. "Please, I can't let you do that."

"All this time I thought our relationship was real, but it was just another fantasy," he says. "Another delusion in my mind."

"You're wrong. It started out pretend, but then it became real."

He barges through the stained glass doors, entering the Basilica as I shadow him.

"Please," I say, tugging his sleeve. "I need you to listen."

"How can I believe you now?"

He begins pushing through the crowd, searching for his father. The Chancellor is seated on stage as people queue to present him with gifts. I look for my own father, but he's nowhere to be seen, probably already on his way to our arranged meeting place.

"Why would you want to protect the Chancellor?" I say, catching up to Oliver. "After everything he's done to you? Stop. Let the truth come out, and let him be judged for it."

He pulls up, uncertainly. Outside, fireworks continue to blaze.

"You've been repressing the memory of her death for so long that you can't remember any more," I say, in a low voice, "but you saw him do it. I saw it in your mind. I made a copy of it. My father has it in his possession."

Oliver shakes his head.

"How could you do that to me? Steal my memory?"

"I did it to save you, not to destroy you. Please Oliver, you have to trust me. This is the only way for us all to be free."

"Is that what Ruben told you?" he says. "You're a fool if you believe him. Do you really think the world will be different with him in charge of it? He wants power, nothing more. They're all the same, and you're no different."

"That's not true. I'm not like them. You know me, Oliver. You know my soul, and I know yours. Let me show you, let me—"

"No. My father told me not to trust you. He was right about that."

My eyes sting bitterly.

"I can't let you warn him, Oliver. I can't let you do it."

He blinks at me, slowly.

"Is that a threat?"

I look to the clock overhead. 9.39 p.m.

"I have to stop you," I say.

"Go on then," he said. "Do your worst."

We stare at each other expectantly, standing in the middle of the ballroom as the people watch on curiously, our voices lost under the music.

"If you tell him, he'll kill me," I say.

He doesn't respond, staring at the ground.

"Maybe you're right. Maybe I can't trust Ruben, but your father is much worse, and you know it. Let's run away together. Just you and me. The Chancellor and Ruben and the Order, let's leave it all behind. We can start over. We can go somewhere else, and be someone new there. No one will know us."

"How can I believe a word you say now?" he says. "You were so convincing. I never even doubted you."

"Please. Go pack, get anything you can't live without, before it's too late. I'll do the same. Meet me at Renato House, in fifteen minutes."

"I can't do that."

"Yes, you can. You will. Just be there. If I ever meant anything to you, you'll be there."

He looks at me, completely torn.

"I love you, Oliver," I say.

"Liar," he says, in a voice that isn't his.

"I'm telling the truth. I swear to you."

His eyes are black voids. His nose is bleeding heavily, drawing the attention of the crowd. Someone gasps.

"I can't trust you any more, Lily," he says.

He quickly flees, disappearing into the darkness that surrounds the dance floor as everyone continues to stare at me.

The fireworks are getting brighter and louder, causing all of the world to flare and shake as the revelation explodes inside me.

As the hands of the clock tick into place, I make my escape.

Lily.

The girl he's still in love with.

The girl he's been mourning…

It's me. It's been me all along.

I awoke with a start.

Somehow, I was back in the Reformatory, tied to a chair in a large empty room with no windows. The Chancellor stood opposite, backed by a line of Inspectors with batons.

"Did you know that the name Renato refers to reincarnation and rebirth?" he said, coolly. "That's why their House animal is a phoenix."

A lean man. His robes had tall, sharp shoulders. He held himself rigidly, gazing at me through those creepy shaded goggles.

"Certainly, you have been born again … from the ashes."

He wore many different rings on his fingers, each with dark stones, like eyes that glinted at me evilly.

"Lily Elizabeth Duffy," he said. "Only daughter of

Ruben Renato, ruler of the fifth house, and Mara Duffy, a lowly servant.'

Lily Duffy. I was Lily Duffy.

It felt right. It fit.

"Your mother tried to raise you outside the Order, outside of Ruben's control. When he learned of your existence, he wanted to claim you as his own. He tracked you down and put you to work – and changed your name, of course. He was ashamed of where he'd laid."

He made a scolding, tutting noise.

"But I saw Lily, in Oliver's memories," I said, thinking aloud. "She looked like Doctor Millefleur's daughter. I saw her picture."

The Chancellor twitched, in irritation.

"After the unfortunate incident, I attempted to have all memory of you removed from his mind. Oliver underwent the procedure in Doctor Millefleur's office. But like a stubborn bloodstain, I couldn't scrub you out. His Shadow tried to preserve you, so that he might remember you again one day. His mind replaced you with the face he was looking at during the procedure. The doctor's daughter, Amelia Millefleur. He already knew her, you see. I tried to arrange a marriage between the two of them, to secure the waning loyalty of House Memoria. Unfortunately, they were never quite enamoured of each other. The false memory corrupted. The mind is a fragile thing. Too much meddling and it begins to degrade. Oliver hasn't been right since his mother's tragic death."

"Her murder, you mean," I said. "I know you killed her. You killed Nadia. She wanted to leave, and take Oliver too. She said no to you, and you don't like that, do you?"

The Chancellor was smiling, as if amused.

"No, I don't," he said.

I was afraid, then. Really afraid. Any desire I had to learn the truth faded away. All I wanted now was to escape.

He moved closer, his fingers gripping the staff.

"How amusing, that you're only now remembering the very thing you sought to destroy me with. Your father had been planning it for some time, hadn't he? His little picture show at the Basilica? Embarrassing that I didn't see it coming. My right-hand man, who I trusted implicitly, undermining us from within. He'd gone to considerable lengths to prepare. He'd taken years over this. He tracked you down, his illegitimate, discarded daughter with tactile gifts, all so you might work as a honey trap for my son, who was already so vulnerable. My greatest weakness. Ruben waited patiently while you gradually wore Oliver down, until you could take advantage of him. And, with the great and good of the Order gathered in one place, Ruben broadcast the memory you stole from my son's mind at the ball on the night of December 24th."

I wriggled against my shadowy restraints but they were too tight, cutting into the skin.

"I admit, I was surprised. Taken off guard. Ruben had established a network of spies, all plotting together to bring me down that night. Most of them I identified afterwards, and eventually they led me to him. I imprisoned him. But I had to work hard to undo his little exposé. I had to remove the night entirely from the memory of everyone in attendance."

The Night That Never Was … that was why all the remnants from that night were wiped clean, why no one could recall what happened.

"You had only just been announced to the courts. Without this night, most people forgot that you existed at all. You were *supposed* to be dead. But somehow, you survived. When I realized you were alive, I knew you would recover that memory eventually. That you would return to destroy me. I had to do everything in my power to stop that from happening. And here we are."

He took a step closer and I recoiled as far as I could.

"Where is he? Where's Evander?" I said.

"Who?" he said, holding one hand to his ear as if his hearing was failing. "I don't know an Evander." He was in his element, tormenting me.

"Oliver," I said, between clamped teeth.

"Oh, Oliver. Would you like to speak to him? Oliver, please join us, won't you?"

A figure emerged from the shadows, his face free of feeling, walking slowly to join his father, his hands clasped behind his back.

"Evander?" I whispered. "Oliver?"

He glanced at me with the same disinterest he had shown at my trial. "It's no good," the Chancellor said. "He won't speak to you."

"What did you do to him?" I said.

He laughed, a joyless sound. "*Me*? I did nothing, Lily. This was all you. Your lies destroyed him. If not for you, he might've been happy. His soul might not be tarnished. But you made him do something terrible."

"What?" I said, the words barely audible. "What did he do."

The Chancellor regarded me coldly. "Don't you remember? After all, you were there too."

On the wall behind him, another memory flickered to life.

I pace back and forth before the balcony in my room, tugging anxiously on the Renato ring as I stare out at the Basilica. Sirens can be heard in the distance as five bright beams of light shoot up in the air.

It's too late to change my mind now. The deed is done.

I look at the clock on the tower across the square. 9.59 p.m. My father has exposed the truth. And Oliver isn't here.

He isn't coming.

Pulling a sheet of paper from the desk drawer, I sit down to write him a letter, something to leave behind to explain my feelings, but the only words that come to mind are: *Forgive me.*

It's no good. Words don't suffice. I stare at the letter a moment before tossing it into the fire, watching as its sentiments burned away.

Maybe it was better to say nothing.

I need to pack. I need to flee. I can't risk sticking around for the fallout, not now Oliver's memories will help condemn me.

But how can I leave without him?

What's the point in being free if Oliver isn't with me? And what will happen, if I leave him behind?

I meant it, when I said I loved him. It crept up on me, like a shadow. I can't remember when it began, when it stopped being make-believe. That first time I danced with him, maybe.

There's something raw about him, something flawed yet brilliant that cuts through the mindless fog, the meaningless drudge. He makes it all seem sharper somehow, in focus, in key.

I'm meant to be at the quarry outside the Fifth Borough. I'm meant to be meeting Ruben and his followers as planned, poised to seize the city in chaos, but now I start to question everything.

Does he really have my best intentions in mind? Is this really the right way to honour my mother?

What am I doing?

Every second I let pass me by is a weapon ready to strike.

The shadows near the door deepen. My masked attacker manifests out of nothing, swinging the staff in its strange, five-pointed shape.

In a chaotic spray of broken glass, I am shattered again,

as the dark beam shoots out of the staff.

Slowly, my attacker removes his mask.

Oliver Obscura stands over me.

The memory faded.

"No," I choked.

"Oliver was the one who shattered you," said the Chancellor. "I am just the one who covered it up. How does it feel, to know the truth at last? If you had a Heart, I'm sure it would break."

I stared into Evander's stoic face, desperate for a sign that this wasn't true, but I found nothing. I saw nothing.

"I don't believe you," I said, vehemently shaking my head. "You can create illusions. You can make people see things that aren't really there, make them believe things that aren't really true."

"I've shown you the truth, yet still you deny it," said the Chancellor. "Stubborn as ever, I see, even at your own expense."

"It's not real," I said, eyes welling.

"Why are you so surprised? What did you expect, Lily? You and Ruben plotted against him. When he learned the truth, he was betrayed. It broke him. He lost control of himself, just like I always knew he would."

He clicked his fingers. "Tell them, son."

"It's true," said Evander, in a monotonous voice. "I did

it. Like I told you. You should've listened to me."

Horror rolled over me again and again, like I was being repeatedly run over by a series of trains.

"I don't believe you. I don't believe you."

My chanted denials echoed loudly in the bare room.

"Whatever romance you thought you had together, it was a fantasy, and it's over now," said the Chancellor.

My throat was thick with hurt.

"Evander!" I screamed, trying to get through. He was still Evander to me, even now. "Tell him it's not true. Tell me it's not true!"

"Son, why don't you encourage our guest here to keep quiet?"

With a sharp twist of his head, Evander turned to me.

"Don't do this," I said. "You don't have to do this."

The darkness in his eyes floated free of his body, hanging between us until it bled into me. I could feel it, so soft and so cold at the same time, like a welcoming death. I could feel the tendrils of shadow clutching at my soul, wrapping tighter and tighter. A terrible chill wormed deep into my bones, giving me a haunted feeling. I would never again know love, or happiness. I would die all alone in a grave without a name...

"That's enough," said the Chancellor. Evander loosened his grip and stepped aside.

I gave a dry sob.

"I always knew that you were dangerous," said the Chancellor. "A common-born girl like you had no business

322

rubbing shoulders with the nobility. Once it was only members of the five families who possessed extrasensory gifts, ancestors of the hallowed founders who unlocked the secrets of psychometry, but now the unwashed masses have developed their own powers. Too much … *cross-breeding*. I vowed to stamp it out. Yet there you were, an estranged love child, the daughter of a servant, with the ability to channel psyche by touch, invited into the heart of the courts. Your appearance risked muddying the purity of the five Houses, which was already in disrepute."

He was ranting, his face reddening.

"And then you and Oliver became … *friends*, if you can call it that. I wasn't sure what game you were playing – but I tried my best to keep you apart, sending him out on trips, filling his days with mindless tasks, distracting him with Amelia Millefleur. It didn't work. I sensed that you were concealing something. I tapped into his Shadow to spy on you, watching you through his eyes. I saw your confession and learned of your deception, allowing me to halt Ruben's plot just in time. I was able to lock the doors at the Basilica, keeping in the guests. I used the oblivion machine from the Reformatory to wipe the memory of every person in the room. Every object. There were crumbs, of course. A window, broken as someone tried to escape. A lost shoe in the stampede. A missing fork. But nothing so incriminating it could reveal the truth. Perhaps I should thank you. If not for your honesty, it might have been too late. Only the beginning of the memory was seen. I was able to erase the events of that evening from all who attended, but it was too late for me to stop Oliver from getting revenge. Poor Oliver. Such a shame."

My skin puckered, hairs standing on end.

"If only he'd obliterated you completely. Instead, he made a mess of it as usual and came running to me for help."

The Chancellor forced images into my head.

Screaming, banging on a dark door.

My head was telling me it was true, but my heart disagreed.

"I had to cover his tracks. But when I arrived at Renato House, your body was gone. You were not quite deceased, as I believed. I had my two most trusted men search for you, but they could not track your psyche. I had your belongings destroyed. The room was refurbished. I tracked down everyone who remembered you and made sure they forgot you, one way or another. I found your father and had him imprisoned, in the dungeons of Obscura House. His wife met an unfortunate hunting accident. His entire household was replaced. All that was left of the Renatos was an old woman with one foot already in the grave. We wiped her mind and kept her alive for appearance's sake. I started to think you might have done the sensible thing and vanished, back to the squalor and obscurity you came from. But then one day, there you were, stealing back your own house ring."

The ring. The moment I'd put it on, I'd sent a sign to them, a message that said, "I'm alive".

"Your soul had not been destroyed, as I intended, but displaced. As long as these reliquaries existed, those vessels of your soul's pieces, your memory left a residue in the subconscious of anyone who'd ever known you, beneath the surface but not entirely out of sight. I won't make that mistake again."

Again? As I intended? Without realizing it, he'd given himself away.

"It was you," I said, my mouth twisting. "You shattered me. You wanted me dead and you used your own son to do it. You heard my confession. It was you who lost control that night."

"I suggest you cease speaking."

"Just like you did with his mother," I said.

The Chancellor's gaunt face tightened.

"You took over Oliver's Shadow. You controlled him, just like you're doing now. You let him believe he'd killed me."

"That's enough!"

"You're pathetic," I spat. "If you can't make someone do what you want, you have to control them. But people still remember. They always will. At least my father knew that. At least he tried—"

The mask slipped. His Shadow grew enormous, looming over me.

"Your father," he sneered. "Your father who locked up your own mother and threw away the key?"

I stared at him, not understanding.

"My mother is dead," I said.

He laughed again, that same hollow sound.

"It was convenient for Ruben, for you to believe that. I'm sure it fuelled your hatred, your desire for revenge. Ruben didn't want her turning up and making a scene, trying to get you back and messing with his schemes. She's been languishing in the Reformatory this whole time. It was him who had her arrested for defecting from the Order, all so he could recruit you for his rebellion plot. He knew you'd have his gifts for tactile manipulation, combined with your mother's talent for encapsulating memories. But you failed. He failed. And as for your mother? Let's just say I've found a better purpose for her."

With that, he turned to go.

"What have you done with her?" I shouted at his retreating back.

He swivelled to face me.

"I will enjoy breaking you again, Lily," he said.

19.

LOST AND FOUND

I was returned to the Reformatory to await my sentence. All the days bled into one. In my dreams, I retraced my steps, visiting every place I'd found reliquaries. Despite all I'd learned, I still didn't know myself.

I was Lily Elizabeth Duffy, daughter of a servant. But I was also Ruby Renato, protégée of House Renato, insurgent, spy. And I was Iris Cavendish too, soulless street thief, dangerous fugitive.

I was too many people, and none.

I was tormented by recurring nightmares, Evander shattering me over and over again, each time causing my heart to restart in alarm before I woke up in cold sweat, my head empty and heavy at the same time.

I missed the button. I wanted my mother. I needed Evander, more than I'd ever needed anything or anyone. I needed him, and he was gone.

I dreamt.

Dragged back to the depths of unconsciousness, I fall through the darkness of the universe within and land in the middle of a familiar carnival, before a giant wheel with carts playing organ music. Oliver is standing next to me.

"I can't believe we're doing this," I say. "I'm going to be in so much trouble when Ruben finds out I'm missing."

"*You're* going to be in trouble? You've met the Chancellor, haven't you? That face he makes is just his regular expression. Imagine what he looks like when he's actually angry about something."

We turn together to face the fair.

"What shall we do first?" he says.

"Let's go eat candyfloss," I say, tugging him on. "Let's hit stuff with mallets and guess the weight of things."

We move through the carnival, spinning on the whirling waltzers as a carriage full of clowns rides by. We watch acrobats in the Big Top while eating popcorn and unsuccessfully attempt to win a goldfish by tossing rings. We ride the carousel horses, pretending to race each other.

"I can't believe I thought you were a bad boy when we first met," I say, giggling as he charges beside me on his pastel pony.

"Don't let the pink bows fool you. Lancelot here is a champion stallion," he replies, patting him fondly.

"Then why am I winning?"

We roar, charging, until the carousel winds down.

"Victory is mine!" I shout.

Climbing off, we wander through the crowds of

fair-goers, passing by an old-fashioned sweet stall.

"Mmm," I say, breathing in the delectable scent of chocolate.

One box is bigger than the rest – heart-shaped.

Evander hands a palm of coins to the seller, who gives me the box.

White. Red ribbon.

I recognize that box.

We depart the fairground for a nearby park, with swans gliding on a silvery lake, the same place where we'd met in dreams. As we sit beneath a tree, far away from the crowd, I open the box, eagerly unwrapping chocolates, laughing as I feed one to him.

"Mmm, caramel crush," he says, tracing one finger down my arm.

He kisses me, so I can taste the sweet caramel too, then wraps his arms around me from behind, making me feel safe. Loved. Little sparks dance through me, making every part of me catch fire, come alive.

"I wish we could stay here for ever," I say.

But the carnival darkens, its rides grinding to a halt. The revellers vanish, fading into the darkness.

I woke up shouting aloud again, reaching out for a love that was already gone.

The box. That was the reliquary containing my Heart.

I had identified the final piece, and yet it did me no good in here.

Wake. Sleep. Wake. Sleep. I cycled through both, until dreams and reality were indistinguishable. The shadows of my body bled into the shadows of the world, until I was nothing at all.

That's when I noticed something.

A thin, silvery thread, no thicker than a cobweb, was illuminated by an invisible source of light. Not a spark this time, but a string. It stretched out in front of me, leading into obscurity. Instinctively, I trailed it.

On the horizon, a small, stony room emerged. I floated into it, as if I were climbing into a painting. I was standing in my familiar monastic cell, but at the same time, I could see myself lying on the floor, fast asleep. I was beyond my body somehow.

There was my flesh and blood, breathing softly, and yet here I was, outside of myself. We were attached by that same silver string. Cautiously, I stuck out my arm in front of me, watching as it passed through the heavy door. I was a ghost, a spirit, but still living. With one giant step forwards, I moved into the hallway on the other side, which was lined with iron cell doors.

Two Inspectors walked towards me, obliviously. They glanced into my cell through the hatch, observing me lying there with my back to them before continuing on, not noticing 'me' at all.

Awed, I moved slowly through the Reformatory, spying

on the other inmates. There were thousands of kids in cages, some sobbing themselves to sleep or banging their heads against the wall.

I could hear a hundred voices echoing.

What if I never get out of here?

My parents will disown me.

I'm losing my mind.

Unseen, I floated further, out through the prison walls and into the streets of Providence, moving up and up, past Cavendish House, to the sky villa owned by Chancellor Obscura. The further I travelled, the tighter the silver thread became. I could only walk slowly, as if deep underwater.

Past the high walls, Obscura House was built of shiny black stone. There were a hundred eyes built into its façade, each with irises made of different coloured gemstones, but none of them spied me. I was invisible again. Inside, the building was gloomy, oppressive, its dark walls displaying various artefacts. The interior decoration was extremely ugly, from the grimacing serpentine statues to the tribal masks frozen mid-scream.

All of the windows were shuttered, drowning out the light.

Past a shrine to Evander's mother and a chilly dining room, I floated down the hall towards the black door at the bottom, the one with an eye-shaped peephole. On the other side was the Chancellor's study, its walls illuminated with scenes from the Eye network.

There was the heart-shaped box, locked inside a glass

and steel cage with a web of fiery energy to protect it. But that wasn't what I had come for.

Evander lay asleep upstairs in a room filled with glittering, expensive things. I floated over him like a phantom, watching his face. Closing my eyes, I allowed myself to sink into him, passing through his skin and into the Shadow that consumed him within. I plunged into him like the sea, drowning in his dark place as a wave pulled me under.

Kicking my feet, I struggled upwards, breaking through the surface.

I floated alone in a stormy ocean, Evander's cloudy soul hanging high above me like the moon. Another giant wave arose, blocking out its light before it crashed down on me, dragging me into the depths below again.

I washed up on a black sand beach, with the black sea on the horizon. Everything was ridden with that same shadow rot. The birds were covered in oil. The trees were blackened and skeletal as if scorched by fire. The sky was full of dark matter smog.

Soaking wet and filthy, I walked on into the thorny woods that lined the beach, feeling my way through the darkness. The deeper I plunged into the haunted forest of Evander's soul, the worse I felt. It was cold and dark. There were no paths. The branches were needle-sharp, scratching my skin.

I saw the Chancellor's face everywhere: in the knot of a tree trunk, in the dark clouds above, in the reflection of the water, in the rocks that sprang up from the ground, forming a spiky mountain.

The climb was steep and unforgiving, but I was determined.

As I scrambled upwards, small stones broke free, skittering down the slope. I kept losing my footing. Wet with sweat, my chest tight, I climbed until my muscles burned and every footstep was like walking on coals. By the time I reached the fortress that sat atop the mountain, I was dirty and bloodied, covered in scrapes and bruises.

The fortress appeared impenetrable, guarded by a dozen different walls and fences, some spiked, some brick, some electrified.

This was Evander's last stand.

I roamed the perimeter, looking for a way in. On the southern-facing side of the building, a single black door was left open. The shipyard around it was abandoned, full of wrecks. I slipped inside, trying not to breathe or think or make a sound, afraid of what might stir.

I made my way through the dark labyrinth within, as dense and unfathomable as the World's End. Its walls were decorated with dioramas, frozen moments in time, displayed behind glass like exhibits at a museum.

In one, I saw his father strike him. In others, I saw the indiscretions of his misspent youth. One of the dioramas depicted our first dance, at the Burning Eve ball. Another depicted our last dance at the Basilica, just moments before our worlds broke apart, like a giant version of the snow globe. One of the final dioramas showed him facing off to the Chancellor as his father's dark shadows poured down his nose and throat. The Chancellor was holding the twisted staff and blank white mask.

It was that Night That Never Was, moments before I was shattered.

In the next diorama, Oliver Obscura was crying, frozen in the act of banging on his father's door. It was much later, past midnight according to the grandfather clock on the wall.

As I paused in front of it, the memory began to play.

"Father!" he shouted. "Open up. Please. I need help."

The door slowly opened, revealing the Chancellor. "I'm busy. What do you want?"

"It's Lily. I think I did something terrible," said Oliver. "I can't remember doing it. I can't remember anything. I woke up and I was there, in her room, standing over her... And she was ... she was..."

He started to sob, covering his face with his hands.

The Chancellor pretended to look surprised, ushering him inside.

"Whatever you did, I will make it go away, as always," he said. "That is just what a father does for his son."

But as Oliver passed by, the Chancellor gave a small satisfied smile.

Beyond, another, smaller diorama was displayed in a cove in the wall. It wasn't as formative as the others, but it was still there: Evander and I dancing at Birdie's party. The night he confused me for Lily. Had a part of him still loved me, even when he thought I was the wrong girl?

I climbed stairs, so many stairs I lost count, trudging slowly towards the glowing vignette in the distance. As I drew near, it turned into a room. It was the living room of Obscura House, with those god-awful statues and masks.

Oliver was a little boy, five years old, looking up at his parents as they fought.

"We're leaving, and you can't stop us," said Nadia.

"You will do no such thing."

The Chancellor's eyes darkened, his Shadow metamorphosing.

"I would rather kill you than let you walk away," he said, pinning her against a wall.

"Papa, no! Stop!" cried Oliver, pulling at him. "Don't hurt her!"

A maid watched from the doorway, half-hidden in darkness, her face warped by fear.

The Chancellor's Shadow came to life, chasing Nadia down when she broke free. There was a struggle, the Shadow pushing her over the balcony. Nadia plunged to the ground as Oliver screamed.

The scene went dark, like the end of an act, before playing again.

That was when I saw him.

The real Evander.

He and his Shadow were trapped together in a cell, like those at the Reformatory, but this one was his own mind's creation.

I shouted his name, but he didn't move. Forced to watch his mother's murder over and over, he was unaware of my presence, guarded by the Chancellor's Shadow: a black-eyed double of his father, with black veins beneath the skin. When it saw me coming, it smiled evilly.

"I killed you once. I can do it again."

Screaming, the Shadow Chancellor broke apart, spreading across the walls, taking the form of a thousand dark birds, like a murder of crows. The flock swooped and dived, forming a tornado of wings that circled, attacking me.

"Oliver, it's Lily! You didn't kill me," I shouted.

The flying shadows zipped past, screaming and whistling like runaway fireworks, knocking me from side to side.

"I'm Lily, and I'm still alive! It was your father who shattered me that night, not you. He was controlling you. I saw the memory."

The shadow beasts were scratching at me with their rose-thorn claws and biting me with viper-sharp fangs. They were tearing at my hair and skin, ripping away layers until there was hardly anything left of me.

Struggling forward, holding my arms crossed and raised up over my face, I got close enough to the cage that Evander noticed me. He looked at me wide-eyed, not moving, while his Shadow stood up to greet me, clutching the bars of the cage.

"Remember the button?" I said.

Evander merely frowned.

"I'm Lily," I said, firmly. "I'm alive. You didn't hurt me. Your memories are all mixed up, that's all."

The dark birds swarmed around us, drowning out the light.

"Don't give up. That's what they want. That's what *he* wants."

He shook his head.

"It's too late," he said.

I felt something burning hot in my chest. I looked down to see that fiery soul, glowing through the skin.

Burning like I burned for him.

"Don't you want us to have another chance?" I said. "That can't be it for us. There has to be more to the story."

I watched my soul ignite. As its light fell upon one of the shadow birds, the darkness disintegrated, burning up into dust that dissipated. Soul fire streaked through the dark army like a meteorite, burning away shadow birds like sugar paper. The air was filled with the specks of their ashes, like a fine snow.

"Lily," he said, and this time it wasn't the wrong name.

I felt myself stirring, beginning to wake as the string tugged.

"We don't have much time," I said. "I need you to know you fought against him. Even though he was in control, you didn't want to hurt me. That's why you didn't kill me like you were meant to. My soul was just temporarily shattered, instead of permanently broken."

He was fading. I couldn't hold on any longer.

"Ruben is imprisoned in the dungeons of Obscura House," I said. "Mr Sharma told me to find him. The Heart of my soul is in your father's study. It's in the chocolate box. Remember?"

I transmitted the scene of us sitting beneath the tree. I showed him the cordate box in his father's study.

"I know you can find it," I said. "I know you can find me, because I found you. We found each other, even after everything."

As he reached for me, I was ripped away, dragged back to the waking world against my will.

"Save me," I cried. "Like I saved you."

Flying backwards through the darkness of the waking world, I landed back into my own body.

Bolting upright, I clutched at my chest.

My heart was pounding, my blood throbbing.

Time ran thin.

20.

OBLIVION

At dawn, the Chancellor's guards came for me. They dragged me down a dark, windowless corridor, deep underground. The ceiling was low, a tangle of bare cables. Letters and numbers were stencilled on the walls next to plain grey doors. The lights flickered as we passed. The hall stretched on for ever. It felt as if the walls were squeezing in, making it hard to draw a full breath. We moved through a series of silver gates, each set thicker than the last, until we reached a dark doorway that made me shiver.

There was something in there. It pulsed and hummed, making my heart skip a beat. I didn't want to go inside. I didn't know why but that room was more terrifying than anything I'd ever known or imagined. I tried to shrink away but the guards grabbed my arms, walking me forward as I squirmed.

They threw me on the floor, a jumble of limbs, locking the door behind them. I scrambled up, crying and clawing at the lock until a noise behind me drew my attention. Turning to face the dark room, I saw an observation panel that ran horizontally along the back wall. A long window of tinted glass.

A panel of white coats sat behind it, including Doctor Millefleur and Doctor Stanford. There were bright lights in each corner of the ceiling, blinking on and off, and in the centre of the room … a void. It floated unnaturally mid-air, like a piece of reality was missing.

Suddenly, I knew. This was the oblivion room. This was where you went to be purified.

As I looked into the void, I found that I could not look away. I was frozen in place by it, like the light of a magic lantern. A tingling sensation passed through me in a wave, from the tips of my toes to the top of my scalp, before a thick heavy, numbing fog settled in. It filled my mind, dulling my senses.

I could hear the voice of Doctor Millefleur echoing distantly, telling me that when I woke up, I wouldn't remember any of this. I wouldn't remember anything, not even myself.

A deafening surging noise started up as the void vibrated. I felt a brief flash of hot blind panic as I started sliding away, bit by bit, fading into oblivion. Crying out, I tried to hold on to myself. The feel of my mother's hand on my forehead as she nursed me through a fever. My father's wrinkly-eyed look of pride as I first descended the stairs of the Basilica as Ruby Renato. Octavia's crushing embrace, our faces in the mirror. Evander and I close together on the attic steps as he wished me sweet oblivion. Evander at my door as I held up the button. Dancing the burning dance with Evander as he created scenery for me to appreciate.

Evander. Evander. Evander.

I would not forget.

I *refused* to forget.

These images slipped through my fingers like grains of sand. I was falling, I could feel it.

An alarm began to sound.

Lights flashed on and off.

"Stop!" came a voice. "Stop!"

A grinding noise sounded, vibrating my bones. The void flickered and vanished. Shaking, barely able to stand, I spun around to see the Chancellor standing in the doorway. The doctors hurriedly exited their observation panel, rushing out to greet him.

"Evacuate the building," said the Chancellor. "Security breach."

"What about the prisoner?" said Doctor Millefleur.

"Bring her here, now."

The white coats hauled me over to him. "Come," he said. "I'm not letting *you* out of my sight."

I followed him, too dazed to protest, along the corridor where the cells were. "Open the cells," he demanded, of the nearest man on guard.

"What? But we're not supposed to—"

The Chancellor's Shadow jutted out like a snakehead, grasping the man around the neck.

"Do you want to read in the papers tomorrow about how the Order left thousands of people to die? *Open. Them.*"

Hands shaking, the guard obliged, unlocking the first door.

"And the rest. Quickly. Get them outside."

Wardens continued to open cell doors behind us, creating a swell of manacled prisoners who were funnelled towards the prison yard. At his urging, I followed the Chancellor instead. We turned down one darkened corridor, then another and another, as I became increasingly confused and afraid.

Distant booms echoed.

The corridor opened out into a large pentagonal hall, where the rest of the Reformatory staff had gathered.

"Chancellor Obscura?" said one man. "Bloody hell. What are—"

"Get everyone outside, now."

The guard nodded mechanically, eyes wide. Two men raised the inner gate and ushered us out.

The Reformatory was blazing, flames jumping and spitting and licking every surface. The roar of a growing inferno ricocheted in my ears, cracking and popping as it claimed its kindling.

The freed prisoners swelled into the yard as the Keepers of the Keys were pushed back, crushed against the gates. Nearby, the Chancellor nodded at two guards in black armour, their breastplates engraved with eyes. Standing next to them were Octavia and Rani, still manacled. Octavia stared at me vacantly.

"What the hell is going on?" said Rani.

Everyone was shouting, screaming, creating a chaotic cacophony.

"Free them," the Chancellor ordered, of his guards.

Without question, they unclipped our manacles.

"This way." He pushed me towards the front gates, his two Obscura guards following behind with Octavia and Rani.

Maybe we could take the chance to make a break for it. I looked urgently for a way out as we neared the gates, but the Chancellor was sure to keep me close, in his sight.

A loud explosion sounded, sending a shockwave through the air and knocking people off their feet. The haze that obscured Octavia's eyes faded, causing her to gasp as if breaking the surface after a long time underwater.

"Someone blew up the oblivion machine!" came a cry.

Several people began cheering as prisoners regained the memories taken from them at the Reformatory, calling out the names of forgotten friends.

"Iris?" said Octavia, in disbelief. "Is that really you?"

"It's me," I said, taking her hands. "Sort of."

A siren began to blare. Always the sirens.

"I said keep moving," said the Chancellor through gritted teeth, pushing me towards the gates. He was beginning to sweat.

Something wasn't right.

On the other side of the prison yard, a man caught my eye. A bedraggled-looking fellow with an overgrown beard, dressed as a guard.

I recognized him with a heart-stopping jolt.

Ruben Renato.

As I watched, he raised his hand. Beside me, the Chancellor raised his hand in response.

That didn't make sense at all.

When the Chancellor looked back at me, the features of another bled through the skin, revealing the face I knew and cherished.

"Evander," I whispered.

I wasn't the only one who noticed. One of the white coats pointed and cried out, "That's not the Chancellor!"

A dozen more heads turned to see Oliver Obscura in the place of his father. I sensed a split second of hesitation amongst the guards, uncertain whether to seize him or not.

In that brief moment, a web of fiery energy streaked out from Ruben's hands like lightning. It snapped in bolts, striking the Keepers and reducing them to a pile of slightly-smoking bodies.

"Now!" he roared.

A group of prisoners rushed forwards, stealing the keys.

Among them, I recognized Ash and the Countess, along with some of the other survivors of the Sanctuary battle and the attack on the World's End. With a thundering roar, the gates burst open, allowing the masses to flee the burning Reformatory, storming out into the streets.

Evander grabbed my hand, I grabbed Octavia's and she took Rani's. We ran, past the moat where a horse-drawn carriage waited, and he bundled us inside. I turned to see Gus and Perpetua emerge from behind the mirages of the Chancellor's guards. Perpetua took the reins and Gus scrambled up beside her. We took off at speed, looking around at each other with delight and disbelief.

"Where are we going?" I said.

"Ruben told me a place to meet," said Evander. "The quarry."

Just like on the Night That Never Was.

History was repeating itself.

"Why didn't he just come with us?" I said.

"He said he needed to make contact with an old friend of his."

I stared at him, memorizing his face. He looked drawn, dark circles under his eyes. The strain of keeping up false appearances had drained him, but he didn't bleed.

I wondered if he remembered it as I did, that moment in our minds and the words he'd said to me.

"How did you ... what did you..." I tried.

Evander produced the heart-shaped box. White with a red velvet ribbon, it was decorated with roses and cherubs and lovebirds.

My pulse quickened, palms clammy.

"My Heart," I said. "You found it."

He pulled out the Chancellor's eye pendant to show me, hidden beneath his dark shirt.

"I found the box in his study, like you said, along with this. I used it to cast his image and entered the Reformatory as him."

"Where is he now?"

"Hopefully still unconscious. I used my Shadow to knock him out. I knew I'd need as much time as possible if I was going to rescue your father, alert the Renato guards, locate Gus and Perpetua and break you out."

There was a twinkle in his eye that hadn't been there before, a spark of confidence.

"Ruben was in Obscura House all this time?" I said.

"For almost a year, in an oubliette in the dungeon. No door. No windows. Just a single hatch in the ceiling," said Evander. "A year he spent in darkness, plotting how to bring down my father. It was his idea to blow up the oblivion machine. He thought the prisoners recovering their memories might incite a riot." As a dozen Order wagons peeled past us in the opposite direction, sirens blazing, he added: "Looks like he was right."

My father was alive. He was free. He was on his way to meet me. I didn't know how I felt about that. Mixed feelings churned within.

Evander nodded at the chocolate box.

"Go on then," he said. "No time to waste."

Everyone waited with bated breath as I placed both hands on it. I closed my eyes, waiting … waiting…

"Nothing is happening," I said.

"Maybe you need to open it," said Evander.

Dramatically, I pulled off the lid. Inside, a single heart-shaped chocolate was left behind, wrapped in golden foil. I rolled it around in my hand, but I didn't feel the answering pull of my soul, calling me to it.

"I think I have to eat it," I said.

"You're serious?" said Evander. "They're a year old."

"I put the ring on my finger. I looked into the mirror. I heard the song of the music box. I think I need to taste this."

Unwrapping the aged chocolate, with a mysterious white bloom, I popped it in my mouth, letting its sugary taste cover my tongue. It had a sweet, salty filling, slightly sour from age, which gave me a strong, festive feeling, warming my mouth. It tasted like … caramel.

As I swallowed, letting the melted chocolate drop down my throat, I followed it, plummeting inside myself. My stomach somersaulted, like the sensation you get when you almost fall backwards in a chair.

As I tumbled through the dark, I saw the light of my soul glowing red and cordate, growing big and fat and tough and pliable. I felt full. I was happy. I was sad. I was frightened. I was confused. I was homesick and grieving and heartbroken and vengeful, and with every passing second, I grew more into myself. The feelings became stronger, almost too strong to bear, the force of them threatening to tear me apart limb from limb. Was it normal, to feel this intensely? It felt dangerous, somehow. Like I might not survive it.

Since I first put on the ring, I thought I'd been feeling things, that I was alive. But reunited with my Heart, those pale, faint impressions faded away. They were insignificant, incomparable to the strong surging waves and plumes I felt now, crashing and erupting inside.

Losing control, I let the feelings of my past romance wash over me as I tumbled through a series of vignettes.

Catching Oliver's eye across a crowded ballroom, my heart leaping even as I whispered plots with Ruben. A secret letter, folded up and hidden inside a copy of the Renato Method, full of intimate confessions. *"I need you." "I want you." "I think of only you when I'm alone in my bed."* A stolen kiss in an alcove at the Basilica. Laughing in the garden. Dancing in the bandstand. Running through the rain. Swimming in the lake at night, when everyone else was in bed.

In my mind, I saw him stroking my hair, falling asleep in my lap, his fingertips tracing my skin as he lay across from me beneath the covers, dark hair in his eyes. A wave of pleasure washed over me.

Coming back to reality and the darkness of the stolen carriage, I found myself gazing into Evander's eyes as my entire body flushed.

In the darkness, we listened to the symphony of sirens, reaching their deafening crescendo.

"You're her," said Evander. "You're Lily. Of course you are."

"Lily Elizabeth Duffy," I said. "That's me."

I liked the way it rolled off my tongue.

"Is that what you want to be called now?" he said.

"Yes," I said, nodding. "It feels right. It feels like my name. What about you? Are you Evander now, or Oliver?"

"I don't know," he said. "I honestly don't know."

My newly-found Heart stuck in my throat.

Maybe it was too late for us. For Iris and Evander, or Oliver and Lily, or whoever we were now. We could never again be what we were then.

When he thought of Lily, did he still see that blonde, smiling girl that wasn't me?

Something wet and itchy tickled my cheek. Suddenly, tears spilled from my eyes in hot, salty waterfalls, before I could stop them.

"Oh!" I said, surprised.

First one, then two, then a flood that pooled under my eyes and in the ridge above my nose.

"It's OK," said Octavia, moving to put her arm around me. "It must be overwhelming, getting your Heart back all at once."

I laughed self-consciously. "This is embarrassing," I said. I could hardly make the moment any more awkward if I tried.

"It's just us," said Evander. "We're not going to judge you."

He wiped one tear from my cheek with his thumb before falling back, his expression soft and open. An explosion of feeling reverberated inside me. Fireworks in my soul. My hand twitched, my fingers drawn to touch his hand, his face... The urge to kiss him was so strong it pained me, making my chest hard with hurt. But I pushed it away.

I slowed my breathing, filling my lungs as I steadied myself.

I had to focus on the task at hand.

"If you're done with romantic reunion, we have revolution to organize," said Perpetua, dryly.

PART
FIVE
THE SPIRIT

21.

FAMILY REUNION

Our stolen carriage pulled up at the disused quarry on the outskirts of the city, surrounded by ghostly shipyards and factory silos. I looked around nervously for Eyes or guards who might sound the alarm, but there wasn't another soul in sight. What a strange place for a family reunion.

Evander had brought a bundle of clothes from the laundry room in Obscura House. We took turns dressing in the carriage, swapping our prison jumpsuits for civilian outfits. I changed quickly, pulling on the black cape of a house servant and fastening its eye-shaped button catch with trembling fingers, before walking to the edge of the crumbling, dusty pit, watching alongside the others as dawn began to break in the distance.

From here, Providence sprawled below us, now aflame with a dozen tiny fires, spreading outwards from the Reformatory as flames jumped from building to building. Sirens wailed while shouts and breaking glass echoed softly, even at this distance. The Reformatory prisoners had dispersed through the streets, creating a dozen different crises for the Order to deal with.

"I can't believe we *broke out of prison*," said Octavia, giddily. "If we weren't fugitives before, we certainly are now."

"All the best people are," said Perpetua, staring stonily down at the burning city. "Consider it a badge of honour."

Nervously, I awaited my father. Had Ruben really locked my mother away? Or was the Chancellor lying, as he lied about everything?

The sound of horses galloping broke the anxious silence. Three carriages emerged from the smog, pulling up in front of the quarry.

"Everyone, stand by," said Evander, positioning himself in front of me protectively.

We watched together as a figure stepped out of the first carriage.

Ruben.

He was surrounded by a group of uneasy-looking Renato guards in red armour with fiery breastplates. Servants of the Reformatory, and of Renato House, they must have flocked to him once Evander had set him free. From another carriage, Lord Cordata appeared. Behind him emerged the survivors of the Reformatory break out, including Ash.

They held back, allowing my father to greet me alone.

"My darling Ruby," he said.

Up close, his face was more familiar than I expected: the wrinkles by his eyes; the smile lines on either side of his mouth; the crook of his nose, once-broken; the rich, hearty boom of his voice.

He gripped my arms, looking me over.

"It is a great relief to see you so well, my jewel. My Ruby."

He was the first person who remembered me, right away.

"It's Lily," I said, lifting my chin. "I just want to be Lily now. The name my mother gave me."

He narrowed his eyes slightly before nodding.

"I need to know what happened the night you saved me," I said. "I remember only fragments. I'm trying to piece them together, but…"

I trailed off, looking at him imploringly.

"Where to begin?" he said, laughing warmly. He put his arm around me, walking us out of earshot of the others. I squirmed, uncomfortable. "That night at the ball, I revealed the repressed memory you took from Oliver's subconscious as planned. I'd stowed it in a brooch that once belonged to Nadia Obscura herself. Its connection to her made it the perfect receptacle. You had performed your duty just as I'd asked, taking the memory from Oliver's head. You were the perfect weapon. I needed someone to infiltrate his social circle and become his confidante. It had to be someone trustworthy, someone gifted, someone desirable to a troubled teenage boy. You worked hard to retrieve it, using intimacy to exploit his vulnerabilities. As I recall, you stole the memory away as he slept beside you."

I looked away, ashamed.

"The Basilica is equipped with magic lanterns, used to broadcast scenes of the Order's many triumphs." Ruben seemed to drip with contempt, as if he didn't think them triumphs at all. "My friend over there set the brooch before one of the lanterns," he explained, gesturing at Lord Cordata, "ready to play automatically at the end of the gift-giving ceremony, at 9.40 p.m. precisely. I made myself absent. I knew the Chancellor would quickly connect me to the crime. Meanwhile, I went to find you here – our prearranged meeting point."

He gestured at the jagged rocks surrounding us and I shuddered, feeling the echo of that night tugging at my soul.

How different things would be if I'd made it here in one piece.

"I showed everyone the truth. I exposed Nadia's murder. Everyone who is everyone was there that night. That part went exactly as we planned. But the Chancellor wiped the evidence of his crime from history, and it was all in vain," he said.

He looked over my shoulder at Evander, standing behind me.

"We planned to rally the other Houses now they'd seen the truth, and finally convince them to help us usurp the Chancellor, but you were not here waiting. I went back to search for you but it was too late. I found you shattered, in your room at our House."

His face was gaunt, his expression harrowed.

"A servant told me she'd seen a masked Observer entering your room. It was clear we'd been discovered. I knew I had little time, so I used the Renato method to guide the five parts of your soul into objects I found nearby, objects you treasured. I used my gift to conceal them from sight. I hoped that there might be a way to put you back together later."

"And you were right," I said. "I reassembled myself."

He looked proud, though whether of me or himself I wasn't sure.

"Inspectors were nearing Renato House. I knew the Chancellor had identified me as the culprit, and that I needed to scatter your belongings. I begged the servant to take you as far as she could. I gave her the music box too, hastily parcelled up with instructions to post it to Birdie. I enchanted the parcel so that none but you could open it. I left the mirror behind in the chaos, but I managed to give the ring to my mother, hoping you would be drawn back to Renato House to reclaim it. I knew you'd only need your Spark to light the way and find the others. I had just enough time to slip the ring on to her finger. When the Chancellor seized me, he took the possessions I had on my person, including the chocolate box, with that necklace you always wore inside it. I watched carefully as he filed my belongings for examination, not knowing he held your soul in his hands. Those that looked harmless were sent to his study and the rest to his vault. His men caught up with the servant but she'd already left you somewhere, to the mercy of the back streets. You were lost, but you were alive, even if the pieces of your soul were scattered around Providence."

"The Spirit is the last piece I'm missing – my mother's

necklace," I said. "I have to find it."

A strange look came over his face, a fleeting sheepishness or guilt that quickly passed.

"And so we will," he said. "I never forgot you. The Chancellor didn't wipe you from my mind, as he did everyone else's. He wanted me to remember what my actions had cost me. He told me you were dead but I knew otherwise. I sensed you still. I waited for you to build yourself whole again, so that you might come for me, so we might finish what we started. Imagine my surprise when his son came to my aid, the same boy I'd bid you to destroy. Now *he* was saving me. It was destiny, telling us now is the time to try again, this time with him on our side."

I wanted to ask about my mother, to confront him with the story as told by the Chancellor, but I was frightened to hear the answers. He seemed to sense the question coming and diverted it.

"I know I did wrong by you," said Ruben, taking my hands in his.

I realized that he could feel my feelings. His gift was my gift.

"I'm glad to have this second chance to make things right with you," he said. "I hope you can come to forgive me some day. But now, we must rebuild our society piece by piece. We must work together to achieve great things. We must lay down our weapons and build bridges. Will you help me?"

"I wouldn't be here otherwise, would I?" I said, slowly.

"Good."

"What about him?" I said, inclining my head towards Lord Cordata, who watched the rebels uneasily.

"Lord Cordata was integral to our plan on the Night That Never Was. He stayed behind to plant the brooch, but he fled as soon as the memory began to play. He knew to expect it. He alone escaped from the room with his memory intact. He did not see the murder play out, unfortunately, but he can testify that the night was wiped from the minds of the courts."

Lord Cordata was the creator of the fork's memory, I realized. He would've been sitting with all the other nobles that night.

"He and his House will stand with us. I have promised he will be second in command when the New Order dawns."

"And who will be first?" I said, though I already knew the answer.

"Me, of course."

I gave him a sceptical look.

"Who else?" he said. "Oliver is hardly prepared for the role. Someone must lead. Let it be someone who understands how to rule a country."

He tentatively kissed the top of my head before he turned, almost bumping into Evander, standing behind us.

"Ah, Oliver!" said Ruben, taken aback by his closeness.

Evander didn't correct him.

"I hope we can put the past behind us, too," he said. "Not my finest moment, using you to get to your father, but we do what we have to when faced with the impossible."

"Consider it old news," said Evander. Despite their amicable words, I sensed a crackle of tension, an unspoken mutual distrust, simmering cold and slow, just beneath the surface.

"There is still much for us to discuss but we have a bigger purpose." Ruben looked around at the others, raising his voice importantly. "Tomorrow we will announce the dawn of a new generation, with a promise to reform our institutions and restore justice. Tristan Obscura is irrevocably corrupt. His soul cannot be saved. His wickedness destroyed everything the Order was supposed to stand for. Once he's removed, I will be announced as Chancellor. There will be peace. Prosperity. Providence will finally become the city it's supposed to be, with me at its helm."

Ruben's confident gaze met mine and I nodded, slowly, ignoring the growing doubt I felt inside.

"Tonight, there will be a ball held at the Basilica of All Souls," he said. "This will be our chance to overthrow the Chancellor."

"They're throwing a party while city burns?" said Perpetua.

"Chancellor Obscura wouldn't have it any other way," said Ruben. "He can't risk giving the impression that he's losing control. That was why he's been using a simulacrum of me to give the impression I'm still loyal. That all ended with Ruby's trial, of course. Now, the rumour mill is in overdrive. People are already suspicious about what else is being kept from them."

"So what's the plan?" asked Ash, clearly ready to fight.

"The memory of Nadia Obscura's murder is hidden in a brooch that once belonged to her," said Ruben. "The Chancellor keeps it in his personal vault, beneath the Basilica."

"How are you so certain?" I said.

"He told me himself, on one of his visits to my cell. He sought to goad me, to remind me of my failures. He keeps all of his most precious and most dangerous treasures in the vault. We need to access that brooch and feed it into the Eye network, so that it will be broadcast on every spectacular across the city. This time, we won't just show the truth to the Order's inner circle, but all the world."

"Can't we just use my memory?" said Evander. "I've recovered it now. I could broadcast it directly. It would save us time."

"An extracted memory is more stable," said Ruben, "less suggestible to manipulation. We would risk your mind wandering, or the memory fading."

Something told me my father didn't trust him not to screw it up. From Evander's face, he was getting the same impression.

"We also need the necklace in the vault," Ruben went on. "Ruby's spirt is inside."

"Lily," I corrected.

"Right, Lily. She must be complete if she is to use her full power."

My full power? What did that mean?

"The Eye network is guarded by a dozen soldiers armed with psychometric weapons," said Evander. "How will we seize it?"

"Leave the guards to me," said Ruben. "Can you get us inside the building without being seen?"

I shot Evander another worried look, recalling the blood running down his face the last time he used his Shadow to turn mind to matter.

Octavia looked just as concerned as I felt.

"I can, but the Chancellor will immediately know our location," said Evander.

Ruben nodded. "Of course," he said calmly. "That's the idea."

A ripple of discontent moved through the group surrounding us. Ruben nodded to one of his subordinates, who quickly stepped forward.

"At the Basilica, we will split into two groups," she explained. "One group, led by Lord Renato, will proceed to the vault. The other, led by Lord Cordata, will access the building through the side entrance, creating a distraction that will draw the guards..."

My father gripped my arm, steering me to one side.

"Do you remember any of your training in the Renato Method?" he said. "I need you at full strength if we are to face the Chancellor."

"I've used my hands to render a couple of men unconscious," I said, with a smug smile. "I didn't really

362

know what I was doing, though."

"It's all still within you, I'm sure."

Ruben walked me through several key moves, including the splayed-finger palm shape and the neck pinch. I found that it returned to me easily, the knowledge I'd known all along. The moves were familiar, well-practised.

"By holding the index finger in your fist as so, you can create the psychometric impression of digits being severed. Highly useful if you need to torture someone for information."

"I shall keep that in mind," I said.

"And here, by grabbing the wrist like this and channelling the pulse, you can cause a person to seize up, as if turned to stone."

I mimicked him, copying the shape of his hand.

"Back when you were whole, your Spark was so powerful you were able to channel soulfire and direct it like a weapon, without even needing to make physical contact with your victim," he said. "It is an advanced art, a gift possessed by very few. Do you think you can still tap into that power, missing your Spirit?"

"I think so," I said, straightening my shoulders. "I'm still connected to it, right? I should be able to use the rest of my soul to channel it."

"Let us try. See if you can cause me pain without touching me."

We stood several feet apart, him braced for impact, me baring my palms in readiness of dealing blows.

"Go on," he encouraged.

I closed my eyes, listening to the crackle of the fire inside, letting its warmth spread through me, until my fingertips were tingling.

"Focus on the face of your intended victim, and imagine what sort of pain you'd like to inflict on them."

I thought about the boy in the red tunic I'd battled on the roof. I'd hurt him, but I couldn't remember how I'd done it exactly. I screwed up my face, tensing every muscle as I tried to project that same burning feeling. Cracking open one eye, I saw that Ruben stood calmly, comfortably, looking in no way like a man who was being roasted alive.

"Nothing?" I said.

"Not yet," he said. "Try again."

"I can do it," I reaffirmed. "I can."

Taking a deep breath, I attempted it a second time, pouring all of my intention into this single act. Again, Ruben remained unmoved.

"Never mind," he said, though he looked disappointed. "You must need to be complete to recover the full extent of your abilities. Don't worry. You're still highly useful to me without it."

I stared into my palms, silently cursing them. Hadn't I created a real fire before? Why couldn't I do it now? I sensed that power working through me but I couldn't get a handle on it. I couldn't control it.

As Ruben went to instruct the others, Evander joined me, standing at the edge of the world as we looked again upon the burning city.

My skin prickled at his closeness. I ached for him again, a nauseating blend of thrill and fear, joy and sorrow, but all of that I pushed down, out of mind, trying to focus on the seemingly unsurmountable task ahead of us.

"It's hard to believe we're really here, isn't it?" said Evander. "Just a few hours ago, I was back in my room at Obscura House, feeling nothing, seeing nothing, trapped in my mind, forced to watch my mother's murder over and over while my father directed my body." He turned to face me. "If you hadn't found me in the Shadow realm, I wouldn't have made it out."

His gaze was so penetrating, it left me dizzy. The world was spinning. I had to look away.

"I'm scared," I said, surprised by my own words. "Scared of getting captured, scared of being killed or of forgetting myself again. You only just broke us all out of the Reformatory and now we're going to take on the Chancellor? We must be mad."

"I'm scared too," said Evander. "I'm always scared, honestly."

He moved closer, reaching out before catching himself, second-guessing it. His hand fell.

"But I don't think we're ever going to have a better opportunity to remove the Chancellor from power," he added. "Now is our only chance."

My eyes pricked with tears. Ever since I got my Heart back, I could hardly keep them back.

"Do you trust him?" he said, tilting his head towards Ruben. I didn't answer for a while, struggling to stitch all those loose threads together.

"I think he lied to me about my mother. He said she was dead, that that was why we were doing what we were doing, but the Chancellor said Ruben had her imprisoned. Between the two of them, I don't know what to believe."

"I'm sorry, Lily," he said.

My heart fluttered. He had called me by my true name.

"Both of our mothers were stolen by the Order, and both of our fathers would rule it," I said, with a dry laugh. "Do you think my father will be a better Chancellor than yours?"

"It wouldn't be too hard."

We smiled at each other. Gallows humour. As every clock across the city began chiming to signal six o'clock, the end of curfew and the dawn of a new day, another round of sirens began.

"I'm sorry," I said. "For lying to you, tricking you. For everything."

He glanced at me daringly, as if afraid to look too close, or too long.

"I'm sorry too. Sorry I let my father take over me, sorry I let him rule my mind, as well as my life. I would never have willingly harmed you."

"I know," I said.

We fell silent, listening to the sirens.

"It might sound odd but, in a strange way, I'm glad all of this happened," he said.

"Really?" I said, disbelieving, amused.

"Maybe now we finally have a chance to be free."

He said free, but I heard "together".

I wanted to bridge the gap between us, but I didn't know how.

He was standing inches away from me but there may as well have been a giant abyss between us.

For a moment, I thought about taking the leap. My fingers twitched, stretching towards him again, until my father's voice interrupted us, calling us to come. It was time.

The distance ached.

22.

ALL SOULS

Our journey to the Basilica was a parade of chaos. As we rolled through the streets, they were thick with people. Prisoners and protestors, rebels and street rats. Everyone who was no one had been drawn out of the shadows, waiting for a sign that tonight was the night. The Inspectors were trying to corral them, trying to clear the roads, but there were too few of them, even with the help of some of the Chancellor's guards.

As we pulled up, I gazed out at the building I'd visited so many times in my memories, its golden cupola domes glimmering in the moonlight.

In the background, the Reformatory was still smoking.

Ruben had explained the vault to us, where he was sure my Spirit and the brooch would be kept. Now, we shivered and eyed the building.

"Only the Chancellor can access it without triggering alarms, so we're going to have to find our own way in," he reminded us.

"How?" I said.

"Being a fire soul has its advantages."

He flexed his hands aggressively.

The evening curfew announcement sounded, ringing loudly and causing the streets around us to clear. In my mind, I pictured Birdie teaching the House dances, lending us her dresses. She ought to be here. Mr Sharma too. Birdie's voice echoed from beyond the grave, stirring up all the fires inside me that told me to fight.

"The hour is upon us," said Ruben.

"Let's do this," said Ash, their grey eyes sparkling.

The group split up, with Octavia, Rani and the Renato guards accompanying my father, Evander and I to the vault, while Ash, Perpetua, Gus and the others entered through a door used by servants.

"We'll meet you in the upper chamber. That's where the heart of the Eye network is hidden," said Ruben.

"Let's hope we make it that far," said Perpetua.

I clasped her hand, just briefly.

We were a rag-tag group of Reformatory escapees and Sanctuary survivors, holding makeshift weapons, faces still dirty from fire soot.

What chance did we really stand against the all-mighty Order, I wondered, looking around at our army.

"Remember, you do not fight alone," said Ruben, turning to regard them and lifting his chin. "Tonight the streets are full of people the Order has hurt. They're angry. Many will be armed. More will join as the night progresses, and it becomes clear that the Order's hold is faltering. Tonight, we fight together. We are many, but we are of one soul. Uno sumus animo!"

"Uno sumus animo," some of them chanted back.

"What does that mean?" I whispered to Evander.

"We are of one soul," he said, his gaze lingering. "Are you ready?"

I watched the darkness in Evander's eyes take over him, pulling us into the basement of the building.

We emerged into a dark corridor, deep beneath the ground. Ruben walked with determination towards the gargantuan vault door beyond, its silver façade decorated with a hundred eyes. He gripped the iron bars that protected it, melting them easily in his hands, before turning his Spark on the revolving lock mechanism.

It made a grinding, squealing noise before a blaze of soulfire caused it to burst from its hinges. The door swung open, revealing the round, portal-shaped entrance into the Chancellor's private vault.

Immediately, an alarm began to sound.

I stumbled clumsily inside, as Ruben resealed the door behind us.

We gazed upon a vast cavern filled with treasures. From floor to ceiling, cabinets of vials were stacked, crammed into every available space, some of them covered in cobwebs. There were remnants here, too – reliquaries, maybe: a giant statue of a headless horse made of serpentine, a mirror so mottled I couldn't see my reflection in it, a chest of blackened silver and tarnished coins, an oil painting of the

Chancellor that looked as if it had been burned and melted. I grimaced, shivering.

As Evander and my father searched for the brooch, a strong and distinctive scent caught my nostrils, making me sniff. It wasn't the smoke, or the antiseptic smell of the vault. It was perfume.

It smelled familiar. Flaring my nostrils, I followed the strange sillage. My ears began to ring at high pitch, drowning out the sound of Octavia and Rani whispering fervently. My skin puckered, flushing hot and cold.

Something was calling to me. Something I knew, and loved.

I followed the flowery aroma, weaving around glass cabinets of vials towards a shelf of small silver security boxes. One of them gleamed unnaturally, shining brighter than the others. I fumbled for it, knocking it down. Something rolled around inside. The catch was stiff and rusty, difficult to shift, but with a jarring scream it flipped open.

I could see a handful of objects – Ruben Renato's identity card, presumably seized at the time of his arrest, a sheaf of papers, a pocket watch…

A single vial glinted at me. It was decorated with flowery filigree patterns, with a flower charm.

My mother's necklace.

With trembling hands, I reached in to retrieve it, reliving the scene in the attic when she had given it to me. It glowed faintly, with a pearlescent sheen. As my fingers found its hinged seal, it sprang open eagerly, releasing a flower-shaped cloud of essence into the air. Opening my lungs, I breathed it in, smelling its fragrance. It smelled like lavender and washing powder, like sugar and the sea. It smelled like cologne and old books, like freshly cut grass and the ground after it rains.

The world closed in, darkened like a vignette. Reality was slipping and sliding out of focus again. My legs buckled, and I toppled to the floor like a felled tree as the ground tilted beneath me. Evander called my name but I couldn't answer; I was falling deeper within myself, until the lights from my eyes were just two distant stars.

I fell into my memory. Not just my memory, but the memories of my entire family tree, stretching out like branches inside of me as their lives played out simultaneously, too many to keep track of.

The woman burned at the stake as a witch. The settler who sailed west for Newfoundland. The cunning man who treated victims of the plague. The actor. The carpenter. The gravedigger. The opera singer. I was every urchin and tourist, every noble and merchant, every salesman, every soldier, every pauper and preacher in the history of my genes.

I saw the women whose tears had been donated to the vial, passed down for generations, so their lives would not be forgotten.

And then, there she was.

My mother.

I remembered her dancing with me, tickling me, singing lullabies as she tucked me in at night. I remembered her wildflower gardens and her towers of books, her shyness and her sarcastic sense of humour. I remembered the sharp look she gave me when I said something daring, the waver in her voice as she begged me to be careful, the crow's feet that increased with every act of rebellion. I could hear the piano scales of her laughter. I could taste the charcoal of her cooking, for no matter the dish she always managed to cremate it…

Her loss pained me like nothing I'd ever experienced before, a vast gaping scream that tore at me with sharp teeth. I replayed the last time I'd seen her, ripped away by Inspectors, as the inner child within cried out for her like Oliver cried for his mother still.

Bit by bit, my vision cleared.

I was kneeling on the floor, slicked cold with sweat, the beating of my heart as loud as cannons firing.

I looked down at my chest. My soul was glowing, its five parts visible, illuminated by a power unknown and unseen. Its light cast reflections upon the faces of my friends, and my father.

The silhouettes of my Shadow waltzed around me, like

the dancing shadows of the snow globe. The spectres of my Spirit formed a protective circle. They showed me growing up, from a baby to a young adult. The melody of my Song played "The Haunted Heart" mixed with the burning dance, broadcast for all to hear. I held Evander's gaze as it echoed. The bittersweet taste of my Heart lingered like caramel. Finally, the golden embers of my Spark formed a ring of fire around me, streaming out like the solar jets of the Sun.

I was whole again.

I climbed to my feet, unsteady as a baby deer, as Evander offered me his arm for support. He looked at me differently, as if he finally recognized me. All of me.

"I…"

I couldn't finish my sentence, my throat closing up. That weight inside me had increased, that fullness, that life. I wanted to laugh. I wanted to cry. I wanted to sing and scream and dance and fight. The richness of Spirit filled my body from head to toe.

Evander crushed me in a hug, the kind of embrace that makes you feel completely held. I melted in his arms, losing myself, bleeding into him. After a long moment, he let go, holding me at arm's length.

"Well? How do you feel?" he said.

For the first time, the inside matched the outside.

I was in my right place, my right time.

"I feel … like me," I said, as a bubble of laughter rose up.

"Yes, congratulations, darling," said Ruben,

absent-mindedly, "but I have bad news. The brooch isn't here."

"It's not at Obscura House either," said Evander. "I emptied the safe before I escaped. The Chancellor must have it on his person."

"That complicates things," said Ruben.

"You'll just have to make do with my memory," said Evander.

I looped the tear-catcher over my head, letting it hang over my chest, in the place where my heart was, armouring myself for what was to come.

Ruben gestured to Evander.

"Let's get on with it, then," he said, sharply.

I watched as the Shadow enveloped Evander again, pulling us with him through the dark tear in the fabric of reality. I was afraid that it would kill him, but this time, at least, he seemed to withstand it without bleeding.

It brought us to the top of the Basilica, beneath those famous golden cupolas, where the heart of the Eye network was concealed. It was quiet in the stony corridor but the sounds of disorder bled in through the cracks in the old walls, drawing us to the balcony to look down on the scene below.

Outside, Providence was burning. The light of the Reformatory fire lit up smashed windows and the empty shells of shops looted by prison escapees, their debris scattered across streets lined with broken glass. On one corner, one of the spectaculars had been shattered, showing a fractured, corrupted picture of Evander and I, echoing a reward for information. The fires were growing, the city echoing with shouts … and song.

"It's time to rise up and shine a light,
We'll take our freedom back tonight…"

A group of street children ran past, waving a ragged flag and singing Birdie's resistance anthem. Beyond them, I saw a burning black wagon, with vagrants gathered around it, cheering riotously. A group of women had cornered a sole Inspector, stripping him of his uniform. A carriage full of nobles from House Cordata passed by, waving their gold handkerchiefs in support of the rebels. A woman in a habit passed out protest signs.

The incident at the Reformatory had been that tiny spark Ruben talked about, that single flame that turned a whole city to tinder. It wasn't just us any more. People had been waiting for this, their anger burning like fuel, keeping them alive so they'd be ready when the day came. Now all of that rage was pouring out at once, seizing Providence in a frenzied rebellion.

Anything was possible tonight.

From the balcony, I could see the steps of the Basilica below lined with Inspectors, standing in formation like a house of cards ready to be knocked down. Their batons crackled with soulfire, creating a live barricade. As a wave of have-a-go heroes surged the building, breaking through the barriers and snatching batons from the Inspectors' hands, Ruben led us on down the hall.

A group of guards waited in front of the chamber that protected the Eye network, one from every house. The Renato and Cordata guards laid down their batons when they saw Ruben, but the Memoria guard swung her lantern, streaming billowing grey smoke.

"Cover your face," Evander called, pulling up his shirt to conceal his nose and mouth.

"What is it?" I asked, copying.

"Redolence," he said. "If you breathe in its scent, you become lost in nostalgia."

Soul fire sparked from Ruben's hands, creating a web that electrified the Memoria guard, causing her to shriek in psychosomatic pain. Evander swiftly incapacitated the Obscura guard, while the Harmonia guard was persuaded to let us pass by a whisper from Octavia.

"Hurry! This way," said Ruben.

A loud droning alarm began to sound, even louder than before. I swung around, a terrible feeling sweeping over me. Sure enough, a ring of black portals swirled into existence all around me, trapping me as the others pushed on, unawares.

From each one stepped an Observer, and each held in their hand a familiar, glinting staff, like copies of the Chancellor himself.

As they raised their arms in sync, ready to shatter me a dozen times, something inside me came alive. My father's words echoed in my mind.

"When you were whole, your Spark was so powerful you were able to channel soulfire and direct it like a weapon."

I was angry. No, I was furious. At what had been done to me, and at what I had done. I despised the Chancellor. I hated the Order. I wanted the whole ugly system to burn to the ground.

Screaming, I allowed the soulfire to rise inside me, coursing through my veins and jetting out from my fingertips in streams, like a living, breathing volcano. Its force was so tremendous it almost threw me backwards, causing me to lose my footing slightly. The web of energy wrapped around my attackers, sparking and spitting and crackling as I imagined what sort of pain I wanted to inflict on them.

Involuntarily, I remembered the sensation of being shattered – of pieces of myself falling away as I struggled to hold on to the last memories of everything I had loved. It was the worst feeling I could recall.

Clutching at their chests, their faces twisted into silent screams, the Observers fell backwards into the black holes they'd appeared from, their portals vanishing along with them.

I pushed on, trying to catch up to the others. Through clouds of smoke, Evander emerged, his eyes black as oil as he disarmed two guards at once, sending them to sleep. When he saw me, the Shadow retreated immediately.

"There you are," he said.

We bumped into Octavia and Rani, fighting alongside

each other. More guards loomed out of the fog, but Evander and I felled them easily. Their armour clattered noisily as they hit the floor.

I stumbled over a huddled shape and found Perpetua, rocking back and forth as tears streaked down her face. She had succumbed to the redolence.

"Perpetua!" I yelled.

"Papa?" she said, her eyes clouded and out of focus. "Is that you?" I pulled her along with us but she was inconsolable with grief, as reality and illusion curdled together, like milk and orange juice.

Several yards on, we found Gus, curled up in a ball, clutching his stomach. I knelt down beside him. "Hurt bad," he groaned.

I wasn't sure if the injury was real, or remembered. "You have to get up," I said. "Just a little further, come on."

The redolence hit me too then, plunging me deeper into the nostalgic fog as my own memories overwhelmed me.

Mr Sharma, offering me his arm as we walked through the gardens. Birdie, cupping Evander's cheek as she spoke of Nadia. My mother, throwing me up in the air as I played with her necklace.

With some effort, I found that I was able to ignore them, focusing on the grim reality in front of me.

Ruben and I battled the guards side by side, father and daughter, gradually making our way along the corridor.

"Everyone OK?" I said, looking around.

The others nodded uncertainly, the delusions that

enchanted them rapidly fading. Torches gleamed on the walls, guiding us into a complex warren of stony catacombs. Layers of holes were connected by rickety scaffolding that stretched up towards the ceiling, like a giant honeycomb. The walls and floors were laid with the yellowed bony remains of departed souls, with teeth and skulls embedded into the cement.

Foreboding filled my veins.

Evander gripped my arm suddenly, holding me back.

"What?" I whispered, nerves on edge.

"There's a good chance we'll lose today, and an even greater chance that one of us won't make it," he said.

"I can always count on you for a rousing pep talk," I said.

"I'm not sure I'll get another chance to say this to you, and I don't want to die knowing I haven't."

"You're not going to die."

"Just in case … I need you to know… I… I…"

He frowned, struggling to find the words.

"Come on!" barked Ruben.

"Just wait a damn minute!" I yelled in frustration, before turning back to Evander. I could feel his heart pounding, throbbing, in time with mine.

"I still love you," he blurted out. "Lily, Iris, Ruby, whoever you are. I love you. All of you."

It took me completely by surprise.

"I still love you too," I said, a smile spreading across my face.

I reached for his hand, and he gave it to me. My emotions

bled into him, showing him how I felt, what I needed, what I wanted…

"Lily," he breathed.

I kissed him, softly and tentatively at first, remembering his lips and the feel of him, then harder, in case it really was the last time. It wasn't just a kiss, but a love letter. It told him everything I wanted to say to him without a single word uttering from my lips.

His kiss was his reply. I could sense all the parts of his soul in it. *Waltzing shadows. The sound of rain. The perfume of old books and the taste of vanilla…*

Being with him again was like rediscovering a precious treasure you thought was long lost. Something old, yet something new.

Ruben cleared his throat noisily. Octavia and Rani were grinning, their hands intertwined. Perpetua rolled her eyes.

"You can kiss and make up *after* we win," she said.

Breaking away from each other, our fingertips lingering, we walked on, reaching an enormous set of wooden doors, carved with the symbols of the five Houses of the Order.

The Eye. The Flower. The Harp. The Apple. The Torch.

"This is it," said Ruben. "On the other side of these doors is the Eye network. We must overpower the soldiers on guard so that Oliver here can broadcast his memory."

"Where are the others?" I said. "Shouldn't they be here by now?"

"They must've been held up," said Ruben. "We'll have to go on without them."

He turned to face the giant doors, producing a key.

"Lord Cordata was kind enough to give this to me. A skeleton key that opens every door in the Basilica. Including this one."

He slid it into the lock, operating its revolving mechanism. The doors creaked open, revealing the cavernous chamber on the other side. The room was full of Obscura soldiers in matte black armour, their breastplates engraved with eyes. They raised their weapons at us, standing in formation – each one equipped with a black baton that cast streams of shadow – but they didn't move towards us, nor us towards them.

On the raised platform beyond, five people were locked in gilded cages like birds, wearing hooded robes that shadowed their faces in the dim light. They were strapped to giant machines, titanic mountains of steel which generated energy, all five machines connected to the giant orb at the centre.

It rotated slowly, a mix of red, black, white, silver and gold.

The prisoners didn't sense our entrance, trapped in a strange catatonic state, twitching as if having a bad dream.

"What's wrong with them?" I said.

"Those the Order cannot purify are drained of their life force," said Ruben. "What did you think powers the Eye network?"

Mouth suddenly dry, I watched the life force slowly trickling from them in streams, feeding into the giant orb.

"But … they can't. They can't do that," I said, stupidly. I struggled to comprehend what I was seeing.

These frail bodies locked in cages were being used as the soul of the Order: its Shadow, its Spirit, its Song, its Heart, its Spark. Human lives fuelled the Eye network, so the Order could watch over us all.

Many more prisoners waited hopelessly in cages at the side of the room, ready to replace the five in cages when their life force was spent.

"They're creating Hollows!" said Octavia, her cries echoing.

My friends looked horrified, yet Ruben looked … calm.

"The Eye network is powered by souls?" I said. "You knew about this?"

"With great power, comes great sacrifice," he said. "Terrible, of course but what can we do? No one can hold on to the empire without the Eyes. It is a necessary evil."

I turned away from him to regard the wretched system in horror, trying to tune out the cries of the prisoners in the waiting cages. I needed to understand how it worked.

The giant orb connected the five cages, tethering the prisoners powering the system. It also created a mass of floating, eye-shaped portals, peepholes through the fabric of reality. These were the eyes of the Observatory, feeding images to the Observers to be captured as evidence. It fed the lanterns and spectaculars, broadcasting urgent messages.

In these brief, gleaming windows, I watched a group of

former Reformatory prisoners topple the steel tower of a Listening Post, while a troop of Memoria guards abandoned their posts. Outside, the fight went on.

The sound of a million inner voices emanated from the orb, talking in fast, jumbled streams, a hundred thousand minds echoing through the chamber. The Listening Posts across the city replayed their voices here, the orb acting as both a transmitter and a receiver.

This was the brain, the engine of the Order.

I jumped as a low rumble cut through the babble. The Chancellor emerged through a dark portal, standing high on a platform looking down on us as his soldiers stood to attention.

A familiar gleam caught my eye, making my fingertips tingle tellingly. I spied the black brooch pinned to his chest.

Everything I'd been through, everything I'd done, it had all been in pursuit of this one single memory. All I had to do now was play it to the world.

Ruben stepped forward.

"This ends today, Tristan," he said.

"Is this it?" said the Chancellor. He eyed us all. "A middle-aged lord, my train wreck of a son, a broken-souled thief, and a handful of petty criminals. The great resistance! Truly, I am terrified."

He raised his staff, and the Obscura guards stepped forwards in perfect synchronicity.

"You didn't really think it would be that easy, did you?"

They copied his movements, their eyes darkened by

his Shadow's control as they formed a human wall. Like a puppeteer, he pulled their invisible strings, controlling all of them at once.

When my father attempted to cast a web of fiery energy, a ring of swirling dark matter swiftly surrounded the Chancellor like an ouroboros, a circle of snaking darkness, sending out one lightning-fast tendril that whipped itself around Ruben in a flash.

My father writhed in its grip, his fire burning through the shadow, sending sparks towards the Chancellor.

"I never thought it would come to this, Ruben," said the Chancellor. "My old friend. And yet – we never did see eye to eye, did we? You never truly understood the importance of order."

"Order? Is that what you call this tyranny?" yelled my father, breaking through his bonds.

Ruben was smiling. He seemed to be enjoying this, on the cusp of claiming that power for himself.

"I should've killed you when I had the chance," the Chancellor said, "but I needed you alive to project your simulacrum. I thought it better to keep up the illusion of the five Houses being united."

"You kept me imprisoned for a year! But I could never forget my mission: to remove you from power and stop you from causing harm!"

As they continued to strike back and forth, Evander inched closer to the orb, reaching out one hand to touch it. I knew what he was doing. He was going to broadcast the memory himself while everyone else was distracted. I bit my lip, willing him on – he was so close…

With a casual flick of his hand, the Chancellor sent two guards to block his path. On the stony wall, I saw Evander's Shadow grow monstrous, rushing forward to greet them.

Looking back to Ruben and the Chancellor, I watched dark ropes wrap around my father's neck.

"From this day forward, there will be no Renato House," said the Chancellor. "I'll kill every last love child you ever sired. I'll salt the earth where you walked, so your seed can never breed. Your line is over."

I lunged forward but a guard grabbed hold of me, clasping on to my wrist so hard something popped. Pain seared through me like fiery needles. Tearing my hand away, I found his head, gripping his temples. I watched the light in his eyes die out before he fell to the floor. With a flicker of numb regret, I turned back to Ruben, now struggling against the dark mass as the Chancellor dominated him.

"What are you going to do about the people in the streets, Tristan?" my father rasped. "How are you going to bring order to Providence? Only a new leader can bring peace. You know that as well as I do."

"And that new leader will be you, I presume?" said the Chancellor. "Too bad dead men can't lead."

With a grunt and a violent thrust of his staff, the shadows punctured my father's chest.

I witnessed the precise moment the light left his soul.

His eyes met mine one final time.

"Ruby," he croaked.

I felt the life inside him snuffed out, shivering uncontrollably. The shadows released their hold, and he slumped to the floor with a weighty thud.

I screamed dully as Obscura guards surrounded his body, dragging him away, the hollow sound bouncing off the walls.

I may not have been certain of his virtue. He might not have been the best leader, or even the best father … but he had saved me. He had made me. He had got me this far.

"Who's next?" said the Chancellor.

His shadow serpents amassed, surrounding Rani, pouring down her nose, her throat.

Shoving past the guards, Evander ran towards the Chancellor. His Shadow sprang ahead, tackling his father, breaking his concentration. Rani fell to the ground, released from his hold, but she didn't get up.

The Chancellor's Shadow began to wrestle with Evander's as their true selves stood on either side of the room, unlaboured.

"You've improved, son," said the Chancellor. "I'm impressed."

"I learned from the best," said Evander, huskily.

"Yes, you could have been a great asset," said the Chancellor, watching keenly as Evander's Shadow parried a blow. "It's such a shame you had to take after your mother. Both of you were nothing but a disappointment, an embarrassment. I should have picked a better wife, and bred a better child."

A portal swirled into existence behind Evander, pulling him into it. For a second, he disappeared, vanishing into thin air as his father looked around in confusion. Immediately, another portal slowly whirled into being behind the Chancellor. With a furious roar, Evander emerged from the darkness, tackling his father from behind.

He first attempted to snatch the brooch from his chest. When this didn't work, he tunnelled into his father's psyche, taking control of him.

The Chancellor stiffened, moving slowly, unnaturally. Evander was the puppeteer now, walking his father's body over to the giant orb. Gritting his teeth in concentration, he forced the Chancellor to touch it with his own hand, causing the orb to turn black.

The Shadow Chancellor was cast enormous on the wall. A skeletal winged figure with sinewy limbs, its flesh rotten, bones exposed, dripping blood from a decomposing, fly-infested mouth. And in the centre of its chest, a gaping hole. Freed from his control, his guards watched in horror.

Through his translucent chest, the Chancellor's rotten, shrivelled soul was visible for all to see. Dark marks and boil-like protuberances speckled a hollow shell, which was illuminated by the dimmest of sparks. Gasps of horror echoed eerily through the hall.

Snatches of the Chancellor's own memories began to play: a furious Nadia, a crying Oliver, Ruben in chains in the dungeon...

But Evander couldn't maintain control. He flagged, losing hold of his father's mind.

The memories ceased as the Chancellor's Shadow broke free from him, pinning Evander against the wall.

"Evander!" I screamed.

Shadows spun like spiderwebs around him, their tendrils acting like ropes, wrapping tighter around his chest and throat as he struggled, trying to draw a breath.

"Let him go!" I ran towards them, flinging fireballs against the web of shadows, but they broke into sparks. One caught the Chancellor in the back of the head, singeing his hair.

Hissing, one hand raised to the burned spot, the Chancellor released Evander, who toppled to the ground, the brooch nestled unseen in his hand.

Chancellor Obscura whirled around to face me.

"You," he said, as I inched backwards. "This is all because of you. You stole the memory from my son's mind. You turned him against me. You should've stayed lost and forgotten. If only I'd finished you off the first time." His shaded gaze seemed to bore deeper. "But I'm glad I kept you alive for this."

The shadow serpents writhed around me, pinning me in place.

"You asked me what I did with your mother," he said.

"Allow me to enlighten you."

He pointed to the five imprisoned souls channelling the eye, and to the caged woman in white who served as the Order's Spirit.

Her hood had fallen back, revealing her face.

A face I knew.

23.

THE EYES OF PROVIDENCE

"Mama," I said, in dread.

Her eyes were white, unseeing.

"You see?" said the Chancellor. "Ruben lied to you all along. It's not me you should hate, but your beloved father. He was the one who tracked her down. He told me he wanted a relationship with his child and I foolishly took pity on him, but that wasn't nearly the whole truth. You had all the gifts he needed, so he stole you from your mother to do his bidding. Then he gave her to me, to dispose of as I saw fit."

I fought against the shadows that bound me, trying to reach my mother, but every step I took forwards, the darkness yanked me back.

"Mama! It's Lily! I'm here!"

"You're wasting your breath," he said. "She can't see you, or hear you. She has no awareness of your existence, nor even her own. It's a mercy really. She pined for you all these years, never forgetting."

"Mama!" I screamed in futility, my throat hoarse.

Tears streaked down my cheeks, unbidden.

"But you forgot her, didn't you?"

The Chancellor smiled, a twisted knife-slash of a smile.

"It's rather poetic, don't you think?" he said. "Mother and daughter reunited at last. It's only right that you leave this earth together." He looked past me to the cages. "I could kill you outright – like I should have done that night. But why waste such a valuable commodity as a soul?"

He gestured at the five cages. The man serving as the Order's Spark had expired, lying motionless. He was removed by two attendants.

The Chancellor's shadows dragged me forward, twisting my arms behind my back and forcing me towards the cage. I dug my heels in, fought with all my strength, scratching and spitting, but they pushed me in as though I was made of paper.

"This time, I want to make sure you're really spent," he said, "every last bit of you."

Shock and sorrow made way for rage. "I'll kill you!" I screamed.

Metal restraints snapped, trapping my ankles and wrists in rings. I watched helplessly as a syringe protruded from the edge of the cage, filled with a thick, black liquid. The needle punctured my arm.

"Lily, no!" cried Evander. He was awake, staggering to his feet, eyes locked on mine.

In the pit of my stomach, a hollow feeling began to grow. The world closed in on me, tunnelling to create a vignette.

I watched Evander's Shadow shoot out to meet his father's, but the Chancellor quickly wrestled control again, forcing Evander up on to the raised platform.

The attendants opened the cage holding the Shadow soul and dragged out the barely conscious woman inside. The Chancellor's Shadow forced Evander, kicking and struggling, into it.

"Why don't you join your beloved, you wretched waste of atoms?" spat the Chancellor, his face unrecognizable with hatred. "If she was worth risking everything for, she must be worth dying for too."

My eyelids drooped. I could feel the pull of the Eye, tugging me under, making it hard to concentrate.

"Finally, son, you will be useful to me. In fact, why don't all of your friends join you? Better your souls be put to something good, rather than wasted on vice and depravity."

He pointed his staff at Perpetua, who cursed angrily as the Shadow snakes wrapped around her. He ordered his guards to force open the Spirit cage that held my mother prisoner. They hauled her out, discarding her on the ground like a piece of rubbish. She didn't move, face down on the stony floor.

I heard Perpetua's scream as the cage door slammed but all too soon she fell silent. Gus yelled out, an animalistic yelp, while Octavia roared.

One by one, we became the Order's Song, its Heart, its Spirit, its Shadow and its Spark.

I sensed their energies, bleeding into mine like different colours of paint in a water jar, the streams of our souls streaking and stretching, writhing around each other like ribbons.

The great and terrible power of the Eye network quivered, shaking our bodies. Evander's Shadow mixed with Perpetua's Spirit, as Octavia's Song met Gus's Heart, and there was my Spark, connecting everything.

In this moment, we were as one.

One soul.

Uno sumus animo.

I felt myself becoming less, my Spark dimming.

I could feel their fear. I could hear their thoughts. Perpetua was praying to the dead in her mother tongue. Octavia was singing a lullaby to soothe herself. Gus was screaming internally.

Evander was thinking about me.

Me.

Lily Elizabeth Duffy.

No. No! They would not take me away from myself again. They would not take me away from Evander. Or my friends.

Show them, Evander, I thought. *Show them the truth. Before it's too late.*

I felt the network shift, expand.

An excruciating pause, then the memory began to play, reflected in every floating eye-shaped peephole. It showed the Chancellor and his late wife Nadia quarrelling, captured by young Oliver's eyes.

"I can't live like this, Tristan," said Nadia. "I don't know who you are any more. I can't stand by and watch you break your own son, like you broke me. We're leaving, and you can't stop us."

She tried to pick up Oliver but the Chancellor pulled her away.

"Mama!"

"You will do no such thing," growled the Chancellor.

"You will let me go, or I will ruin you," she said, as he held on to her wrist. "If I told the people what I know, they'd crucify you."

The Chancellor's eyes darkened, his Shadow metamorphosing.

"I would rather kill you than let you walk away," he said, pushing her roughly against the wall.

"Papa, no! Stop!" cried Oliver, pulling at him. "Don't hurt her!"

The Chancellor's Shadow branched out and came to life, a faceless silhouette that stalked towards Nadia, faster than a human man. She ran in terror, her dark hair spilling everywhere. Looking back over her shoulder, she stumbled, clutching at nearby objects to fight off the Shadow but it caught up with her, overpowered her.

Her eyes turned black. She stopped fighting.

The Shadow pulled her to her feet, lifting her up to the balcony's ledge before pushing her over the edge.

She fell, her face eerily free of fear, free of feeling.

Nadia hit the ground as the Chancellor watched coldly, pausing only for a few seconds before his eyes returned to normal.

There was no guilt in his expression. No regret. No humanity.

The haunting image of Nadia's murder reflected on every lantern, every orb, every shining billboard across the city. Every eye that had once spied upon the people now projected the sins of their keeper.

The network hummed as I felt myself drawn deeper into it.

Opening myself up like a vessel, I let the energies of everyone who'd ever stood in this spot pass through me one by one, soaking up the remnants of centuries of psyche.

I lived through every birth and death, every kiss and heartbreak. I fought in every war, and celebrated every new year. I knew the loneliness of every prisoner and the fear of every child. I could taste every drop of blood spilled. I could hear a symphony of voices, all laughing and crying and screaming and singing. The sound broke apart, turning to whispers. We knew everything. We were everything. The Order's secrets echoed across the capital.

The Chancellor killed his wife...

Children are being tortured at the Reformatory...

House Memoria has been erasing memories of the Order's crimes...

Broadcast by the Listening Posts, these confessions rang aloud down every street, ricocheting endlessly.

The answer came to me suddenly, just a distant, faded ember at first, juxtaposed against the endless night of the dark place, before blooming brightly into view, shining clearly through the void.

We have to destroy the Eye network, I thought, hoping the others could still hear me. *Burn it to the ground.*

The light flared hotter and brighter as if some invisible tinder had been ignited, causing fire to arc in orbiting loops.

Help me destroy it, I begged. *Once and for all.*

Maybe it would take our lives. Maybe the effort would burn us up. But if we were doomed anyway, we had to try.

Let the truth destroy it. Let our sacrifice set people free.

Evander seemed to register my silent plea, Shadow arcing out in streams. Perpetua's Spirit formed a cloud that wrapped his Shadow and my Spark inside it, before the golden glow of Gus's heart throbbed at its centre. Octavia came last, the Song of her soul vibrating ripples through the air.

In the darkness of my mind, I relived the sensation of my soul's shattering, imagining the Eye network shattering apart. I sent the image to every eye in Providence, projecting my attack across the city.

The energy of the network began to groan and strain, as the ethereal threads that kept it alive began to fray and snap.

Just one last push, I thought. *Together, everyone. Now!*

The orb glowed like a supernova, breaking through the darkness. The last thread snapped.

Inch by inch, a blinding flash of light bathed the chamber. A deafening, tremulous, long note resounded, shaking the walls and shattering the windows. The atomic force of it reverberated, ricocheting through Evander, Octavia, Perpetua, Gus and me. Then, just like that, the Eye network imploded, folding itself away into a black hole that shrank to a pinpoint and vanished.

One by one, the eye-lights of the city went out, plunging Providence into preternatural darkness. The cages that contained us burst open, freeing us from our restraints. We staggered out, falling to our knees.

Silence followed, deathly quiet and cold.

The Chancellor angrily swiped his staff through the air towards me, but nothing happened. His weapon had been linked to the Eyes, that same power we had just destroyed. He stared at it incredulously, just a useless ornament now.

And the Chancellor was just a man.

"Everyone, return to your positions," he cried. Some of his guards fled, abandoning their posts, bolting through the doors in a repentant mass. "I will have order!" he shrilled, licking his dry lips. But no one listened.

The thundering of footsteps rumbled the ground. Loud, angry shouts carried along the hall. Lord Cordata appeared, waving a ceremonial sword I recognized from the wall of the ballroom of the Basilica.

"We saw what you did!" he cried.

"We all saw," echoed Lady Memoria, right behind him.

Chaos erupted in seconds.

All around me, people were fighting, brawling bare-knuckle like people did back in the Stone Age, creating a chaotic melee of writing bodies. Distantly, I saw Ash deliver the final blow to the Chancellor, dragging him towards an empty cage. In a blur I moved through the crowd. Among the mass of strangers, I spied several people I recognized, including the Countess, the Sanctuary runaways, the escaped prisoners and the street kids: Eyepatch, Bird's Nest and Shoeless, all working together to battle the Obscura guards.

Finally, through the scrum, I caught sight of my mother, still dazed on the ground. I flew through the crowd, flinging myself down by her side.

"Mama! It's Lily!" She lifted her head, staring at me blankly.

I tried to feel her feelings, to access her memories, but her mind was clouded by a strange fog. It shrouded everything, keeping me out.

"Your name is Mara Duffy," I said, taking her hands. "You're my mother, and I'm your daughter."

Nothing.

"I've always been yours, and you have always been mine. I have loved you for every moment I've been alive."

Her clouded expression seemed to clear slightly. "You were a good mother. You protected me." She began blinking rapidly. "You once told me, *never forget who you are*. We were standing in the attic of our old house, the one in Green Valley surrounded by fields, with washing on the lawns and birds on the roof. Don't you remember?"

Closing my eyes, I pictured our last embrace.

"You said the tear-catcher would bring me back to myself," I said, "and back to you. Well, it did." I clutched her hands tighter, pouring myself into her. When I opened my eyes again, I saw myself in her pupils. Something in her expression shifted.

"Lily," she said.

"Mama," I exhaled, hugging her tightly.

Her memories rushed through me, her thoughts filling my mind.

As a child, I collected things. A pretty conker. A paper flower. A key. A ruby earring. I had a talent for making memory capsules, using special objects to preserve my favourite moments as remnants.

Autumn leaves. The spring dance. My first kiss.

My mother gave me the tear-catcher, explaining that it had been carried by the women in our family for decades.

Never let anyone in, Mara, she said. Never let yourself be truly known. Or the Order will punish you for it.

But I didn't listen. I thought I knew better.

I wanted to live, to experience things.

I moved to the city and got a job working for the very people she told me to fear. I made remnants for Renato House, concealing their secrets. By removing their incriminating memories, Ruben was able to pass the Chancellor's inspections. Ruben was gregarious and tactile, charismatic and fearless. He knew just the right words to say and in the right order to make me fall for him. But he was expected to marry into nobility. He would not turn his back on his birthright. Not for me, not for his daughter, not for anything. His embrace made me feel safe, but he cavorted with other lovers behind my back.

My heart grew bitter. When I looked in the mirror, I no longer recognized myself. The memories I concealed in remnants were ever more sinister, as Ruben's mission to deceive the Chancellor drove him to darker and darker deeds. I didn't know what I would become if I remained. I came to fear the Order, and what they would do if they knew the doubt in my mind. I ran all the way back to the place I came from, to raise the baby already growing inside me.

You, my Lily.

Reality flooded back, planting us in the present.

"Am I still dreaming?" she said when she saw me.

"You're awake. We're awake."

She was changed from my memories, but when she smiled, it was my same smile. My mother. She looked like me. Freckles and wide-set eyes, a heart-shaped face and a small pert nose.

"There's so much we have to catch up on," she said.

"I missed you," I said, in a small voice.

"You'll never have to miss me again, I promise."

Octavia ran over to me, out of breath.

"Come quick!" she said, her expression filling me with fear.

"I'll be right back," I said to my mother.

"Go," she said.

Octavia led me over to a dark corner where Evander was lying, sprawled on his side. His eyes were closed, his face pale, blood congealing around his nose. We knelt beside him together.

"His thoughts are quiet," said Octavia.

I laid my head on his chest. I could hear a heartbeat – weak, barely a flutter – but it was there.

I urgently tried to recall what I had learned back at Renato House under Ruben's tutelage, moving my hands in different positions, drawing thin wispy threads of fire between my fingers as if stitching together a torn garment, but I had no idea what I was doing. Ruben hadn't thought it worthwhile to teach me the healing part of my craft, only the destructive part.

I became aware of the others, gathering around us – Gus and Perpetua, Rani and my mother, supported by Ash – all staring helplessly.

This wasn't how it was supposed to end.

My soul was shattering all over again.

What was the point of having a soul, if the one you loved was gone?

Octavia started to sob. Rani pulled her close. My mother put her hand on my shoulder.

"You can't be gone," I cried, as Gus gently tried to ease me away. "I can't lose you, not when I just found you again." I shook Gus off and tried again, and again, and again, as the crowd watched me working through the throes of desperation and despair. Concerned voices rose around me.

"Enough now."

"Leave him."

"There's nothing more you can do."

A single tear fell, streamed down my cheek, landing on his chest, in the place where his heart was.

With a sudden raspy gasp, Evander's eyes sprang open.

At first, they were full of darkness, but it bled away as black tears. His vision cleared, allowing him to focus on me.

"You're OK!" I sobbed.

"I'm fine," he said. "It's just a little blood, that's all."

I kissed him before he could say anything else, but drew back when he made a small, pained noise.

"Sorry ... I didn't—" Before I could finish my sentence, he was pulling me close, kissing me back, his lips soft and warm.

As before, they felt as if they belonged there.

With one hand, he cupped my cheek, and with the other he held the back of my head. My own hand tangled into his thick dark hair, running down to the nape of his neck. When he shivered at my touch, I felt the spark of chemistry, the invisible thread that had been suspended between us all along.

Energetic. Ethereal. Electric.

After a long, lingering moment, we broke apart.

"Lily," he said.

The fighting had stopped. The survivors beheld the collateral of bodies scattered on the ground, but there was no one to lead, no one in charge. Guards stood around with no orders, abandoned by their Houses. The Renato soldiers looked to me, while the Obscura soldiers had mostly fled.

Lord Cordata was in the perfect position to step forward,

with Lady Memoria right behind him.

"Tend to the wounded," he directed of his own guards. "Summon the rulers of the other Houses."

"We will form an emergency council," said Lady Memoria, "just like in the good old days."

For tonight, no one person ruled the world.

I stood beside my mother, who squeezed my hand.

"I can't believe you're real," she said. "You *are* real, aren't you?" Tucking a strand of hair behind my ear, she reached forward to button my black cape, resting her hand on its button clasp a moment.

I laid my hand on top of hers.

I was loved.

I was treasured.

I caught Evander's eye through the swell of guards and rebels who had traded places, wanting to run to him.

"Are you hurt?" asked Ash, of my mother, with Octavia and Rani standing beside them.

"Just a little," she said, looking herself over.

"Better to be sure. Come on. I'll sort you out."

I looked back and forth, between Evander and my mother.

"Go to him," she said, seeming to read my mind. "I'll go with your friends here. We can meet later. I've waited this long. I can last a few more moments without you, I'm sure."

I smiled gratefully, happiness flooding through me.

Evander and I moved towards each other, meeting in

the middle.

"Do you want—" he began, at the same time I said: "Shall we—"

We laughed, awkwardly.

"Let's get out of here," I said.

"Good idea."

We drifted outside into the gardens, where several topiaries were smoking. The lawns were thick with injured people and spectators, including lesser nobles of the other Houses, who eyed us with mixed fear and suspicion, all jostling for position behind those who would take power, I assumed.

Lady Cordata was among them, already telling the heroic story of her beloved husband's triumph.

But I would worry about that later. For now, it was time to be Lily and Evander, not the new leaders of House Renato and House Obscura.

Standing before the rose-shrouded bandstand where we'd danced our first and last dances, our entire history played out in my mind.

We climbed the steps where we'd first fallen in love, simmering in comfortable silence.

"Where will we live?" said Evander, abruptly. "What will we do for money? Who will run the country? What if—"

"Let's just … have a moment," I said.

"Sorry," he said, mussing his hair. "I feel oddly nervous

right now."

"Why?"

"Just being around you."

"You've known me for ages," I teased.

We stared out at the still-smoking Basilica.

"But you're not just Lily to me now," he said. "You're Ruby and Iris as well. And who am I? Oliver or Evander or someone else? When I try to imagine the future, it's just an empty space."

I gently laid my hand over his.

"Maybe an empty space is a good thing," I said. "You can put whatever you like in an empty space."

He smiled ruefully.

"What about you?" he said. "How do you feel?"

I took a moment to think about it, reaching out to those soft, secret places inside myself where my emotions thrived.

"I'm a lot of things at present," I said. "Most of them good. Some of them bad. I'm happier than I've been in as long as I can remember, but I'm more frightened than I've ever been too. I'm sad but I'm excited. I'm angry, and grieving, but I'm at peace. Maybe that's just what it's going to be like from now on, being human."

"Yes, that sounds about right."

Our fingers crept closer together, entwining again.

"What happens next?" he said.

"We live," I said, with a shrug.

I kissed him. I must've kissed him a hundred times before but it was always like the first time all over again.

Evander extended his hand. I took it, allowing him to pull me into the middle of the bandstand. Though there was no music, we danced to our song in our minds, drifting back and forth in the middle of the pavilion, repeating the moves we'd made long before.

As we spun and swayed, snow began to fall. I wasn't sure if it was an illusion or not. Evander's Shadow danced along with us, perfectly in time and synchronicity, just like mine.

His feelings flooded through me in waves. Concern. Contentment. Grief. Love...

Though the Eyes were closed, the magic of the soul was still alive within us, within everyone.

The world was still, just for a minute in time.

ACKNOWLEDGEMENTS

Apologies in advance. This is going to get mushy.

To my parents. The biggest, truest, realest things are always the hardest for me to put into words, which is why I write such rubbish birthday cards, but that love so deep it scares you? That's the love I have for the two of you. Can you believe you're reading this? In a book? This is all because of you, and for you. But also a little bit for the cats. One day they might learn to read.

To my agent Hannah Sheppard, at D H H Literary Agency. This book simply wouldn't exist without you. You so patiently and gently encouraged me over the best part of a decade, never allowing me to give up, even when I really wanted to. You changed my life. To everyone at D H H who helped make this a reality, thank you for taking a chance on me.

To my editor, Sophie Cashell. I always knew that editors were talented and hard-working but the real truth is that editors make books. They are the real masterminds of stories. So many of the best parts of TGWNS came from your prompts, your questions, our imaginations combined. You subtly pushed me to the best of my ability. It's been an honour and a pleasure.

To Yasmin Morrissey, who never forgot the idea. When you asked about it years later, you set in motion a chain of events that led us here. You were the Spark! I'll never forget that first video call with you, Sophie, Hannah and Lauren Fortune. I was trying not to cry as you said the most amazing things to me. Even now, I can't quite believe it. Thank you all. Thank you for seeing the magic.

To Genevieve Herr, whose feedback was instrumental: Perpetua is way cooler because of you. Your notes were so insightful, illuminating parts of the story I hadn't yet fully grasped. Thank you for speaking up for Shadow.

To Hannah Love, to Hannah Griffiths, to Sarah Dutton and everyone else at Scholastic: I am so lucky to have had the chance to work with you all. You have made this process so enjoyable. To Jamie, who designed the cover, thank you for bringing this story to life so beautifully!

To Danielle and Jessica, my best friends. You were two of the earliest champions of this story despite me never letting you read it. I swear this only happened because we did that ritual in your garden where we put the good vibes out into the universe. Thank you for listening to oh so many rambles. To Hope: I'll make sure your mommies give you a copy when you're old enough.

This is also for Catrin, my heathen sister and mentor. You taught me so much. You took me from my little dark room and set my mind on fire. It's so typical of us that we haven't spoken for a while and yet you messaged me while I was writing this very paragraph. I wouldn't be me without you.

To Pat and John. You made me want to live an interesting life. You made me want to be smart and cultured. I didn't necessarily succeed in any of those things but you were the inspiration all the same.

There are so many people I want to thank. To Katie and Lucy, the other corners of the Impenetrable Triad of Doom. To Ethel, to Alice, to Saz, to Mat. To Emma Bradley, specifically. To Sarah, Heather and Savannah. To Christine. To Mary, Jonathan, Kevin and Loni. To Nan. To Waterstones. To the people unfortunate enough to have known me since I was a child. To the Uber drivers who kept me alive. To my Animal Crossing pals. To all the writers I've ever loved. To every single person who pre-ordered. To the Debut 2022 group: strap in!